Night of the Predator

Also by Christopher Sherlock

Hyena Dawn

CHRISTOPHER SHERLOCK

Night
of the Predator

HEINEMANN : LONDON

William Heinemann Ltd
Michelin House, 81 Fulham Road, London SW3 6RB
LONDON   MELBOURNE   AUCKLAND

First published 1991
Copyright © Christopher Sherlock 1991

A CIP catalogue record for this book
is held by the British Library
ISBN 0 434 67864 3

Typeset by CentraCet, Cambridge
Printed in England by
Clays Ltd, St. Ives Plc

To Karen with all my love

The worst lie was our hope:
Perpetual teatime and the colour
   green.
Fantasies always suffice
But we returned to the lie,
The dirty towns, the insensitive people.
Endless teatime and the colour green.
But we can forgive this remembering
One promise: driving through
Long grass at night, the scratch
Of the grass on the truck,
And in our headlights a continent,
An Africa within. An Africa beyond.

Exiles
by Patrick Cullinan.

Prologue

Kalahari 1950

Tracey shivered. The cold, dry air pulled at the folds of her khaki jacket and she drew it tightly round her. Gently, Kotuko took her hand. He stood only as high as her breasts, the grey crinkled hair growing across his head like thorn bushes on the bare veld.

God, what had she done! David would kill her if the child was dead. Why had she done this to her baby? But she had only to look into the old man's eyes to know the answer to her question. Behind those dark, impenetrable orbs lay the secrets of a culture that had been a part of Africa since the beginning of time.

This was a place where David loved to come and hunt leopard. He hadn't known about her relationship with the Bushmen – or San people – he had been surprised when he discovered she could speak their language, and horrified to find that she treated them with equality. But Tracey had grown up here, in the Kalahari; it was her home; she was one of only a handful of white people who could speak the Bushmen's language.

Her first child – hers and David's – had been weak since birth. The European doctors said he might never be able to walk, but they would only know for certain as he grew up: it was a matter of waiting, hoping. It had been entirely natural for Tracey to come here, to bring her baby to the medicine man. He had picked up the bones – two flat, two round, and the other misshapen. He had cupped them in his hands, thrown them on the sand and raised his arms into the air. Then he had examined the way the bones had fallen and consulted with the other Bushmen. Finally he had made his pronouncement.

1

'It is because the Great God loves him that he makes this child a cripple, and if he loves him even more he will take him to himself.'

Tracey had shivered. And she had shivered even more when the medicine man told her what she had to do. Could she live with her baby's death?

Now they came over the rise, she and the old man, Kotuko, and her baby lay still on the sacking where they had left him, in the blazing sun, the day before. The tears began to stream down her face. She ran, the breath bursting from her mouth. The little bundle was lying still against the sand, his face chapped and burnt. When she dropped down on her knees, she found the baby smell was gone, replaced by the pungent, sandy smell of the desert. Sobbing, she sensed the Bushman come up behind her.

'Why you have no courage?'

He picked up the baby and talked to it. The baby's eyes opened, it let out a stifled cry. Tracey grabbed her baby from him, tore open the folds of her jacket and pushed his lips against her breast. He drank and drank.

The Bushman smiled. 'Now he is Africa. We will call him Kaikhoe, the fighter.'

The smell of blood filled the hot, dry desert air. In the heat-haze a tree wavered on the horizon; above, the sky was crystal blue without a single cloud to blemish its intensity. The smell alone made Tracey want to vomit – but she could not turn her eyes away; away from the emaciated yellow body that was suspended from a crude wooden frame used for skinning game. The cords bit into the skin of the wrists and blood oozed out around them. The body was splayed out, naked and powerless, the prominent buttocks red with blood flowing down from the torn flesh of the back.

Nearby, a coffee pot gurgled, resting on two metal rods above the glistening coals of a small fire.

The young man in the immaculately-pressed safari kit studied his victim with detachment, weighing the sjambok in his right hand. David Loxton always managed to control his emotions, and now was no exception. The cool grey eyes beneath the dark, bushy eyebrows betrayed little of the anger that dwelt within. Again came the swish of the whip, the smack as it contacted with

2

the old man's flesh. The white of bone showed through the fine cuts in the dark flesh.

'Oh my God! David! Stop!' Tracey screamed out the words, then ran to her husband who was about to raise the bloody sjambok again to the old man's back. 'It was a test, don't you see? We always knew the child was weak, but this proved he was strong enough to survive. David! Could you have lived with a cripple?' She flung her arms around her husband of only a year and stared desperately into his eyes. All she saw was that cool grey stare, the look of a stranger.

He broke her grip, then savagely rammed the butt of the buffalo whip into her solar plexus. She doubled up with the pain and collapsed into the hot sand, coughing and gasping for breath. Again the sjambok sang in the air, then tore into the open flesh of the Bushman's back.

'Heegh!' The breath burst from Kotuko's mouth, but there was no scream of pain, no begging for mercy. The old man's teeth showed between his lips.

Tracey looked up into his eyes from where she lay, helpless in the sand. He returned the glance, and she could read the silent communication – this is not your business, stay away, I will handle this.

'You old kaffir! Try to kill my son, you heathen bastard? Scream for me! Beg for your life!' Again and again the sjambok came down, and Tracey, staring into Kotuko's eyes, saw the life force slowly fading.

Hatred tore into her soul. It was not enough that she would never let David touch her again; his son must learn to know his father, understand the savagery that lurked beneath the cultivated exterior – learn how to hate him, and avenge the man who was being beaten so mercilessly. This was suddenly very clear to Tracey. The nature of her life from this moment came into focus: it would be a continuing battle against this man she had loved and married, to whom she had borne a son. And yet, even as she thought of her revenge she knew that she was trapped. What could she do against the power of a man like David Loxton? A power which still the old man resisted, though the back of the thin yellow body was latticed with bloody weals.

David, sweating, walked round and stared into the Bushman's eyes. 'Beg for your life, kaffir!' The spittle hit David in the face.

3

'Never!' Kotuko's wrinkled lips pronounced the word clearly, quietly.

A faint smile crossed David's face. He dropped the sjambok and walked across to the fire where the coffee pot boiled and bubbled, the coffee hissing as it hit the coals. He took the pot and poured himself a cup, sipping at it meditatively, contemplating the old Bushman and Tracey.

He put down his coffee and pulled one of the metal rods from the fire; it glowed, angry and red, like metal from the blast furnace. He pushed it close to the old man's nose and saw him stiffen. Without saying a word he walked round behind the spreadeagled body, then slipped the rod slowly up the old man's rectum.

'Agggh! Eeeh!'

The smell of burning flesh and faeces hit Tracey with the old man's scream.

She stared again at the dead body of Kotuko, the old man who had been her closest confidant for the last few weeks. All around them lay the bare, rolling veld, above them the intense, everlasting blue of the sky.

'You killed him, you bastard!' Her scream died on the hot air.

She heard the sound of David's feet approaching. His shadow fell across her where she lay on the sand, and he pushed the bloodied whip against her face. Its acrid smell made her gag. His cool grey eyes bored down into hers.

'No, Tracey, it was you who killed him. It was your stupidity that caused that kaffir to leave our child in the desert. Now get up, I'm hungry.'

She lay still, resisting him. He grabbed her hair and yanked her to her feet. Twisting her hair tightly, he forced her to look at him, ignoring her whimpering and the tears streaming from her eyes.

'Obey me, or I will flog you.' The precise, clipped tones of the upper-class Englishman.

She felt the full force of his brutality directed against her, and closed her eyes. But this was no nightmare, this was reality, and as he pulled her towards him, forcing her to kiss him, she knew the horror that was to be the rest of her life.

BOOK I

One

The sun was merciless. It beat through the tinted windscreen and the Zeiss lenses of his sunglasses. When he switched off the air-conditioner and opened the side window, the wind came in with a roar and he drank in the hot parched air. He loved the burnt smell of Africa, it gave him a lift like a drug. He glanced down at his watch: he'd left later than planned. The meeting that morning had taken forever. He'd forgotten that bankers worked on a different time-scale from other people – the men from Zurich had too much influence and too much money to be threatened or dismissed, though Max Loxton would dearly have loved to have done both.

He listened to the hum of the big Buick V-8 engine, ramming the square white aluminium body of the Land-Rover against the hot air. The engine had been designed to cope with far worse conditions than this and was quite happy pushing two tons of metal at 130 km/h in the burning heat. All the same, he wasn't taking chances. But when he glanced down at the gauge, the engine temperature was fine. He'd had this Landy for a year now, and already it had done two arduous safaris. He thought back to them briefly, longingly. This would be the way he would be going if he were heading to the north of Botswana, to the Okavango swamps. But on this journey he wasn't going to see any big game. His objective was to take steps that would protect the wildlife of Botswana and stop the rape of the land.

Already, less than two hours from Johannesburg, he was in another world. Gone were the tall skyscrapers and the golden

7

sands of the mine dumps, the men turned old by the lust for money. Now he was in farming country, the home of the Afrikaner; the true Boers, the fighters – a tough breed, the biggest men in the world. Of those he knew, Max Loxton loved some and hated others, but almost all he respected. He thought now about one Afrikaner in particular – Kobus van der Post, his mentor. Things had been happening very quickly for Kobus. The South African State President, P. W. Botha, had been ousted in a series of dramatic moves made by his own Cabinet, and Kobus van der Post had replaced him. Max had not previously suspected government dissension; Kobus had never mentioned the senior Cabinet members' growing concern over Botha's behaviour. Now, with Kobus van der Post running the country, Max guessed there would be big changes and that they'd be happening very fast.

Max let the Land-Rover out a little, and stared across the flat lands before him. A sign popped up, breaking the monotony of the stony verge: Zeerust 5km. At least he was getting closer to the border. He wouldn't need to fill up with petrol – he'd had both the long-range tanks filled by his driver before he left his headquarters in Johannesburg. Perhaps he should have used the Lear jet? That would have caused problems, though – the media would have been onto him the moment he left. That was the price you paid for success. But behind the darkened glass of the Land-Rover's windows he was anonymous, just another tourist heading for Botswana.

Besides, this drive gave him time to set things in perspective, to run through the arguments again in his mind. He thought about the cases filled with plans and drawings, stacked up in the back – years of work. Those documents were the expression of a dream – a dream begun while he was still a child, a dream nurtured by his mother, Tracey.

It had been a hard battle to persuade Phillip Trengrove, the world-famous environmentalist, to leave Berkeley. Max had travelled again and again to California to plead with him, and eventually Phillip had come with him to see the Okavango swamps, Botswana's uniquely beautiful wetlands. Phillip had fallen in love with them on that trip, and today the two of them shared a common dream – to turn Botswana into a giant game farm. Many thought they were crazy, but knowing what would happen if they could not make their vision a reality, Max and Phillip were in deadly earnest.

Max glanced quickly back at the other cases stacked in the Land-Rover; they were filled with gifts, essential for the opening of any discussion in Africa. When he turned his attention back to the road, lines of worry creased his deeply tanned brow. He knew the men he was to talk to, and he understood why they would not want to listen to him. It was because of men like his father, David Loxton; men who'd stripped away the dignity of those to whom Africa had first belonged.

Max swore out loud. There was so little time left to achieve his goal, the Okavango Delta was shrinking every year. The place was part of his soul – its gradual destruction was like a cancer eating into his own body. Every day he failed to get his plans into action, was a year off the life of the Delta.

Only four kilometres to Zeerust now. Zeerust had begun as a mission station founded by two Frenchmen who were driven away by an invasion of the Matabele. As so often happened in the strife-torn history of South Africa, the warriors were chased off in their turn, and it was the Voortrekkers who finally established themselves in Zeerust, the first town of the Transvaal, older even than Johannesburg or Pretoria. Max could see one of them now, beside the road – or at least, the modern-day version. A big man, this Voortrekker, standing beside his German car and giving orders to his black farmhands. Speaking the African dialect, no doubt.

Voortrekker. Roughly translated into English, it meant 'pioneer', but to anyone who knew the story of South Africa well, it meant a lot more. The Voortrekkers had come north, to get away from the British and to create their own isolated, Calvinistic society. The ones who came to Zeerust found rich lands and plentiful game; unchallenged, they had settled here. Later came the problems, the diamonds, the fortune-hunters, but the Voortrekkers had survived. Now they called themselves Afrikaners, the white tribe of Africa. They had ruled South Africa with an iron hand since the Second World War, a white minority ruling a black majority; and despite sanctions and universal condemnation, they fought to preserve their power. But Kobus van der Post, the recently appointed State President, was determined to make radical changes in the government, to

9

achieve full democracy in South Africa, and to gain international acceptability. Max knew just how hard that would be.

He pulled up in Zeerust, feeling thirsty. The café here was filled with cooking pots and kitchen utensils, not like the chrome and plastic places in Johannesburg. Max picked up the *Star*, along with something to drink. Back inside the Landy, he read the main headline a second time, not quite believing it.

'Napoleon Zwane to be freed!'

So Kobus was getting to work already! A broad smile spread across Max's face.

Arrested in the 1960s, Napoleon Zwane was South Africa's most famous political prisoner. He had been convicted of conspiracy, of plotting to overthrow Verwoerd's government by violence, and the sentence had been life imprisonment. He had spent the next twenty-eight and a half years of his life incarcerated on the notorious Robben Island prison, some nine kilometres out to sea from Cape Town. Botha, the former State President, had then had him moved to Leeukop Prison, halfway between Johannesburg and Pretoria.

Napoleon Zwane had become famous throughout the world, as a man who refused to give up his beliefs for the promise of an early release. He was a living legend now, the man everyone saw as the natural leader of the African Freedom Council – the movement that had fought long and hard for black representation in parliament. According to what Kobus had confided to Max, the release of Napoleon Zwane would be just the first stage in a revolutionary process of change. Soon the unbanning of the African Freedom Council would be announced – an act of supreme courage on Kobus' part.

Max turned the newspaper pages to find the share prices – but it was too soon for the news of Napoleon's impending release to have affected them. Once it was known, however, South Africa would receive an immediate inflow of desperately needed foreign money. One particular share price caught Max's eye. Yes, his new hotel venture was doing well, the shares were strong, and over the next few months should grow even stronger. He smiled. The more money he was worth, the more he could raise to push his Botswanan plan through. He started driving again, slaking his thirst, as he drove, with the cool drink he'd bought at the café.

Why did he always think of his wife when he was on his own? The marriage hadn't worked, one of the few things in his life that

hadn't. She hadn't been able to accept Max for what he was –
rich, powerful, charismatic and successful. He'd never had an
affair while he was married to Shandy, yet she had constantly
accused him of it. Was it his fault that women found him
attractive, were always making eyes at him? It was so stupid, her
suspicions were entirely groundless, but it had driven them apart.
Maybe she hadn't been right for him in the first place. She'd
entranced him at first, she'd had so much energy, such a zest for
life, but with marriage that had vanished. She said it was his fault
– and that had hurt. He remembered the day he found her in bed
with Rod Niven, one of his mine managers. Rod had actually
come at him, stark naked and fists flailing – and Max had
flattened him with a well-placed left hook. Shandy had gone
berserk, but he hadn't touched her, simply told her to get out.
Yes, it had hurt, though he found it hard to admit it.

Shandy had not remarried after their divorce. She was still a
beauty at forty, a tall woman with an air of sexual mystery that
made men turn as she walked. She had dark hair and passionate
eyes – eyes that had flashed in the darkness when he made love
to her – cat's eyes. And she'd sold their story to every woman's
magazine in the country.

The border post came up quickly: wire gates, white buildings
and parked cars. Max pulled over, reached for his passport and
jumped down.

Cornelius Coetzee, First Lieutenant of the South African Customs,
Kopfontein, paged idly through the passport of the man standing
over the counter from him. Dr Max Loxton, a familiar face. Thirty-
nine years old, divorced, regular traveller. Wealthy, by the look of
his clothes. A big man with a broken boxer's nose and a scar down
the right side of the face. Brown hair streaked with blond, big,
bushy eyebrows, heavily tanned. But the feature that was really
unusual was his neck, as wide as the face above it and taut with
muscle. It gave this Max Loxton a bull-like aspect. Lieutenant
Coetzee sensed the crystal-clear piercing blue eyes watching him as
he made these assessments, and couldn't help feeling intimidated.

'Dr Loxton, your passport's in order. Tell me, are you any
relation to the Minister of Justice?'

To his surprise, Max Loxton grimaced. 'Yes, he's my father.'

'Good man.'

'I hate his guts.'

11

The lieutenant stared in confusion as Dr Loxton snatched up his passport and walked out into the sunlight, the muscles on that big neck tight with anger. He couldn't understand what he had said to upset the man; his sudden rage was obvious, and frightening. He himself would have been proud to have David Loxton, the Minister of Justice, as his father, so why was his son so riled? Odd, definitely odd.

Max leapt into the Landy, slamming the door shut. The sweat was running down his face. Only fifty metres to the Botswana side, and then he could put this nasty little incident behind him.

He drove across the short stretch of road to the Botswanan side of the Kopfontein borderline, scanning the country to right and left. The land was covered with dense, thick bush and hot dry, sand; it was inhospitable, impenetrable. Parked at one side of the road was a Buffel armoured personnel carrier, reminding him of the army camps he'd been on, year in, year out, for ten years after he'd done his compulsory year's military service. How he'd detested those camps! He'd been a member of the elite reconnaissance commando, holding the rank of major, but it gave him no pride that he had been the youngest citizen-force soldier ever to be accorded this rank. If the army had been impressed by his will to win, they had also been impressed by the fact that his father was a cabinet minister.

Max knew how carefully this border was guarded: the number of weapons and explosives being illegally carried across it into South Africa was steadily increasing. Terrorist incursions across the border were increasing too, but these were nothing more than pin-pricks in the side of the South African army, the sixth largest fighting force in the world. No, it was not terrorist attacks that frightened the South African army, it was the possibility of a revolution within South Africa itself, fuelled with weapons from across its borders. Max knew that Kobus intended to curb the power of the army, which stood in the way of change like a great grey monolith. Many of its high-ranking officers would consider the release of Napoleon Zwane a supreme act of stupidity, and there had even been talk among them of the necessity for a military coup.

These thoughts evaporated as Max pulled up outside the dusty border post and walked into the Botswana Customs Section, bracing himself for the inevitable formalities.

In the past, the South African military had taken to making raids across the Botswanan border in order to hit the offices of the banned African Freedom Council in Botswana's capital, Gaberone. On the first couple of occasions, the Botswanan Defence Force had tried to stop them, but their soldiers had been mown down by the gunfire of the seasoned South African professionals. Now the BDF merely stood aside in the face of such formidable fire-power, but their hatred of the raids was as strong as ever, and as a result, everyone entering the country from South Africa was meticulously searched. This time Max had to open up all the Landy's tool boxes as well as the bonnet, and he cursed silently at the delay. Still, he could imagine the wrath that would be heaped on this customs official's head if he was found to have let a South African commando cross the border disguised as a tourist.

'Busy today?' Max asked.

'Yes, a lot of trucks. It's hell searching them.' The man eyed him suspiciously. 'You have a Land-Rover, but you're not going on safari?'

'Not this time unfortunately,' Max said. 'I'm here for business in Gaberone.'

'What kind of business?'

'Environmental conservation.'

'You work for Euro?'

Max laughed: the inevitable question. Euro owned a large percentage of South Africa's gold mines, most of its profitable diamond mines, and controlled seventy per cent of the companies listed on the Johannesburg Stock Exchange. No, he did not work for Euro, though Euro had tried to buy him out time and again. Max's holding company, Loxton Exploration, was highly profitable, and very good at what it did – finding new mines. But Max had no intention of working for Sir Julian Wehrner, the man whose name spelled God in the oak-panelled boardrooms of Euro Pacific at 55 Wehrner Street, Johannesburg. Besides, Max had other interests quite apart from mining. The hotel and game-ranching business he had started ten years before was growing at a spectacular rate.

'No, I don't work for Euro,' he chuckled, 'I work for myself.'

'Max Loxton? The heavyweight boxer!' The man's eyes lit up and he pumped Max's hand warmly.

'I haven't boxed for years . . .'

13

'Everybody remembers that fight. You could have turned professional, been world champion.' There was awe in the official's voice, and a new look of respect in his eyes.

'I've got bigger battles to fight these days,' Max said, with a hint of regret. He had liked the power he'd enjoyed in the ring; just him against the other man, no one else to worry about.

'Well, Max Loxton, I'm sure you'll win them. Enjoy your stay in Botswana.' The customs official smiled, gesturing him to drive on.

Max breathed a sigh of relief. Searches always unsettled him; you never knew what might cause suspicion, and the last thing he needed was to be arrested. It could happen so easily – even the possession of something as innocuous as a South African army water-bottle could do it.

He accelerated away from the border post, the difference between South Africa and Botswana hitting him visibly. Now the roadside was bare and dusty, because the grass that should have held the verge together had been eaten away by goats. The country looked desolate; he saw very few trees, the occasional tin shanty. He slowed down as a group of goats crossed the road in front of him. The contrast between this and the carefully managed South African farms was enormous. Here, the thousands of subsistence farmers were raping the earth. The possibility that all this might soon be a wasteland was suddenly very real to him.

Predictably, five kilometres later, at the edge of Gaberone, there was another road block. Max's eyes scanned the soldiers manning it. He made a swift calculation in his head, and reckoned he could have wiped the lot of them out on his own. Their lack of discipline was evident – badly creased uniforms, brass buttons unpolished, weapons held sloppily. The commanding officer swaggered over and rummaged through Max's suitcase, eyeing an aerosol can of deodorant with suspicion.

'You may proceed.'

He pulled away, and drove towards the sprawling capital of Botswana – Gaberone.

The Gaberone Oasis had changed dramatically since Max had acquired it the year before. Then it had been a sad reminder of a bygone era – a grand old colonial-style hotel in the process of gradual decay – but Max had seen the potential in it. He was

14

building a number of hotels across Africa; deliberately avoiding the uniformity of the international chains, he was creating each hotel as a unique architectural statement, and he had seen that the Oasis could fit the pattern. Now the tired traveller approached it along an imposing avenue of classical white columns, topped with a wooden pergola and covered with bougainvillaea. Underfoot were giant terracotta tiles, and through the columns could be glimpsed green palms and fountains. There was a feeling of coolness within a tropical setting.

Max smiled with satisfaction as he strode through the white colonnade with its twining crimson blossoms. The architect and the landscape gardener had surpassed themselves. He was looking forward to testing the level of service – this was a surprise visit, and no one was expecting him.

The large, airy reception area was paved with black and white tiles, and at its centre was an elegant fountain with two white cherubs on top, perched as if about to dive. A big skylight overhead gave the whole room a feeling of light and space. The first thing Max noticed was a couple of black women, standing as if waiting for someone. When their eyes lighted upon him, he frowned at them, and they immediately shifted their attention elsewhere. Like ladies of the night the world over, they were definitely under-dressed, and examined the men passing through the foyer with undisguised interest.

He'd reserved a room under a fictitious name, one of the best suites on the upper level, with a view over the hotel's splendid gardens. The receptionist looked down at his letter of confirmation, then up. She smiled pleasantly. 'You'll be staying on after the weekend, Mr McDowell?'

'I'm not certain. Could you hold the room over for me for the moment?'

'No problem, sir. Would you like tea or coffee in the morning?'

'Coffee. And the newspapers.'

'We get the Johannesburg papers a day late, but our local newspaper will come with your coffee. May I wish you an enjoyable stay.'

Once at his suite, Max unpacked his suitcase and then decided to take a shower; the cold water would wake him up after the heat of the journey. Then this evening he'd run through the reports he'd brought with him. He did not underestimate what he was up against; Euro already had an almost monopolistic

15

control of Botswana's mines, and what he was proposing wouldn't go down well with them at all.

After an invigorating shower, he towelled himself dry and poured himself a neat whisky. Then he threw open the balcony doors and looked out across the garden. The sun was setting; brilliant orange on the skyline, above, across the fading blueness, jagged streaks of dark cloud edged with white.

Botswana, he mused, had a lot of potential. To the current big investors that meant mining and cattle farming – a way of making the most money out of the country before anything went wrong, like a revolution in neighbouring South Africa. But Max Loxton saw riches in Botswana that most of the big investors ignored or discounted. The game reserves to the north, together with the Okavango swamps, comprised one of the most impressive and unspoilt wilderness areas in the world. Max dreamed of preserving this paradise. He knew that in the future it could become a tourist attraction rivalling the best in the world. But the tourism would have its own natural checks and balances.

There would be giant game farms where people could hunt – but only in limited numbers, so that while a vast amount of revenue was earned for the maintenance of the game park, the delicate balance amongst the animal population was maintained. There would be spectacular hotels, too, in the middle of the swamps, where visitors could sit and gaze into paradise or be poled around the luxuriant waterways in mokoros, the traditional wooden boats of the swamp people.

Max took another sip of his whisky. The alternative was to see the whole country reduced to the kind of wasteland he had just travelled through, destroyed by bad farming practices; to see Gaberone become a modern city in a dust bowl; to see money going out of the country instead of coming in. If the big cattle farmers, who wanted the game around the swamps removed in favour of cattle, had their way, it would take ten years, maybe less, before Botswana was ruined.

As the sun set, and with these thoughts in his mind, Max went back into his room and read through the first of his reports – as convincing an argument as ever, he thought now, for replanning the Botswanan economy. The crux of his proposal was that he should take control of Botswana's mining operations. He was amply qualified, already running two sucessful mines of his own, one near Johannesburg and the other in Namibia. The way he

16

would organize it, Botswana would gradually scale down its mining – but would, at the same time, levy higher taxes on the mines remaining, thus drawing a larger revenue than it currently enjoyed, but drastically reducing the damage to the environment. Max's plans also involved opening other avenues of employment for the men who would be laid off from the mines that closed down.

This way of organizing Botswana's mining, it seemed to Max, was infinitely and obviously better than the way the South African companies mining in Botswana ran their operation; they were here simply to mine the hell out of the country and then get out before there was any big trouble – like a coup d'état. The difficulty was, it might be hard to persuade the Botswanan government to ditch the big South African consortia, especially if one of them, as was more than likely, was helping to build the country a new university, say, or a new airport. Well, that was something he would find out tomorrow, when he met some of the key Botswanan government officials. He reckoned he had quite a lot going for him. He spoke several African languages, and through his involvement in boxing had earned the respect of the black community. Max believed that leadership potential was developed through sport, and had worked hard and long for the promotion of black South African boxers in the international arena.

There was a knock on the door of the suite. Max walked through from the sitting room and opened it. A black woman, dressed in a white blouse and dark skirt, walked into the room and sat down on one of the easy chairs. Fairly attractive; he would put her in her early twenties. She lit a cigarette and looked seductively into his eyes. He stared at her, nonplussed.

'For a hundred rands . . .'

Max angrily tightened the cord of his towelling robe. His relaxed mood, and his concentration, were both gone. 'Get out!' he said. He must talk to the manager. Someone on the staff was obviously running a prostitution racket.

She felt the front of her blouse fall open to reveal her pendulous breasts. 'If you don't like me . . . I've got friends.'

He grabbed her hand and yanked her towards the door. 'You shame your people,' he said. Taking a wad of pula notes out of his pocket, he pushed them into her handbag. 'Take that, and get off your back.'

She spat in his face. 'You dirty South African son-of-a-bitch!' Then she ran off down the corridor.

He slammed the door and went into the bathroom to clean his face. All the problems of the continent, he thought, summed up in a single incident.

He had dinner in his room, working as he ate, skimming through each of his reports and looking for errors or omissions. Max was a perfectionist. In his first business, geophysical surveying, tiny errors had made the vital difference between failure and success, and spotting one of these on a geophysical survey many years before had enabled him to find copper where no one had thought it existed. The result had been an open-cast copper mine that had made him an overnight millionaire.

Just before midnight he put down the last of the reports, and decided he'd earned a break. He freshened up, then put on a jacket and tie. The casino would provide a brief distraction – gambling was one of his few addictions. Anyway, he told himself, he wouldn't be able to sleep immediately after such an intense working session, even if he tried.

Leaving his suite, he found to his surprise that the hotel was still busy, with a steady stream of people moving through the foyer. The casino lay across lawns, beyond an illuminated oval swimming pool. Max looked up into the clear evening sky, listening to the sounds of Africa around him – the continuous buzz of crickets, the bark of a hyena. Again he felt satisfaction at the renovation of the hotel – the atmosphere was perfect.

As he walked through the mirrored glass doors of the casino, a black woman bumped into him. He made to apologise, then realised that the 'accident' had been intentional: another hooker. She stared at him coldly, then turned on her heel. He guessed the word had got around that he didn't have much of a predilection for prostitutes.

Inside, the casino was a blend of cigarette smoke, mood music, and muffled conversation occasionally punctuated by a gasp of satisfaction or disappointment. Max went over to the cashier. He knew that to draw money he'd have to reveal his identity, but the need for anonymity was over. He'd seen enough already to make an accurate judgement about the level of service at his newest hotel.

'Good evening. One hundred thousand pula, please.' He

passed his cheque over the counter, and saw that the cashier was about to query it until she noticed the name.

'Dr Loxton!'

'I've come for a little roulette.'

Quickly she pushed the money across the counter, and as he left he noticed her reach for the phone. That was good. The manager would no doubt be on top form when Max saw him in the morning.

He crossed the floor of the casino, heading for the Salon Privé. At the end of the main casino was what looked like a solid wall of mirrors. Only a few – including Max himself, who had had a hand in the design – knew of the concealed door.

A tall man dressed in black tie blocked his path. 'Sir, this is a private room for serious players.' Discreet but firm.

Max produced the card that was only issued to those who could afford to play for high stakes. As he read the name on it, the man looked up with surprise, and swallowed. 'My apologies, Dr Loxton.'

The man bowed, and Max, smiling pleasantly, walked through into the Salon Privé.

It was a beautiful room. An open picture window, all along one wall, looked onto a private garden with a fountain. Inside, the deep-pile wool carpet, subtle lighting and period furniture completed the effect of grace and luxury. Max moved across to the roulette table and stood watching the trend of play for a while, then he sat down at the table and took P25,000 of chips from the croupier. There was no thrill for him unless he gambled with a significantly large amount, and at the Salon Privé he was guaranteed to be playing with people who felt the same way. As he moved some of his chips across the baize, he noticed a strikingly attractive dark-haired woman watching him from the other side of the table.

The game went well, and he had soon trebled his initial pot. A few more people came to the table. He felt the excitement building, felt himself in the grip of it – and at the same time resented its power over him. He noticed the woman again. She was dark and mysterious, leaning forward so that he caught a tantalising glimpse of her cleavage. He pushed P200,000 of chips across the board and suddenly, everyone went very quiet. The wheel took a long time to turn. Max stared at the woman and she returned his gaze. Everything risked on the chance of a

19

moment, that was the way to live. Attractive green eyes, a full, sensual mouth, the black silk dress clinging to her body. He wanted her.

There was an intake of breath. He glanced back at the table. He had won.

The adrenalin was surging through him now. He caught her gaze again: she was challenging him. He shifted everything he'd won across the green baize, put it all on one number.

A trickle of sweat ran down the croupier's face, and the room fell silent. Players at other tables, sensing the excitement, moved across to share it, mesmerized like Max himself. The wheel turned, the black ball skipping lightly across its undulations. Max suddenly remembered how it had been when he was in the ring – how every time he'd seen his opponent's fist coming at him, he'd reached inside himself and found an extra reserve of strength.

The wheel stopped. The ball was on the black and he had won over a million pula. He turned to look at the brunette. She was smiling enigmatically.

Silence still held the table as he walked over to her. 'Like to celebrate?'

'Honey, I never celebrate with strangers.' The voice was American, husky and deep.

'Max Loxton.' He stared into the sparkling green eyes.

'My name's Saffron. Let's party, Mr Loxton . . .'

He couldn't remember exactly what time they had come back to his room. Against earlier resolutions, he'd drunk a bottle of Moët, and now he was lying on the bed, still dressed, watching her.

He still didn't know who she was; perhaps the wife of a visiting diplomat or businessman, who like a fool had left her alone for the evening. She was electrifying. She was undressing slowly, taunting him with those green eyes. For a moment he had memories of Shandy – but no, this one was different. He was usually in control when it came to women, but he wasn't now.

The dress slid off and she stood naked before him. It was as if she'd never worn clothes – she was unashamed of her nakedness, so sure of her sexuality. His eyes fell from the fine dark hair cascading over her shoulders to the triangle of dark hair between her legs.

She walked towards the door. 'Sweet dreams, Mr Loxton.'

20

He sprang up like a cat. She turned, her eyes never shifting from his face, and he pulled her across the room and down onto the bed.

'Goddamn it, is this your idea of seduction?' she purred, her dark tongue running across her lips. Then he was kissing her, feeling young again, remembering his first kiss, the intensity of love without fear.

She pushed him away. 'Look at me,' she said softly. 'And tell me what you see.'

He kissed her on the forehead, rising from the bed and undressing slowly. Naked, he peered into the depths of her soul. 'Everything I've ever wanted in a woman,' he said.

Her mouth locked across his and he felt himself deliciously lost, unable to think, swimming on a sea of emotion.

Consciousness was eddying and flowing in him, like the tide on a moonlit night when there is a cool wind blowing amongst the palm trees. The elixir of love brought memories, long forgotten, flooding back to him. Then came an image of a woman with dark hair, wielding a sword, her green eyes flashing as storm clouds rushed across a darkening sky. Was this a dream or could it be real?

The sharp buzz of the alarm clock woke him and he smashed it off the side-table. Instinctively he reached out for her, then realised she was no longer with him. He felt a deep sense of loss. He staggered into the bathroom, turning the shower on cold and diving in underneath it, letting the freezing water take effect. Shivering, he strode back into the room.

The training routine he'd used when he was boxing at university seventeen years ago hadn't changed. First, he did two quick sets of press-ups. Then he pulled a skipping rope from his case and went out onto the balcony, the leather cord singing round his head as he danced on his feet. He skipped faster and faster, crossing his hands and alternating from foot to foot. After half an hour he was sweating heavily and took another shower – this time a hot one. Now he was feeling stronger. But his mind and body were still filled with memories of the previous night.

He went to the batch of files he'd prepared the evening before – they were all in order – and it was only then that he noticed a message smeared in lipstick on the dressing-table mirror. 'When love beckons, follow.'

He was unnerved. He had not been in charge of what had happened with Saffron the previous night; it was something quite beyond his normal experience, and he had to see her again.

There was a knock on the door, and a maid appeared with his coffee and papers. He took them out onto the balcony. The cool morning air, the fresh coffee and the memory of the night before, made him feel very good.

He ran over his portfolio in the stocks and shares section of the paper, hoping that his broker had listened to his instructions the previous day. With the imminent release of Napoleon Zwane there had been an upswing in confidence on the Johannesburg Stock Exchange. He paged through the rest of the paper, which was full of articles on Zwane and had an editorial praising Kobus van der Post for arranging his release. Max also saw that there had been unrest in Soweto. His forehead wrinkled with concern as he read the report. Why violence now? It didn't make sense. A mindless anarchy seemed to be taking control of the township; in ten separate incidents people had been burned to death – a frightening pattern of violence.

The Botswanan news was tame stuff by comparison. Max saw that his arrival in the country had been noted. There was also an excited article about the possible development of new mines. Max grimaced at its short-sightedness; no one here seemed to care about tomorrow.

He put the paper down and took a sip of coffee, remembering his winnings of the previous evening. The hotel manager would definitely not be sleeping in late this morning – he'd probably have to contact the bank to raise the extra funds. Max chuckled to himself; after all, he was only taking money from himself and his shareholders. He reflected that at least the guests of the Salon Privé would be discreet – if he'd made that money in the main casino, the story would have been all over the local papers.

He shaved, dressed quickly, then drove into Gaberone to begin the serious business of the day.

Over the course of the day, Max managed to see everyone he wanted to see, including the Minister of Mines and the Minister of Commerce. His proposals were treated with apparent disdain – but he hadn't expected much more than this initially. At this stage he wanted merely to plant ideas, in particular the possibility of increasing revenue by heavier taxation on fewer mines. He would proceed slowly, winning support little by little. Only when he had this support would he really put pressure on the Botswanan government.

He was back at the Gaberone Oasis by six, and found the hotel in full swing, coping with a sudden influx of South Africans. He was relieved that he wouldn't be eating here this evening; in his jacket pocket he had a stiff manilla card with gold edging, an invitation to dinner at the President of Botswana's residence. It was better than he had hoped for; he might well get an opportunity to talk to the President himself.

Before going back to his rooms he had a short meeting with the hotel manager – at which he was not the least bit conciliatory. He made himself quite clear: if he saw any more evidence of prostitution, he would give the manager his marching orders. The man knew better than to argue, and Max was fairly certain that he would handle the situation efficiently. Back in his suite Max took a long, leisurely bath. He thought of Saffron. They'd meet again, and soon. He'd make it happen. And then he thought of Shandy, the wife who'd cheated on him. The bitterness always crept up on him at times like this, when he was least prepared to resist it.

He knew there were other people like Shandy – people who didn't like the man he was. They thought of him as a wild card. He knew he drove himself hard: the mining exploration business, the gold mines and now the hotel chain – each of these he'd attacked with the same furious energy, and all to achieve one goal: his Botswana project. And then he hated being tied down, fettered by convention. He was a free thinker, and that determined his political outlook – he'd always detested apartheid. How could you build a country on a constitution that judged a man by the colour of skin? Freedom – that was a magic word. And for him, Botswana represented freedom; it was a country that still retained its wildness, the essential quality of Africa, and he would fight to keep it that way.

Max had fought for his own freedom since he was a boy; boxing had given him his first taste of it, the knowledge that he could hold his own against any man. It had also given him financial independence, an essential step on the road to freedom. His father was an enormously wealthy man, but from an early

23

age Max had decided he wanted nothing from his father. He would not taint his hands with David Loxton's blood money.

His mother would have understood that if she had still been alive, but she had died tragically in a car accident when he was eight. Tracey: he had a photograph of her standing next to the Bushman, Kotuko. He wished he knew more about her; he often wondered how she could ever have loved his father. Always he felt as if she were with him in spirit.

After her death, and until his father married again five years later, he and his two sisters, Vicky and Lucinda, had been brought up by a succession of housekeepers. It had been a bleak, loveless childhood, and he had been glad to leave it behind.

He pulled up outside the front gates of the President's private estate just after 8.15 pm, where an armed guard carefully checked his invitation against a typed list before allowing him to proceed up the drive. The house was half a kilometre away, surrounded by a game reserve; the President was as passionate about wildlife as Max himself, and Max hoped to capitalise on this. Of course, he reflected, as he drove up to the enormous thatched mansion, the wild animals that prowled around the estate were also excellent security – far better than guard dogs or surveillance systems.

He was relieved to see that he was by no means the last to arrive. The main reception room was alive with the buzz of conversation and the tinkle of glasses, and men and women in evening dress stood silhouetted against the darkness of the African night. A waiter handed him a glass of champagne, and among the throng he caught sight of Solomon Khoza, Deputy Minister of Tourism, a known advocate of free enterprise.

'Solomon, how are you?'

Several guests turned round in surprise, for Max spoke Setswana, the language of Botswana, as if it were his own.

'Ha. Max Loxton. You never give up, do you?'

Solomon eased Max gently away from the crowd, out through glass doors and onto the lawn beyond. 'Now let us talk,' he said softly, and Max saw his eyes flash in the darkness.

'Any reaction to my visit to Gaberone this morning?' Max asked in a low voice.

'Reaction? You've stirred up a hornets' nest. You know the

24

President favours your plans, but his cabinet think very differently.'

Max respected the courage it must have taken for Solomon to tell him this. 'Well,' he said, 'I just hope I got a few people thinking.'

'Thinking of ways to get rid of you! Conservation is not regarded as an important issue here. And it's a question of power, Max. You and your country are seen as a threat to us. It is felt that you have no right to interfere.'

'But Kobus van der Post is letting Napoleon Zwane out of prison, and he's talking of big changes that will favour your people – surely the pressure is off?' Max found it hard to keep his irritation under control.

Solomon moved closer to him. 'Don't be a fool! Zwane was put in prison thirty years ago – he's a spent force. Times have changed, my friend. There are new forces to be reckoned with.'

Max cursed silently. This was something that had worried him, but which he hadn't really taken seriously. It was true that many of the more radical black freedom fighters believed the African Freedom Council and Napoleon Zwane had lost their edge. They felt that the AFC, with its temporary headquarters in Zambia, was out of touch with the reality in the townships. 'You're talking about the Comrades?' he said.

'Yes, my friend. And they're bound by the blood of oppression. They're not interested in democracy – only in power.'

'You believe they have power, here? And that they're against my plans?'

'Your proposals were well prepared, but you're another white face – no better, no worse than the rest. Besides, there are others with more money.'

'Euro?'

Solomon nodded.

'Are you people fucking crazy!'

Solomon looked up at him in silence. At five foot six, he was not an imposing figure, but his face reflected the powerful mind that lay behind it. Now he put his finger to his lips, and Max looked round into the darkness. 'Be careful what you say, Max. Euro has a lot of influence here. I'm glad that at least you kept your anti-Euro sentiments out of your reports – they would have doomed them to the rubbish bin.'

'There's seven years of work in those reports, and they point

25

to one indisputable conclusion – unless you take action, your country will be a wasteland in ten years' time, a goddamned dust bowl. I'm not in this for myself – don't you understand?'

Solomon gripped his shoulders. 'I trust you like a brother, Max. I know what you say is true, but a man can die for saying such things. Listen, there is something I must tell you.' He paused. 'Euro are going to drain the Okavango Delta. They're planning a gigantic new mine there!'

Max felt himself in turmoil. This was appalling news. He saw his dream beginning to fade away, and the boxer in him wanted to lash out at someone. Solomon's eyes never left his face, and he realised suddenly that in telling him this, Solomon Khoza was probably risking his life.

'The ethics of Euro,' Max said, spitting the words out, 'are those of the British imperialists of the last century. There is total arrogance masquerading as modesty, courtesy that conceals a ruthless self-interest, and a fierce elitism that pretends to a democratic openness of mind.'

Solomon grimaced. 'Your father sits on the board of Euro.'

'You don't know about my relationship with my father? We hate each other's guts.'

'There's nothing you can do there, then?'

'When will Euro make a public announcement about its delta project?'

'When it happens, my friend.'

'And what happens if anyone finds out about this conversation, Solomon?'

'I will die.'

There was a sound behind them, and they both turned to see a man striding across the grass towards them. Max saw a ripple of fear cross Solomon's face.

'You guys are speaking that funny language of yours again, how about a little English for us foreigners?' The voice was American, deep and booming. Max recognised the man as the owner of the world's largest TV network, Packard Vision. 'Hi. Packard's the name, John Packard.' He stretched out a big paw, and Max, then Solomon, shook it, making their introductions.

'Sorry if I broke up your party, guys. I came out here for a little light relief.'

'You find our President boring?' Solomon interjected.

'Hey, slow down, Mr Khoza.'

Max studied the American TV magnate closely. He was of medium height, with greying blond hair swept back from a prominent, almost square forehead, and deeply recessed, pale blue eyes. The effect was distinctly Teutonic; he exuded power. Max already knew a lot about him. The son of a movie director and a famous actress, he'd realised early that the smart money was going into television, and after business degrees at Berkeley and Harvard he had persuaded his father to lend him the money to start his own television production company. By the time he was twenty-four, John Packard was a millionaire, by the time he was thirty he'd made a fortune. He'd written a book all about it, *The Packard Way*.

Someone else came out of the darkness, and Max breathed in a musky scent. 'Honey, you haven't found any lions to shoot?'

'My wife, gentlemen, likes to live dangerously. Saffron, dear, meet Dr Max Loxton – hotels, mining and so on. And Mr Solomon Khoza, Deputy Minister of Tourism for this beautiful country.'

She took his breath away. She was dressed in a man's black-tie suit without a shirt, so that her breasts were all but exposed. Her long black hair was pulled back to reveal the striking lines of her deeply tanned face. He knew, suddenly, that he could not live without her.

'Mr Khoza, Dr Loxton, a pleasure to meet you.' She spoke softly. Her eyes caught Max's and he returned her gaze, spellbound. Fighting to regain control, he managed to pull his eyes away and stared into the darkness. What did she feel about him? Had it been a one-night fling for her? He wanted her now more than he'd wanted anything in his life. And she was married to one of the most powerful and ruthless men in the United States.

John Packard glowered. He did not like other men ogling his beautiful wife. 'Your mind seems to be elsewhere, Dr Loxton?'

Max stared into Saffron's green eyes again. 'Are you on holiday here?' No woman had ever had this effect on him before. He positively ached to have her naked flesh against his own.

'Max, I'm directing a feature.'

The pieces suddenly fell into place. Saffron Packard was one of the talented new breed of independent film directors. No doubt he was just one of a procession of lovers. He felt despair riding over him like a dark horse. 'A film about Botswana?' he

27

managed. He saw that Solomon was looking at him oddly. Were his feelings as obvious as that?

'Yes,' Packard said, 'though I doubt that as a South African you'd approve of its subject matter.' There was a glint in Packard's eyes now. He was actually enjoying the effect his wife was having on Max.

Solomon butted in quickly. 'Few men have done more to fight apartheid than Dr Loxton. You do him an injustice.'

Max took a deep breath, while a startled expression registered on Packard's face. He was obviously used to making people squirm, but, recovering, he playfully held up his hands. 'Whoa! My apologies! The politics of this land are hard to get to grips with.'

Max was hardly listening. Saffron was still staring into his eyes.

'Saffron! Come, the President's interested in your film.' And Packard guided Saffron away, holding her arm a fraction too tightly.

Solomon slipped back into his native Setswana. 'Are you all right, my friend?'

For a moment Max stumbled over his words. 'You can't let Euro drain the delta . . .'

'Max, if one word of our talk tonight gets out, I'm dead.'

After a few minutes' conversation with her husband and the President, Saffron Packard excused herself, slipped away from the crowd and made her way down an empty corridor. She was looking for somewhere where she could be alone, somewhere to think. Opening a door, she was pleased to find a room in darkness, and she slipped inside. As her eyes grew accustomed to the lack of light, she made out a bed, and beyond it French windows opening onto a balcony. She curled up on the carpet by the windows and stared up at the stars, her mind in turmoil over Dr Max Loxton.

She'd acted completely on impulse the previous evening at the casino. She'd had a tough day trying to get everyone functioning on set, and then, at dinner, she and John had started arguing over their first glass of wine. He disliked the subject matter of her new film. Frankly, he'd said, she was wasting her energy on it – and they'd ended up having one hell of a row. By the time they got back to the hotel, they weren't speaking to each other; John had gone to sleep and she had gone to the casino.

Now this bull of a man, Max Loxton, totally dominated her thoughts. She liked his modesty – he hadn't boasted about his winnings at the casino. She guessed they were a fraction of his real wealth, though in fact, he hadn't told her anything about himself at all. So different from John with his brash self-assertiveness, John who was driven by an insatiable desire for both money and power. For some time now, though she was fiercely independent, Saffron had been feeling neglected by him – the woman in her needed attention. She sensed that Max Loxton had a gift for making people feel special, that he could provide her with plenty of emotional support. But really this was just a rationalisation, because the fact was that she had fallen head-over-heels in love with him. She didn't know if he was married, or had some other attachment, and she had no idea what to do next; all she knew was that she wanted to be in his arms more than anything else in the world.

Suddenly, the light in the room was switched on. Springing up like a cat, Saffron had opened the French doors in a moment, and was out on the balcony. She drew up against the wall, adrenalin coursing through her, beads of perspiration on her forehead. Danger was something she'd always relished.

She heard the door of the room shut, and footsteps coming towards the French windows. Cornered, she looked down at the drop below. She could hear herself breathing. But whoever it was stopped short at the open windows and turned round.

'You are wasting my time,' Saffron heard a German voice say. There was the click of a lighter, then she smelt cigarettes. 'Sit down, my friend.'

A softer male voice, a Botswanan, she guessed, said, 'You have been paid a small fortune. You can afford to listen.' The German laughed. 'You did not pay me, and this contract is none of your business. Your orders were clear – you were only to contact me in case of an emergency.'

The other voice was agitated, frightened. 'Yes, but we don't want him killed on our soil.'

'What does it matter where the corpse rests?' There was almost a chuckle in the German's voice. 'We both want him dead, and that is what he will be tomorrow morning. You're ashamed of your dirty work, black man? It's a pity none of you has the guts to do it.'

'Then you will not listen to us?'

29

'No.' The finality with which the German said this indicated that further discussion was pointless, but the other voice said desperately, 'We have pictures. We'll reveal your identity!'

The German almost growled. 'I will kill him here. Then I'll dump the body over the border. OK?'

Saffron heard sounds of a struggle, followed by a cry of pain. 'Please!' The Botswanan's voice was a squeal.

'You people are scum,' came the response. 'If we had ruled, you would all be dead. And you, you know far too much.'

Something fell, hitting the floor. 'Goodbye, Schwarze,' Saffron heard, and then the door closing quietly.

Beating the steering wheel of the Landy with rage, Max drove back to the Oasis from the President's house. His mind was in a ferment. He had spent the rest of his time at the dinner consolidating the relationships he'd established earlier in the day, in Gaberone, and he had even managed five minutes with the President. But now he knew that his listeners were only humouring him; after what he'd learned from Solomon Khoza, he knew they weren't really listening at all.

On top of all that, there was Saffron. He had to have her, it was as simple as that.

He got back to the Oasis at two in the morning, strode past the revellers in the main dining room and up to his suite, where he stripped off his evening dress and threw open the balcony doors. The full moon shone brightly. Botswana and Saffron, he was in love with them both. He had to act, and act fast.

When he woke the next morning, they were still in his thoughts, but now his mind was set. He would stop Euro from draining the swamps, and he would take Saffron.

He was glad of the expected knock at the door – coffee and the papers were just what he needed. But instead of the usual maid, he was surprised to see a smartly dressed man facing him, holding the coffee tray. A white waiter? No, not possible.

Suddenly the man's right foot shot up and hit him hard in the groin. Max staggered back and the man moved into the room, throwing the coffee tray to one side. The silenced pistol was out and pointing.

Max threw himself to one side, and the bullet slammed into the floor next to him. He rolled over, and over again as his assailant moved forwards. Max was leopard-crawling behind the

30

bed now; a bullet grazed his head, hitting the giant glass mirror and sending glass shards flying round the room. He picked up the bedside lamp and hurled it towards the gunman. The porcelain base erupted into tiny pieces as, with frightening accuracy, a bullet caught it in mid-flight.

The only thing to do was to get out. The glass shattering as he hit it, Max dived head-first through the side window, rolling into a ball and dropping a storey into the gardens below. Even as he dragged himself out of the line of fire, another bullet thudded into the earth beside him. Death was only seconds away. And now the gunman leapt from the window, dropping his pistol as he fell. Max was ready for him now, the fight had really started, and as he hit the ground, Max landed a punch in his right ear. The man crumpled to the earth, then rolled over, grabbing his pistol and firing. The bullet sang across Max's throat, tearing the skin open. He dived towards his attacker before he could let off another shot, and in that brief moment of surprise, managed to connect a punch to the gunman's ribcage.

Dimly, vaguely, somewhere at the edge of his field of vision, Max could see hotel guests running towards them. Bloody fools, they'd only get hurt.

The gunman was gripping his ribcage in agony, his pistol lying on the earth. Max moved in for the kill – but the gunman's left foot came up without warning, smashing into the side of his skull. Max reeled back with the force of the blow, then, recovering his wits, landed two more punches in his opponent's belly. The gunman shrugged them off, backing into a karate stance.

Max smiled grimly: now he knew what to expect. He was back in the ring now, every nerve tingling. Another blow caught Max on the side of his skull and he shot forwards, smashing the bare knuckles of his right fist just below the gunman's heart. He followed through with more punches that lifted the gunman into the air, and as he came down Max moved in again, with two more blows to the ribcage and then a pile-driver in the centre of the face that almost broke Max's left hand.

Max's attacker staggered up again, now weaving from side to side. This was it, this was his chance. Max lost control, smashing his fists again and again into the man's head, sobbing with exhaustion, and his attacker keeled over onto the lush green lawn.

Max dragged himself back and leaned against a tree – but

there was a sudden searing pain in the back of his hand. He looked down. Christ, a throwing knife! The bastard had been faking! Christ, the pain! He spun round to see the gunman sprinting away across the lawns.

Max wrenched the blade out of his left hand, then he was away, blood pouring from the open wound. But he didn't care any longer, he just had to get this crazy bastard who was trying to kill him. Sirens wailed in the distance. The man was quicker on his feet than Max, disappearing into the bush as the shadow of a helicopter passed over them, the noise of the rotors blanketing out all other sounds.

The chopper came down in front of Max and two uniformed men leapt from the hold, sprinting towards him, their hair flattened by the wind from the rotors. 'Follow the bastard!' he yelled. But, incomprehensibly, they kept on running towards him, and now his hands were being pulled up behind him, cuffs clicking onto his wrists.

'It's not me, it's him!' But his scream faded as they roughly dragged him back to the chopper.

He focused blearily on the brunette, and reached out. To his surprise, she took his hand. Now he saw her more clearly: deeply tanned face, hair parted in the centre, glittering green eyes watching him closely. Painfully he raised himself up and kissed her softly on the lips.

The taste of her roused him. He was conscious of the exotic fragrance she was wearing. Then, looking round, the sight of the crude bench and the black metal bars brought memory flooding back. Her perfume wasn't strong enough to disguise the smell of urine.

'Easy, honey. You've taken a hell of a beating. What happened?' Saffron whispered.

'What happened? Some bastard tried to wipe me out!'

She held up the local newspaper, and he saw that there was a picture of him on the front page. Where the hell had they got it? It was an army photograph from fifteen years before. 'Mad Max' read the headline. He ripped the paper from her hands and read the article. He had apparently run amok in the grounds of the Oasis hotel with a machine-gun.

'What rubbish! It was a silenced pistol!' He was shaking with anger.

32

She placed a finger to her lips, leant closer to him. 'I know.'

She was wearing a jet-black jumpsuit that emphasized her sensuous curves, the beauty of her long, full legs and her pert, thrusting breasts. The zip was pulled down slightly at the top, revealing the soft dark skin of her throat, and her face was lightly made-up, with a sheen of pale lipstick on her lips. Was she real, or did she exist only in his imagination?

The thick black bars brought him back to reality. 'Get me out of here before they kill me!'

'Quit worrying, Max, you're free to leave.'

She helped him to his feet, moving him towards the open cell door. Unsteady, he followed her. 'How long have I been in this hole?'

'Twenty-four hours. It's Monday morning.'

At the desk he was handed a cardboard box containing his belongings. His watch was missing, but judging by the look on the policeman's face, it wasn't worth complaining about. Only when they were outside the police station did his anger really surface.

'This is bloody ridiculous! Some madman tries to kill me and I end up in jail!'

'Cool down, goddamn it! I had to pull every string I know to get you out.'

'You bailed me out?'

'Yes. Now let's get out of here.'

They got into her car, and he leaned against the side of the seat, totally exhausted. As they drove, sunlight bounced off the bonnet of the car, temporarily blinding him. The smell of the leather upholstery and Saffron's perfume mingled together, driving the stench of the police cell from his memory. In the distance he saw a small boy playing with a ball, his shape dancing in the heat-haze. Saffron took his hand. 'You must see a doctor – those wounds are dirty.'

'I want to go to the central government offices. To hell with the doctor!'

Saffron pulled the car up with a jolt and turned to face him, her green eyes flashing with anger. 'I've lost a whole day's shooting because of you, I've bailed you out, and now you act like a fucking fool! Don't you understand that they want you dead!'

He pulled her towards him, ignoring her efforts at resistance, and brought his lips to her mouth. The kiss went on and on. She closed her eyes, relaxing in his arms. What lay behind the passion in her kiss? Did it mean that she cared for him as much as he cared for her? She drew back at last, and kissed him on the throat as he stroked her long black hair.

'Saffron, I'm sorry.' She looked up into his eyes, and he said: 'I'm crazy about you.'

'Max Loxton, I guess I've chosen the worst man on earth to fall in love with.'

It was then that Max had a sudden vague feeling of unease. Looking round, he saw a car parked behind them with two men inside. He was sure he'd seen the same car outside the police station. Shit! Saffron was right, they were after him.

She followed his gaze. 'We're being followed?'

'Drop me off at the hospital, then get my Landy from the Oasis. I think we should disappear.'

Max studied the thatched roof above him with a certain detachment, and chuckled as he thought back to the men in the car trying to follow him and Saffron through the bush. He'd lost them in just five minutes – the Landy had been a good idea. Now here they were together, Saffron lying over his left arm, her head across his chest and her long black hair cascading down over his body.

This place was far away and very private. It had come as part of the deal when he'd bought the Oasis – an exclusive game reserve thrown in, one hundred kilometres north-east of Gaberone, quite close to Francistown. From time to time he needed a place where he could come and collect his thoughts; this was where he always came – and now was such a time.

He thought now about the attempt on his life. It wasn't the first time he'd faced death. In the army, he'd fought for his life – but that was war. In the boxing ring he'd fought too, but that was not like fighting for your life against an unknown assailant; then, it was a battle of wits and strength, where you and your opponent faced each other openly. That was when you really lived, walking the knife-edge between victory and defeat. Had he been a fool to give up boxing? He had to admit he enjoyed the knife-edge experience, it made him feel very alive.

But this last time, he knew, he'd missed death by a hair's breadth. And the police hadn't wanted to hear about it! They said that he and the other man had been fighting over gambling debts, that Max shouldn't think he was above the law merely because he owned the Oasis. He had been charged with assault, and with bringing a weapon illegally into the country. They had a simple explanation for what had happened, and that was all that mattered to them. Life was cheap in Africa.

He looked again at Saffron. She'd completely exhausted him – John Packard was a fool to neglect her. Her eyes opened. 'Mmmmmm. Max, I can see that brain working overtime again. Who owns this wonderful place?' Her voice was still husky with sleep.

'I do. When I bought the Oasis, the reserve, and this little game lodge, came with it. I had the place re-fenced and re-thatched. I keep it for myself, and special guests.'

'Am I a special guest?'

He drew her close to him, feeling the softness of her against the matted hair of his chest. 'For a lifetime.'

She pulled away from him and folded her arms, looking at the thatched reed ceiling, angry. 'Did you have to say that?'

He drew her to him again, ignoring her opposition, but she wrenched herself away. Her strength took him by surprise – she was like a leopard, lean and wiry, strong, and with a natural agility. He caught her, saw the rage flash in her eyes as she realized she was no match for him. Now they stood facing each other, naked. He held her by the wrists, pulling them together in a praying position.

'Look at me.'

The flashing green eyes focused on his.

'I love you. I want you.'

'Want to keep me locked up like some zoo animal? Parade me in front of your friends?'

'No. I love your independence, your spirit.'

He was less sure of himself with her now. She drew him back to the bed, lay down beside him, stroking his hair.

'All lovers make promises, Max. Promises made in the heat of the night, then forgotten in the morning.' She held his face between her long, slim fingers. 'I live for what I do. John also promised me independence, but all the time he tries to wall me in. I'm not going to let any guy do that to me. Life is for fighting, for living every day as if another will not come. That's why I'm here with you now instead of on set. Today's worth the hundred thousand dollars in lost shooting time.'

Max chuckled. 'So you think you're getting value for money?'

'Every woman pays a price, takes a risk.' She kissed him on the lips. 'Honey, you've said the words I wanted to hear, but can you honour them?'

The silence hung between them like a storm cloud over a mountain – dark, brooding, intense. Max looked out of the window at the rolling veld in the late afternoon sun. He thought of a lifetime of not knowing her, of opportunity lost and an eternity of regret. There was no doubt in his mind now. 'I'll fight for you. Every day I'll find something new about you. I'll make you only one promise. If you marry me – I'll always let you be yourself.'

He'd played his hand, now he must see if life had dealt him the right cards.

She kissed him long and passionately, and he felt the sap rise within him. Her hands explored his body, instinctively knowing what aroused him. Rolling her over, he ran his lips across the deeply tanned flesh of her back and she let out a sigh of ecstasy, her flanks rising and falling in expectation of him. Still he held back, teasing her, building her passion to fever-pitch.

'Yes, oh yes.'

He glided inside her. The force of his feeling shook his body, and he could no longer control himself, the pleasure exquisite as he felt her shuddering against him. Her body was alive, her climax shaking her deep within.

'Hold me, goddamn it, hold me!'

He held her tightly, frightened at the feeling he had unleashed in her. Gradually she relaxed, tears running from her eyes. Then she curled up small against him, nuzzling his chest.

He watched the sun setting across the veld, a pale yellow light suffusing the bedroom. As the day faded, the trees and bushes beyond the window took on a magic quality, every colour intensified. He felt whole again. She had given him her answer.

He woke in the darkness and slipped softly from the bed so as not to disturb her. There were questions he had to have the answers to. He went into the study and switched on the light; his papers were neatly piled at one side of the desk, his address book in the drawer. He rang the number, drumming his fingers on the desk as he listened to the tone. At the thirtieth ring, when he was about to put the receiver down, someone picked up the phone at the other end – but there was silence.

'Hallo?'

'Who is it?' A faint female voice.

'Mrs Khoza, I have to speak to Solomon, I believe he is in great danger.'

He heard a sob, and fear shot through his body. 'Please, what's wrong?'

'They've taken him, the secret police.'

Max felt his blood run cold. 'When did this happen?'

'Early yesterday morning.'

'Give me your address,' he said. 'I'll be over straightaway.'

'No, we must meet somewhere else. The house is being watched.'

He looked at his watch; pondered on a place where they wouldn't look conspicuous at that hour. 'The casino,' he said, 'at the Oasis, in an hour.'

'I'll be there.'

He turned over in the bed to see that Saffron's side was empty – and then he smelled the wonderful smell of coffee brewing. He was very tired after his middle-of-the-night meeting with Solomon's wife at the hotel. She had had no idea where her husband had been taken, and she was thoroughly overwrought – Max had told her to ask her doctor for sedatives. It was too much of a coincidence that Solomon had been abducted almost at the same time as he, Max, had been the victim of a murderous assault. Someone must know they were both aware of Euro's plan to drain the swamps; someone must want them dead.

Naked, Saffron came into the room, carrying the coffee. 'Can't complain about the quality of the room service!' Max joked, but just as she was about to reply, peace was shattered by the sound of a car hooter going full-blast. Max angrily snatched up his dressing-gown and sprinted round to the back of the lodge.

What he saw at once was that a dusty white Peugeot 404 had smashed into the back of his Land-Rover. The driver of the car was slumped over the wheel. Max ran over and tore the door open.

'What the . . .?'

The words died on his lips. The driver was covered in blood

and hardly breathing. Max grabbed the body and carried it out on to the grass, then pulled off his towelling robe and made it into a pillow for the man's head.

'Max! Oh my God!' He heard Saffron's voice, tremulous behind him.

'Get some blankets and some water. He's almost gone.'

'Oh Max! It's Solomon Khoza!'

My God, she was right; the face was so dreadfully disfigured that he had not recognized him. The eyes stared desperately from bloody sockets, and the whole face was so covered in hideous burn-marks – huge black and blue scorches across lips and nose – that it looked like an abstract painting.

Saffron was back with the blankets in seconds, and they wrapped them round the tortured body. Max saw now that all Solomon's fingers were mangled and broken; they looked as if they had been crushed in a vice. She handed him a hip flask – 'Brandy. Good for shock.' – and he trickled the amber liquid between the black man's lips. Almost immediately Solomon's eyes opened, and he let out a long, shuddering sigh. Max held his hand, silently praying, hoping, praying.

'Be careful, Max . . .' The words came with great difficulty, punctuating the spasms of pain.

'Euro?'

'No . . . This is deeper. You must leave it alone, Max. Go away.'

Solomon's voice was fading now. In a last desperate effort to hang onto life he raised himself up, pulling Max close to him. The bloody eyes stared at him with frightening intensity. 'Go away.'

'I will get them, whoever they are. Just tell me.'

'No. Go away!' Solomon gasped, and fell back onto the grass.

Saffron watched Max's big hands fumbling with the buttons of Solomon's shirt. Gently, tenderly, he put his hand over the heart. There was no need to say anything; they both knew.

It was then that Saffron caught sight of the dead man's stomach. For a moment, caught off guard, she staggered back, screaming in horror, but quickly regained control when Max grabbed her arm. She turned to him. 'I have seen this before,' she whispered. 'I investigated a Satanic cult for a movie once, and there was something just like this – a sort of ritual killing. I can't quite believe it.'

Max stared down at the mass of congealed blood and burns that was Solomon's stomach. 'But that is gone from here!' he shouted. 'That old, primitive part of Africa is dead!' But even as he said it he knew it wasn't true.

That evening, Max, Saffron and Johannes, the chief black worker at the lodge, dealt with Solomon's mutilated corpse. Though Max had spent most of the day on the phone to the relevant authorities, no one would touch it, and Solomon's wife, when she saw it, had become hysterical. At first Max and Saffron had planned to bury the body on the farm, but Johannes – a fine man, loyal and a hard worker – had refused point blank. 'Bury him on this land, baas,' he said, 'and I leave.'

It was Saffron who had understood Johannes' deep fear of supernatural evil, and who had known what they must do. On a rocky buttress, out of wooden poles and strips of animal skin she had constructed a strong frame with a webbing platform, and on this strange bier they had laid Solomon Khoza's body, an offering to the gods.

The three of them stood there for a long time in the dying light, watching the sun settle behind the long line of low hills. The sky was an eerie blue now, streaked with long white clouds, the air unmoving. It was as if time stood still.

'What is it, Johannes?' said Max quietly. 'I do not understand why we have to do this.'

'It is not for you to know,' the black man said. He pointed to Saffron. 'She knows.'

'But you're a Christian, Johannes. What are you scared of?'

Johannes stared into his eyes. 'Evil,' he said.

Saffron spoke softly. 'Stand a minute,' she said. 'Pray that the spirit of this man lives in peace.'

Later Saffron lit a small fire, and as they drove back to the lodge, Max, taking a last look back, saw the small glow of it, and the lonely burial structure standing out black against the fiery red evening sky. This evil had been created by men – and he would hunt them down and destroy them.

Afterwards, he and Saffron ate outside, the hot coals of the braai glowing red in the darkness, the steaks sizzling as he dropped them onto the fire. Saffron had spun her long dark hair into a plait that nestled sensuously against her back, and was wearing black shorts and a T-shirt that clung tightly to her dusky skin. They did not talk of Solomon, although his death was with them in all they did and said.

Saffron touched his face. 'What happened to your nose?'

'It was broken in my first bout.'

'Did you win?'

He stared into the darkness, and Saffron could not guess if he was thinking of his fight, or something else. 'Yes, I won. I started boxing at school. Strangely, I've always found it helps me to relax.'

'Honey, you are crazy.'

He ignored this. 'Boxing requires absolute concentration,' he said.

'Like making love?'

He pulled her close to him, her lips locking against his own.

'That evening,' she said huskily, 'at the President's house. I couldn't stand being near you and yet not being able to touch you – I had to be alone. I found an empty bedroom and lay down to gather my wits – and then two men came into the room, a German and an African. They didn't see me, they were talking about the German killing someone. Max, I think that someone must have been you.' She clung to him tightly. 'I'm scared, Max. I don't want anything to happen to you.'

Later, they made love. She sat over him, her legs on either side of him and her taut breasts pointing down towards his face, while he moved his hands gently up and down her body. Then he was penetrating her. He was swimming in sensuality, and the feeling of total abandon almost scared him. They moved rhythmically together, stretching out the moments until their passion climaxed, then feeling it ebb and flow until it finally lapped away. He held her tightly, loving her, revelling in her, till she cried with the intensity of it.

'I'm sorry.' He was scared that he might have hurt her.

'No, no. Honey, I love you.'

Then there was silence between them. Tomorrow he must return to Johannesburg, while Saffron stayed filming in Botswana for another month. He felt his heart almost stop beating at the thought of it. If he lost her now . . .

'John is not going to take this well.' She took his face between her hands. 'I'll leave him, of course, but it's just that . . .'

'. . . You think I've got enough enemies already.' He looked

40

deep into her eyes. 'What's another? John Packard can't touch me.'

Only much later would he learn to regret those words.

Next morning, Saffron left early for the day's filming. Max was packing the last few things into the Landy when a car pulled up behind it and a black man stepped out. 'Dr Loxton?' He took Max's outstretched hand and shook it. 'The name's Gideon Sisulu,' he said in a firm voice. 'I'd like to ask you a few questions.'

'I'm not answering any questions. I'm leaving.'

'So Mrs Packard told me.' The dark eyes looked at him intently. 'I doubt if Mr Packard would appreciate the fact that you have spent the last two days here with his wife.'

'Shouldn't you be trying to find who wanted to kill me instead of playing peeping Tom?'

'As a detective inspector, it's my job to know what the people I am investigating are up to. You have been charged with public violence, Dr Loxton.'

Max towered over Sisulu. 'It won't stand up in court!'

The policeman stood his ground. 'It is my belief, however,' he went on, 'that you were the intended victim in a case of attempted murder, and I am trying to find a motive. Sexual jealousy is obviously a possibility.'

Max relaxed a little. Gideon Sisulu had guts, and he respected that. 'Perhaps we should have coffee inside?'

The sliding doors that formed one complete wall of the lodge's kitchen were drawn back, and outside the grasses of the rolling veld glistened with the last of the early morning dew. Sisulu smiled, sipping at his coffee. 'I have never been here before, but I have heard a great deal about you, Dr Loxton. You have a feel for, an understanding of our country. What you have done with the Oasis is nothing short of a miracle . . . But come, we must get down to serious business. The man who tried to kill you, can you tell me what he looked like?'

Max paused, thinking how to answer. This man could be anyone, in anyone's pay – Euro, Packard, his father. 'It's in my statement,' he said at last.

Sisulu leaned across the table, dark brown eyes boring into Max's. 'Don't be a fool, Dr Loxton. Solomon was my best friend.

Officially I may be here to ask you to return to Botswana for your trial – but unofficially I am here to avenge Solomon's death!'

He pulled out his wallet and removed a photograph. It was of three young men in casual clothes. Max stared at the picture, then at Sisulu.

'The man on the left is Solomon Khoza,' Sisulu said. 'The second is myself, and the third is your friend George, son of the famous Napoleon Zwane. This photograph was taken at Fort Hare University in 1961.

'You were all members of the African Freedom Council?'

'*Are* members, Dr Loxton. Take the photograph, show it to George, send him my regards.' He leaned back in his chair, stretched out and relaxed. 'You love this country, I know that. You have big plans. But you, like George and myself, are beginning to be old news, old hat, Dr Loxton. There is a new force at work.'

'The Comrades?' ventured Max.

Lines he hadn't noticed before furrowed Sisulu's forehead. 'You saw how Solomon died. It is happening everywhere – no one knows who's behind it. And anyone who gets too close, dies.'

Two

Home at last. With a sigh of pleasure, Max pulled into the long avenue of oak trees that led up to his house – a big mansion set in five acres of private parkland in Inanda, one of Johannesburg's most exclusive suburbs. Max loved the sentinel oaks, the guardians of his privacy – but now, to his horror, as he reached his front door, an avalanche of reporters burst out from between the trees. He was surrounded. Everywhere he looked, cameras were clicking, microphones were at the ready. Cursing, he got out of the Landy to face them.

'Dr Loxton, do you believe the attempt on your life was the work of the Botswanan government?' A dark-haired woman reporter stared quizzically at him through her glasses.

He forced himself to relax. As the head of several mining companies and a hotel chain, the last thing he needed was a hostile press; and a good photograph of him losing his temper would give extra credence to the claim that he'd run round the Oasis trying to shoot everyone in sight.

'Listen,' he said. 'I'm exhausted. I'll make a full statement tomorrow morning.'

A flash bulb went off, and a male voice said: 'Dr Loxton, how do you feel about the release of Napoleon Zwane from Leeukop prison, which will take place at four this afternoon?'

Another voice chimed in: 'Have you spoken to your friend George Zwane, yet?'

Max felt his mind reeling. For the last two days he hadn't paid any attention to the news at all. 'It's great news,' he said. 'No conditions were set for Napoleon's release?'

'It was unconditional, Dr Loxton.' It was Harold Collins who

43

answered, a seasoned reporter whom Max knew well. 'Harold,' he said. 'Tomorrow I'll give you an exclusive on the Botswanan project. But now, ladies and gentlemen' – he turned to face the rest of them – 'I've been through a harrowing experience, and please, I need a little peace and quiet. I'll be available for questions at my office tomorrow morning, nine o'clock sharp.'

There was a reluctant murmur of assent, and as they began to disappear slowly down the drive, on cue, the front door opened and an ebony face looked out and gave Max a beautiful smile.

'Welcome home, Dr Max.'

She was more like a second mother to him than the most efficient housekeeper in the world. 'Tuli!' he said. 'It's good to see you.'

As always, she was dressed in bright clothes. Tuli. A big woman who carried herself with the elegance of a dancer, whose boisterous spirit had weathered four husbands and was looking out for a fifth. Her loyalty to Max was unswerving; she would not allow a bad word to be said about him.

'Dr Max, you must be careful.' As she spoke now, a frown creased the soft, radiant skin of her face. 'I told you not to talk to them in Gaberone, it's not a good place.'

'Tuli, if I listened to you I wouldn't go anywhere!'

But she remained serious. 'All this that happened to you – a bad business. And what if you had died? What about me?' Then she moved closer and whispered conspiratorially, 'Now, did you meet a wife?'

To Tuli it was unacceptable that Max should remain unmarried after his divorce. She herself had nine children and considered that he should sire at least as many.

'Yes, I think I did.'

At these words Tuli broke into another broad smile, and Max realised he'd better qualify his announcement or the house would immediately be prepared for the wedding. 'But she is the wife of another man, Tuli,' he said.

'You are bad Dr Max, very bad!' And she burst into laughter and ran out of the room, her bright red-and-black shawl disappearing into the kitchen. He wondered what he had ever done to inspire such loyalty.

When he followed her, ready for the enormous lunch that she would inevitably have prepared for him, she was ready with more questions.

'Is she beautiful?' She stood next to the long refectory table and served him.

'Yes.'

'Does she have children?'

'I don't think so.'

'You meet a woman, you fall in love and you do not ask if she has children, Dr Max?'

'We met at the casino.' He spoke between mouthfuls.

Tuli frowned. For her, gambling was the work of the devil; her first husband had run a shebeen selling liquor and girls, then he had become a gambler and lost everything, including Tuli.

'Her husband, is he wealthy?'

'Very, very wealthy.'

'Tch. There are so many beautiful women who would have you, Dr Max. Why do you always fall for the ones that belong to someone else?'

The tall woman in the perfectly tailored dark-blue suit walked briskly away from the Johannesburg Supreme Court. Her face showed little emotion, but inside she was seething with anger. She couldn't quite believe what she had just heard: only a day before, she had obtained the release of a man who had been detained for twelve months under the emergency regulations, and now he'd been detained again, re-arrested on another technicality, on the personal orders of the Minister of Justice. She felt like screaming, like raking the public prosecutor's eyes out with her nails. But naturally none of this anger had surfaced in court, its officials had merely been treated once again to the cutting remarks of the remarkably attractive blonde with the icy smile.

Advocate Victoria Loxton was over six foot tall; she had the willowy figure of a ramp model, and just the same poise and composure. Bimbo – that was the automatic male reaction until the soft, sensual mouth opened and spoke. Now, ignoring the admiring glances of a junior counsel, she went quickly to her rooms. Here, at last, she could give vent to her feelings. She picked up one of the hefty legal volumes from her desk and hurled it against the bookcase, and books and shelves collapsed in noisy confusion. Temporarily relieved, she sat down on the leather sofa and kicked off her Italian shoes – but almost at once the door opened and a short, dumpy man with greying hair slowly entered the room.

'May I?'

Vicky tried to get up but he gestured to her to remain seated. 'I'm sorry, Ken,' she said. Her fingers drummed against the arm of the sofa. She was embarrassed. Ken Silke was her mentor, the most famous man in the South African judiciary.

'I gather from your behaviour that your father rearrested Mr Khumalo?'

'I've had enough, Ken. We uphold the law, we get the people out of prison, and then they just change the law and rearrest them.'

'I think you overreact, Vicky. Remember that Kobus van der Post is making some big changes soon. Napoleon Zwane will be a free man by this evening.'

Ken Silke knew that if he were twenty years younger he would be hopelessly in love with Victoria Loxton, but age and experience told him that this might not be a good idea. To her colleagues she was known as the Ice Maiden. Now, as she pulled her legs up underneath her, he caught a brief glimpse of her long, sensuous thighs. Why had God decreed that one so beautiful should also be so intelligent? He stared at her sympathetically; he knew the kind of conversation they were about to have.

'I'm tired of the charade, Ken.'

'Vicky, if you're threatening to emigrate, don't tell me. Rather let your father know and see what his reaction is.'

Her dark blue eyes focused on him and he realised that he had already won the argument. But he could see the hatred in them.

'You're right. My leaving would give him immense satisfaction.'

'This thing is between you and him, Vicky. I almost feel you shouldn't stand in certain cases because he may intervene personally to the defendant's detriment.'

'An advocate can't refuse a brief from an attorney,' Vicky muttered stiffly.

'Don't play games with me, you know what I mean.'

'It's not my fault my father's a bastard.'

He saw her left eye twitch with tension, and wished he'd never mentioned her father. But at least, he thought, it looked as if David Loxton's days in the cabinet might be numbered. Kobus van der Post's ideas ran directly counter to David Loxton's, and it could only be a matter of time before the two of them fell out. And then, mused Ken Silke, he was sure that David Loxton would be the loser.

*

David Loxton walked up the steps of the Union Buildings in the hot midday sun. This was the finest building in Pretoria; when he was a boy his father had brought him here once, when they came down on holiday from Salisbury, and ever since it had been his ambition to work here, to belong here. His father had been sarcastic about the Afrikaners, but David had felt differently; he had sensed their power. And look at what had happened. The Rhodesians were no more, but in Africa the Afrikaners ruled supreme, and he, David Loxton, was one of their number. He was the only Englishman in the whole cabinet; he was the Minister of Justice.

And a few months ago his ultimate goal had seemed within reach. He had come so close! P. W. Botha had been grooming him as his successor, it was all arranged – and then, because of dramatic shifts of opinion within the cabinet, Botha was forced out and Kobus van der Post, a former academic and Minister of Home Affairs and Education, was put in his place.

David Loxton watched the heat haze wavering in the distance over the University of South Africa – another impressive building in the modern style, perched on its koppie. He loved this country. He owned vast farms, factories and mines, and though he was not as powerful as the Werhner-Beits, the family who controlled Euro-Pacific, he was close. And even more power had been almost within his grasp . . . But now everything had changed for the worse. As far as David Loxton was concerned, Kobus van der Post was weak-willed, a sell out. He was supposed to keep control of the country, not let it go! No red-blooded Afrikaner would ever have voted for the government in the last election if they'd known Kobus van der Post would be State President.

He looked down at his watch. Twelve thirty on this sweltering summer's afternoon: why did the State President want to see him? He hurried up the stone steps and inside, into a long, cool corridor where he was stopped by an armed soldier. This was not token security; if he tried to push past the State President's guard he would be shot down, and no questions asked. Security had been an obsession with South Africa's leaders ever since the assassination of Verwoerd, over twenty years before. Ah, Verwoerd, he thought to himself as he hurried on, now there had been a man after his own heart. Tough as old shoe-leather, none of this liberal shilly-shallying. You knew where you stood with Verwoerd.

47

Here was the ante-room to the President's office. He walked in slowly, savouring the air of the rooms that *he* should be occupying. The President's secretary gestured for him to proceed, and he rapped smartly on the double doors of the office.

'*Kom binne*,' the voice boomed out in Afrikaans. 'Come in.'

'Good afternoon, sir.'

'Be seated.'

He sat in front of the enormous desk and stared at the man opposite. Kobus van der Post might be old in years, but he had the body and the brain of a much younger man. His face was smooth, with an almost childlike quality about it, and he had a full head of grey hair. As he stared back at David now, his mouth was drawn into a tight-lipped smile, his eyebrows arched over eyes like grey steel. As soon as David was seated, Kobus had stood up – a deliberate tactic to unsettle his visitor.

'Loxton, I am faced with a problem. I am afraid I must ask you to stand down.'

The blood rushed to David's face. Who was this Van der Post who a few years before was not even rated as having a political future? It was outrageous! 'After the sacrifices I've made for this country!' he barked hoarsely. 'The years I've worked for this government!'

Van der Post moved closer, the sharply etched lines around his mouth betraying his anger. 'I am tired of your behaviour, Loxton. You're openly defying me, you're persecuting the judiciary. Why, just today you acted against a man rightly freed by the new legislation. And I believe you did it just to spite your daughter! Your successor will be André Joubert.'

'What? He's totally unsuitable!'

Kobus van der Post sat down again behind the desk, keeping his eyes on the Minister of Justice. 'How dare you contradict me!'

For David, the reality of the situation began to sink in fast. André Joubert was only forty; he came from an irreproachable Afrikaans background and had the respect of everyone. David swallowed, and said in a more reasonable tone of voice: 'You're making a serious mistake, sir.'

'I'll be the judge of that, Loxton. Today I release Napolean Zwane from prison after nearly thirty years, and hot-headed behaviour like yours is the last thing I need.'

Hell, thought David, the man's crazy. 'I would ask you to

allow me to carry on till the end of this parliamentary session, sir.'

'You will accept the post of Minister of Tourism.' Van der Post smiled grimly. 'Perhaps, in that position, you will find yourself able to exercise a little diplomacy.'

David rose to his feet. He was shaking. A lifetime of work for the party, and now they were betraying him! Well, he wasn't going without a fight. 'Have you consulted the rest of the cabinet, sir?' It was a subtle reminder that he, too, had his supporters in the cabinet, as well as Kobus.

Kobus' fist smashed hard down on the table. The State President's face was puce with anger. 'Don't try your strong-arm tactics on me, Loxton. What do you think you have achieved in your ten years in office?'

David lifted his chin. 'I have kept this country free from violence and unrest. I have eliminated most of the black protest movements.'

'What you have done,' said Kobus, 'is to blacken the name of this country throughout the world. You've built up a police state here – you've made us comparable with the Nazis. Your militarist policies are anathema to me, Loxton – not least because they're specifically designed to benefit your own arms business. But all that is about to come to an end. Joubert's approach will be entirely different.'

David Loxton said nothing. He would not give Kobus the pleasure of seeing him rise to provocation. He thought about Dolph Klopper and his Afrikaner Weerstandsbeweging – the Afrikaner Resistance Movement, now the official opposition. David admired their determination and had secretly cultivated their support. Now was obviously the time to start using it.

'To be honest, Loxton,' Kobus was saying, 'you have betrayed this government.'

His next course of action was clear: to get rid of Kobus van der Post as quickly and efficiently as possible. But for the moment, he must play the game. 'I never considered Joubert as an equal,' David said reasonably. 'I suppose, though, he might handle the responsibility – but he's so young.'

Van der Post's face softened. 'Make things easy for yourself, Loxton – it would be embarrassing to have to officially retire you. Tourism is important to this country, there's real work to be done. And doesn't your son own one of this country's fastest-growing hotel chains?'

The jibe was subtle but effective. 'I will take the post you have offered me. I will not disappoint you.'

'Very well. And bear in mind what I've said.'

David Loxton nodded and turned on his heel, leaving the room as quickly as he could.

Max stood beside the narrow tarred road that led from the front gates of Leeukop Prison to the prison buildings some half a kilometre beyond. In the distance brown koppies formed a barrier across the horizon; in front of him his shadow lengthened, pointing to the east. Nearly a hundred thousand people were standing around him, waiting for an event that no one had ever dreamed would happen: the release of the world's most famous prisoner, Napoleon Zwane, after thirty years in prison. Above the vast crowd fluttered the green, gold and black flag of the African Freedom Council: green for the land, gold for the country's mineral wealth, black for its people. Was this the beginning of a new era? Releasing this man would unleash a wave of euphoria through the black population of South Africa. Would this mean an end to the violence in the townships? Please God, it would.

Max watched a man dressed in animal skins move forward out of the crowd, towards the gates of the prison. This was the praise-singer, the *Imbongi*. Just as the witchdoctor, the *Isangoma*, acted as an intermediary between man and the supernatural world, so the *Imbongi* acted as an intermediary between a chief and his people. Napoleon Zwane was a great chief, and now the *Imbongi* began to sing his praises in a rapid-fire style, not standing still for a moment, lifting his staff high in the air, and chanting constantly, raising the excitement of the crowd to fever pitch as his movements became more and more frenzied.

It was now three thirty: the release must be taking longer than expected. Minutes earlier a limousine had flashed by carrying George Zwane, Napoleon's son; Max guessed that George had been organising his father's schedule after his release – there would be interviews lined up with media people from all over the world. But the most immediately important event would be Napoleon's speech to the people of Soweto at the Jabulani Stadium, planned for six this evening. Standing there in the hot

50

afternoon sun, Max realised that now he felt more optimistic than ever before about the future of his country. Kobus van der Post had already re-established links with foreign governments; perhaps, in spite of everything, South Africa might sort out her problems peacefully

Indistinct in the heat haze, a black limousine emerged from the cluster of prison buildings. The crowd started chanting wildly, following the *Imbongi*, whose animal skins were shaking up and down with his frantic gyrations. Now the atmosphere was charged with an emotional electricity that infected everyone. Slowly, slowly, the limousine drew nearer, grew larger. After what seemed an eternity, it pulled up just inside the prison gates. A solitary figure emerged, dressed in a dark suit, walking confidently towards freedom.

Napoleon Zwane was not a tall man, but there was a natural air of authority about him. Though over seventy, with his grey hair cropped short, it was clear that he was as strong as ever. The prison warders swung open the gates and he stepped through them, a free man after more than thirty years. The *Imbongi* moved forwards, spinning wildly, and Napoleon Zwane flashed a brilliant smile to the crowd. Everyone was hypnotized by the moment. It was then that Max saw something flash beneath the *Imbongi*'s skins. Dear God, no. Not . . .

He began sprinting forwards even as he saw it happen. The *Imbongi* threw the animal skins aside and pointed a Scorpion machine-gun. Max pumped every ounce of energy he had into his legs, sprinting between the menacing figure with the gun and Napoleon Zwane, who, ignorant of the danger, was waving at the crowd, giving his salute. As Max launched himself into the air, going for a flying tackle, the *Imbongi*, sensing Max's attack, smiled, pivoted – and red flecks blossomed across Napoleon Zwane's black suit.

Bullets tore into Max's left shoulder as he thudded into the earth, and screams erupted from the horrified crowd. Max dragged himself over to the crumpled form of Napoleon Zwane, screaming at the onlookers to give chase to the *Imbongi*, who had flung down his weapon and was disappearing into the seething crowd – but people were so mesmerized by what had happened that they had forgotten the attacker and were surging towards Napoleon Zwane, now writhing on the ground.

'Air, air, air!' Max shouted. 'For God's sake, give him air! Get back, get back!'

He bent over the dying man; the brown eyes locked on his own. Max felt the tears running down his face. 'A doctor is coming, Napoleon. For God's sake try to hold on.'

The gnarled black hand gripped his. 'They are against me, they are against you.' It was nothing more than a whisper. 'Max, you must fight them . . .'

'Who has done this, Napoleon? Is it the army?'

An attempted shake of the head. 'The enemy is in the townships. He is waiting for you . . . You must find him before he kills you too.'

'Who?' Max bent lower to catch the answer. There was an intake of breath, a faint smile, and then Napoleon Zwane's eyes closed for ever, and Max and the crowd were alone with their dead leader.

The two of them sat out on the stoep of the old farmhouse. The evening was thick with the sounds of crickets; below them, far in the distance, the lights of Pretoria twinkled. David Loxton liked this farm, which belonged to General Jurie Smit, the tall, lean man sitting opposite him. He liked the General, too; he might be in his fifties, but his physical condition was that of a man of twenty. General Smit was the commander of the South African army. David leaned forward earnestly. 'My son continues to be an embarrassment. Those pictures of him trying to save Zwane – most unfortunate – they've made him a hero! And his friendship with Van der Post disgusts me!'

'I hate Van der Post, man. But there's nothing we can use against him. Don't underestimate him.'

'That's the last thing I would do, old chap.'

The General rose from his chair, picked up the ultra-modern rifle that lay between them on the table, and sighted it on something in the darkness. 'This weapon is a masterpiece, my friend. If we'd had it in Angola, it might have made all the difference. And who knows what we mightn't do with it here – if that sell-out Van der Post wasn't in power.'

There was anger in Jurie's voice, as he said: 'My budgets have been cut – I cannot order this magnificent weapon from you.' He paused.

David did nothing to disguise his own annoyance. 'The country is heading for disaster, Jurie. Van der Post has betrayed us all. He must be removed.'

'My friend, I wouldn't worry too much.'

The rifle cracked, and there was a muffled scream in the distance. The General looked carefully through the sight. 'Brilliant, brilliant.'

'A perfect shot?'

'Yes, one of my kaffirs.'

They both laughed, then the General laid down the rifle and took up his drink. 'An unfortunate accident . . . Yes, accidents can happen. Obviously, when they happen to a kaffir people don't ask questions. But when they happen to a State President . . .' He leaned closer. 'Now is not the moment to dispose of Van der Post. It would be too obvious. We must wait – but our time will come.'

George Zwane sat on the back porch of his house and watched the sun rise over the horizon. Another day had come, another life had gone from this world for ever. George's father had been his mentor, his inspiration; he had lived for his release – for the moment when he could embrace the man who had been taken from him when he was ten years old. Now, the dream was over, hope was dead.

In the distance the tin roofs of the township glistened in the early morning sunlight. Today there would be violence: who knew how many would die in the rioting? His father had been released to create peace in this strife-torn land – his father would have negotiated with Kobus van der Post for black representation in the government. His father was dead. And now?

George smelt coffee, and turned to see his wife Brenda holding out a steaming mug. 'My love, are you feeling a little better?' she asked. He was sitting just as she had left him the night before.

'No!' he groaned. 'No! It is not better.' He raised his hands knocking the coffee over. 'All my studies have been for the purpose of promoting peace. I have striven for peace in every aspect of my life. That is what my father did. Then, when his striving bore no fruit and in despair he turned to violence, they arrested him. Now, when he agrees to peaceful negotiation, they kill him!'

Brenda put her arms around him, trying to soothe him in his distress. 'I wanted to be with him!' George cried. 'I wanted to

53

know what it's like to have a father! How can this have happened?'

The noise of a car pulling up outside startled them. There was a knock on the front door which at first they tried to ignore, but when it became more insistent, George silently indicated to Brenda that she should answer it. Opening the door, she found herself staring at Max Loxton. His left arm was in a sling. Max was a regular visitor to the Zwane household; he and George had met through boxing at university, they were old friends.

'He's been sitting out on the porch all night,' Brenda whispered. 'He's desperate.'

'I must speak to him in private,' Max said. 'Do you mind?' Brenda smiled and shook her head, and Max went through to the porch.

As soon as he saw him, George got up and grasped Max's uninjured hand. 'You tried to save his life; I am deeply indebted to you, Max, and grateful beyond words.' He dropped the hand and slumped back in his chair. 'But he is still dead. My father is still dead.'

Max sat down and stared at his friend. 'We must talk, George. Your father's murder has changed everything. Van der Post made an official announcement last night: he said your father's life and ideals should be honoured, and he's asked for other black leaders to come forward to begin talks. But George, although Van der Post appealed for peace and warned people not to overreact to what's happened, there's already rioting right across the country, and Loxton wants to declare martial law. Van der Post wanted to remove Loxton from the Ministry of Justice, you know, but the way things are at the moment, he can't do it, it would be taken as an act of weakness – and now Loxton's putting pressure on him to take a hard line.' Max paused. 'But there's worse, George. Your father spoke to me as he died. He spoke of his murderers.'

The furrows on George's forehead deepened as he listened, and he clasped his head in his hands. 'I have heard rumours about these men – the Comrades. They will stop at nothing.'

'But why kill your father?'

'Because he was a man of peace, because he stood for law and order, for the resolution of our problems through negotiation. These people we are talking about – his murderers – they want to return to primitivism. It is said that they were the ones who

54

introduced the necklace. If these people take control there will be violence on a scale you've never dreamed of. Massive ritual killings, infant sacrifice, bestiality – a reign of terror that will sweep across Africa.'

'Is there any action you can take against them?'

George was silent. 'Yes,' he said at last, 'but only at enormous cost to myself.'

He got up and walked across the porch. 'My father lived for freedom, and I cannot allow him to have lived in vain. It is time for me to act. This may be the last time we see each other, Max – as friends. I will have my revenge on his murderers, and somehow I will find a way to foil their evil purpose. I must go into a world you do not know – that, thank God, you will never know. More than that, I will not explain.'

'Is there nothing I can do?'

George shook his head. 'It is goodbye, Max.'

'I know I could do more . . .'

George cut him short. 'You will hear things about me that you do not like – things that will appal you. Max, pray that I may not descend into hell.'

Kobus van der Post eased his Mercedes into the outside lane and put his foot hard down on the accelerator. The harsh light of the midday sun caught his eyes, and he reached into the dashboard cubbyhole and pulled on a pair of dark glasses. He was going to Napoleon Zwane's funeral. There were no security guards with him, he was alone – a deliberate tactic on his part: he would expose himself to risk in front of an enormous black crowd, in the hope that his courage would be rewarded with their trust, their faith in his leadership. Already he was losing the backing of the cabinet, and he was realising that by speaking to David Loxton the previous day he'd overplayed his hand. Perhaps the pressure was getting to him. God, he had so much to achieve, and so little time in which to do it!

The Minister of Justice was a dangerous and wily man, capable of resorting to the basest means to get what he wanted. He would have to have Loxton's phone tapped and his movements monitored; he had to stay one step ahead of him. André Joubert, now, was much more his sort of person. He'd been right to start grooming him as his successor – Loxton must never become State President.

Suddenly, Kobus's vision started to blur. The needle, he managed to see, was right up at 160 km/h – shit, he'd better slow down! He didn't seem to be able to see out of his right eye at all now. What the hell was happening? Then there was blackness.

Speeding motorists saw with horror how the Mercedes saloon swung in front of a huge truck that pushed it down the highway like a giant bulldozer. Other cars spun off the tarmac to avoid the chaos. Acrid smoke rose from the tyres of the truck as the driver desperately wrestled with the controls, until at last he brought it to a halt and leapt out of his cab. As the truck driver struggled with the tangled wreckage of the Mercedes, trying to open the driver's door, he could hear the scream of ambulance sirens in the distance.

Three

David Loxton looked at the note that had been brought to him, and his face tightened. The rest of the cabinet was still in close discussion.

'Gentlemen!'

Every face at the table turned towards him. This was his moment.

'I have terrible news,' he said, slowly and deliberately. 'Half an hour ago, on his way to Napoleon Zwane's funeral, our State President lost control of his car.' David relished the words 'lost control'; when he was in power, he would never lose control. 'First reports indicate that he had a stroke.'

The room exploded with cries of horror and consternation, while Loxton looked on with grim satisfaction. Now was the moment to take control and never let go. He banged his fist on the table. 'We must elect a leader in Van der Post's absence. I pray that he will recover, but in the meantime, unless we act quickly, violent elements in the community will try to capitalize on the fact that our country is now rudderless!' He spat the words out, making eye contact with every man in the room. Joubert, he was pleased to see, appeared to be in a state of shock.

Barend Viljoen, the Minister of Defence, rose noisily to his feet. He was a big man and an imposing presence. 'Gentlemen, I propose we elect a successor immediately.' He studied the stunned faces round the table, then looked quickly at David, who nodded. 'Control is now vital,' Viljoen went on. 'These are troubled times. Napoleon Zwane's death has been engineered by violent black elements, and now our President has succumbed to the stress of the situation with a stroke. We need a strong leader to guide us through this difficult period. I propose David Loxton as acting State President.'

A sea of hands rose, and David Loxton stood up. Viljoen counted the hands, then spoke again. 'And those against?' Anxiously, he counted the upraised hands. One of the reasons why he had moved so fast was that he hoped shock would cause a number of ministers to abstain – and certainly it looked as if some of them had not voted. David Loxton was a man after his own heart; with him in power, the proposed cuts in the defence budget certainly wouldn't go through.

Viljoen's heavy face broke into a smile. 'You have decided, gentlemen. David Loxton is our acting State President!'

When the meeting was over, Viljoen waited until the last of the ministers had left then, closed the double doors silently behind them and walked to the window, where he stood looking out over Pretoria. He was very pleased. Loxton was the perfect choice, and in the next election he would carry the English vote as well as the Afrikaans. Within the government, though, as he well knew, there were still many who would rally behind the charismatic Joubert.

He watched David walking down the steps outside – a tall, good-looking man with black hair only just tinged with grey. What was he, fifty-seven, fifty-eight? He looked more like forty-five. The face was unusually long, with cool grey eyes beneath bushy black eyebrows. Loxton had the gait of a military man, proud and erect, and always cut an elegant figure at parades. He was enormously wealthy, and had married a fine young Afrikaans girl some twenty years before. His commitment to the country was unquestionable. He was intelligent and ruthless, but he had the smooth manners of a diplomat.

Viljoen thought of the foreign governments that had imposed sanctions against his country; and he thought of Kobus van der Post, who believed that if they negotiated a new constitution to allow blacks into the government, sanctions would be lifted. What a fool the man was! But now all this foolishness could be stopped. As he pulled out his pocket diary, he thought that yes, the future did indeed look a lot more rosy. He must give General Smit a call.

Outside Johannesburg Hospital, reporters and cameramen jostled for front position as Dr Len Oblowitz emerged from the front entrance, with an anxious-looking Max Loxton at his side. As Max held up his hands for silence, a brunette with long legs and a determined look on her face launched the first salvo: 'President Van der Post is alive, but can he ever rule again?'

Max grimaced, and Dr Oblowitz gestured for him to remain silent. 'President Van der Post has had a left brain stroke. I shall have to do more tests, however the results of the brain scan were pretty conclusive.'

'But is he all right?'

'He's still unconscious, but off the danger list.'

As in some medieval pageant, the line of horses marched up towards the granite steps of the vast monument. The rider in front held the flag high, at his side a service revolver, and in the gun holster of the saddle, a Mauser rifle. He was a young man with white-blond hair that blew in the faint breeze fluttering upwards from the mauve jacaranda trees below.

A black man, who had been walking along the pavement, darted fearfully into the bushes. The young man saw this and smiled a sickly smile. '*Uit my pad uit, kaffir!* Get out of my way, kaffir!' he screamed. The bushes were sparse and the man's face was visible between the branches. One of the white horsemen spat, and the spittle found its mark and trickled down the black man's face. The other riders roared with laughter as the man cowered down even lower.

The blond young man turned to the rider behind him. 'When we come to power they will no longer be allowed to walk the streets of Pretoria. And nor will that *kaffirboetie*, Kobus van der Post.' He looked up at the flag, a bold reverse swastika, the symbol of the Afrikaner Weerstandsbeweging.

A deeply tanned man, wearing khaki fatigues, dismounted and strode up to the foreign news crew who were filming the procession. 'Who are you people?' he asked defiantly, tugging at his closely cropped blue-black beard.

'CBS news, Mr Klopper,' replied a blonde-haired female reporter.

He looked at her faded denims and T-shirt with obvious disgust. 'If you're going to film me, I demand the right to state my case.'

'Go ahead, Mr Klopper.'

'I founded the AWB in 1973. Since that time, we have grown from strength to strength. Our rise, our growing support, have been a direct result of the Nationalist government's attempts to dismantle apartheid. Many of us whites saw what was happening – we were losing out to blacks. Now let me tell you, this is our country. For us it is a matter of principle, of faith, that we should never be ruled by blacks. We have created separate states for them – but this land is ours.'

The reporter was about to ask a question but Klopper lifted his huge hands, indicating that silence should prevail. Now he turned his eyes towards the vast granite building which soared towards the heavens – the Voortrekker Monument – and the rider carrying the flag leapt from his horse and strode athletically up the steps, the pennant fluttering gaily in the air behind him. The rest of the troop dismounted, standing to attention, while Klopper followed the young rider up the steps. Then he turned to address his followers.

'We are a nation of heroes!'

The men raised their rifles. His dark eyes held them in awed silence.

'We who are pure in the eyes of God will never mix our blood except in battle! Let God be our guide and our judge. Our fore-fathers trekked into this promised land, and it is ours to rule. The Lord has spoken. He has taken the life of Napoleon Zwane, he has struck down Kobus van der Post. But there are still others who speak their viper's language, and I say they must be overthrown!'

A faint chant began that grew and grew in strength, echoing up the granite walls. 'Kill them! Kill them!'

Klopper drew his revolver and fired it into the air. The silence was instantaneous.

'Those who are not for us are against us. We are the backbone of the new volk, and our duty is clear. We must mobilise, and eliminate the traitors.'

The men cheered in unison. After this, a group of young boys went inside the base of the monument, where, watched by Klopper, they draped the Voortrekker tomb – the resting place of the first Afrikaners who had trekked north from the Cape – with the flag of the AWB. Then they all broke into song. Klopper looked on, his dark eyes gleaming. Never had things looked so hopeful. The battle was on, and he had been born to lead it – to take his people into the promised land.

He walked out of the tomb into the fierce sunlight. A young boy in khaki handed him the reins of his horse, and he mounted and looked across at the Union Buildings in the distance. From there he would soon command South Africa, and rule it as God intended.

He'd seen her jeep from the air, had flown round in a circle and then come in. Now, in the blistering heat, he brought the plane down expertly on the salt pan and got out to wait for her, smelling the wonderful smell of the hot air, relishing the isolation of the place. He felt the excitement coursing through his veins as he watched her jeep moving towards him through the heat haze, felt his heart beat faster as she pulled up. As always, she was dressed in black. She came over to him and they stood staring into each other's eyes; then their lips made contact. This thing between them was frightening in its intensity. Eventually Saffron drew away from him, sweeping her long black hair back. It made him ache to see the strong lines of her face, the mesmeric green eyes, the smooth light-brown skin. It was the combination of strength with beauty that made her so irresistible.

'Honey,' she said huskily, 'we can't go on like this. I can't concentrate on anything.'

He drew her to him again, and felt himself harden. She stared coolly into his eyes. 'We've got the whole day – my movie's finished. I want you to show me the wetlands.'

He wanted to tear the clothes from her body, to knead her flesh against his own, to hear her sigh, then scream his name. But he also sensed the need for a deeper, spiritual bond between them, something more important than the purely physical. He placed his hands around her waist, hoisting her up to the cockpit, and though she giggled with the contact, she said seriously: 'I'm feeling what you're feeling, Max. But I want to see this place you're always talking about. I want you to show it to me.'

He knew now, even more certainly than before, that if he lost her he would be devastated.

He climbed into the pilot's seat and gunned the twin-engined plane down the pan. As they rose into the air, he felt almost giddy with excitement – in the distance, the green of the Okavango beckoned them . . .

And only a little while later she was watching the shadow of the plane running in front of them as they crossed the swamps, the irridescent spreads of water interspersed with patches of intense green – each island a private paradise, unspoilt by man, teeming with life.

61

Max shouted above the roar of the engines. 'The Okavango delta's a unique geographical feature. During the winter months water floods down from the Angolan Highlands, creating these flood plains and an ecology all its own, which is the Okavango Delta – sixteen thousand square kilometres of waterways.'

Saffron smiled across at him. 'You're in love with this place.'

He looked away from the controls, staring directly at her. 'I am. That's why I'm so concerned – because there's hardly any time left, and if the Botswanan government doesn't take action soon, this paradise is doomed. I've shown them how they can preserve the delta and the wilderness surrounding it, and still make money, but they don't want to know.'

'But it would still be less dollars in the government coffers, wouldn't it?' Saffron paused. 'Do you think it's because of your plan for the delta that someone tried to kill you?'

Max went quiet. He'd blocked that incident from his mind, but it was still there in his subconscious, disturbing him. 'All they have to say to me is "no",' he said.

'And Solomon Khoza?'

'I don't know, I just don't know.'

She looked at him closely. He was a man under threat of death, yet there was a solidity about him that made you think he would live for ever. She saw the corners of his eyes crinkle, and he turned towards her. He leant across the cockpit and they kissed.

An immense wave of regret swept over Max as he kissed her: if only he'd met her years before. What would he not have given, then, to trade those years of unhappiness and isolation for times spent with someone he loved, someone who understood him, someone to whom he could confide his dreams!

In the distance he saw the island, and his pulse quickened. This was the one important thing that Tracey, his mother, had left him – this pearl, this special place. But he would not tell Saffron about it now. No, he would save it, take her there when he knew she was his for life.

A flight of birds broke across the waters below them, scattering before them, light dancing from their wings. He pulled the plane round hard, heading back towards the south. He had needed this flight, to reinforce his determination to succeed. For now he had a plan again, a new plan to save this water paradise that was a part of his soul . . .

Towards evening they landed and made camp. As the sun disappeared under the horizon, the white fabric of their tent fluttered in the light breeze, and the hard wood of their fire crackled, filling the air with the pungent smell of burning. Saffron watched Max squatting in front of the fire, coaxing the flames. He was wearing only khaki shorts, and she could see that his neck and back were latticed with cords of muscle – there was not an ounce of fat on him. He stood up, and his legs were long and lean, complementing the hard, muscled torso.

Saffron unzipped her jumpsuit and walked up behind him. She kneaded his neck with her hands, and he turned, his eyes flashing as he saw her nakedness. Then her mouth locked against his, and she leapt against him, her legs wrapping round him. They dropped slowly to the ground, and she eased off the shorts, sighing as she saw him.

'Please, now.'

But he did not accede to her demand. Instead he caressed her, adoring her body, his fingers touching her so that she cried out with pleasure again and again. Then, when she could stand it no longer, he penetrated her, and she screamed aloud with the passion of it, the relief and the ecstasy.

Then they lay together on the sand, still after the moment had passed, the crackling of the fire celebrating their love. Her head rested against his chest, her hands around his shoulders. Anything without her, Max thought, would be half-living. Nothing had prepared him for the overwhelming physical and emotional longing he felt for Saffron; already he wanted to go back to the moment of fusion, and capture it again and again.

She touched his face. 'I want to be part of you, but you're hiding things from me. You flew over that island . . . I know it meant something to you, but you wouldn't tell me . . .'

'I'm scared.' Max spoke almost too softly to be heard. 'I've never wanted someone as badly as I want you. I can't live without you – I want a lifetime of loving you. I will tell you about the island, but wait; let me wait until I feel the time is right.'

After they had eaten, they lay naked under the stars. They did not want the night to end. It was as if they were part of eternity.

George Zwane worked feverishly in his office. His preparations were almost complete – although, of course, everything must look as though the moment he'd been planning for weeks had occurred purely by chance. He could tell no one what he intended to do, not even Brenda, his beloved Brenda. His partner could run the practice, and would provide more than enough for her to live on. Not that she'd need it; Brenda was strong and resourceful, she'd be able to survive no matter how tough the going got.

George got up from his desk, and went over to a photograph of his father on the wall. Then he moved on to stare at his degree certificates, and finally to a photograph of himself sparring with Max Loxton when they were both much younger. Now it would be his physical strength and endurance that kept him alive, not his skill with words.

He moved back to the desk, picked up the phone and dialled the number of police headquarters in John Vorster Square. He knew that over the past few days, since David Loxton had taken control of the government, there'd been a tightening-up of security: the army and police were having a field day. Now he picked up a coffee cup, angling it towards the mouthpiece to disguise his voice, making it deeper and more resonant.

'I want to inform you of a secret meeting you might be interested in.' He put fear into his voice – the fear of the informer.

The voice on the other end of the line encouraged him to go on. He told them about a meeting planned to take place in Alexandra in two days' time. When the voice asked him who would be there, he pretended to hesitate, and the voice assured him of absolute confidentiality.

'George Zwane and Seth Naidoo,' George said rapidly. 'George Zwane is the trouble-maker, he's planning violent protests in Alexandra township.' Then he put the phone down, bathed in sweat.

He knew how easily his plan could backfire on him, but he'd carefully planned his movements over the next two days so that the police couldn't arrest him before the Alexandra meeting. They would be there, he had no doubt of it – so now it was just a matter of waiting.

He thought of the townships that surrounded Johannesburg, where black people lived without decent sewage, without lights or water. They were people with nothing to lose, and the Comrades moved among them like a virus, whipping up hatred, encouraging division, witch hunts for government supporters and informers. People's courts meted out back-street justice: the

64

lightest sentence was a few cuts with a leather whip, the ultimate penalty was death by stoning or by fire.

It was into this maelstrom that George Zwane was about to descend.

Dolph Klopper turned off the smooth dust road onto the two-lane track that led towards Rustenberg and the upward slope of the mountains. The sun hung low in the western sky, the bush taking on the picturesque hues of the late afternoon – green scrub set amongst red sand – land that was prosperous and well-tended.

The farm always brought back memories of his boyhood – his initiation, as he liked to call it. Not for him *tok-tokkie*, leap-frog or the other carefree games children play; instead the black-coated figure of his father had given him daily instruction from the huge leather-bound Bible that lay permanently open on the bare wooden table in the dining room.

'You were born to lead your people.' The words echoed through his mind again now; they were a permanent part of his subconscious.

And every Sunday he was shown the pictures, of Tant Cilliers, Boetie, Klein Jacob, Erasmus and many others – all members of his family who had died in the concentration camps of the hated British during the Boer War.

He had been sent to boarding school early, the Hoër Volks-skool in the town of Potchefstroom, where he had also attended the university – the only university in South Africa with a racial discrimination clause built into its constitution: no blacks, no Jews, no Indians, no Chinese; only white Christians. His immense strength had made him a legend on the campus. Every day he had trained with weights, honing his body to perfection, and become South African weight-lifting champion, bringing honour and glory to the university and his people – and he had represented South Africa in Europe and America.

He had served his country with pride in the army, volunteering to serve an extra year and working in the State President's guard. After the army he had joined the police force, rising to the rank of major. Finally he had turned to politics and the career that was his life's purpose.

He pulled the car over under a huge acacia tree and got out. He loved the smell of the bush, the smell of Africa. He smoothed down his khaki fatigues, the uniform of his party, and ran his eyes over the property, jet-black eyes that missed nothing. This farm was all that was left of the Klopper fortune, and a bitter reminder of their former wealth.

Even here, Klopper knew, he could not be too careful. There were many who would like to see him dead, who were afraid of his power and his popularity with the people. As he turned his smooth, deeply tanned face to the setting sun, his features looked almost childlike; he had a mane of jet-black hair and a clipped, black and silver beard. He commanded both fear and respect from his followers, and in women he often triggered an atavistic desire – a desire based on the power he exuded.

He approached the old farmhouse with a certain caution, moving lightly on his feet, making little noise, like a predator stalking its kill. The house had white, stuccoed walls and a thatch now grey with age. The windows were shuttered, so that it looked as if the place was deserted, but Dolph Klopper knew better.

Passing the sleeping stone lions on either side of the massive front door, he walked in, into darkness. He reached for the paraffin lamp that was always kept just inside the door, and struck a match. The smell of damp assailed his nostrils as he walked forward, the floorboards creaking under his weight. He knew his way – nothing had been moved since his childhood. The dining room was on the left, and there he would find his father.

'Pa?'

'Come here, my son.'

The room was dominated by an enormous tapestry depicting scenes of the Great Trek, the Vow and the sacrifices of the Boer War. In the dimness Dolph could just make out his father, dressed in black, seated at the head of the table, his old gnarled hands resting on the dark wood. Dolph sat down on his father's left, and took his hand.

'Are you well, Pa?'

'God cares for the righteous.'

His father's faith was awe-inspiring. The old man had never once blamed the Lord for his blindness. He had been almost proud of it, saying it was a sign that the Lord had singled out him – and his son – for greatness.

'Did the meeting go well? Did you lay the flag on the tomb of our forefathers?'

'Yes, Pa.'

'Just like the time with the thirty pieces of silver, eh?'

Dolph tugged at his beard, smiling to himself. A month before he had laid a child's coffin and thirty pieces of silver on the steps of parliament. It had been a gesture to remind the nation that the government were a bunch of weak-willed sell-outs who had betrayed their country by acceding to the demands of the Europeans and the Americans. It had been a demonstration against a government whose policies would lead inevitably to the death of them all at the hands of the black hordes.

'Yes, Pa. The press laughed, but soon they will laugh on the other side of their faces.'

'You have done well.'

'Every day, more and more come into the fold. Only my party can give them work.'

Dolph was reciting the catechism of his party. He had schooled himself well in the art of keeping his political creed down to a few simple statements, which, endlessly repeated, had the power of hypnotising those who listened.

'The Church is behind you?'

'As always.'

They referred to the Herenigde Gereformeerde Church, the bastion of Afrikaner belief, the hub of most rural communities. Certain divisions of this church taught that blacks were inferior to whites, and claimed they had support from the Bible: 'The children of Ham were born to be servants' – Dolph knew the words off by heart.

The old man smiled, then looked up, as if to survey the room with his sightless eyes. Nothing had been moved here since he had gone blind; everything was where he imagined it to be.

'You must stop the dark tide, my son. The mud races are sweeping across the world.'

Dolph leaned closer. 'The AIDS plague is the sign, Pa. It will destroy half the blacks in this country – maybe more.'

'The time is right. You must take power.'

'As long as I live, Pa, there'll never be a black face in the government. Our death squads are already at work, wiping out the trouble-makers.'

'Good, very good. How is Marie?'

Dolph smiled with pride as he thought of Marie. She was fifteen years younger than him. Her fairness matched his darkness, and her blonde hair and bright blue eyes symbolised the racial purity he so desired for his country.

But his father's face had hardened. 'You must have a son. And you must bring him up in the traditional way, just as I did you. He must learn to ride before he can walk, administer the sjambok. Learn to keep the blacks where they belong.' The right hand bunched itself into a gnarled fist and smashed against the table.

After that they sat in silence for a long time, the old clock ticking noisily over the cavernous fireplace. Eventually Dolph spoke.

'I have the support of the army and the police force, Pa. I'm ready to establish a *Blanke Volkstaat*, an all-white state. Blacks and Indians will live in their own areas: we will stand supreme.' He leaned back a little in his chair, visualizing it, relishing it all.

'But you must tread carefully, my son. There are traitors everywhere.'

Dolph nodded. 'Like Kobus van der Post – who, unfortunately, seems to be recovering. And I fear there are now so many kaffir-loving whites in the government that he might even succeed in allowing blacks into parliament. He is an embarrassment. He draws support from the weaker elements in our nation. I will back David Loxton for the moment.'

The old hand gripped Dolph's arm tightly and the sightless eyes burned into his own. 'If Van der Post is a problem, he must be disposed of quickly. God will forgive us if the cause is just.'

'No, Pa, no. The time is not right.'

The old man slumped back into the high-backed magistrate's chair, but his hands pressed against the table. 'You must not be faint-hearted, my son. Never forget, we cannot lose. We made our vow with God, and He will not betray us. You have merely to be strong, and the others will follow you. Tell me, are our young children still being properly educated?'

'The government is weakening, there is talk of admitting blacks into white classes!' Dolph shuddered as he spoke.

'It must be stopped!'

'Pa, it shall be.' Dolph looked around him. 'Is there anything I can do for you, Pa? Is there anything you want?'

'Your leadership of this fair and pleasant land, my son, that is all I desire.'

Marie knelt in front of the enormous bedstead, put her hands together and closed her eyes again. 'Please give me a son. Oh Lord, I want so much to please him. Give me a son.'

She thought back to their whirlwind romance. She had met Dolph at a party meeting some two years previously; just eighteen years old, she had come with her mother and father. It had been a great experience for her, actually to see the movement in action, and she had been so proud of her father, looking handsome in his dark suit, obviously much respected by the other men.

The first time Dolph had looked at her, she had blushed terribly. She knew who he was – he was famous – and she had been afraid of him because he was so powerful. Such a fine body he had beneath the folds of his light blue suit. The pictures she had seen of him did not do him justice, and the eyes set in that heavily tanned face – you never really noticed them in the photographs. This was a man she could love. She would become his strength and support, help write his speeches and guide him in his career. The women whispered that he was a devil in bed – and even now, two years later, the smell and the touch of him still made her shiver to the core.

She remembered everything he had said to the meeting that night, but most of all what stayed in her heart was the fact that he actually looked at her for a moment, actually smiled at her.

She had seen him again when he came to their house to discuss business with her father. Dolph had needed financial backing, and her father Tertius van der Vance, a wealthy cattle farmer, was prepared to give it to him. In the following weeks he became a regular visitor to the Van der Vance household, and Marie noticed that he always made a point of speaking to her. He even touched her hand occasionally, and this made unthinkable thoughts come into her head. Half-heartedly she would pray for these thoughts to go away, but they kept coming back – even in church – and soon she could think of nothing but Dolph Klopper. She had childish dreams about him coming to rescue her from the English on a white charger, she imagined herself holding onto his back as they rode away together. One night she dreamed he was undressing her and her body became hot, then suffused with pleasure. She had to have him.

One Sunday Dolph came to church with them, and afterwards her father asked her to drive Dolph around the farm. She couldn't believe her luck, and took as much time about it as she could. They had gone down to the wide flowing river where she had played as a child.

69

It happened without warning. She had turned to him, and their eyes met. The next moment they were kissing. Waves of passion swept through her body, she never imagined she could be so happy. His big arms enfolded her, she felt the massive strength of him; the smell of his clothes, his masculinity aroused her deeply, so that she felt powerless against him.

But then he had pulled away, and she had trembled, terrified that she had done something improper and offended him. His dark eyes bored into hers.

'I must speak to your Pa.'

'But Dolphie, why?'

'Don't be afraid, I want to marry you. I must ask his permission.'

'Oh, Dolphie!'

They had kissed again, longer and more fervently. Her hands unbuttoned his trousers, he ran his lips across her naked breasts. The electricity between them was frightening, a passion that threatened to consume them both. She was not a virgin, though to Dolph she pretended she was – but with him she felt as if she had never slept with a man before. His body was dark and mysterious to her. She kneaded her fingers into the hard muscle of his shoulder blades, and slowly he penetrated her. For Marie the pleasure was exquisite. Everything he did to her sparked off fresh passion. There was nothing she would not do for this man, this man who made her feel like an angel.

Much later she had driven him back to the farmhouse, and the fields looked as they had never done before, their colours and textures touched with a new beauty. Her world was transformed. She was in love.

It was only later that she began to ask herself a few questions – though she never voiced them. Why, for example, had Dolph not asked her if *she* wanted to marry *him*? It was as if she had no choice in the matter. Of course she wanted to marry Dolph Klopper more than any man in the world, it was just that she would have liked the opportunity to say 'yes', or even 'no'.

Events happened very quickly after that. She graduated from high school with such good marks that she was offered a scholarship to study at the university, but she told herself that her studies could wait till after she was married. Dolph and her father decided that the wedding should be in April, in the autumn. The ceremony would be conducted by the Reverend

Cilliers at the family HG Church, with the reception at the farm. She grew excited at the prospect of buying a wedding dress, and in Pretoria, with her mother, chose a beautiful white brocade dress with a high collar and a long, flowing train. It showed off her bountiful figure in all its glory, and Marie felt proud that her new husband would see her in such a dress.

Dolph came to the farm again the next Sunday, going to church with them and then sharing the traditional Sunday lunch. Then they went for a walk in the orchard behind the main house, and she literally tore his clothes off him. Afterwards they lay naked in the grass, under an old oak tree. For a long time Dolph was silent, and Marie sensed that something was troubling him.

'Dolphie, what's wrong?' Perhaps he was tiring of her.

'It's your wedding dress . . .'

She had wanted to surprise him. 'My Ma showed it to you!' In spite of herself, an edge of annoyance crept into her voice.

Dolph rolled over and pulled her against him. 'My love, you do not understand, do you? I must lead our people through example.'

'Yes?' She could not understand what her wedding dress had to do with Dolph's mission.

'You have a beautiful, full, Aryan body, and that wedding dress – it's indecent. You must wear something simple that befits the wife of a leader not obsessed with carnal things.'

The coldness in his voice was frightening. 'But Dolphie – it's my wedding!'

His eyes flashed angrily, and for the first time, she was scared. 'I will not argue with you,' he said coldly. 'Your father and I have chosen the dress you will wear, and you must return to Pretoria on Monday so that the seamstress can arrange a fitting.'

She had felt like hitting him in the face. But then she had imagined what life would be like without his dark body, and she had lain back and smiled at him, and he had taken her in his arms and kissed her passionately. She had forgotten about the dress – until now.

Now, kneeling next to their bed, Marie prayed a second time that she would bear Dolph Klopper a son. The gynaecologist had examined her and said that there was no reason why she should not have a child. He had then suggested that perhaps Dolph might take a few tests? When she mentioned this to Dolph, he had exploded with rage. He had insisted that she re-read certain passages of the Bible and remember her role in the family. She

71

had stiffened with anger as he shouted at her; he made it so clear that he regarded her as his possession, and she bitterly resented that, without being able to put it into words. Recently, too, she had become aware that there was another side to her adored Dolph. He could be like a raging bull, chasing after whatever he wanted, with no thought for the consequences. And she hated his blind father. When they had first visited his farm, he'd asked to touch her, and Dolph had laughed as the frail old hands explored her body. The experience made her feel like a breeding sow being assessed for value. The old man did not come to the wedding.

All these resentments had built up in her so that when Dolph refused to see the doctor, she finally lost her temper. 'Well, don't keep blaming me,' she had shouted, 'if we don't have a child.'

Eventually he had gone and it was as the gynaecologist guessed – Dolph had a low sperm count. She had felt like laughing at him, him with his arrogance and his racial prejudice; most of the black men he despised could father as many children as they pleased.

He took his revenge on her in the most savage way possible. He would force her to make love when she did not feel like it, penetrate her roughly so that the pleasure was all his. She liked him to face her so that she could see his pleasure, but now he insisted that she turn over for him. And it never took more than a couple of minutes now. Then he would roll off her and return to his own separate bed, collapsing, exhausted, into a deep sleep. She wanted him to hold her tightly in his arms, the way he used to.

Dolph's sperm had been artificially implanted in her, but still there was no sign of a child. She dreamed that with a baby, Dolph might come to love her again. Perhaps everything would change then, and she would grow to respect him once more.

'Oh Lord, give me a boy.'

When she had finished her prayer, she got up from beside the bed and wiped away her tears. She went down to the kitchen where dinner was cooking on the stove and Anna, her maid, was stirring the soup: Anna, who was only a year older that Marie; Anna, who was pregnant with her fourth child. Marie had talked to Anna like a friend when she first set up house, but Dolph had scolded her and told her that she must not talk to 'kaffirs' as if they were white, so now Marie only talked to Anna when Dolph was not present. Anna was in love with her husband, Joseph.

Sometimes he came to see her, a tall, proud man who worked on the mines. He joked with Anna and touched her often. Marie felt herself jealous of their intimacy – resentful of her own failing marriage.

She would pray harder in church on Sunday. God was merciful. Surely He would reward her with the child that Dolph so badly wanted?

Max stared across the sea of tin-and-board shanties, their roofs glistening in the early morning sunlight. Saffron was walking slightly in front of him, the compact video camera hugged up against her right shoulder, her right eye looking through the viewfinder. There was something rather erotic, Max thought, about a woman using high technology equipment. He was glad she was here, helping him. Together they were making a film for Kobus van der Post about what his government had achieved so far.

Max had returned from Botswana to learn of Kobus' recovery, but he was still worried. Kobus' health was now seriously impaired, and every day in parliament was a strain on him. He had a great deal to achieve, and he had to do it fast so that David Loxton could never seize power again. In particular, he had to block the passing of the new security bill, and over the last few weeks, as he sparred with Loxton in parliament to defeat it Kobus had aged visibly.

David Loxton believed that this bill, if passed, would enable the police to stem the rising tide of violence. Kobus knew that the new legislation would turn the country into a police state and make Loxton invincible . . .

Saffron zoomed the camera in on Max, who began his prepared speech.

'People living like this make up twenty per cent of the population of this country, and they're not going to go away.' He squatted down on his haunches and looked up to the camera. 'It's easy to criticise these people – they can't fight back. They have no money to fight back. They may be forcibly evicted from their homes at any moment, their makeshift houses destroyed by bulldozers.'

Max got up now, the camera following him as he moved towards some unoccupied land. 'But where are they supposed to live? Where do they go when they've been forcibly removed? They move on to create another squatter camp. Is this a problem without a solution? No. There is a solution – one that big business

73

and government can effect right now. And now I will show you proof that this solution works.'

Saffron lowered the camera, and the two of them got into the Land-Rover and bounced along the dirt road towards another township. After his speech for the camera, Max was quiet.

'What's wrong?' Saffron asked.

'I hate those places.'

'Go easy on yourself – you can't carry the blame for all of that on your shoulders. It started long before your time. And besides, you have an answer . . .'

Saffron never finished the sentence. As they came over the rise they were greeted by clouds of smoke issuing from the township in the distance. Flames were pouring out of the tiny houses, people were running everywhere.

Max gunned the vehicle forwards, heading for the edge of the fire. He caught sight of a black man pouring kerosene from a metal drum against the side of a house, men with automatic weapons standing guard on either side of him. Saffron, resisting the urge to scream, coldly lifted the camera to her eye.

Max was out of the door and running. One of the men opened fire on him, and now Max was rolling, jumping and weaving his way forwards. Saffron dropped the camera and tore open the locker at the back of the Land-Rover, reaching for the Musgrave hunting rifle. The windows exploded around her as she was raked with fire.

Max bore forwards, a bullet grazing the side of his skull. He moved in on the man with the metal drum – then reared back as he saw that one of the automatic weapons was pointing right at him. He could see the gleam in the gunman's eyes. No, not now! For God's sake, not now!

Suddenly the gunman rose in the air, flying backwards, the automatic rifle spinning from his hands. As Saffron lowered the smoking rifle from her shoulder, Max bolted forwards, ramming a hard left into the side of the arsonist's head, so that the man staggered back, running off into the smoke and flames. The second gunman, too, had vanished.

Wary of further gunfire, Saffron kept the hunting rifle in her hand as she leapt out of the Land-Rover and ran over to Max. 'Goddammit Max, what the hell's going on?'

He was examining the body of the gunman. Now he looked up at her, his face twisted. 'These bastards were firing the new township! This is the place we were going to film, Saffron. The people were given the right to own the land they squatted on; they were able to buy materials cheaply – able to build better houses. There was fresh water here, a proper sewage system . . .' He stared at the smoking ruins, in his eyes a cold hatred.

'Sweet Jesus,' he said. 'Why?'

Saffron lowered the rifle, staring at the destruction. 'Who did this?'

'I don't know. There's a tide of violence running here, a drive towards anarchy that obviously sees this order, this new township, as a threat. The people behind it want a revolution – and if the squatters living here see their chance to live decently destroyed, they *will* revolt.'

'But who are these hell-raisers?'

'If I knew, I'd kill the bastards with my bare hands.'

They looked into the smoke and the flames – into an abyss from which there seemed to be no return.

Four

The area looked like the surface of some strange planet. The early morning light intensified the deep reds and oranges of the sand, the brilliant blue of the sky. The air was cold and invigorating. At a distance stood a solitary figure; black and inanimate, it dominated the inhospitable desert landscape. A faint breeze picked up the folds of its clothing so that they fluttered in the wind.

Suddenly the silence was broken by a violent staccato noise, deafening in its intensity. The figure erupted into pieces, disintegrated and fell, and the noise ceased. All that remained in the distance were bits of material and sawdust splattered against the red sand. David Loxton walked forward and nodded approvingly at the destruction.

A brute of a man in a black overall stood holding the still smoking weapon. He spat out of the corner of his mouth. Behind him was an elegant man in a white laboratory coat who wore steel-rimmed spectacles, his white hair combed back from a high forehead. The man moved forward, arriving at the tattered remains at the same moment as David Loxton.

'Dr Preusser,' Loxton said, 'I am impressed.'

Dr Preusser ignored the compliment and bent down to look at the disintegrated dummy. 'Perfection, *ja*?'

'Yes, absolutely perfect.' David Loxton had immense admiration for this German engineer. He always delivered. 'How many rounds?' he asked. He liked to keep the man on his toes, all the same.

'Ten or twenty. But you hev ze choice of single or continuous fire with any standard shotgun load. One shot is all zat is needed to kill the average man. Or *Schwarze*.'

Preusser was a professional, one of the best weapons designers in the world. He worked full-time at Terminal, David Loxton's weapons business. David Loxton had good reason to feel content at the moment. The arms business was the biggest money-spinner in the world – bigger even than drugs – and his huge manufacturing and selling operation ensured that his massive fortune could only increase.

Dr Preusser hailed the man with the weapon. 'Carl! *Ja*. Come here.' Carl ambled towards them slowly, the thin blond hair on his ugly bullish head fluttering in the wind. 'I told you I vanted a tight grouping, *ja*. So why do you massacre ze dummy? You fool!'

Carl stood smiling dumbly and the doctor wrenched the weapon from his hands. 'And ze remaining rounds?' he snapped.

Carl handed him two boxes of shotgun shells from his pocket.

'Walk away from me,' the doctor ordered. 'And next time, listen to vat I say. *Ja?*'

Carl ambled off, and Loxton watched as the doctor fed the ammunition into the base of the weapon – a sophisticated tube with three handles jutting from it. The doctor then pushed in the back handle, which had an action like a bicycle pump, and moved a selector switch on the side of the weapon. Then, without warning, Dr Preusser swung round, aimed, and fired the weapon at Carl's retreating back. The noise of the shot at close range made Loxton's ears ring. Carl fell forwards, lying still on the sand.

Then the big man gathered himself up and ran for Dr Preusser – but stopped when he saw that the weapon was aimed square at his chest, the doctor's immaculately manicured finger resting lightly on the hair trigger.

'*Ja*, you fool. Next time I vill kill you. Listen to vat I say and you vill learn to shoot as accurately as I do.'

David Loxton sucked in his breath. Dr Preusser had missed Carl by a fraction of a centimetre, there was blood at the base of the man's overall where he had been grazed by the shot. And Preusser wasn't bluffing: if Carl moved closer, he was dead.

'All right Carl, clean up ze mess.' Carl turned and started cleaning up the remains of the dummy. 'Vy do I employ such fools, that is vat I ask myself.'

David and Dr Preusser walked slowly towards their cars. David

77

was pleased with the development of his latest weapon. 'There is no danger of copyright infringement, Dr Preusser?' he asked.

'Herr Loxton, ve have discussed zis before, *ja?* I took ze British Arwen anti-riot gun as ze basis for my design – an excellent veapon in basic form, but as usual vith all zat is British, totally unreliable, *ja?*'

David nodded his head, and the doctor, pleased with this acknowledgement of British incompetence, continued. 'Our new weapon, ze Aardwolf, is far superior to any other currently in production. It has four times ze shot capacity of ze British, vill be better made and more reliable.'

David smiled as he thought of how much money could be made from the sale of this new weapon. 'How soon can we begin production?'

'Six months' time, maybe earlier. Of course, you understand it has a variety of uses. It can fire a plastic baton projectile and CS gas pellets, for use in riot control. Then of course zere are ze more powerful combat loadings, armour-piercing ammunition, high-explosive fragmentation shells. Zis is a very versatile veapon.'

'And why the name "Aardwolf", Dr Preusser?'

'Because, like ze aardwolf, for its small size it has a devastating liddle bark!'

David was still laughing when he got back to his car.

And he deserved a good laugh, he told himself as he drove home, because this morning's paper, *Business Day,* had certainly been nothing to smile about. He had already been disappointed by Van der Post's recovery and his swift resumption of the presidency, but this new move was devastating.

'Kobus van der Post invited to USA to meet President,' ran the headline.

David had read on grimly. This kind of coup would decide the fence-sitters in the Cabinet to plump for Van der Post rather than him, David Loxton.

Driving now through the gracious streets of Waterkloof, Pretoria's most exclusive residential suburb, David turned into the long, curving drive that led to his house, a sprawling white Georgian-style villa set in large grounds. With its frontage of immaculate lawn, its tall columns and curving steps, it looked, as one friend had remarked, as if it came straight out of *Gone with the Wind*. In fact David would have preferred to live all the time in Cape Town, but parliament only sat there for six months of the year – the other six months it moved to Pretoria, the nation's administrative capital. This split parliament was a hangover from the days when the Cape had been just as influential as the Transvaal. Those days were over now, of course; the Transvaal, with its mines and its industry, was now the economic power-house of the country.

A valet opened the door of the car as he pulled up, and David walked across the gravel and strode quickly up the semi-circular staircase to the big black double doors of the entrance, where Betty, the Loxtons' black housekeeper, was waiting for him.

'Good morning, Mr Loxton. The Madam is waiting for you.'

He smiled at her cursorily, hurrying across the hall to the breakfast room, where Hanli sat reading the papers. He kissed her affectionately on the cheek.

Hanli was twenty years younger than himself, and an exceptional beauty even at thirty-nine; she was still slim, and her skin was smooth and unblemished. Hardly a week passed when she was not the leading light in some woman's magazine. She was the perfect asset. Secretly, David wished that she could have stayed seventeen, the age she was when he first met her, but even he had to admit how lovely she still was. Her long dark hair cascaded sensually over her shoulders, and her hazel eyes looked out from under long black lashes. Standing beside her now, he imagined her in one of the beautiful, low-cut ballroom dresses she loved to wear to state functions. The other ministers' wives hated her because she looked young enough to be their daughter and drew amorous glances from all the men. Even more galling for these women, Hanli was one of their own kind, an Afrikaner by birth and by education, daughter of Jan de Villiers, the former Prime Minister.

It was David's marriage to Hanli that had made him acceptable to Afrikanerdom. He was a Zambian by birth, and a former minister of the Rhodesian Cabinet. As the son of the legendary big game hunter, Liam Loxton, he had inherited little except the desire for a big bank balance, and a political stance that was as far to the right as you could go. An education at Eton and Oxford had had absolutely no effect on his views, rather it had confirmed his belief in the decadence of the West, and his longing to return to the golden age of Imperialism, where might was right. There were two categories of people in David Loxton's book: those who did the fucking, and those who were fucked.

79

With the small amount of money he'd inherited from his grandfather, David had bought a small tobacco farm. Everyone said he'd go broke in the first year, but instead he made enough to buy a cigarette-making machine. Then when, he talked of marketing his own brand of cigarettes, everyone said he'd truly lost his head, but five years later he was a multi-millionaire, and when people talked about him now it was in hushed and reverential tones. His ruthlessness had become legendary, as had his ability always to make the right decision.

Then he had met and fallen in love with the wildlife artist and celebrated beauty, Tracey Butler. It had been a whirlwind romance. They had been married above the Victoria Falls, in the rainforest overlooking the Devil's Cataract, and the reception that followed at the Victoria Falls Hotel had been attended by over a thousand people from across the world.

David thought back to Tracey, with her little girl's face and her lion's heart. But he would not think about her for too long, it brought back too many memories – memories that were best forgotten. He'd had three children by her: Max, Victoria, and – But no, he would not think about that.

'How's the gun, sir?'

He turned with a start, his train of thought broken. It was Rory, his youngest son by Hanli. The boy was grown-up now, a curious-looking young man only just over five foot tall, with a freckled face, intense brown eyes and curly red hair.

'Better than I expected, my boy,' David said. 'Dr Preusser is worth his weight in gold, it's a fine weapon.'

'When can you start production?' Rory asked eagerly.

This was the one he would leave his fortune to, David thought, not for the first time; Rory was the one who, after his death, would make the Loxton companies even larger, even more profitable. Young as he was, business was something he understood – he was always on the look-out for fresh opportunities. And yet, David thought, Rory was so different from himself. He looked at the loose, creased shirt his son was wearing, the unfashionably wide tie, the badly fitting trousers and the stout black shoes. Rory certainly did not cut a particularly rakish figure.

'Production will start in six months,' he said. 'The export potential is excellent. I have guaranteed orders from both the army and the police.'

Rory smiled, proud of his father's success. Then he sat down at the table and tucked voraciously into his breakfast plate of ham and eggs.

Hanli glared at Rory angrily. 'Where are your manners? You eat like a pig.'

'I'm in a hurry,' Rory muttered, gulping down another mouthful.

Hanli got up from the table, thin-lipped with anger. 'I'm not going to eat at this table with you, my boy. Tomorrow you can eat with the servants – and every day after that, too, until you learn better manners.'

While Hanli stormed out of the room, Rory continued eating without concern. When she had disappeared, he looked up at his father, and David said harshly: 'You must show your mother a little more respect.'

'I'm twenty this year! I've got my first degree! I don't have to take her nagging!'

'As long as you live in this house, you'll abide by its rules. If you don't like it, get out!'

Rory was silent. He knew when he was beaten. He wanted to succeed in business with his father before he struck out on his own – and if he had to be polite to his mother in order to get on with his father, then he would. But he would get his revenge on her in the end. Rory hated attractive woman – they never gave him a second glance. As far as he was concerned, their manners were totally false, they cared only about appearances. He knew his father had several young girls on the side, and he suspected Hanli knew about it, but since her life-style wasn't threatened she kept her mouth shut. How could you respect behaviour like that? Rory, like his father, admired strength and detested weakness.

Hanli, hurrying along the corridor, thought how much she had disliked Rory since he had reached puberty. He had never paid her a single compliment or shown her any love since that time, and she knew that to Rory women were lesser mortals, like servants.

In the hall, she ran straight into Dirk's arms. Her oldest son kissed her affectionately on the cheek and she smelt the exclusive aftershave he always wore.

Mother!' He stepped back to admire her. 'Stunning as usual.

How do you always manage to look so beautiful?' Then he saw the set look on her face. 'Something wrong?'

'Oh, it's nothing, Dirk.'

'No, it's not nothing, is it? I bet it's that slob, my younger brother.' He held her shoulders in his strong hands and looked her straight in the eye. 'Isn't it?'

She nodded, and her dark hair fell forward. Dirk thought that if she wasn't his mother he would have bedded her there and then.

'I'll speak to him, he has no manners. He's a disgrace to the family.'

'Your father respects him.' Hanli knew this would spur Dirk on to give Rory a beating. She liked men who responded to her, like Dirk.

'Only because he can analyse a balance sheet in six seconds, the little creep.'

Hanli looked at Dirk's handsome face. He was even better looking than his father. He had long, straight dark hair and a finely chiselled jaw, an elegant, aquiline nose and mysterious dark eyes – eyes that seemed to penetrate to the depths of a woman's soul, to see what it was she secretly wanted. Today he was wearing a pale blue shirt, thin black leather tie and a dark blue Italian suit. He looked devastating, much older than his twenty-two years. This was her true son, Hanli thought, Rory was just some strange aberration of nature. She could sense Dirk's powerful body beneath his clothes, the lattice-work of finely formed stomach muscles, the huge masculine organ beneath them. Dirk was a film producer with his own company financed by his father. He had hired the best director in the country, and they already had a successful local film to their credit. Women went for Dirk as if he was the last man on earth.

Now he took his mother's chin in his hand and kissed her on the lips again. 'Don't worry. I'll speak to Rory.'

When Dirk reached the breakfast room David Loxton had already left and Rory was noisily slurping his coffee. Dirk went straight up to him and knocked the cup from his hands, then gave him a sharp clip across the ear. Rory was up in a second – but Dirk kicked his legs from under him, then pushed his foot down heavily on his right hand.

'You're breaking my fucking fingers!'

82

'You upset Mother again, creep, and I'll break every one of them.'

'Fuck off.'

Dirk put his weight down on Rory's hand until he screamed for mercy; then he relented, and Rory rose painfully to his feet, tears streaming from his eyes.

'Just remember, you be nice to her or I'll ball Amanda.' Amanda was Rory's first and only girlfriend. He had been going out with her for nine months and Dirk knew that they'd never had sex. He also knew that Amanda was crazy about himself.

Rory stormed out of the room and Dirk sat down at the table, shaking with laughter.

The airport terminal was packed with reporters, but Kobus van der Post and Victoria Loxton kept close together, heading towards the car that was waiting for them. Senator Dan Hill had been as good as his word: everything had been laid on to let them get away from the terminal as quickly as possible. They watched Kobus' entourage including his security men step smartly into a waiting bus. Now the chauffeur held the door of the stretch bullet-proof limo open for them, and they sank gratefully into the thick upholstery. As they sped through the streets of Washington, they had time to think about what lay in store for them.

'I've got to be very careful about what I say, Vicky.'

Kobus looked across at his companion, this woman he'd heard so much about but never really got to know well. She was Max's sister, so like him in some ways, so different in others – aloof and controlled where Max was passionate and energetic. Victoria was dedicated to her cause, the pursuit of justice. With her encyclopaedic knowledge of the judicial system, and her reputation as one of South Africa's foremost civil rights lawyers, she would be his ideal back-up on this exacting trip.

'You've got nothing to be worried about,' she said now. 'The Americans like what you've been saying, and they're right behind you. But you've got to work quickly and watch your back.'

Kobus grimaced. 'Every minute I'm away Loxton will be working on some angle to get me out of office. And he has a big following here – he comes across as British, and a gentleman. He's very persuasive.'

'All you have to think about is what will happen if you lose,'

Victoria said. 'Men like Napoleon Zwane will continue to be imprisoned; I'll emigrate, and so will Max; and the country will turn into a police state.'

Kobus smiled weakly. 'How is it that you always manage to hit a nerve-ending, Vicky?'

'It's because I understand our people so well.'

He looked at her, perhaps for a fraction too long. The blond hair was swept back from the sculptured face, revealing the high cheek-bones and the lustrous blue eyes, the full, passionate lips and the almost perfect aquiline nose. He wondered about the real woman behind all that self-control. But there would be no time for him to discover that woman now, he thought, as he turned to look out of the window at the busy streets of Washington. He was fighting, now, for the future of his country.

Two days later, Kobus van der Post was sitting outside the famous oval office in the White House. It felt as if it had taken him a lifetime to secure this opportunity – to talk to the President of the United States, perhaps the most powerful man in the world.

The newly elected American President carried one of the most famous political names in America. He could have been a pro football player – but politics had proved more attractive. His nickname in the Senate was 'Bulldozer', and he was a man who fought tooth and nail to get exactly what he wanted. He had a reputation for being an autocrat but also for being scrupulously fair. His staff believed in him with a passion.

Kobus, sitting on his elegant, spindly chair, stared up at the high white ceiling. The President was highly critical of South Africa, and was being pushed by many black senators to continue American trade boycotts and sanctions – which were doing irreparable harm to South African business, especially to the mining houses, which were the cornerstone of the economy and paid over seventy per cent of the country's taxes. What Kobus wanted from this meeting was approval of, and support for, his own new initiative. He had done a lot of groundwork: he'd been interviewed by most of the major networks, and thanks to the influence of Saffron and John Packard, had achieved very positive publicity. Now, if luck was with him . . .

The secretary gestured for Kobus to walk through into the President's office. As he got up from his chair, Kobus wondered if the gaunt-looking man with the thick glasses ever slept – he never stopped answering the telephone and sifting through correspondence, and the look he gave Kobus as he opened the door to the President's office for him was distinctly harassed.

'He's ready for you, sir. Remember, you have one hour.'

David Loxton, sitting on the sofa in the bedroom, looked at the headline again and felt the stabbing pain between his eyebrows intensify. This time, Van der Post had pulled off a masterstroke. Beside him, Hanli glanced across at the front-page photograph of Kobus.

'He's an attractive man.'

'He's a bastard! The bloody man is doing everything he can to block my security bill and oust me from power.'

Hanli had never considered before the worrying possibility that her husband might be kicked out of the cabinet. 'But darling, no one in their right mind would reject your legislation.'

'That's where you're wrong. Parliament is divided on the issue, and Van der Post is accusing me of trying to change the constitution – of putting more power into my own hands.'

'But darling, you are.'

He lay back and closed his eyes. In his mind he repeated one of his favourite tenets: In order that I succeed, others must fail. He wondered if it might not be time to issue a few new orders to Major Hurst. It was the sort of approach to the problem that Van der Post would never even think of.

The air was hot and the sunshine intense; he might almost have been in South Africa, Max thought, if it weren't for the stretch limos pulling by him, the big studio names he kept passing. If there was one place on earth he had thought he'd never visit, it was Hollywood.

The building he wanted came up suddenly, taking him by surprise: the Packard Picture Company. Saffron had said her husband's company was big, but that had been an understatement. Max pulled up at the gate, and a man wearing an immaculate uniform and dark glasses strode up to the car and peered through the window.

'Dr Loxton?'

'Yes,' Max replied, and then curiosity got the better of him. 'Tell me, how did you know my name?'

'Well, sir, I was given your photograph. Security here is very tight, you see, sir. One small leak about a new picture could give the competition the edge on us.'

Max was directed to an underground garage filled with exotic motor cars. He noted a black Porsche convertible parked under the Saffron Packard name-plate. Saffron had left South Africa shortly before he had, but they'd agreed to meet again, here in Hollywood. He hated to admit it, but he felt apprehensive; her world was obviously so different from his.

He took the elevator to the tenth floor of the main building. The elevator was all glass, and through a sound system dulcet tones delivered a short history of the Packard Picture Company. 'The Packard Picture Company is now the largest motion picture producer in the world. Started in 1971 by John Packard, the company has produced a sequence of blockbusters. Films like *The Fighter*, *Viet Vet* and *Lost World* were the largest grossing movies of all time. Today, through growth and acquisition, the Packard Picture Company dominates the world TV networks . . .'

Max got out on the tenth floor, to a breathtaking view of the Hollywood skyline, and a platinum blonde receptionist wearing a strip of cloth that was obviously meant to pass for a mini-skirt.

'Dr Loxton, Mrs Packard apologises, but her meeting is lasting a little longer than expected. Some coffee?' The long lashes fluttered. He wondered if she'd been born in Hollywood, or just created here.

'Thank you. Black, no sugar.'

He strolled over to the huge glass windows and looked down over the studio buildings below. He was just wondering whether Saffron had made it here on her own talent or her husband's influence, when he heard a voice through the wall beside him, and realised that it was hers. He moved closer, straining his ears.

'I don't give a damn, Henry,' he heard. 'The release date is in a month's time.' There was a mumbled reply, and then: 'Meet that deadline or you're out!'

'Your coffee, Dr Loxton.'

Max spun round to see the receptionist offering him his coffee. He grinned at her, and inclined his head in the direction of Saffron's office. 'Problems?'

'Mrs Packard is just giving a few of our executive producers a dressing-down.' Her eyes told Max that she'd like to know him better. 'Mrs Packard doesn't believe in problems, she's a woman of action.'

The double doors of Saffron's office opened, and four men in suits strode out, the tallest red-faced and flushed. 'I told you, you weren't going to get away with it,' one of them was stammering. They disappeared into the elevator, and Max found himself staring at Saffron.

'Max, I'm sorry!'

The radiant smile betrayed none of the anger he had heard a few moments before. 'Belinda, we are not to be disturbed,' she said to the receptionist, and led him into her office and closed the doors behind her.

Her lips touched his, and they kissed long and passionately. Then she drew back, and they sat together on a long white leather couch.

The office was designed to impress. The high ceiling was of pressed steel, and the huge glass windows looked out over the studios. On the bare white walls hung a number of originals by French Impressionists, and two pieces of Middle African sculpture. The whole effect was minimalist, and very striking; Max admired her good taste.

'You like it? I spend a lot of time here – it's where I plan the pictures I'm going to shoot. Those assholes were trying it on. Schedules in this business have to be kept to.'

The sensuous curves of her body were clear through the thin material of the black jumpsuit. She swept her hair back, and leaned closer to him. 'I've wanted you so badly. Just to hold you, have you near. It's been unbearable. But I knew that if John found out about us it would have been disastrous in every way: it's through John's contacts that Kobus has had such a lot of media coverage while he's been over here.'

'But that doesn't alter what's between us?'

She walked across to one of the big windows and leaned against it, facing him. 'Of course it doesn't. But I'm explaining why I haven't been able to tell him yet. If John had known about our relationship, he'd have done his damnedest to wreck Kobus' American tour.'

Max looked at her with renewed respect. He could see the pain reflected in that beautiful face.

'And now?' he asked.

She went up to the couch, sat on his legs and took his face in her hands. 'That danger's over now. Whatever happens, John can't undo the discussions Kobus has had with the President. It's just that . . .'

'Yes?'

'It's just that I know he's not going to let me leave him. He'll do everything in his power to get his revenge.'

They were silent for a moment. Then Saffron kissed him, and smiled. 'I love you, Max. I want to be with you. I want to come and make films in Africa. John's away at the moment, he's negotiating to buy an interest in one of the European TV networks. I'll tell him I'm leaving him when he gets back from London.'

Soon after that they left the studios together, not noticing the car that followed them at a discreet distance.

They had spent the afternoon in bed, then driven up the coast and gone swimming in the sea. It had been a wonderful day. And now, after a marvellous dinner, they were sitting drinking their coffee in the tiny seaside restaurant Saffron had chosen, listening to the distant sound of waves crashing against the shore. The combination of the chardonnay and the seafood had made Max sleepy. Saffron was sitting next to him, leaning on his shoulder.

Suddenly there was a scuffle down at the back of the room, and Max saw a big man push the restaurant owner out of the door. There were two other men standing in the middle of the wooden floor, and one of them was John Packard.

'Come here, Saffron!' Packard bellowed.

Max rose to his feet, saw the anger in Saffron's face as she spun round to confront her husband.

'Stay away from me!' she screamed.

The big man moved forward, and Max quickly sized up the two toughs. No problem – but he wasn't going to let that show. He stared at John Packard, immaculate in his dark double-breasted suit, his grey hair combed tightly back and the look of power clear in his blue eyes.

'Saffron, go out to the car. I'll sort this out,' Max whispered.

She ignored him, and squared up to her husband. 'John, I'm not your possession. I'm leaving you!'

Packard laughed. 'No way!'

'You were attractive once, John, but then you became obsessed with power and money. You don't love me! I know all about Yvonne.'

Packard swayed a little on his feet. 'Who's she?'

'Come off it, John. She's that bimbo you've been screwing for the last sixteen months!'

Max had never seen her so angry – beautiful in her fury. 'I was loyal to you,' she said, 'even when the love had gone. I owe you nothing.' She turned to Max. 'Let's get out of here, I don't like the company.'

Packard gestured to the two toughs, and as Saffron walked past him, one of the men caught her by the waist, then hit her in the stomach, and she collapsed to the ground.

Packard chuckled. 'Nice try, dear!' He turned to his men. 'Take her outside.'

It was then that Max moved forward, the muscles in his neck rigid with anger. He saw the confidence in Packard's eyes as his men closed in on him.

The first came directly at him. Max connected a hard right to the man's skull that lifted him off his feet and sent him spinning across the floor. Then, the other picked up a chair and swung it – but instead of trying to avoid it, Max pressed forward, the wood splintering across his face as he landed a trio of punches to the man's torso. Then Max moved right in, repeatedly smashing his fists into the man's face till he collapsed across the floor. Now it was Packard's turn.

'Touch me, buddy,' Packard yelled, 'and you'll spend the rest of your life regretting it!'

Max glanced at Saffron lying on the floor, then drove his fists into Packard's face – and kept on driving. He didn't care any more.

Saffron was screaming. 'Max! Stop, for God's sake!'

Max stared into Packard's eyes, he was still conscious. He took Saffron by the hand and led her out of the restaurant.

Geneva was very cold. Max looked across the lake and saw the fountain shooting a single icy spume of water towards the azure sky. In the distance a line of birds was strung out along the horizon. Max undid the top button of his overcoat and turned away, walking through the slush towards the modern office block that housed the Proust Bank. In his hand he carried a large briefcase.

The satisfaction of beating up John Packard had come at a high price. Still, he did not regret it, and if he had the chance he'd do the same again – but Packard had retaliated swiftly. Fortunately, as Saffron had pointed out, he wasn't able to undo what Kobus had already achieved; but his first act, the following day, had been to ban Saffron from the premises of the Packard Picture Company. Then, as Max looked for American finance for his Botswana venture, he found every avenue blocked. At first, he hadn't made the connection. It was Saffron who pointed out that Packard's influence was enough to shy any bank off.

But here, in Geneva, Max knew he was beyond Packard's reach. And now, as he crossed the road, he saw Saffron standing on the pavement waiting for him. It was only the second time he'd seen her in a dress – the first had been at the casino – and she looked ravishing, especially with the diamond choker round her neck.

He kissed her softly on the lips. 'You look good enough to eat,' he whispered.

'Let's hope the bankers are impressed.'

Proust was one of the oldest banking families in the world, and the association between the Proust and Van der Post families was strong. Proust had financed the expansion of Kobus van der Post's vineyards, and it was on Kobus' recommendation that Max had approached them. Initial discussions had shown the bank and some of their clients to be very interested in his project.

Like everything else in Switzerland, the lift moved with precision, taking them to the twentieth floor where Mr Proust was in reception to greet them. He was a short, plump man with closely cropped grey hair and an infectious smile.

'Dr Loxton, Mrs Packard, it's a pleasure to meet you at last. Please come through to my office.' His English was excellent.

Once they had been served with coffee, Proust eyed both of them and then opened a report on his desk. 'I bring you good news. A respected client of ours, with the means to provide the investment capital you require, has shown considerable interest in your project. However, he requires a major stake in your operation – at least twenty-five per cent.'

Max breathed deeply and looked across at Proust. 'That leaves fifty-one per cent for myself, and twenty-four for the Botswanan government. I must meet this man – he'll have to be as dedicated to the project as I am.'

Proust removed his reading glasses and leaned back. 'Money and morality do not go hand in hand, but I think you will be

90

favourably impressed. My client will arrive in ten minutes' time to see your presentation. Shall we set up in the main boardroom?'

The presentation went better than either Max or Saffron could have hoped. Her film on the Okavango swamps and the threat to their existence clearly impressed Proust's client, Shelton, a major British financier, as did Max's plans for the largest hotel and entertainment complex in the world, to be set amongst the waterways of the Okavango. They discussed the project for an hour, then Proust carefully moved on to the matter of funding.

Shelton, a short, dapper man with fine black hair, removed his black-framed glasses and stared at Max. 'Your experience and your reputation in business are both very, very good,' he said in his measured, public school accent. 'However, Africa as a continent is not considered a good risk. I am sold on your project and I believe in its viability, but I would have to ask for a thirty-five per cent stake in it, at the very least.'

The way Shelton said this made it plain that the figure was not negotiable. Max smiled affably, disguising the unease he felt. He wanted control of the operation himself, but under Shelton's terms the Botswanan government, with their third-party share, could give control to whichever investor they chose. For Max, the project was an enormous risk – he was backing his side of the operation with his entire fortune.

He saw the roulette wheel spinning in front of him, and somehow he knew that this was a risk he had to take. The sum required for the project was enormous; not many investors were going to be interested.

Max looked across at Shelton. The man's cool grey eyes did not shift from his, and in them Max could see nothing suspicious.

'We have a deal,' he said.

Kobus van der Post sat in the darkened London theatre next to Victoria Loxton as the last act of Andrew Lloyd Webber's wonderful musical drew to a close. The last notes died away, and the audience were applauding wildly; beside him Victoria rose to her feet – he'd never seen her so animated. He would have got up too, but the American trip had taken its toll of his health, and he felt terribly tired, though he would not have dreamed of admitting it to Victoria or anyone else. Of course, he understood the reason for her euphoria. His meeting with the British Prime

Minister had been an overwhelming success, and then, just before they left the Dorchester, Max had phoned to tell them of his success in finding backing for his Okavango project in Geneva.

Now, in amongst the crowd of departing theatre-goers, Victoria kept close to Kobus. He felt giddy on his feet, and was very moved by her demonstration of affection. 'Let's go back to the hotel,' she whispered. 'Thank you for taking me to the theatre . . . I realise how tired you are.'

They collected their keys from reception and took the mirrored lift to their floor. As its doors closed on them, Victoria adjusted Kobus' collar affectionately.

'That was wonderful,' she said. 'I feel so good when I'm with you.'

Then the lift doors opened, and she was gone.

Kobus walked tiredly towards his suite. In love at his age? No, he couldn't possibly be.

General Feisal watched the Lear jet circle above the shimmering desert sand, then drop like a bird towards the distant concrete runway. He turned to his aide and said softly: 'The time has come for us to show our power. If the weapon is right, we shall be in a position to cause immense trouble for our Israeli friends – just as they think we're becoming complacent.'

Feisal and his aide stepped into the white stretch limo and sped towards the plane as it taxied to a halt down the runway. As it came to rest, the desert air was filled with the pungent smell of aviation fuel, and a line of steps snaked out of the side of the plane and down to the runway concrete. A well-dressed business-man appeared, closely followed by a silver-haired man in a white coat and a gorilla-like figure in a black overall.

Feisal moved from the car, adjusting the wide sleeves of his djellaba. He knew David Loxton by reputation and he wanted his co-operation. He looked into the cool grey eyes as they shook hands.

'Mr Loxton, I have heard so much about you. I look forward to the pleasure of doing business with you . . .'

Later, General Feisal examined the Aardwolf. David Loxton stared at the inscrutable brown face with its precisely trimmed moustache. For a long time there was silence, then Feisal looked up.

'It looks so simple. Why is it so expensive?'

The words hung in the air, and David smiled. He always encountered resistance – that was what told him the price was right. He turned to Dr Preusser, and the doctor, recognising his cue, launched into his sales talk. 'First, sir, zis weapon is not a pressing, it is milled from steel. You could drive a truck over it, it would still fire properly, *ja*?' Preusser's clipped tones seemed out of place in the stillness of the desert. 'You hev a truck, Mr Feisal?' he asked.

The Arab smiled.

Half an hour later, a huge articulated lorry rumbled over the horizon line and meandered towards the runway. To Feisal's surprise, Dr Preusser smiled with satisfaction. '*Ja*, zat is very good.' He turned to the man in the black overall. 'Carl. Load ze weapon, then put it under ze wheels of ze truck.'

They watched as the demonstration took place. David winced as he watched the great wheels of the lorry run over his beautifully crafted rifle, but Dr Preusser only gave a tight-lipped smile and turned to Feisal.

'A veapon needs to be tested. Who vould you suggest ve kill?'

'The truck driver,' Feisal replied. From the expression on David Loxton's face, he guessed that the truck had completely destroyed the gun. He disliked the German, and looked forward to humiliating him.

'Carl!' Dr Preusser barked. 'Shoot ze driver.'

Carl smiled with satisfaction and walked across to the Aardwolf. As he picked it up and slid back the bolt, Feisal rose in his chair to call a halt to the experiment, but Carl, pointing the snout of the gun at the cab, let the weapon explode into life. Glass and metal showered across the runway as the shotgun shells tore the cab apart. The driver staggered from the door, to be massacred by the avalanche of bullets.

Feisal dropped back into his chair, laughing, and Dr Preusser smiled contentedly. 'It is good, *ja*?'

'Very, very good,' Feisal exclaimed with awe. With this weapon they could decimate the Israelis.

That evening David Loxton signed a contract to supply the Aardwolf to several Arab states. The profit on the deal, big enough to satisfy the wildest dreams of avarice, was for him only another step on the road to power. He laughed as he thought of Kobus van der Post trekking through Europe and America, drumming up support, and wondered if his opponent would sleep as easily if he knew of the agreement David had made with Dolph Klopper a few days before. It guaranteed that his security bill would be passed in parliament by an overwhelming majority.

General Jurie Smit opened the suitcases to reveal the piles of used bank notes, and looked across at Major Hurst. Hurst, dressed in a pinstripe suit, looked the epitome of the successful businessman, and actually bore a striking resemblance to the actor Sean Connery, with dark hair and a broad wrinkled face. Behind the dark eyes, however – eyes without a glimmer of light – lurked a mind obsessed with killing.

'I have more work for you. And this time the deaths must look like accidents – we've had enough violent killings.' Jurie Smit gave his orders quite without emotion.

Major Hurst took the list of names, his eyes narrowing as he ran over them carefully. 'Disposed of in this order?'

'*Ja*, and on the dates specified,' Smit growled. 'And no bugger-ups like Max Loxton!'

'Loxton was not a bugger-up,' Hurst snapped. He put the list of names down on the table and glared at General Smit.

'Then what was it, Hurst? You tell me,' Smit said, not in the least intimidated. He knew how to control Hurst; he could give him what he needed most – the power to kill.

'My man was supplied with insufficient information on the kill. How could we expect a subject to react as vigorously as Dr Loxton did?'

Smit sat back in his chair. 'A fairly acceptable excuse, but you've made it impossible for me to go near Dr Loxton again. A full investigation has been launched in Botswana to try to get to the bottom of the incident. You realise what will happen to you if we are found out?'

Major Hurst looked at Smit evilly. 'You wouldn't dare touch me.'

'I have details of every kill you've made, Hurst. Try anything, and you'll hang.'

'And you'll walk away a free man?' Hurst stammered.

'Naturally. There is nothing to link us.' Smit smiled reflectively. 'There was one particular hit squad I used, I remember, that gave me a lot of trouble. That was about five years ago . . . Eventually I buried them.'

Five

George Zwane drove his car along the narrow crowded street in the centre of Alexandra township. Alexandra – a black ghetto, one square kilometre of slums and overcrowding, and only two kilometres away from Sandton City, the most exclusive shopping centre in Johannesburg. As usual, thought George, the white man had secured his supply of cheap labour and hidden it carefully away.

Driving past the wretched shanties, he went over his plan of action again. He felt like a man coming to his own funeral, strangely detached from what was going on around him. Even at this stage he could still pull out, take the easy road and let things be. But then he thought about his father, the great Napoleon Zwane, and all he'd stood for and believed in, and knew that he could not pull out. Because of his father, this was the only course he could take.

He saw a man leading a small cow along the sidewalk, and remembered back to the time when, as a child, he had been a herdboy in Zululand. That was a long time ago now. It had been an honourable task – traditionally, it was the sons of the royal family who were given the task of looking after the tribe's livestock. But now he had turned his back on all tradition; he must move into a new and violent world, without values.

He drew up outside the small trading store. He had planned everything down to the last detail. The timing was right – he glanced down at his watch – this was vital, so that the police should not suspect anything later. His reason for being here was also cast-iron: as his firm so often did, he was acting on behalf of the Indian storekeeper, to recover unpaid bills, and having recovered the money, was bringing the cheque to his client. Not that the police had any right to ask him what he was doing here, it was just that he was a marked man.

George was Secretary of the African Freedom Council in the Transvaal. Only months before, the government had encouraged the AFC to come out into the open – but now, with Kobus van der Post abroad, the Minister of Justice, David Loxton was taking power into his own hands, and two days ago he had declared the AFC illegal. It was only a matter of time before he arrested its key members, including George. This had put George at a crucial crossroads in his life. It would be so easy to take the low road, to renounce his membership of the AFC, to keep on as a lawyer, building up his practice and his name. But he had a commitment to something deeper than personal success; it was the reason he'd studied law in the first place – to free his people from the shackles of oppression. In addition, he now knew that the Comrades were taking control of the townships, and that this heralded a downward spiral into anarchy – the law of the street courts and the necklace.

George stared as a child in torn clothes crossed the street. He thought of his own children. For their sake – if not his own – he must infiltrate the Comrades, confront the mind behind the violence, the man who'd had his father killed. But to gain acceptance, he'd have to throw away the present, everything he believed in. All his life he had opposed violence, trusting implicitly in Gandhi's ideal of passive resistance, but he had come to see that against this new movement in the townships, it would be entirely ineffectual. He was forty, but recently he had felt like an old man.

He closed the car door, leaving his keys in the ignition – he wouldn't be needing a car where he was going. He walked in through the crowded store. From behind the counter an enormous Indian woman in a sarong smiled at him. 'Good morning, George. Seth is in his office,' she said in her high-pitched Indian voice.

'Thanks, Priscilla.' Guilt, at using their store for his plan, was strong in him.

He passed through the beaded curtains and along a dark passage that smelt strongly of incense. At the back was a small room where a handsome young man sat at an old desk, poring over a ledger. He looked up as George entered and they shook

96

hands, the gesture of an old and trusted friendship. God, George thought, what am I doing?

'I have brought you the money from the Levy case,' he said.

Seth looked at the cheque and smiled. 'Perhaps I should have written it off, it's less than your fee.' Then his face creased into lines of worry. 'George, I'm frightened at what's happening. What will the AFC do now?'

George glanced down at his watch. Where the hell were the police? And then he heard a noise at the door.

George was out in the passage in seconds – but then he realised that there was no way out except through the front of the store. This was all to the good: he would confront the police, then make his getaway.

But suddenly Priscilla was there, blocking his way. 'George! The police have come to arrest you! Get in here, in here!' She opened a sliding door in the wall to reveal a tiny alcove the size of a coffin. He couldn't object, so he pressed himself inside it and Priscilla closed the door behind him. He heard her whisper from outside: 'George, there's a panel in front of your face, you can slide it back for air. But be careful!'

Then there was a scuffle in the passage outside, and he remained absolutely still, listening to the tramp of men's feet. Furtively he raised his hands and found the panel. Slowly he moved it back.

The opening looked out into the store's back room, the room he had just left. In front of him he could see two blue uniformed backs. He smiled grimly – it was the police all right, they'd obviously listened to his tip-off. Seth must be seated at the desk where he'd been earlier, and perhaps Priscilla had gone back to the front of the shop. George heard the sound of a paper being unfolded, and a heavily accented Afrikaans voice said: 'Mr Naidoo. We've received a tip-off that an illegal meeting is being held here. You must come with us.'

George shuddered. This was not what he had planned at all. As he had envisaged it, the police, alerted by his tip-off, would surround the store, expecting to arrest George Zwane, the noted AFC activist, who could now legitimately be imprisoned. He, however, would elude them – and his status as a wanted man, a fugitive from justice, would then gain him admittance to the ranks of the Comrades. But it looked as if his plan was going badly wrong.

'What have I done for you to arrest me?' Seth's voice was controlled, not showing any fear.

'*Meneer*, it's not for you to ask. Come.'

Seth knew his rights. 'Tell me what I've done. Then I'll go.'

'Listen, you cheeky coolie!' the policeman snarled.

'Sergeant sir, he's within his rights.' This time a younger, more tentative voice.

'Don't tell me about his blerry rights, Van Tonder. Give these cheeky coolies any line and they'll wrap it around your neck.'

'It seems he knows the law better than you do, sergeant,' Seth butted in.

Again the younger policeman was conciliatory. 'Sir, I think you must tell him the reasons for his arrest.'

George saw the sergeant's neck muscles straining – Seth had better watch it. 'All right, Mr Naidoo. What you've done is, you've been funding the African Freedom Council to the tune of over R20000, to be exact.'

'It's been unbanned – I've done nothing illegal.' Seth's voice was calm, controlled.

'Now listen, coolie, shut your blerry mouth. Come!'

Seth rose into view and George saw the constable put the cuffs on him. Then, as Seth started to walk to the door, the sergeant drew out his truncheon and hit him a heavy blow in the kidneys. 'Now, coolie, apologise!'

Seth lay on the floor groaning. George heard the truncheon smash across his friend's face. 'OK. Let's hear you sing, coolie.'

His body shaking with rage, George burst from his hiding place. The constable turned towards him, drawing his revolver, and George gave him a right hook that sent him sprawling on the floor. The look of surprise was still on his face when he went down.

The sergeant lumbered towards George now, an ugly smile on his face. 'Try me.' For a moment he stared at the tall, good-looking black man who was dancing in front of him like a professional boxer, then took a slug at him, but George feinted, then came up again, and hit him hard in the face, once, twice, and then a third blow in the chest. The man sank forwards – and then grabbed George, trying to head-butt him in the face.

Now George was in the swing of it. He hit the sergeant again and again, seeing the blood begin to froth around his mouth. Each blow was perfectly placed, so that the man was battling to

98

stay on his feet, and George didn't notice the constable rise up behind him with his baton. The next moment he received a savage blow on the back of the head and staggered forwards onto the floor.

The sergeant now came over to him and kicked him savagely in the side of the head, then in the groin. George pulled himself up, and saw the sergeant move forwards again.

'Eat this, kaffir!'

The boot hit George square in the face, breaking his front teeth, and he sagged to the floor. Blow after blow came down on him, and his body burned with the pain. Everything had gone horribly wrong . . . Then, out of the corner of his eye, he saw the sergeant's revolver lying cocked on the floor.

George rolled over and grabbed it. His life was in the balance. He pulled the trigger, the .357 Magnum kicking back in his hands.

The sergeant catapulted up in the air, the bullet taking him in the ribcage. His blood spattered across the white wall behind him. George coldly pulled the trigger again, watching the face explode. As Priscilla came in, screaming uncontrollably, George pirouetted round, saw the constable cocking his weapon, and squeezed the trigger again, watching the incredulity on the young policeman's face as the force of the bullet tore away his right arm.

Seth looked up in horror. 'George, they'll hang you,' he whispered hoarsely.

Priscilla, cradling her husband's head in her hands, looked at the bloody corpse of the big policeman and shuddered. Then she glanced at the constable who was still slumped on the ground, barely breathing. She could hear George breathing deeply behind her, and she looked up at him, her face stricken with agony. 'George! Get out of here!'

George towered over her, his hands still shaking. 'Tell my wife that I won't be coming home.' As he spoke, there was the noise of sirens in the distance. Priscilla touched his cheek – and then he was gone.

Outside the shop, he saw the yellow police van approaching in the distance. There was a sickness in his stomach; no going back now. He lifted the gun and fired a shot at the driver. The windscreen shattered, then went red, and George darted down a

99

side street, running as he had never run in his life. There were dogs barking, shouts. They were after him.

Down another street, with feet drumming on the tarmac behind him. He was losing wind, beginning to slow down. To die now, after the sacrifices he'd made . . . Suddenly, someone grabbed his arm and yanked him off the street. A young black face stared into his. 'Lie down, Comrade. The *boere* will not find you.'

He plunged into the bin of offal. He could hear very little and he lay quite still, concentrating on trying not to vomit.

Suddenly, his life had changed beyond all comprehension.

Victoria Loxton pulled up outside Rivonia police station, and got out of the car. The black guard looked at her sourly over the barrel of his assault rifle; another wealthy housewife reporting a burglary, he thought – and no doubt this beautiful woman would say that it was her gardener or her maid who was responsible. She gave him a cursory 'Hello', then walked into the station.

Victoria had returned from Europe only that morning, riding high on the success of the trip and her growing closeness to Kobus van der Post. But as soon as she landed, the reality of South Africa had broken in on her; she could feel the tension in the air, see the despondency on people's faces. While she was away she had read of the terrifying new wave of violence spreading through the black townships.

And then a journalist friend of hers, Karen, had telephoned and told her of the incident involving George Zwane. George was one of Victoria's oldest friends, and she simply could not believe it – it was totally out of character. He had always avoided violence, any kind of confrontation with the police. There was something wrong about this; something fishy. She had gone quickly round to Seth Naidoo's shop and spoken to Priscilla, then she had come straight here.

Now she banged angrily on the charge counter, and a black constable ambled over towards her. 'Can I help you, madam?' he asked, a supercilious grin on his face.

'I want to see Seth Naidoo.'

'Who?'

'Seth Naidoo was brought here earlier today. I am his legal representative, and I demand to see him.'

The constable sighed. This white woman meant trouble. He decided to call the station commander. 'Will you wait a minute?'

It was actually ten minutes before Major Pretorius appeared, looking distinctly unwelcoming. There were few senior police officers in the Johannesburg area who were not wary of advocate Victoria Loxton.

'Yes, Miss Loxton?'

She could hear the edge in his voice, and was pleased. She knew Major Pretorius, and knew she was right – Seth Naidoo must still be here, in detention.

'Major Pretorius, I demand to see Seth Naidoo.'

'Who?'

'Don't play games, Major. I know he's here. Has he been allowed to call me?'

She could see the Major weighing up the options in his head. She knew from Karen that the evidence was cast-iron against George Zwane, but that Naidoo was in the clear. However, he would be a vital witness in the case if the young constable, now fighting for his life in Johannesburg General Hospital, did not recover.

'You may see him, Miss Loxton. He is being held as a state witness.'

It was another quarter of an hour before she was led to the cell used for consultations. Seth was brought in and sat opposite her at the small table; he looked shaken, but otherwise fine.

'They haven't touched me, Vicky. Is Priscilla all right?'

Victoria knew she must treat him gently. 'She's just sick with worry, Seth. She told me what happened.'

Seth shook his head in despair. 'I wish George had never come to see me. It was bad timing. I didn't realise he was so on edge after his father's death.'

'He got away, Seth – they can't find him anywhere.' She paused. 'Of course, you know why they're treating you reasonably well?'

Seth held his head in his hands. 'They want me to testify against George?'

She inclined her head.

'Never!'

'You don't have a choice, Seth.'

'If they catch him they'll hang him!'

'They won't catch him,' Victoria said. She got up from her

101

chair and paced round the windowless room; it would be bugged, of course.

'They arrested me on a totally trumped up charge,' said Seth. 'Can you believe it?'

'They didn't have a warrant, your arrest wasn't legal, Seth. You must just make a statement about what happened, and then you'll be released.'

Seth stared at her, anguish written across his face. 'My statement will condemn him to death. The fuckers were beating me up, you see. George couldn't stand it, he went berserk.'

Victoria nodded her head sadly. It all made sense now: the bottled-up hatred of years had been released in an instant. She looked at Seth Naidoo, an old client of hers, whom she was very fond of. 'Seth,' she said. 'You must give them a full and accurate statement. Please. For Priscilla's sake.' She knew Seth's love for his wife was all-encompassing.

'But what about George?'

Major Pretorius came in; he had been more than generous with the time he'd given them. Victoria got up and touched Seth's hand.

'Do as I say.'

'I will. But I'll hate myself for it.'

George's beard was now four days old, and already he felt changed. The successful attorney, the civilized urban man had become a warrior, like the generations of his forebears. The Comrades had taken him in as a blood brother, a fellow killer – and killing a policeman had automatically elevated him to the highest level among them. They'd given him a gun, and protected him, and now he was sitting with them in a people's court.

The room smelt of wood smoke, and early morning sunshine blazed in through a broken window. Outside, he could hear children playing in the street, the noise of cars, but inside it was very quiet. This court was nothing like the ones he had been used to in Johannesburg. This was Orlando, a suburb of Soweto, and this 'trial' was being held in a tin shanty whose walls were brown with rust.

In the dock – or rather, sitting on the floor in the centre of the room – was a young woman accused of being a police informer. She was dressed in old clothes and her face was a patchwork of bruises. George could smell that she hadn't washed, but it was her eyes that frightened him – dull, lifeless, without hope. George and the Comrades sat on a long bench behind a table. They heard the story from witnesses, then the young woman gave her version of events.

The Comrades reached their decision within five minutes. George shuddered at the severity of it – but then, he realised, they had no jails; and being a traitor to the people was the lowest crime of all. The sentence was inevitable. Death.

The woman begged for mercy. The faces of the Comrades were stony, but in the heart of George Zwane she found sympathy, and he cried inside for her at the injustice of the sentence. Moments later she was dragged screaming out into the street, and the whole court followed. They let her go, and she began to run, faster and faster, stumbling in her haste to get away.

Then the stones began to fly. Several hit her, one on the side of the skull. She staggered and fell over, then rose, her face covered in blood.

A young boy whom George guessed to be about fourteen ran up to her and pointed. 'Informer! Traitor!' And the crowd took up the cry, so that it rose and fell like the sound of the sea. From nowhere a length of barbed wire appeared, and two men bound the woman's hands behind her back with it.

She screamed when she saw the car tyre being rolled towards her. George smelt petrol, strong and pungent. Her dress and underclothes were ripped from her. The young boy mounted her from behind, penetrating her roughly as the crowd cheered him on. He eventually staggered back, a sickly grin on his face.

'Burn the bitch!'

She screamed out, but relentlessly they closed on her, swarming eagerly about her. The barbed wire was wound round her neck, two long pieces left dangling down to the ground. Two young children doused the tyre with petrol, then they heaved it upwards and over her head.

She staggered around, the tyre supported by the wire and hanging round her, just above the elbows. George shuddered, muttering the word to himself: 'Necklace.' Now her screaming became desperate. The crowd watched silently, dragging it out, enjoying her agony, watching the face of the woman who had informed on one of the Comrades.

Suddenly the tyre exploded into flames. She cried out in agony

103

as she fell to the ground. George smelt the sickly smell of burning flesh. He wanted to run forwards, help her, but instead he stood transfixed amongst the crowd.

He had thought it would be quick, but it was not. She lasted a long time, but when the screaming stopped he was sure she had ceased to feel any pain. People who were necklaced generally died from suffocation, the flames drinking up the air around them. He made the sign of the cross – and turned to see himself staring at John Mtshali, the man he had come to know as the unofficial leader of this section of the township.

Mtshali was a lean man with a close-cropped beard and the glint of power in his eyes. He had the habit of talking very softly, and George had to move forward to hear him properly.

'You do not like our justice, Comrade Zwane? You feel pity for that bitch?' It was a threat, not a question.

'"Justice" does not enter into it. She was guilty before she was accused.'

'You speak like the Afrikaner dog, traitor!'

As Mtshali spat the words in his face, George gripped him by the front of his black windcheater and hauled him close. He sensed the crowd moving in, watching as he challenged this powerful township leader; keen, perhaps, for another necklacing.

'This is what they want,' George said icily. He looked deep into John Mtshali's cold, dark eyes and searched for the man behind them. 'They want us killing each other like dogs. You know what a man in Europe thinks when you burn a woman to death with a car tyre?'

'He is afraid, he knows that we must be left alone to rule ourselves.'

'No, you fool, he is horrified. He thinks we are savages. Kaffirs!'

'Traitor!' There was a crazed gleam now in John's eyes. George hit him hard in the head, and let him fall. But then he felt someone grab at his shirt: the crowd was against him.

'Comrades!' He screamed it out, and the crowd fell silent at the power of his voice. He waited for quiet.

'You want to burn people every day? You want them to scream as the fire eats their flesh!' George shouted with all his strength.

He caught the eyes of the dissenters in the crowd, and turned in a slow arc, looking at each one of them in turn. Always it would be like this, having to prove himself again and again.

'I will lead you on a path of blood . . .'

Now the crowd was quiet. This was the language they wanted to hear. George looked down at John Mtshali lying unconscious on the ground. He must take this man's place, try to find out who was pulling the strings – hiding behind the Comrades.

'There will be no more killing for today,' he shouted. 'But tomorrow there will be a harvest of blood!' George was gaining momentum – the crowd was with him. 'We will turn our anger against the white government! We, the people, will overcome and destroy them!'

He sensed a change of mood in the crowd, and a wave of euphoria came over him. He had them in his power. He felt that power, heady, intoxicating . . .

'You will follow me. I will show you the way. I will give you freedom, whatever the cost.'

Then he shouted it out, the cry of freedom, his fist clenched in the salute. '*Amandla*! *Ngawethu*!' The power. Be ours.

Comrade Mtshali staggered to his feet and joined in the cry – and George felt the primitive side of himself powerfully stirred. Never in his life, perhaps, had he felt like this. To have power . . . This was what his forebears had lived for – to be warriors.

Without warning, John Mtshali turned on him, drawing a long-bladed knife, moving in for the kill.

The crowd drew back, their chanting of the freedom cry rising higher and higher, and George raised his fists. He was back in the ring, sparring with his friend Max Loxton, the man who had defeated the heavyweight champion of South Africa. The knife flashed against the sunlight, and the blade caught the skin of his torso.

George dropped back. Then he felt a prod from behind, and glancing round, saw the young boy who'd pulled him from the street a week before. In his hand was a knife. George grabbed it, and turned to face John Mtshali. Now they were equal. All his life had been directed towards this moment, he knew it instinctively.

Mtshali moved in like a cobra, striking again before George could react, taking a slice from his face, and George felt the warm blood running from the wound, the adrenalin coursing through his veins. Another wound like that and Mtshali would gain the upper hand. George moved in, slicing down at Mtshali's

105

arm. As expected, his opponent dodged to the left, and George caught him with a punch to the skull.

Mtshali staggered back and George turned his knife upwards, ripping into his opponent's shirt. As a line of blood opened up on John Mtshali's chest, the crowd screamed with excitement. The foam was bubbling from his lips now, his eyes glazed. But George was wary of this gutter fighter – and rightly, for suddenly Mtshali's knife flashed in the sunlight, and before George could avoid it the blade penetrated his stomach. He screamed out in agony, and saw the look of delight in his opponent's eyes. That was when he lost control. Throwing caution to the winds, he closed in on Mtshali, pushing his blade into the man's face and sliced off a piece of his ear. Then he dropped the knife and moved in with his fists, driving the blows hard into the skull so that blood puffed up under the eyes.

George drew back, and as Mtshali lunged at him he stepped aside and wound a pile-driver into the side of his head. Mtshali screamed out in agony, and George kept the blows going, hearing the bone breaking beneath his knuckles. His opponent's face was now a mess of mangled bone, but somehow he kept coming. George bent down, picked up his knife from where it had fallen, and rammed it into Mtshali's guts. Mtshali let out a final scream as blood gushed into the dry red earth. Then he staggered forwards and gripped George one final time as he died.

Now the crowd knew. Here was a warrior who could lead them as none had done before.

The silken curtains of the huge marquee swayed gently in the evening breeze blowing off the Okavango River. Beautiful people mingled, champagne corks popped, in the background a full orchestra played soft music.

Glancing round, Max saw Mick Jagger and Jerry Hall making a dramatic entrance. Another flashbulb burst, and he saw several people looking furtively about them, hoping that their faces might appear in *Stern*, *Paris Match* or even *Time*. It was all going better then he had dared to hope. And the real coup was to have secured the presence of the distinguished-looking man standing next to one of the tables with his world-famous bride, a man who was as devoted to conservation as Max himself. The heir to the British throne and his glamorous wife had made the journey specially for the occasion. As head of the World Wildlife Foundation, the Prince was able to bring all his influence to bear in helping the project come to fruition.

Max moved out of the enormous tent, past the diesel-driven generators and out into the open. This was the greatest achievement of all, to be hosting the event right in the centre of the Okavango swamps, airlifting everyone in and entertaining them in a style that could compare with the world's finest venues. And so much of it was due to Saffron. She had pulled every string she knew to ensure this evening's success.

Max glanced at his watch. Almost time for the big surprise – again Saffron's idea. None of their distinguished guests had any idea what they were in for – as far as they were concerned, the function was already a spectacular success. Max noted that even the head of Euro, Sir Werhner-Beit, had attended. He was glad he'd extended the invitation. Once his project had been given the go-ahead by the head of the Botswanan government, he could really put the pressure on Euro. What he had in store for his guests now was his opening salvo in what he expected to be a long and difficult fight.

He walked back inside, to find Garth Cilliers waiting for him. Garth and his wife Suzette had made a fortune out of producing spectacular car launches, and Max had left the organization of this evening's events to them and Saffron.

'It's almost time, Max,' Garth said now.

Suzette smiled at Max. 'That lady of yours is a genius – wait and see.'

Max frowned anxiously. 'It must work, that's all that counts. If it doesn't, the Okavango will exist only in history books, as an example of the failure of conservation projects.'

Suzette touched his arm. 'You don't have to worry. Go back to your guests, the show's about to begin.'

Max left them, and went looking for Saffron. She wasn't hard to find; she looked devastating in a long black dress that clung to her like a second skin. He went up to her and took her arm, and as he did so, the whole interior of the marquee darkened and the sounds of the night began to intrude. By the time it was pitch black, all conversation had stopped. On cue, the voice of one of the world's great Shakespearian actors began to unfold the Okavango story.

'We are standing in one of the world's greatest miracles, a

107

place where wildlife and rare plants flourish, a landlocked water paradise that has a peculiar magic of its own . . .'

On a massive screen at the back of the marquee, beautiful images of the Okavango swamps appeared, while the orchestra played a rich classical theme.

'Today, we have an opportunity to preserve this paradise for ever, to turn most of Botswana into a giant game farm and to build perhaps the most magnificent hotel on earth. From organised hunting and a continuous inflow of tourists, the country will secure a revenue that can be utilised to further the development of the Okavango into the world's premier tourist attraction.'

As the voice-over continued, the photographic images gave way to architect's drawings of the proposed hotel, sculpted within the swamps. Every room would have a view, yet the whole low-lying structure be almost invisible from the air, and carefully designed to blend in with the landscape. A huge subterranean dining room with glass walls would give guests a breathtaking underwater view of the waterways.

'Satellite hotels, dotted throughout the swamps, will cater for those looking for a more individual experience. Expeditions on mokoros will take guests into the very heart of the swamps. Around the swamps will be hunting lodges and game farms . . .'

The beautiful images on the screen began to fade, and were replaced by others, less beautiful: the trees of the swamps being felled with power-saws, areas being drained of water, poachers massacring the vast herds of elephant and buffalo. The music became feverish, and Max could feel the tension building in the audience. The narrator continued: 'Botswana's future hangs in the balance. Tomorrow the waters of the Okavango could run dry; drained by mines to the north and south, this area could be lost for ever. But the potential is here, to turn this beautiful wilderness into a place of inestimable value to us all. An opportunity for scenes like this . . . to last for ever.'

The orchestra stopped playing and, spellbound, the audience watched the sun setting over the swamps. It took some minutes before people began to realise that one whole wall of the marquee, with its screen, had been removed, and they were actually viewing a real sunset.

Gradually everyone moved forward, onto a promenade deck that had been built out over the waters. As waiters began to circulate with bottles of champagne, a deafening applause broke out. Tears started to Max's eyes; the production had been magnificent.

Someone grabbed his hand and was pumping it. It was Kobus van der Post – looking terribly tired. Max wondered how long his friend could stand up to the pressures of government after his illness. `

'Max – magnificent! I had no idea of the size of your project! It *will* succeed. I will give you all the support I can muster.' Kobus' voice was charged with emotion.

Max was amazed to see that the woman with Kobus was his sister, Victoria. She had her hand tucked under Kobus' arm. Max had never seen her display such open affection to a man before.

'Vicky, I'm so pleased you're here for this.' He kissed her on the cheek.

'Saffron is the lady of the evening,' Kobus exclaimed, giving her a kiss.

Not far away, Shelton stood looking out over the water's edge, his fine black hair slicked back and his heavy black-framed glasses perched on the end of his nose. As Max approached, he moved towards him.

'I'm frightfully impressed, especially by the kind of people you've managed to involve in the development of our project. I feel my money is very well invested,' he said in his precise, public school English.

Max's smile tightened a little. Shelton's money was still on standby, for it was one of the conditions of their agreement that Max should use his own money to take the project halfway to completion, and only then would Shelton step in to finish it.

'I'm very pleased. Perhaps we could discuss an up-front payment soon?'

Shelton slapped him on the back good-naturedly. 'All in good time, old chap.'

Max felt ill at ease. Sometimes he had the impression that Shelton was playing him out like a trout on a line. 'But, Mr Shelton,' he said, 'it will have to be soon.'

'Dr Loxton, are you implying that I'm not a man of my word? You still have adequate funds, just relax.'

Max took another sip of champagne and cursed himself. He'd been overreacting.

At the other side of the promenade deck, no one noticed one of the audience slip away from the crowd and move towards the back of the marquee. Lithe as a cat, he slipped out of an exit and disappeared among the shadows of the palm trees, and out into the bush. He followed a game path, eventually coming to a clearing in which he could just make out the shape of a helicopter. In the cockpit he could see the red glow of a cigarette. He gave a bird call, and Rory Loxton called lazily, 'Welcome back, Comrade.' The ugly lines of his white face were barely visible in the darkness, but his voice was full of power and conviction. 'What did you think?'

The black man stripped off his dress suit and pulled on a checked shirt and jeans. He was lean and tall, with the body of an athlete. The moonlight reflected against the shiny blackness of his skin, and his eyes flashed in the darkness.

'I thought it was a great shame,' he said, half-laughing. 'This land is not for dreamers, it is not for the lovers of peace. I will bring instability to Botswana, I will bring riots. I will break this country. Then I will rule it, and I will not have game parks and big hotels.'

'What will you have?' asked Rory, his red hair now partially visible as he stepped out of the shade and into the moonlight.

The black man stared at Rory Loxton. He had often wondered how one so young could be so corrupt.

'I will have cattle farms and mines, but most of all I will have power. My control will be absolute,' he said coolly.

'Let's get going. You guarantee me payment – I'll supply.'

The helicopter rose up like a bird of prey, and flew away to the south.

The guests were thinning out now. Max saw Victoria looking out over the running waters, a champagne glass in her hand. She was alone. 'You've enjoyed the evening?' he asked softly, going up to her.

She shuddered and then turned to him, the trace of tears in her eyes.

'Vicky, what's wrong?' he whispered, instinctively drawing her close to him.

'Oh my God, Max. I'm in love. And I know he's dying.'

Max stared across the dark waters. Kobus van der Post had been an inspiration to him all his life.

'He's twice your age, and – '

'You don't have to tell me. Oh, why do things happen like this? Max – ' she looked around anxiously ' – George has killed a policeman, and seriously wounded another. I have to tell you, Max, but I didn't want to. I didn't want to ruin this,' she exclaimed, with a sweep of her hand.

George Zwane a killer? It was appalling news.

'What happened?'

After she had told him, he was silent for a long time. 'This continent, what is it doing to us?' he said at last into the darkness.

'It's not Africa, Max, you know that,' Victoria muttered, 'it's men like our father. They are the destroyers.'

'Vicky, I feel there's more. You're keeping something from me, aren't you?'

She looked into her brother's eyes. Could she tell him? Yes, of course she could. 'George has joined the Comrades.'

'Jesus.'

'Max, you've said often enough that if you were black you'd be with the Comrades.' She gave him a brief, faint smile. 'Listen, Max, Kobus has to get Father out of the cabinet. If he doesn't, then in a few years the situation will be unsalvageable. There's a race being bred in the townships that only knows of violence – at least now there are still black men who are prepared to talk.

'Kobus can do what he wants to do if he moves fast. He can change the course of this country's history. I love him, Max. I love him more than I believed I could love anyone. And I know that what he has to do will kill him.'

Max took her hand and looked her in the eyes. 'If you love him, you'll help him to achieve his dream before he dies.'

When nearly all the guests were gone, Max took Saffron in his arms. For a moment, earlier, Saffron had thought that Victoria was a lover, not a sister, and this evidence of her vulnerability had stirred him deeply. He led her off, now, behind the marquee and into the darkness. They kissed, a long kiss in which they communicated exactly what they felt about one another. Slowly Saffron sank to the ground, and he followed her downwards.

In the darkness he saw a pair of eyes watching them. It was a leopard, and the danger of the moment thrilled him. He worked his body down on Saffron's and she sighed out loud. He kept his eyes fixed on the leopard's – and he felt himself rising to a height of passion he'd never experienced before. Her body convulsed beneath him, in long shudders of intense pleasure. Then he too could hold out no longer, and came within her.

The leopard growled and then leaped forwards. Saffron, still sighing, clung to Max, staring at the cat in wonderment. The animal came close to them, sniffed at their bodies and then walked away into the darkness. They lay back on the raw earth, looking up at the stars, and wished that the moment could last for ever.

David was working late in his study at home, but he was finding it hard to concentrate. Today's *Star* had carried a photograph of bloody Van der Post looking more distinguished than ever. After his US trip he had been welcomed home as a messiah.

If his security bill went through, then everything would be fine. He'd have the power he needed for the moment, and could just sit back and wait for Van der Post to have another stroke. With Van der Post out of the way, then he could seize the Presidency. David frowned. Meanwhile, however, Van der Post was drumming up more and more support to block the security bill. Still, David reflected, at least he now had the support of Dolph Klopper and his AWB party.

And there was another score he had to settle: he wanted to bring George Zwane to justice. George Zwane, the man of peace who'd turned to violence, the man who'd killed a policeman. With the best defence in the world, Zwane would hang, and David would get the benefit of all the publicity, and that would further convince key members of Dolph's AWB party that he was a man after their own heart.

He thought back to the phone call he'd received the night before. It was very bad news. They were letting her out again. Of course, she would stay with Vicky, that was where she always stayed. She'd never said anything to Vicky or Max. He could not understand why, unless in her condition she'd forgotten about it permanently.

God, if that got out he would be finished. It didn't bear thinking about.

Six

Marie couldn't quite believe it was true. She walked out of the surgery feeling happier than she had felt since her wedding day. Dolph would be so proud of her! She hurried along to her car, and wasn't even concerned about the pink parking ticket that was stuck under the windscreen-wiper.

It had been such a surprise! She went for a check-up every three months, and had grown to hate them because she wanted a child so desperately and there was never the faintest sign. She'd nearly fainted when Dr Jacobs told her – she was nearly five weeks pregnant. He'd examined her carefully and said that he couldn't foresee any problems. She had wanted to kiss him, but of course that wouldn't be correct for the wife of someone as important as Dolph Klopper . . .

Dr Jacobs, looking down from his rooms and watching Mrs Klopper get into her car, smiled pleasantly to himself. Dolph Klopper was lucky to have such an affectionate, loving wife. Apparently he was under considerable stress at present; Mrs Klopper had said he was constantly campaigning, and it was even rumoured that Dolph Klopper might be the next State President of South Africa. Yes, then the blacks would laugh on the other side of their faces. Not that he had anything against them, it was just that, well, blacks had their place, and it wasn't in parliament . . .

She wouldn't drive straight home, Marie decided, she would go into town and look at baby clothes. Already she could imagine their son in a romper suit – for Dolph had said that, when they had a baby, the Lord would bless them with a son. A bouncing little blond-haired boy.

It was all so exciting. There would be the baby shower, the christening, and lots of new friends. The wives of Dolph's friends all had children, and it was difficult to talk to them because she had no experience of the problems of motherhood. Now, she promised herself, everything would be different.

The room was gloomy. The windows had been boarded up long before, and a solitary naked bulb hung from the ceiling. Below it, round a long, stained table, sat seven men. They said nothing, their heads bowed.

Eventually the man at the head of the table rose and opened his eyes – old brown orbs in a mottled white jelly. His hair was cropped short, though the greyness of it was still visible; his face was creased with lines like a Bushman; his teeth yellow, stained and rotten. But the face was hard, for Alfred Gumede had spent seventy years living off violence, and had earned himself a fortune in the process. Men were scared to look him in the eye. And he controlled the township.

He had been there, at Leeukop Prison, to watch the release of the world-famous Napoleon Zwane, watch him take those first steps to freedom – steps that the Comrades had controlled entirely, as a puppeteer controls the strings of his puppet. The Comrades were not going to allow Napoleon Zwane to wrest power from them. Alfred Gumede had smiled as the assassin gunned him down.

But now he faced a different animal: Napoleon Zwane's son, a man of violence like himself.

The Soweto Comrades needed a young warrior to lead them, and George Zwane had shown that he had the ability to make men tremble at his words, and to kill with his hands. Yes, now he must be put to the test. Alfred Gumede looked around the table.

'Comrades, we must elect a new leader. We often forget what leadership means – it is to rule like the lion, to rule by terror. And that rule only ends when the old lion is defeated by a stronger. Now we have one amongst us who has shown us he has the mettle.'

George Zwane went cold. He had been called to this meeting, expecting some sort of promotion amongst the cadres, but not this. Mtshali's death was still fresh in his mind. Would he have to kill again?

114

'I pass my leadership', Alfred Gumede said, 'to George Zwane . . .'

George was the last to leave. These meetings never took long and were never held at the same venue, and the members knew about them only hours before the event. That was the only way they could operate, because the township was riddled with government informers.

Outside, it was early morning. This was one of the poorer areas of Soweto; the tiny box houses seemed to stretch off into infinity. As George began the long walk to the side of town where he was living, a crowd of children gathered behind him. Perhaps it was wrong to call them children, he thought to himself, for young as they were, there was nothing childlike about them. They knew who he was, and they began chanting in unison.

He was their leader. He must give them blood.

Both the children were at Waterford, the exclusive multi-racial school in Swaziland. It was better that way, thought Brenda Zwane, especially now. Life was not too easy. Seth Naidoo had been to see her a few times, and had brought her money, but he could not come more often because of the police. The police harassed her day and night; three times she had been taken in for questioning, three times they had put her in solitary confinement. But it hadn't broken her. On the contrary, each time they threatened her, they made her stronger. She would never betray George to them.

But now she sat alone in what had been their home. He could never come back now, now that he was with the Comrades. She shuddered. He was such a strong man, but was he strong enough to run with them? She had a sudden premonition of long, lonely years ahead, but she pushed it away. She had known when she married George that he was different from other men, driven by a higher purpose, and that her life would not be an ordinary one.

There was a knock at the door.

Brenda froze, terrified that it was the police again. Another knock. There was nothing to do but unlock the door; if she didn't, they would break it down. She went to the door and undid the catch – and found herself staring at a tall, dark figure, the face covered by a black balaclava mask.

Oh, my God. What now?

The man pushed past her and closed the door behind him. He

115

tore the mask from his face – and she rushed into his arms. He smelt of sweat, but most of all there was the smell of the man she loved.

'George! How I've missed you!'

He held her tightly, tears running down his face. 'And I have missed you, my wife,' he answered softly.

'You must be careful, George, the police come almost every day to look for you.' A note of fear rose in her voice. 'It is not safe for you to stay here.'

'I have had this house watched for days. Only now did the children tell me it was safe to enter.'

She looked at him closely. He was a warrior now, a far cry from the smooth-talking, well-dressed man she had fallen in love with at university. She was overjoyed that he had come; she knew that there were many beautiful girls with the Comrades, and sometimes the thought disturbed her. But she could not stop worrying, straining her ears in case there was another knock at the door.

'Relax, my wife. There's no one outside except the Comrades, and if anyone comes they'll give me the signal.'

'Tell me what happened, George. What really happened with the policeman?' She wanted to hear it in his own words, so that she could be a part of the event that had made him an outcast, a fugitive from justice.

He swore her to secrecy, then he told her the whole story. He could see how important it was to her to know the truth. He admired her, wanted her. She was a Zulu beauty, a tall, round-faced woman with smooth pearly skin. She had an ample bosom, still firm after two children, and wonderful eyes with an almost oriental slant to them – big, dark eyes, full of the sensuality that was an essential part of her nature. When he was alone, after his night-long meetings with the Comrades, he always thought of her, and that gave him strength.

She led him by the hand into the bedroom. She knew there was little time – that this might even be their last time together. Slowly she undressed in front of him and then knelt down at his feet. He tried to raise her, but she resisted and began slowly to undress him. Finally she revealed the massive organ and held it tenderly in her hands. This was hers, and she pushed him gently down onto the bed and climbed onto him, her body shivering with excitement.

116

Rhythmically he moved inside her undulating body, and felt the pleasure that was hers. His hands worked over her breasts, exciting and teasing her, but his eyes never left hers. Most couples would have a lifetime of making love, they had only one night.

He felt himself soaring, an eagle leaping from a high cliff and effortlessly floating on the wind. For a few precious moments he was aware only of her and the feelings she aroused within him.

They lay in each other's arms, sated. This was the best it had ever been. They both drifted off into a deep sleep . . .

When the whistle came, long and piercing, he was up and pulling on his clothes in seconds. How long had they been whistling, warning him? Brenda watched him dressing, savouring their moments together. Then she pulled on her dressing gown, kissed him softly on the mouth and moved towards the door.

It was just at that moment the banging started, the whole house echoing ominously as blows rained on the front door. George was gone in an instant, out of the back and across the fence. After that there was darkness – they would never find him in the labyrinth of Soweto. So she must not rush, Brenda told herself. Just remain calm.

She stood still next to the door, and took a deep breath. She knew, irrevocably, what lay before her: a lifetime of struggle. Well, she had chosen to marry George Zwane, she would stand by him and what he believed in till the day she died.

As she slid the latch back, the door exploded towards her and knocked her flying onto the floor, and three black constables charged into the room, all with their guns drawn. A fourth man, a big, fat black man whom she knew only too well from his regular visits over the past few weeks, waddled into the room after them. As she pulled herself to her feet, she could hear the sound of things being broken in her kitchen. All she had to do was fight for time for George to get as far away as possible.

'Mrs Zwane, we've had reports that he's here.'

She stared at him defiantly, this man who was hunting her husband like a dog. She felt like spitting in his face – but why should she grace him with her spittle?

'Captain Mboya, this is my house. You come in and charge through it as if it were your own.'

'Harbouring a murderer is a criminal offence, Mrs Zwane. Now tell me, is he here?'

117

'I wish he were,' she said defiantly.

'Mrs Zwane!' the Captain snorted like a bull, 'you think you can get away with murder. Well, you can get properly dressed, you're coming in with us now, for questioning.'

There was a burst of automatic fire outside the back of the house, and a man screamed. As Captain Mboya drew his pistol, she saw the fear in his eyes. He hesitated for a moment, then sprinted towards the back. Brenda Zwane walked into her room and calmly began to dress. She hoped the Comrades had got some of them.

There were more shots outside. Another scream, and then silence. No lights came on in the neighbouring houses; no one appeared. Soweto had the highest murder rate of any city in the world, and none of its residents that evening had any desire to figure in police statistics.

Captain Mboya walked straight back into the bedroom and grabbed Brenda, still half-dressed, by the arm.

'All right, you bitch. Come.'

She smiled. There was blood running down his arm, they had hit him. Behind him was one of the black constables, limping from a bullet wound. The other one, though she did not know it, was lying dead across the porch.

They hustled her out to the police van and pushed her roughly into the back. There were two other men inside, and it was not right for a woman prisoner to travel in the back with men. They leered at Brenda and she drew her dressing-gown tightly round her. One of them moved forwards, his intentions clear. She stared at him. 'My husband is George Zwane – touch me, and he'll get his revenge.'

The man paled, and slunk back into his corner, and Brenda relaxed. The extent of George's influence was terrifying; she just hoped that he wouldn't be corrupted by it.

Brenda began to sing softly, then louder, and the men joined in with her. Mboya glared angrily, but there was nothing he could do to her now. How she hated him! The ride in the truck was bumpy and she was thrown around inside the back. Eventually she and the two men worked out a way of staying in one place. They had no idea where they were going, and they continued to sing even though Captain Mboya kept on banging on the partition behind him.

*

118

The prison was worse than Brenda could have imagined. The cell was small and cramped, scarcely longer than she was tall. There was a sanitary bucket in one corner that was already half-full when she arrived, and a simple mat on the floor where she was supposed to sleep. A solitary 40-watt bulb burned high up on the ceiling, and above that was the open grid of the metal walkway that allowed the warders to keep a constant eye on the prisoners below.

The smell from the bucket was overpowering, but eventually, through sheer exhaustion, she collapsed on the mat and fell asleep. She dreamed that she and George were getting married again. Everything was perfect, but then, just before the ceremony, a police van arrived and she was pulled away from him. There was nothing she could do. They dragged her towards the police van, and then George turned his back on her . . .

A banging noise finally intruded on her sleep and she opened her eyes. The door of the cell opened, and a huge woman warder came in with a plate of inedible-looking food. Before Brenda could protest, the woman took the lid off the sanitary bucket, turned it over and then put the plate of food on top.

When the cell door closed, Brenda started to gag. She crawled into the corner: the smell from the bucket lid was nauseating. Then and there she decided that she would not eat their food; they would have to force-feed her if they wanted her to eat.

Victoria Loxton couldn't believe that the police had arrested Brenda Zwane again. She had protested immediately, but the terms under which Brenda was held made it impossible for Vicky to see her. She was afraid for Brenda's life. There was just one person who might be able to secure her release, and that was Kobus van der Post. However, the security bill was to come before parliament the next day, and she knew he was under great strain.

With considerable reluctance, she picked up the phone. At least this way Brenda might have a chance.

Kobus van der Post walked with great difficulty down the wide steps of the Houses of Parliament in Cape Town. The huge contingent of press reporters respectfully made way for him and he gave them a warm smile. He needed to be on his own for a

119

few minutes, and saw with relief that his chauffeur was waiting for him.

Once the car was in motion, Kobus relaxed, and ran over the morning's momentous events in his mind again.

They had debated Loxton's security bill, prior to taking the vote. With thoughts of Brenda's arrest still fresh in his mind after Victoria's late-night call – and ignoring the hostile glances from Dolph Klopper – he had spoken passionately against the proposed legislation. Loxton had countered that if the bill were not passed, the country would descend into anarchy and violence. They had voted, then taken a short break while the votes were counted.

As they returned to their places, Kobus had noticed that the Speaker was white-faced and tense. When all the members were seated, he rose to give them the result. 'There are an equal number of votes for and against the bill. I must ask you to vote again.'

Kobus had remained rock-steady, staring at David Loxton, who was sitting tight-lipped as several of his supporters conferred with him. They had voted a second time, and waited tensely as the votes were counted. The Speaker rose again, this time visibly shaken. 'By the rules of this house, since the voting is again equal I must call a national referendum on this issue.'

Kobus had found his hand being shaken again and again by his supporters. As he rose to leave, he had caught David Loxton staring at him. The look had made him feel distinctly uneasy.

Now, in the solitude of his car, Kobus realised that it was a good result. The referendum might be about the passing of the security bill, but it was also a test of David Loxton's power. If the country rejected the bill, in effect they were rejecting David Loxton, for good.

'Why was she arrested?' Kobus demanded.

David Loxton felt a bead of sweat run down his forehead and fall onto his immaculately laundered, hand-tailored shirt. Over the last few months they had been detaining hundreds of people every week without trial – it was common knowledge. Van der Post had chosen to question him about this particular incident just so he could rub his nose in the dirt after the security bill vote.

120

'We needed her for questioning, sir, a perfectly valid reason,' he said curtly.

'But she was always available for questioning. I've talked to her lawyer about that.'

David felt his hackles rise again. 'She was not proving co-operative, sir,' he stated angrily. He paused. 'Is that all?'

'No, it is not!' Kobus slammed his fist down on the desk. 'You will release her immediately!'

David Loxton was silent. He would have to release Brenda Zwane – but not in such a way as to jeopardize other such arrests. The power of arrest without trial was important in maintaining security.

David looked at the smooth face opposite him, with its eyes like grey steel. He had underestimated Van der Post; the stroke might have affected his body, but it had not touched his mind. And now he could see that the bastard was sizing him up for another blow. 'Loxton, you must instruct the National Intelligence Service to find out who authorised that arrest.'

David rose from his chair, bristling with anger. 'No!'

Van der Post sat back, his hands behind his head. 'Your days in the cabinet are numbered, Loxton – '

'I'll get my bill through,' David hissed. 'And when that's done, you will be history . . .!'

Seven

Dolph Klopper straightened his father's black jacket and stood back. The old man looked impressive in his dinner suit, even though he was well over sixty years old, even though his eyes were sightless.

'Pa, it is perfect,' Dolph said proudly. 'You will have a fine time.'

'If only he were alive – the greatest leader the world has ever known! Now he is vilified and condemned, but if we had just had a few more weeks . . . We had almost perfected the bomb. Then we would have shown them all.' The old man spoke with awe in his voice.

Dolph wished he could have been there. To have served under the Führer would have been an unimaginable honour. He had studied every book about him, every film – because the Führer had galvanised the people to fight against a common cause, and Dolph was determined to unify his people in the same manner: to fight against poverty, oppression and unemployment. His father had served under the Führer and been with him during the last hours of his life – and tonight his father would celebrate the Führer's birthday. Dolph wished he could have attended the function, but it was only for those who had served in the SS.

He handed his father his overcoat and helped him drape it over his shoulders. Then they went out to the car – the long Mercedes-Benz Pullman saloon that was housed in the barn behind the house.

Once they were ensconced in the back seat, and the long journey to Pretoria had begun, Klopper turned to his son. 'Pieter's a good kaffir,' he said, gesturing at the black chauffeur

122

who sat out of earshot, beyond the glass partition. 'He knows that he was born to serve. As long as they know we are in control, they are a docile people. Remember that.'

Dolph nodded. The blacks were a problem. One didn't want to live with them, but they were needed to run the mines and other essential industries. One answer would be to let them live in separate states, and then come in to work in the all-white state. Some of his more rabid supporters believed in concentration camps for blacks, but Dolph considered them naive. Certainly, it might be advisable to reduce the numbers of blacks considerably, but as his father had told him, from experience, the mechanics of mass killing were complex. Anyway, mass extermination was not only biblically repulsive, it was unnecessary; the AIDS virus would do their work for them. In his heart of hearts Dolph knew God had made the white man superior. Whites must rule, that was what God had decreed. And Dolph lived by the word of God.

They arrived at the house just after 8 p.m. Outside were several large, luxurious cars, most of them Mercedes-Benz and BMW models. Dolph helped his father to the door, and saw inside the crowd of grey-haired, dark-suited men.

His father squeezed his arm. 'They will look after me now, they will make sure I get back to the farm. Remember that they will always help you, too, if anything should happen to me. Tonight I will ask them for funds for your party, and for their support.'

'Pa, it is not necessary,' Dolph pleaded, 'there are more important issues.'

'There are few like you, they know that. Now go home, I will have good news for you in the morning.'

Dolph moved away from his father as a tall man wearing pince-nez moved up to him. He heard the snap of the boots, and his father followed suit, for even though he could not see, he knew what that sound meant.

'*Heil Hitler!*'

The cry burst across the African night, and Dolph Klopper made his way back towards the car. With such a force behind him, the future would be his for the taking . . .

Inside the house, Klopper was guided into a room where men were seated round a long table. He was steered to its head, and though he could not see his colleagues, he could hear that they had all risen for him.

Having reached his place, Karl Klopper cleared his throat and waited for silence. Then he spoke slowly, in fluent German.

'Gentlemen, this is a miracle, that over forty years after our leader's death we still celebrate his birthday. I think the time has come to ask why? The reasons are very simple.

'I remember his last words, the words of a man tortured with guilt. The Führer felt he had betrayed us all by losing the war. He took the loss on his own shoulders, but he pledged me to ensure that his ideals never died.

'After nineteen forty-five came the humiliating experience of the Reconstruction. The Allies raped our war-ravaged country, they took our best men to work in their factories – and yet today the German Democratic Republic is an economic miracle. They call it a miracle, for they forget how close we came to ruling the world. Now I can tell you what the world will soon hear. West and East Germany are becoming one. We will rule again!'

He heard the snap of the men saluting. He knew they were all still standing.

'Across the world, in every country, groups like ourselves are celebrating the Führer's birthday. We all remember our allegiance. We have brought up our sons and daughters to continue it.

'My son is close to power. Already he has had secret discussions with the Minister of Justice. You must help Dolph, as will our friends throughout the world. We still have great power, and we shall have more, and greater. This is no dream, this is the future – and we can all be part of it.'

There was tumultuous applause, and Karl Klopper sat down, the rest of the men following suit in precise order of SS rank.

He began eating the *sauerkraut* and *eisbein* on his plate, and sipping some of the fine Rhine wine from the silver goblet embossed with the swastika. The man next to him spoke.

'It is good to see you again, Karl.'

'Ah, Rudi, it has been a long time, *ja*?'

'Yes, too long a time. Karl, I can help your son when he comes to power. You know the head of the United Nations?'

'You mean Dr Ulrich Klee?'

'He was one of us,' Rudi said.

'And now a traitor?' Karl asked.

'Unfortunately, yes. He thinks he has covered up his past. But it is we who helped him, without his knowledge, to rise to the head of the United Nations.' Rudi leaned closer as Karl Klopper stuffed another forkful of sauerkraut into his mouth. 'We have assembled photographs from our files,' he said. 'He killed Jews personally, with his pistol.'

'A great man, then.'

'We have contacted him. We have told him we will release the pictures to the press if he does not follow our line.'

Karl laughed. 'Thank you, Rudi. That will be of great use to Dolph. And how is your son?'

'Eric is fine,' Rudi said proudly. 'He continues to live in Argentina, and his business interests are extensive, but he will never achieve what Dolph can achieve here. I think he would like to work for Dolph, should your son come to power.'

'That will be arranged.'

They ate on in silence, the music of Wagner filling the long room. There were no black waiters, only young Aryan boys dressed in immaculate white tie, who moved carefully among their high-ranking seniors.

After dinner the men stood round in groups while Karl Klopper sat on a chair in one corner, like a king on his throne, talking to his subjects. He rose to leave half an hour later, and gave his final salute. Then one of the men helped him out to the waiting car. He was well pleased. It had been an exhilarating and rewarding evening.

Dolph Klopper rose early and pulled back the curtain to let the light into his hotel bedroom. It was a pleasure to be in such a room – the quality of the furnishings was outstanding, and he had been very impressed, too, by the service in the dining room the evening before. Here in Munich he felt as if he had come home, and in his soul there was a sadness; he would be happier living here in Germany than in Africa. But he had work to do in Africa, work that he had been called to do by the Lord.

The phone next to his bed rang and he snatched it up. '*Ja?*'

'Herr Klopper, your taxi is here.'

He looked at his watch. Six fifteen precisely, just as he had ordered. Grabbing his kit-bag, he went down to the waiting car and was soon being whisked through the streets of Munich.

The young taxi driver handled his Mercedes-Benz expertly, and Dolph decided to make conversation. 'This is a wonderful country . . .'

125

The driver turned and smiled at him. 'Yes, it is. But I thought you were German?' The young man spoke with interest. He was in his late twenties, with blond hair, blue eyes and a strong face.

'Of German descent, yet. But I am a South African, my father fought for Germany during the war.'

'We've come a long way since then,' the young man answered heartily.

Now they were speeding down the street past the Odeon Platz where the Führer had given some of his most powerful speeches.

'A pity you didn't win the war,' Dolph continued. He failed to notice the tightening of the young man's lips or the way his fingers began to drum on the steering wheel.

'I would have been ashamed,' the driver said.

The comment caught Dolph unawares. 'No, you would have been proud. We would have ruled the world. No more Jews . . .'

'German Jews,' the young man muttered.

'Jews are not Germans,' Dolph replied angrily. This fine young German must have become a victim of the new education system. His kind would not last long if Germany regained her pride.

The conversation was at an end, and Dolph contented himself with looking at the buildings along the way. They passed the four gigantic cylinders of the BMW building, then turned off to the left and headed towards the Olympic stadium. When they pulled up and Dolph asked what the fare was, the young man shook his head.

'I will not take your blood money,' he answered, not looking at Dolph.

Dolph wrenched the door of the taxi open and hauled the young man out by his shirt collar. He tried to resist, but was no match for Dolph, who pushed him against the bonnet of the car and then tightened his grip round his neck, pressing into his windpipe.

Dolph waited while the young man weakened, then he shifted his grip, grabbing a handful of blond hair. He rammed the young man's face hard into the bonnet again and again, till red streaks of blood cascaded down the white paintwork. Now the taxi driver was groggy, tears streaming from his eyes. Dolph grapped his mouth with his left hand, squeezing hard and bringing the bloody face towards his own.

'Listen, cub. Learn to keep your mouth shut. Now drive!'

Dolph watched the taxi driver drag himself behind the wheel, then drive off slowly. Weakness, that was what had destroyed that young man. That was what was destroying South Africa.

The gymnasium, when Dolph reached it, was the finest he'd ever seen, a huge, airy vault packed with the latest equipment. A tall, fair man walked up to him, naked save for a pair of shorts. The man was nearly a foot taller than Dolph, and was as fair as Dolph was dark. His body was tanned and perfectly muscled, his physical development a match for Dolph's, and the hardness of his jaw reflecting a formidable determination. He spoke in German.

'Dolph Klopper?'

Dolph shook the outstretched hand. 'It is good to see you.'

Reinhold Steiner was almost the same age as Dolph, but he had lived in Germany all his life. His father had died on the Russian front and he had been born just after the German surrender. His name had been changed to Krupp, and it was only when he was twenty that he learned from his step-parents that his real father had been not only powerful, but also extremely wealthy – Reinhold Steiner was heir to a fortune waiting for him in a Swiss bank account.

By this time he had graduated as an automotive engineer, and to his step-parents' horror, used the money to fund a factory specialising in the development of high-performance engines. Five years later came a formidable string of wins in Formula One racing, and Steiner engines became an option offered on many of Germany's most famous sports cars.

However, for Reinhold Steiner this success was just a stepping-stone to higher things. He opened other factories outside Germany, owned by nominees, and gained a reputation as a weapons manufacturer in the first league. Then he started acting as a weapons broker, buying any military equipment he could find, from planes and tanks to nuclear warheads, which he then sold to the highest bidder. As a result, he was one of the richest men in the world. Now, using men like Dolph Klopper, he intended to become one of the most powerful.

Steiner and Klopper worked out together for the next hour, pushing themselves harder and harder till they were drenched with perspiration. They said very little during this time, collecting their thoughts for later. It was only when they had showered, and were in the steam room, that Steiner, leaning back against the white tiles, stared straight at the man from South Africa and said: 'What are your chances of taking power?'

Klopper's dark eyes flashed. 'Very good. But we have only got this far through much negotiation and planning. Our government has weakened. However, I have the support of David Loxton, the Minister of Justice.'

'Yes, but . . . if Loxton should have his bill thrown out in this referendum? If Van der Post should dismiss him?'

Steiner posed the questions carefully, constantly assessing and evaluating Klopper as he made his replies.

'I have contingency plans . . .'

Steiner chuckled. 'I know David Loxton well. I do not think he can be trusted.'

Dolph smiled uneasily. 'You are right, but I believe I can use him.'

Steiner shifted his towel and lay back against the wooden slats of the bench. He did not reply for a while, and Dolph felt uneasy. He needed Steiner's support and his money.

'All right,' Steiner said at last. 'But get rid of Loxton when the time is right. The political environment in Africa will change rapidly – AIDS has been a blessing to us. I have people working for me who are cultivating the virus; it is for sale – you can buy it to solve your over-population problems.' Steiner turned on his side and stared at Dolph. 'If one word of this should escape your lips, you are a dead man, my friend,' he said quietly.

Dolph leant forwards. 'Your ideals and mine are the same.'

'Show your loyalty in deeds, not words.'

'Loxton will be removed when the time is right. When I have power, I will nationalise the gold mines . . .'

Now there was a dreamy gleam in Steiner's eyes, and Dolph let the silence linger for a few minutes, then he pressed on.

'I need your money, your influence.'

'You will get both. I am already addressing the problem of the United Nations, so you need not worry that they will bother you. Now, what will you do about Van der Post? He's got a lot of support in the United States.'

Dolph tensed. He was worried about the President, there was no denying it. 'Loxton hates him. I don't think he'll last long, he's had a stroke.'

'And if he defeats Loxton's legislation? If he should recover his health?'

'I have made arrangements.'

The young black man stared out of the windows of his study at Berkeley University. He was thinking of the land in which he and his father had been born. At thirty-five he was a professor of politics, an international celebrity and the father of two wonderful children. His beautiful wife of ten years was a doctor, and the marriage couldn't be better – yet with all this, he was unhappy.

He looked down at the newspaper again, at the photograph of his older brother, George Zwane. George had always been the difficult one; he, too, had won a college scholarship to the United States, but he'd turned it down. Now their father was dead, after thirty years in jail, gunned down in cold blood on the day of his release. And George, the successful lawyer, had killed a policeman . . .

Malcolm Zwane stared down at the young people milling around on the immaculately manicured lawns of the campus. But in his mind's eye he saw gutters overflowing with rubbish, slums and skyscrapers, burning veld and rolling grasslands, and he could suddenly smell the warm, moist Transvaal dust after an afternoon thunderstorm. Had he betrayed his own people by leaving his country and living here?

He held his head between his hands, wracked with guilt. But his wife and his children, he couldn't take them into that, they were not prepared for it.

There was a knock on the door and he spun round.

'Professor Zwane, are you busy?' a voice asked from the passage.

'No. Please, please come in.'

Then there she was, grinning wickedly at him, in the doctor's white coat that could do nothing to disguise her glorious figure.

'Alice, how nice . . .'

He kissed her for a long time, drawing her close to him. Then she looked into his eyes.

'What's wrong darlin'?' she asked in her Southern drawl.

'Nothing.'

She glanced down at the South African newspaper on the desk, and recognised the brother she'd never met. She sat down in Malcolm's chair and stared up at his handsome face. Sometimes

129

she thought she knew him so well, but he hid things from her, too, things he thought might disturb her.

'Malcolm,' she said, taking his hand, 'we've got to talk.'

He grimaced, but she would not be put off. 'You're holdin' things back from me. I know you have problems to face, Malcolm, but I can face them with you.'

He shook his head.

She leaned forward, touching his hand. 'You want to go back . . .? I'd go with you.'

'You would!' His face was transformed.

'I love you. Don't you think I understand?'

But he shook his head again, shamefacedly. 'Malcolm, my family came here as slaves – you don't forget the meaning of that word in a hurry. I know I may have to make sacrifices for you – that's OK – I owe that to my father and grandfather who paved the way for me to be where I am today.'

He looked down again at the open newspaper on his desk, and then at the letter from the African Freedom Council. Then he stared into Alice's dark brown eyes.

'Yes, I will return to the country of my birth. But not yet. When the time is right, I will know,' he said quietly.

He turned to the window again and stared down at the young people, and Alice came up behind him and put her arms around his waist.

'I've always known that one day you would lead your people,' she said.

Ken Silke swept back the little grey hair he still had and drew Max to one side. They had just left the packed Gaberone courtroom, and Max was obviously seething with rage. 'Calm down, Max,' he said. 'Those were serious charges that were levelled against you – and they've all been dropped.'

Max looked down at his advocate, the short, tubby man whose ability to take command of supposedly unsalvageable cases and turn them around was legendary.

'I'm sorry, Ken, I owe you an apology. You did get me off – but what bothers me are all the things that haven't been explained. Who was trying to kill me? Why was he allowed to get away? And why aren't they searching for him? And why is everybody lying?'

Glancing behind him at a man who'd moved too close for

comfort, Ken drew Max a little aside. 'You have done wonderful things, Max,' he said earnestly. 'Your mining business, your hotels . . . But you are also a very political person. You talk openly with radicals, with foreign leaders who don't like our country, and you also fund a great many projects aimed at giving oppressed people a chance in life.'

'So . . .?'

'There are a lot of people who would like to see you out of the way.'

Max's plane was waiting for him at the airport. He made the last-minute, pre-take-off inspection very carefully – and then, the moment he was in the air, he felt all his troubles and anxieties drifting away. He headed northwards, the descending sun to his immediate left. It was good to be on his own, it would give him a chance to collect his thoughts. The dry lands and pans stretched out below him as he headed towards his spiritual home.

Much later, the dry lands gave way to a beautiful expanse of water, lush vegetation and tiny islands dotted with palms. Max was always filled with awe when he saw this, the jewel of the Kalahari desert. He landed just before sunset, on the tiny airstrip next to his camp close to Chief's Island, in the centre of the Okavango swamps. She was there to meet him in the battered old jeep.

He killed the engine and climbed out of the cockpit into her arms. Immediately he was conscious of the sounds of the bush – and he was pleased that she wasn't wearing her usual perfume: it showed that she understood the place, the spiritual quality of it, its apartness from the urban existence they were both used to.

He held her for a long time. The sexual passion of their early relationship had now given way to deeper and more powerful feelings. He needed her now, it was not enough any more just to see her occasionally.

She drove the jeep along the long, winding track that led into the deep foliage of the swamps. Every now and then the track disappeared underwater, and there was a swish from the tyres as they cut through. He was elated that now he could show her all this, his most sacred place.

Saffron pulled up quickly as they saw a shadow in the distance. She switched off the engine and waited, the water all around them. Sure enough, after some minutes a pride of lions walked past them, brushing against the sides of the vehicle as they padded through the water. First came three lithe females, alert for a possible kill, then an old, battle-scarred male, his powerful, menacing head surrounded by its dark mane. When they had passed, Max gestured to Saffron to start the engine, and they followed the pack into the undergrowth.

'We're lucky to see lion here,' he whispered to her. 'Usually you find them on the big islands, but not on a small one like this. See how they've adapted to this environment; they pad through the water quite contentedly, and they'll even swim from island to island. Be careful as we get closer to the water's edge, now. I don't want to go for an underwater drive with the crocodiles.'

He pulled out a hand-held spotlight from the cubbyhole and switched it on, so that the beam penetrated the darkness and pinpointed a section of the bush in brilliant white light. He caught sight of the back flanks of one of the lionesses, and they crashed through the bush after her. The lionesses had split up into a wider group now, hoping to catch a buck as it returned from drinking at the water's edge. Saffron could not believe they were not irritated by the jeep's presence.

'They aren't even aware of us,' Max whispered again. 'We don't fit into their frame of reference because we're in the jeep, but if you got out now and started to walk, they'd be on you.'

'Thanks. I just hope we don't have a puncture.'

She fell silent as they moved into a clearing and a small buck appeared in front of them. The animal was standing still; its senses were alert to the presence of danger, but it was unsure what to do. Then it turned, having obviously decided to return to the water.

Saffron screamed as the lioness charged out of the undergrowth, a great mass of energy and muscle bounding effortlessly towards the fleeing buck. As if in slow motion, she moved towards her tiny prey, bringing it down with one flick of her huge front paw. Now the other lionesses moved in to feast on the raw flesh. The old lion, leader of the pride, was left the choicest pieces. He ate silently, watching his females as they prowled around him. Then Saffron heard a noise, and looking into the darkness, saw a pair of menacing eyes.

'Hyena,' Max said softly. 'They're waiting for the lion to go, then they'll move in on the carcass. The bush is incredibly efficient – nothing is ever left to waste. Let's go.'

She started the jeep and they headed back through the

undergrowth towards the track. The night did not seem so friendly to her now, and Max, sensing this, put his arm around her shoulders.

The camp, when they got to it, was lit by strings of bright bulbs suspended from the trees and extending down to the water's edge, where several wooden makoros, or canoes, were moored beside a small pier. Max could hear the sound of meat cooking, and when he went into the reed enclosure, the boma, there was the little grizzled old man cooking meat on a glowing fire.

'Gumsa!'

The old man jumped up and turned, then ran towards Max and clasped his arm. He spoke in the Bushman, or San, tongue, spoken by only a handful of white men and characterised by its distinctive click sounds.

'The stars said you would come, Kaikhoe.'

'The stars never lie.'

Max's name amongst the Bushmen people was Kaikhoe, because they knew the legend of his birth: how the *Shaman*, the medicine man, had laid hands on the sickly child and told his mother to leave him in the open, so that the evil spirit within him might leave. And how, after a rising and setting of the sun, and then another rising, the mother had returned to find the child alive, and they had all wondered at the fighting spirit of the baby. They had called him Kaikhoe, meaning fighter.

Now the old man's hand ran across Max's face, and he stared up into his eyes. 'Kaikhoe, the stars have also seen that you have many problems. This woman with the dark skin and the hair like the night, she is now yours?'

'No, she will never be completely mine.'

He knew that he would never be able to possess Saffron completely – there was an elemental wildness about her. Perhaps that was what attracted him to her. 'Kaikhoe, no woman can resist you,' Gumsa said, then added proudly, 'I have taken her on the waters.'

'In the makoro?'

'Yes. She was a little scared at first, but now she laughs. I like her. She will produce many fine children for you.'

'Children, Gumsa?'

'A man must have children.'

Max squatted on his haunches, staring into the bright coals of the fire, smelling the good smell of the meat cooking in the three-legged pot.

'We go hunting for our food tomorrow, Kaikhoe. You will find me a kudu bull?'

'I will find a bull such as you have never seen.'

Max got up and walked out of the boma, back into the centre of the camp. To his horror, he saw Saffron standing by the water's edge, and he ran across and pulled her away.

'Why so rough?' she exclaimed, as he grabbed her arm.

He hadn't meant to hurt her, but she'd just about scared the life out of him. 'The crocs aren't choosy, you could end up being their dinner!'

His eyes lingered on the curves of her body beneath the loosely fitting safari shirt. She moved nearer to him, sensing his need, and he pulled her close.

'Do you always kiss with your eyes open?' she asked.

'I like to see what I'm kissing. I like to see you.'

'You're like a predator, do you know that?' She looked up into his eyes, and continued: 'You're different here, I guess. I knew that there must be another side to you.'

'I see you've already captivated Gumsa.'

'He showed me around. It's such a weird name, how did he get it?'

'Ah, the curiosity of the film-maker! The Bushmen always name their children after some incident that happens shortly after the birth. Gumsa means hole, because his mother fell into an ant hole.'

They walked hand-in-hand into the boma, ready for the food that Gumsa had prepared for them. An open bottle of wine and two glasses were standing on a tree trunk in the corner of the enclosure, and Max went over and poured each of them a drink. He handed her a glass.

'To love.'

He saw the brilliant green eyes watching him. She smiled.

'To us.'

There was a thatch and reed hut built on stilts by the water's edge, and here, on the old double bed, they made love. Each time they were together now, like this, made the pain of their separation worse for Max, intensified his longing for them to be together always. But he would not force her; she must make her own decision in her own time. He understood the spirit that made her what she was, the reckless urge to defy convention, to

134

live life to the full. She represented so much of what his mother had stood for.

He thought back to the last time he had seen Tracey, when he was eight years old. She and his father had been arguing violently – he still remembered perfectly the terrible shouting and screaming. Then she had run out of their bedroom, tears streaming down her face, and into his, and had bent over him, kissing him on the forehead. He remembered the words she had spoken in the language of the Bushmen people she loved.

'Kaikhoe, be strong. Do what you believe is right, live for what you think is important. I love you.'

Then she had gone. He had heard the car going off down the drive.

The phone call had come later that night. He remembered his father, ashen-faced, scarcely able to stand, tears rolling down his face. They had known that their mother was dead – he, Victoria and Lucinda – and they had blamed their father for it, and still did. And though it was apparently a car accident that killed her, Max knew it was suicide, and he knew that his father was responsible.

He had all her photographs and paintings. She left them to him in her will, along with the island.

The makoro slipped through the water as easily as an arrow through the air – silent and purposeful. Gumsa stood on the back of it like a gondolier – except that this was not a Venetian canal, and if he fell off there would be no danger of polluted water making him ill because the crocodiles would kill him in seconds.

He pushed the pole into the reeds again, and the makoro shot forwards. Max raised the binoculars to his eyes, then handed them to Saffron, who sat cross-legged in front of him. Through the field-glasses she could see a kingfisher sitting on one of the branches of a knobthorn. The little bird's bright blue plumage stood out against the surrounding green. When she took the glasses away from her eyes and looked down through the clear water, she could see the thousands of waterlilies resting on the surface, and the thick beds of papyrus all along the sides of the narrow channel. Gumsa gestured for her to look to the left, and she saw a group of crocodiles sunning themselves on the bank. As they passed, the crocodiles slithered into the water, ready to investigate a possible source of food.

They came back to the camp late in the afternoon, when the air was hot and thick with the sounds of buzzing insects, and Saffron welcomed the hot shower in the reed enclosure behind the camp. The dense greenness of the wetlands at once attracted and repelled her. It threatened her, because she knew that alone, she would die in this place in a matter of hours, but it attracted her too, because she had never been anywhere quite so beautiful.

That night, over the camp fire, she broached to Max the subject that had been troubling her for weeks.

'Honey, I don't think you believed me when I said I'd never had an affair.'

His heart skipped a beat. 'I believed you.'

'You see, I loved John at first. It was only later that I realised I had become his ultimate possession – that I wasn't a person to him, but an object.'

'But you still remained loyal to him?'

'There was no one else I wanted: none of the men I knew were as strong as John. Then . . . I met you.'

She stoked the dying fire with a branch. 'Max,' she said, 'I . . . I can't take it any longer.' And when he took her in his arms, she burst into tears, her body shaking with unhappiness. 'I don't know what to do. I'm so scared that you might leave me, and then I'd have nothing. I need a man – not just a lover.'

Holding her tight, he stared out into the night, probing the dark air for an answer. He was frightened, too. He remembered his own disastrous marriage. He had been in love at the beginning, too, but the love had faded once they were legally bound to one another. He had decided never to marry again, but now he was changing his mind.

Saffron turned her face up to him and they kissed, a long, desperate, seeking kiss. It was as if they were one, and scared to part because, separate, they became lesser people. At last they drew apart and she sank back into his arms, staring at the glowing fire. The reddish light lit up their faces and cast strange shadows on them.

'Saffron . . .' He looked up at the stars and said a silent prayer that this time it would be for ever. 'Will you marry me?'

She watched the flames. 'Yes,' she said softly.

His face relaxed in the redness of the firelight. He turned her face towards his and wiped away the tears.

'Max?'

He bent to kiss her on the forehead. 'This is what I've been wanting, hoping for,' he said.

Then they made love in the sand, next to the glowing embers of the fire, and were more together than they had ever been before.

Eight

It was almost time to go. Her cases stood packed in the little room that had been her home for so long; Victoria was due in a few minutes. She couldn't quite believe they were going to let her out again. It frightened her. How many times had she been discharged, only to be readmitted a few days later?

She looked at herself in the mirror, brushing her long red hair. All she saw was a pale, freckled face with dark brown eyes that had tiny worry lines round them. She was still unaware of her beauty – of the perfectly sculpted face with its aristocratic jaw-line and its high cheek-bones. She did not know that she was bewitching from any angle; that the pale lipstick and musky fragrance she always wore fatally added to her attractiveness. Her eyes held a naive charm that hid the torment in her soul.

She was a painter. She painted with a fiery energy, in a vigorous, frightening style that surprised all who saw it. Savage brush strokes, vivid colours; faces glaring from the canvas, a world run amok. The psychiatrists had studied her paintings, trying to find a clue to the source of her distress, but they could not discover what it was that drove her over the edge into her strange, secretive world.

She picked up her cases and went out into the corridor, and stood there, smoothing the pale blue dress over her body. Her perfect breasts pushed against the thin material, and the line of her slim hips turned the otherwise quite ordinary dress into something sensuous and special. She saw Dr Spratt walking towards her, and smiled, remembering his attempts to understand her, and how carefully she had fielded every question he asked.

138

Dr Spratt looked at her longingly. He was in love with her. It was a tragedy that someone so perfect should be so fatally flawed.

'Are you feeling good, Lucinda?' he asked carefully.

'I always feel good when I am permitted to leave this place, Dr Spratt,' she replied harshly.

'You can do it, Lucinda. You need never see the inside of this hospital again.'

'I don't want to. I never wanted to.'

He saw it then: the tension, the inner rage. But the hatred was subdued now, as it had been for months; she was in control.

He escorted her to the front door and squeezed her hand. 'Lucinda, you don't belong in here, you know. You deserve to be loved.'

'Love? Who the hell needs love?'

Again he glimpsed her rage. What was behind it? They could not find out, its cause was locked inside her brilliant mind, and until she admitted it, released it, she would never be free from the fatal tendency to imbalance – he didn't like 'madness' or 'insanity'.

'Goodbye,' he said sadly, watching her walk down the steps to the waiting car. She got inside without giving him a single backward glance.

Inside the car, Victoria gripped the steering wheel tightly. Lucinda's beauty always took her by surprise, disconcerted her. She was tongue-tied – she, Vicky Loxton, who never put a word wrong in the courtroom and sparred with some of the keenest minds in the country, was terrified of her own sister. She concentrated her mind on the driving.

'Where's Max?' Lucinda asked quickly. The first question from a mind that never stopped asking questions.

'In the Okavango, at the camp,' Victoria replied, staring ahead at a big truck that had just pulled out in front of them.

'Mummy's camp?'

'Yes. Her camp.'

Why, wondered Victoria, could Lucinda never forget the past? Most people forgot the bad experiences of childhood and only remembered the good. With Lucinda it was the other way round.

'When will he come back, Vicky?'

'I . . . He has business in Gaberone. I'm not sure.'

'Something's wrong, isn't it?'

Victoria had already promised herself that she would hide nothing from Lucinda now, she would treat her as a normal human being. So she told her about the man who had tried to kill Max at the hotel in Gaberone, and about the court case in which Max was accused of public violence.

Lucinda made no comment on all this, but asked, 'Is he still on his own?' Her voice seemed to echo round Victoria's head – it reminded her of her own potential for madness.

'No,' she replied, trying to remain calm, 'there's someone new.'

'How he could have married that bitch! But then he's always been impulsive.'

'Max doesn't give a damn what anyone thinks,' Victoria answered. Then she said: 'I've prepared a section of the house for you.'

Lucinda smiled. Freedom at last! Now she could go wherever she wanted to, walk in the park, talk to anyone. 'I want to be on my own,' she said, 'but I'll stay till I can find a job, anyway.'

It wasn't a good idea for Lucinda to work; Victoria was hoping she would start painting again. 'You don't have to work,' she said. 'You have a permanent allowance, you know.'

Without warning, Lucinda screamed out loud, her face contorted with rage – Vicky almost swung into a car on her left. Desperately she aimed for the side of the motorway and pulled up onto the grass. Then she jumped out and ran round to the other side of the car. She dragged Lucinda, still screaming, through the door, and pulled her down the steep embankment. There was a shallow stream running at the bottom, and she threw herself into the water, pulling her sister with her.

Gradually Lucinda calmed down and her breathing became normal. They climbed back onto the bank, and lay soaking wet in the hot midday sun. It was some time later that Victoria opened her eyes to see a traffic policeman looking anxiously down at them.

'You can't stop here, lady.'

'My sister isn't feeling well,' Victoria said, 'can't you see?'

The policeman looked uncertain. 'Well, all right. But you must move on as soon as she's OK.'

'I will. Now please,' Vicky steadied her voice, 'leave us alone.'

Lucinda lay quite still after the policeman had gone; her rage had subsided. Suddenly she leaned up on one elbow and looked down into her sister's eyes. 'I will never take his money,' she said. Then the beautiful face exploded into tears. 'Don't take me back there,' she begged. 'Please don't put me back there, please, Vicky.'

'I won't, I promise I won't.'

John Packard smoothed his white hair back. There was a slight tremor above his right eyebrow, but otherwise the long, finely-lined face was calm, and the light-blue eyes never lifted their gaze from the photographs that lay scattered across his desk like confetti. They were photographs of two naked bodies intertwined in the passion of love – Saffron in the hands of this animal, Max Loxton.

The day after the fight with Loxton in the restaurant, Saffron had come to see him, on her own. That was her way, never afraid. He still thought he could keep her, even then.

'You'll get nothing, Saffron,' he had said. 'You will be penniless if you leave me.'

'You bastard, what do you think I am? One of your tarts? Two hundred and fifty dollars for a fuck and I should be grateful!'

He smiled. 'You cost me a lot more than that.'

'I'll go to the *New York Times*. The story will match anything on your networks. How about "The Highest-Paid Fuck In America"?'

That had ruffled him. 'You wouldn't dare!'

'Try me. You called me a whore last night – well, seeing I'm a hooker, I'm going to get paid.'

The battle had raged in his mind. He knew the damage she could do him. 'Saffron,' he said. 'I love you.'

'The way you love money, or a good picture. Perhaps you should keep me in a bank vault.'

He'd wanted to hit her then, beat her to a pulp, but he knew Max Loxton would kill him. He'd have his revenge on her, though, all the same.

Now he gathered together all the photographs and then fed them slowly into the paper shredder. The last picture of Saffron he fed in slowly, gloating as the machine cut her face into long horizontal slashes; then he strode back to his desk, touching the intercom key as if it were the trigger of a pistol.

'Show him in.'

Now he'd shred Max Loxton.

*

141

Saffron felt as she had felt the day she left college and all the world was before her. She had been working in London; filming had ended yesterday, and last night, on impulse, she had taken a British Airways flight to Johannesburg, and now here she was, in the blazing early morning heat, driving a hire car to Max's house. She had not told him she was coming – that she was coming for good. Since she'd left the Okavango the last time, she'd only been able to think of one thing and that was Max. Now she had made her decision; she was coming home, home to Max. As she turned into the long, tree-lined drive she could feel the pulse of excitement beating in her head. He had to be home, he had to be!

But when she knocked at the door, there was silence. She rapped on the big wooden panel again, and this time the door opened – and she found herself looking at perhaps the most beautiful woman she had ever seen, dressed only in a petticoat.

'Yes, can I help you?' the woman asked, as if the house was her territory.

'Where's Max?' Saffron stared at the woman with the flame-red hair cascading over her shoulders like tongues of fire. What a fool she'd been! Max had just found her temporarily interesting, a momentary distraction. How could she have been so naive as to think that she was the only one?

She heard his footsteps in the hall, then his voice: 'Who is it?'

Saffron felt the blood running from her face. Now she was cold with anger. 'You goddamned cheating bastard!' she spat.

Then he had his arms round her, and he was laughing, his whole face crinkling up. Even in her rage she had to admit that he was the most handsome, most rugged man she had ever met.

'Saffron!'

'Bastard!'

'Is this her?' the redhead exclaimed, her voice dark and husky.

God, thought Saffron, the woman's a bitch. She obviously wants to complete my humiliation.

'Lucinda,' Max said softly, as if speaking to a child, 'leave us alone, there has been a misunderstanding.'

Lucinda grinned. 'I'm the mad sister,' she said. 'I'm sure you and Max have a lot to discuss. I'll come back later.' And she walked past them and out into the garden.

Now it was Saffron's turn to laugh. 'This isn't a very good start!'

'Start?'

'I've come to live with you, Max. I've come for good.'

Nine

There was no moon and it was almost impossible to walk without running into thorn trees or thick scrub. Still, to switch on a torch would have been tantamount to suicide. Somewhere ahead of them was the strip of open land they had to cross. There were patrols every fifteen minutes – but that gave them plenty of time, really. The problem was getting across without leaving any tracks.

They had come here more than eight hours ago, in mid afternoon, and had lain in hiding ever since, waiting for the dead of night. The men with George were frightened – not frightened of death, but frightened of being caught, and especially of being tortured: the Botswanan army hated the Comrades. But where they were going, they would learn how to fight with advanced weaponry – radio-activated bombs and hand-held rocket launchers. George and the others had been selected for this special training, a great honour; their mission was to learn how to create terror.

In the distance now they heard the wheels of a Ratel armoured personnel carrier, and lay flat on the ground. The noise grew, and the beam of the searchlight combed the bush above them. George smelt urine: one of the Comrades had wet himself. He knew the man; he had been abducted by the security police and they had attached electrodes to his testicles.

They watched the vehicle disappearing – and then they were up and running towards the sandy strip that marked the border between Botswana and South Africa. They walked across slowly, in long, wide steps, and the last man brushed the earth carefully behind them, but it was too dark for them to see clearly whether all the tracks had been obliterated. Mindful of this, they moved quickly. If tracks were discovered, helicopters would be called in with searchlights, and after that the Bushmen trackers, who could follow a man for days, it was said, even into the townships.

The smell of the bush excited George's senses. It was as if he had become one of his Zulu ancestors, he thought – the greatest warrior race in Africa. Against his side he felt the cold metal of the .38 Special revolver he always carried with him. Even here he had to guard against betrayal; many of the Comrades were weak-willed, and the offer of money could easily swing their loyalty. And of course, there was the constant fear that they might encounter Botswanan soldiers, who disliked the Comrades almost as much as the South African army.

Dawn was just breaking when George and his party found the pick-up point. They hid in the bushes, waiting, and sure enough, just after six a delivery lorry pulled up at the side of the dirt road and the driver got out. George sucked in his breath. Heart pounding, he walked towards the back of the lorry, silhouetted against the angry red sun of the dawn, and took a red handkerchief out of his pocket. This was the signal. The men sprinted from the bush and dived into the back of the truck, hiding behind the canvas side-panels.

A minute later the driver got back into the cab and reversed round, so that they were heading towards Francistown. The men with George Zwane were laughing and joking now, but he did not join in. He knew that the danger was never over – it was impossible to relax. The tentacles of the South African National Intelligence Service spread throughout Africa.

Thrown around by the pitching of the truck on the rough dirt road, they all had to hang on for dear life. This was the way he would return, George knew; also under cover of darkness – but without many of these men. Only the bravest of the brave would return with him, because he would be bringing arms and explosives back with him across the border. This act would be the final proof of his loyalty to the Comrades, and with any luck would be his ticket of admission to the ranks of the unknown men who controlled them. Then he might find the madman who had killed his father.

The truck hit tarmac at last, and suddenly the ride was smooth and George dropped into an uneasy sleep. Just after eleven, they were all woken by the driver banging on the wall of the cab. What was wrong?

They knew soon enough when the back tarpaulin was untied, and a black face with a green beret on top of it appeared over the tailgate. An officer of the Botswanan army peered at them. 'Get out!' he screamed.

Several of the Comrades stared at the officer, then at George in disbelief. To George the brutal greeting was not unexpected. The Comrades with him were naive if they thought that their brothers across the border would greet them with open arms; as he well knew – though it was never mentioned in the media – the Botswanan army had sent several Comrades back across the border to appease the South African government.

'Get out!'

This time they obeyed the order. Out in the bright sunlight, they saw that they were the only ones at the road-block apart from five members of the Botswanan army – and all the Botswanan soldiers were pointing guns at them. The road was deserted, and dry bush stretched off to the flat horizon. The heat haze caused everything in the distance to shimmer.

'Drop your pants. All of you.'

George and his men hesitated, but when they heard the metallic click of a safety-catch being released, they undid their pants quickly and let them slide to the ground.

'And your jockeys.'

Now they stood naked from the waist down in the burning sun. George felt a cold sweat running down his back. They could be shot now, and no one would know what had happened to them. He centred his mind on one thought; survival.

The commanding officer came towards him and stuck his rifle barrel beneath George's testicles. Then he yanked it up sharply, and George dropped to his knees, stifling the cry of pain that almost burst from his lips. He looked up into the officer's eyes.

'What do you want?'

'Who are you?' the officer demanded.

George watched the officer hug his automatic rifle, just the way a child holds a toy. His uniform could not conceal the layers of fat that hung around his stomach.

'My name is George Zwane.'

'Zwane. Why do you come here?'

'I am travelling to Francistown.'

'You are from across the border?'

'Yes.'

The officer spat in George's face. 'Get back in the truck.'

George climbed back into the truck, controlling his rage. From his vantage point he watched as the officer questioned the other men. Eventually the officer came to Mchunu, a short, thin man with a terrier temperament.

'Name!'

'Comrade. That is my name. I fight in the struggle for South Africa, that is all you have to know.'

'Comrade? That's not a name! Give me your name, dog!'

George could see the beads of perspiration dripping off the officer's forehead. Shit, Mchunu was a fool to have admitted they were Comrades. He had riled the officer and he had put them all in danger.

Mchunu said to the officer: 'You call yourself a soldier? You're not a fighter, not like us in the townships. We take the real risks. What's your name, soldier?'

The officer gestured to one of his men, who came forward and took the officer's rifle. The officer took a hard black rubber truncheon out of his waistband, and without warning hit Mchunu hard across the side of the head. Mchunu did not waver.

'Kneel in front of me, Comrade.'

The last word was spat rather than said. Mchunu contrived to stare at the officer defiantly. Then the officer hit him again, and this time blood ran down from Mchunu's ear. Next the truncheon was rammed into Mchunu's stomach so that he sagged halfway to the ground.

A curt command, and Mchunu's attacker was handed back his rifle. Mchunu collapsed on the dirt. As the barrel came up viciously between his legs, they moved in then, kicking him roughly. At first it seemed that that was all they would do, but then the officer gestured for two of his men to drag Mchunu to his knees. They forced him up, and tied him spreadeagled across the bonnet of the truck, while the officer took a pickaxe handle from the back seat of his Land-Rover.

'Watch now, Comrades!' the officer screamed at George and his men. 'You must learn that this is not your country. You come here, and the white bastards follow. You will obey our laws or we will kill you.'

He swung the axe handle down hard and hit Mchunu in the small of the back. Mchunu sagged. The next blow hit him in the skull, and the next at the back of the knees. The blows carried on until Mchunu stopped screaming. They untied him and thew him down, then the officer pulled out his Makarov pistol and walked over to him. Looking at George, he pointed the barrel at Mchunu's head.

The shot echoed across the road, and Mchunu rolled over, his skull covered in blood. The officer smiled and stepped back.

'Any other Comrades here?'

George felt the sweat trickling down his back. No one said a word.

The officer holstered his pistol. 'You may go.' He gestured to the driver of the truck to pull away.

The Comrades stared at George as the truck pitched along. They wanted him to say something, to tell them why. But he had no explanation to give.

It was pitch dark because there was no moon. The little house at the edge of Francistown seemed as familiar to George as the one he had been born in; they had been watching it for several long, uncomfortable hours and it was now nearly midnight – long enough. This was the moment they had been waiting for.

George was the one who walked boldly to the door and knocked on it. After some time it opened to reveal a pretty young woman. For a moment George felt pity for her; then he thought of Mchunu, and his spirit hardened.

'Yes?' she asked.

'I have to see your husband.'

He felt the coldness of metal being pushed into his side. He swung round, grabbed the rifle barrel and kicked the man in the shin. The woman's husband – the officer they'd encountered two days previously – fell on the floor. The woman started screaming, but George slapped her hard across the face and she was silent. She began to step back down the passage, her eyes big with fear, darting from George to her husband, who was now on his knees.

'Get up,' George said roughly, yanking the man's elbow. He was whimpering softly, but George steeled himself to feel no compassion. This man had killed Mchunu, his good and loyal friend, and the Comrades must have their revenge.

As George's men came in now through the front door, he shifted his gaze from the officer to his wife. 'Have her,' he said, almost choking on the words. He would show no mercy.

They grabbed the officer's wife, ripping the nightdress from her body. Each of them had his turn with her as one held a knife to her throat. Now the officer was crying.

George waited while the last man zipped up his pants. 'Take him outside,' he ordered, looking coldly at the officer.

When they had gone, he turned to the woman. He could not let her live, it would be seen as weakness. She stared at him, her big eyes full of hope.

'Look away from me!' he screamed. Then he moved up to her, placed the pistol to her head and squeezed the trigger. As blood spattered across the hall, George had to resist the urge to vomit. He walked outside into the cold night air, where the officer was spreadeagled over the front of his car.

'What have I done?' he whimpered. He had obviously forgotten the incident of two days before, but George Zwane hadn't forgotten it, he'd thought of little else except the savage killing of Mchunu.

'Remember the man you shot at the road-block?'

The officer shivered as he remembered. Now he knew why they had come for him. 'He attacked me!' he whined.

'He was my brother,' George replied, using the language of the Comrades. 'You must pay.'

'No!' the officer stammered, looking desperately into the darkness for help.

George gestured to one of his men to come forward. 'Use the hammer, Victor.' Victor took a small hammer from his pocket and moved up to the officer.

'Take off your clothes.'

The man was fat; rolls of flesh overflowed his belt. When he had stripped, Victor made him lie face down on the concrete drive of his home, arms and legs stretched out. Then he brought the hammer hard down on the officer's right hand, breaking each of the fingers in turn, and then the thumb.

'Oh, my God! Oh, my God! Please, no!'

The officer was screaming uncontrollably. Victor smiled, and moved to the other hand. George tried not to watch. In five minutes the officer's hands and feet were a bloody pulp.

George gestured to Victor to stop. He stepped forward and rolled the crippled officer over so that the man was facing him.

'Tell your men they must support us. Tell them we are on the same side. Those who are against us will die.'

Then Victor moved in again, and George saw the knife flash in the moonlight.

'Just the one,' he reminded Victor, who then neatly cut off the officer's left testicle.

They drove away slowly, the screams echoing behind them in the darkness.

Later, when the Comrades were asleep, George staggered out into the blackness and retched. How far down must he go? he asked himself. What level of degradation would he reach before he made contact with the man who was the power behind the Comrades?

Dolph Klopper surveyed the crowded hall before him and thought that this was his greatest achievement yet. This was not a rabble of poor whites – these men were amongst the most powerful in the country, top officers from the police force and the army. More than any others, these were the men whose support he needed. Of course, they could not see him, he was hidden behind the curtain at the back of the stage. He would make his appearance at the psychological moment, when the Reverend Cilliers had prepared the ground.

And now the black folds of the dominee's cloak rustled like leaves in the wind as the holy man moved across the stage to stand before the wooden stand and make his opening address.

The dominee was old and white-haired. He was a hardened Calvinist, and among the crowd assembled in the hall, his word was regarded as second only to the Lord's. The assembly was silent, all eyes now intent on the grim figure who dominated the room. He spoke in Afrikaans.

'Brothers! We made a vow, a pact with God. He gave us the power to defeat the black threat, and we pledged our support to him for ever. Why do you think, therefore, that our present government is so divided?'

No one dared to answer the question.

'In our cinemas we can now watch films where naked flesh is visible. Books containing evil messages are freely available, and our children listen to music that is the very voice of Satan. Our young women wear clothes that would be more suitable for whores!'

The men in the hall were silent, because these things were true.

150

'Our Lord has deserted us! And rightly so! We have sinned in his eyes. But our God is a God of mercy, a God of forgiveness! There is still time for us, though our time is running out. If we do not change our evil ways, we will be damned for eternity. Our race will perish from the earth.'

He was silent, and he let the silence linger.

'Bow down your heads in shame! Pray for forgiveness! Pray that the Vow will not be forgotten. Pray for power.'

Every head in the hall was bent and every pair of eyes was closed. Every heart was filled with guilt and remorse. It was now that the Reverend Eldad Cilliers gestured for Dolph Klopper to move forward to the podium.

'There is one amongst us,' he pronounced, 'who has been chosen. A man marked since birth as the leader of our people. He is the one who brought all of us here tonight, and it is his message that you must take into your hearts and make a part of your soul. In answer to the weakness that is crippling our government, he brings strength. In his words you will find the answer you have been searching for.' And now he stepped back and pushed Dolph towards the lectern.

When everyone in the hall had opened his eyes, Dolph stared down at them, and at that moment he knew he had them.

'Do you understand that we might be driven from this fair land?' he called down to them. 'Driven from this land our forefathers fought and died for? The rest of the world says we have sinned, and that we should pay for our sins, but this is hypocrisy. We have earned our right to live here with our blood. Remember the twenty-seven thousand men, women and children who died in the camps at the hands of the accursed British who tried to take our land from us. But the Lord is with us, and he chased them from our land.

'Today we face a greater evil – lawlessness. And if our government, the government we elected, does not pass the new security bill, this country will descend into chaos!'

There was a wave of applause now, then silence as Dolph held up his hands.

'David Loxton – he is loyal to our cause. But Van der Post? The man is a traitor. He wants to give the black people the vote. Do you know what will happen then? Do you? Exactly what happened over a century ago – they will slaughter us!

'You know what I stand for. I stand for our power, our

151

freedom, our right to a decent living. I will never sell you out –
but Van der Post will!'

The hall was filled with cheering. Klopper allowed himself a
smile. Now it would be easy to get them to do what he wanted.
He raised his hands, and once again the hall became silent.

'You cheer for me as if I were your leader. I am not your
leader . . . yet. But when I do come to power, I have many
powerful friends abroad who will support me.

'I want your votes. I want, too, the vote of every man who
serves under you. I want the votes of your sons, daughters,
wives, parents and friends. Every vote will push us closer to
power.'

He stepped down from the podium amidst deafening applause,
and immediately the Reverend Cilliers led the assembly in a
rendition of 'Sarie Marais', the unifying anthem of the old Boer
republics.

Afterwards there were drinks. Dolph made sure that he spent
a little time with each of his important guests. Then he made his
way towards the imposing figure of Jurie Smit, the commander
of the South African army, a lithe, tough, whippet of a man with
closely cut hair and the look of an American marine – except for
his metal-rimmed spectacles.

'Fine words, Dolph, man.' The General slapped him hard on
the back and smiled good-naturedly, taking another sip of his
whisky and soda.

'Thank you, sir. You're a loyal supporter, I know. I know that
many who came tonight, came because of your influence.'

'No, you brought them here. Your words are music, beautiful
music to a people who are sick of being sold out. But enough –
where's that pretty wife of yours, eh?'

Dolph was so proud of Marie. Only four weeks to go now, and
then he would have the son he had always dreamed of.

'She's resting,' he said. 'The little one is kicking to get out.'

'Ach. A fighter, eh, just like his father. Well, let's hope for a
son – and let's hope, too, for a victory for David Loxton. I
admire the man. I must leave now, but we will meet again soon.
I have much to talk over with you. There are new developments
that I know will meet with your full approval.'

A few minutes later the General was relaxing in the back of
his limousine. He smiled to himself. With a man like Dolph

Klopper pulling the strings of power, the rest of Africa – of the world – would know exactly who was boss.

David Loxton was also on the move that evening, though he was driving himself. He was feeling particularly pleased with life, after reading a very full private intelligence report on Dolph Klopper. In his long political career David Loxton had survived many changes of policy, and the falling from grace of many a leader. It was a good bargain he was striking with Klopper – an association that would show profit very quickly. As for Klopper's aspirations to overall control, well, let the man have his dreams; David would put him in his place in time.

It wasn't a long drive to the Prester John. He handed his car over to the car park attendant, and went inside.

David Loxton had created the Prester John himself – a club whose entry fees were so high that only the wealthiest people in the country could afford them. Membership also meant taking a vow of silence: what went on behind the walls of the Prester John was to be strictly the business of its members and no one else. He had already had one well-known Johannesburg society hostess removed from the register after she let some indiscretion fall to an ambitious journalist who immediately reported it in a gossip column. The woman in question had made every possible effort to rejoin the club, including inviting David to sleep with her. He had accepted the invitation, but had not reinstated her.

He found the club was an excellent venue for entertaining his business colleagues. There was a small private casino on the premises, and he'd imported a croupier from Monte Carlo to make sure that the heavy gamblers who frequented the tables were well catered for.

Now he looked in through the slightly open doors of the card room and was pleased to see that there were plenty of seasoned gamblers in evidence. Roy McCracken, head of Johannesburg's biggest chain of motor dealerships, was at the head of the table, his bushy eyebrows tightly knit in concentration. McCracken didn't play unless the stakes were over R10,000, so the takings that evening would be good.

David looked around a little more, then moved up a flight of stairs to the top of the Cape Dutch house in which the club had its premises. This floor was only open to certain members, and the woman who ran it was a mistress of discretion. She greeted David now with a peck on the cheek.

One of Johannesburg's most notorious ladies of ill repute, Antoinette Fontaines was still sexually attractive at fifty. She was an enormous woman with a huge bosom, dark, lustrous hair and succulent skin. Despite her profession, Antoinette somehow managed to have a clean police record, and as her latest full-time employer, David Loxton made sure it stayed that way.

He pinched her bottom affectionately. 'David, *mon cheri*,' she said. 'How are you?'

'Glad that I'm here. The referendum is boring.'

'But of course you will win?'

'Naturally.'

'I had no doubt of it.'

'Save the charm for your other clients, Antoinette. Now, what do you have for me?'

'It was not easy. You are a demanding man, and it is not easy to meet your very special requirements. But . . .'

She guided him along the dimly lit corridor till they arrived at a locked door at the far end. He almost snatched the key out of her hand in his excitement.

She was sitting on the edge of the huge double bed, innocent and afraid, but very beautiful. He heard Antoinette whisper behind him as she closed the door: 'Enjoy, *mon cheri*.'

Ten

The cramps had got worse in the last week and Marie found herself short of breath, having to sit down often. She was so enormous now that when she looked at herself in the mirror she couldn't help thinking it must be twins. But she tried not to let her size interfere with her ordinary activities, and today, as every day when Dolph was away campaigning, she was taking the sackful of letters that had been delivered at home to the AWB headquarters in Main Street. Anna drove with her, though she always refused to go into the AWB offices, preferring to stay in the car.

Marie was greeted by Eugene Kruger, an eager young man wearing heavy, black-framed glasses. Kruger's thin, pale face was topped by thickly Brylcreemed hair flecked with dandruff. She had tried to like him, but was always put off by the smell of stale sweat that lingered about him.

'*Môre*, *Mevrou* Klopper. Jis, a full sack of letters again, eh?'

'Yes, Eugene.' She was pleased to see that everyone in the office was hard at work.

'Did you see Dolph on TV last night, *Mevrou* Klopper?'

'No. We don't have a TV.'

This disconcerted Eugene for a moment. He had forgotten that Dolph regarded television as an unnecessary luxury. 'If you'd like, *Mevrou* Klopper, I have a recording you could see.'

She was ushered into a darkened room, and Eugene switched on the video recorder. There was the tail-end of a commercial, and then the picture cut to a podium in a packed hall, with Dolph speaking to the crowd. His eyes shone, and his voice boomed

155

insistently. The words seemed almost meaningless, it was the intensity with which they were delivered that was everything.

'. . . And lastly, I want you to ask yourselves a question. What future does our country have when Kobus van der Post opposes the very laws that guarantee our security? You know what Van der Post is? I'll tell you – a sell-out!

'David Loxton is fighting for your security. If you want to live in peace, to give your children a future, vote for his security bill!'

She could not believe it was Dolph. She felt she had been watching someone greater than the man who slept beside her every night. He had become a prophet, the very embodiment of the hopes of her people.

'What do you think, eh?' Eugene's voice brought her down to earth, and once more she was conscious of the discomfort caused by the child inside her . . .

'He's like a star, Eugene. He's our leader, not Kobus van der Post.'

Eugene was still nodding assiduously as she walked back into the street and across to her car. Anna was sitting on the back seat with the groceries, and her face lit up with a huge smile when she saw her mistress.

'You feeling better, *Mevrou* Klopper?' Indeed, she had not seen *Mevrou* Klopper looking so elated in weeks.

'I saw him on television, Anna. Dolph, you know. He's backing David Loxton. They're going to win, there's no doubt about it.'

She pulled away quickly from the kerb, and did not see the anxious look on Anna's face. It would not have concerned her if she had. And Anna would not have dreamt of telling her that in the church she attended every Sunday in Mamelodi, Dolph Klopper was regarded as Satan.

'The prince of darkness,' Max muttered.

Dolph Klopper's face and voice faded as Saffron switched off the television set, then returned to her place between Max's knees on the couch. 'Max, do you think people get taken in by that sort of rhetoric?'

'Unfortunately, yes. But I hope the people in the townships won't take it lying down.' He took a long sip from his glass of red wine, his forehead furrowing with concentration. 'The trouble is, the people in the townships are their own worst

156

enemies. Most of them have only known a life of submission, and for many of them, fighting back seems an impossibility.'

He looked at her, his eyes full of anguish. 'But if only Kobus can defeat this bill, then he can kick my father out of the cabinet. And then he'll push big changes through – he'll curb the power of the army.'

Saffron pulled herself up between his legs and sat on his lap. She kissed him seductively, hoping to distract him, and he felt her against him, lithe and passionate. It was all he could do not to think about her the whole day long. He could scarcely believe that she had now been living with him for nearly a month.

John Packard hadn't been the threat Max had feared; the man had backed off after their showdown in the restaurant in California. Max smiled to himself. Things were going very well with his Okavango 2000 project. True, Shelton had demanded he sink even more of his own money into it, but with the international support it was getting, it seemed destined to become the success story of the nineties. He'd been inundated with enquiries from travel agents from all over the world. Okavango 2000 had already been featured in the *National Geographic*, and the BBC were making a documentary.

He moved on top of Saffron, and the warmth of her full breasts pushed up against his chest. Though she was smaller than him, her body was strong and finely muscled. Already he was hard with excitement, but he did not hurry; he liked to draw out his love-making with her, to savour it. Now she slowly unbuttoned the front of his shirt and pushed her face into the coarse, thick fur of his chest. It had a masculine smell that aroused her so much she hardly knew what she was doing. Her legs twined around his torso like a cat climbing a large tree.

His tongue sought hers and they played with each other, tasting, testing, to see how long the other could resist a full kiss. Her eyes closed as her mouth locked around his and she felt his hands running down the insides of her thighs. Her body began to ripple with excitement.

The phone started to ring, long and insistent. They ignored it at first, but it refused to stop, and at last Max reluctantly unwound himself from Saffron and padded across the floor.

'Gideon! . . . No! Of course I'll come. You can arrange landing permission for me? Good. They'll know my call-sign.'

He put the phone down, his face white with agitation. For a

157

moment he seemed lost in thought. 'That was Gideon Sisulu in Francistown, Botswana. It seems that an hour ago, a crack commando unit from our glorious South African army flew in by helicopter and rocketed three houses – apparently they'd heard that members of the African Freedom Council were living in the vicinity. What they didn't know was that the President of Botswana's son was staying in one of the houses. Now the lad's on the critical list – suspected brain damage.'

Saffron was aghast. 'The boy needs expert medical attention,' said Max, 'and I'm going to get it for him – the best in the country.'

'Why don't you fly the President's son here?'

'Saffron, he's hanging on to life by a thread – I've got to get to Botswana tonight.'

Max stood uncertainly in the corridor outside the operating theatre. Its doors were closed; there was nothing more he could do. He had played his part – hired a plane, picked up Dr Oblowitz and brought him here. Now it was up to medical skill, and fate, whether young Paulus lived or died. He ground his teeth with rage, thinking of the stupidity of the South African raid, the mindless carnage. His own father had probably been behind this particular piece of action. He thought about the headlines that would appear next day in newspapers throughout the world. More fuel on the fire for those who wanted further sanctions imposed against South Africa.

He walked outside into the darkness and lit a cigarette. For a few moments he thought of his hotel being built now in the swamps. Already the excavations were finished and the complex foundations were being laid. He would need money from Shelton very soon. Most of his own had already been spent on materials. Yes, at least that was real, at least that was progress.

He became aware of someone else out here in the darkness. He saw the shape of a man, and smelled the animal smell of him.

'Do you have a cigarette for me, white man?'

Max had a sense of *déjà-vu*. The accent was familiar but he could not place it. He pulled the cigarette packet out of his pocket, and the man took one. He struck a match, and in the brief flare saw the dark, majestic face of George Zwane.

'George!' The shock of it made Max speak too loud. In the

darkness the two of them shook hands, the long handshake of close friends, the handshake of trust.

'Why are you here, George?' Max spoke in barely more than a whisper now.

'I heard about the attack,' George said softly, in Zulu. 'Paulus was at an AFC meeting in a private house when the bastards rocketed it.' He looked away. 'Of course, you'll never hear that on the news. It'll be announced that there was an explosion in Francistown – no explanation given.'

'George . . .'

'I heard about the blast. I laughed. The AFC is a spent force, but still your father attacks it. Then I heard about Paulus. I know how much the President loves his son. Detective Inspector Gideon Sisulu is an old friend, and I got him to call you.'

'You knew I'd come?'

'You always come.' He was silent. Then he said, almost inaudibly, 'Why do you bother?'

'Because I believe, George, that if every man tries to make this world a better place, there's a chance it will happen. Besides, I need the President's support for my Okavango project – this is my chance to express solidarity with him.'

Looking across at his friend in the darkness, Max remembered the young George Zwane, remembered him laughing, tears of sweat running down his face as they stood in the gym. Now everything had changed, and George stood alongside those who perpetrated violence and destruction in the townships.

'Vicky told me what happened to you,' Max said. 'I wish that it had not.'

'I made it happen. I do not wish to be like my father – a martyr. I would rather be a Castro. Alive.'

'You trained as a lawyer, a man of peace.'

'I trained as a black man. I learned to take insults every day of my life, and not to fight back.'

'But what have you achieved by joining the Comrades, George?'

George was silent for a while. 'There was no other way,' he said. 'I have to find the man who killed my father. I have to find the mind behind the anarchy. I have to destroy it.'

'Death's no solution.' Max's voice was soft.

'Because I am a black man, death is my friend. It is the one freedom that no man can ever deny me.' He paused. 'But, Max,' he said, 'let us forget these things for the time being. Tell me how you are.'

So . . . Divided by politics, but still held together by friendship. Max thought he must be the only white man whom George might still regard as a friend. He did not want to lose him.

'I am well. I'm in love, George.'

Love. Something that must be absent from George's life. Max thought of Brenda Zwane, alone in the township.

'I saw a picture of your woman,' George said. 'She is the wife you deserve. She will bring you many sons.'

Suddenly a guard from the hospital shone a flashlight on them. He walked across to ascertain their identities, his machine-gun at the ready. The light shone into George's face, and Max saw the guard start, then turn and walk silently back to his post.

'You see, that is how I live now,' said George. 'I create fear, for I must lead men into a battle that cannot easily be won.'

'How did our troops know where the AFC were?' Max asked.

'I will find out. Always there is someone,' George said quietly. 'I despise informers.'

Max said: 'Van der Post wants you to come back. He wants you in the government. He wants to talk about peace.'

'You dream foolish dreams, white man.'

'Maybe. But while men still dream, there is hope.'

'I gave up dreaming a long time ago.'

'Then I will dream for you.'

Max saw Dr Oblowitz come out onto the verandah in his green operating gown.

'Your doctor has finished his work,' said George. 'He is looking for you.' He started to walk away, but Max went after him, confronted him and wrapped his arms round him.

'George, what's happening to us?'

George pushed him away. There were tears running down his face. 'It is Africa. You are white, I am black. We have to fight to live.'

And with that, he vanished into the darkness.

'He'll live?' Max asked. He stared down at the figure on the bed, swathed in bandages.

'Well, there's still a two-centimetre piece of shrapnel embedded in his brain, and anyone who tries to get that out will kill him.'

Max gripped the cold white rail at the end of the bed. 'But he'll be all right?'

Dr Oblowitz was silent for a moment. 'I'm sorry, Dr Loxton. Maybe it would have been better if I hadn't been able to get here. Death isn't always the worst thing.'

Max felt himself go cold with fury. This was what the South African army would want, an example. 'What are his chances of being mentally normal?' he asked quietly.

'Zero, I'm afraid.'

'Is there no way that you can let him go?'

Dr Oblowitz started. 'What do you mean?'

'Why let him live? It will only cause terrible anguish for everyone who loves him. His father's too distraught to even speak to you.'

'It is my job to preserve life,' the doctor said in a low voice.

'What would you do, if you could?'

'An injection.' The doctor was almost inaudible now, and he turned away and headed towards the scrubbing-up room. Max followed. 'Just tell me how to do it,' he said.

The doctor stared at Max Loxton, stony-faced. A conflict that had started at medical school and never been resolved raged in his head.

'For God's sake!' Max's voice was hoarse with emotion.

Dr Oblowitz reached into his bag and took out a vial and a syringe. '50 mls of this, into the buttock. You know how to inject?' He gripped Max's arm, but Max pulled away and walked down the corridor.

When he emerged from the ward five minutes later, Dr Oblowitz was dressed and waiting for him, and they walked out in silence to the waiting car.

They did not speak on the journey to the airport, and when they reached passport control, a man was waiting for them.

'Dr Oblowitz? I am sorry, but I have to tell you that the President's son had a relapse and died ten minutes after you left the hospital.'

As they walked out across the tarmac together, towards the plane, Max felt the doctor's hand on his shoulder, and turned to look into his dark eyes.

'It's my responsibility, Dr Oblowitz,' he said.

'I just want you to know that I wish I had your courage. You did the right thing. It was I who was wrong.'

On the far perimeter of the airfield George Zwane stood silently in the darkness, watching the plane disappear to the east.

There were times, now, when he was afraid he might be overwhelmed by the sea of violence and destruction into which he had plunged. When he began, he had had a clear objective – to penetrate the Comrades and destroy them. But sometimes, now, he felt lost, adrift on a dreadful tide of death. And there was no end to it. Yesterday, he had been interviewed by a sinister man who was almost certainly assessing him for further promotion within the Comrades' ranks.

He stared after the lights of the departing plane. Only faith in a man like Max Loxton could keep him from finally descending into hell.

The pains had been coming all morning, slowly at first, but now they were faster and more regular. They did not worry Marie; indeed, she welcomed them, for she knew that the small person within her was at last about to emerge. Anna had said she should keep moving, but she had wanted to lie down, and Anna couldn't contradict her – though the thought had crossed Marie's mind that her maid was far more experienced in these matters than she was. She could hear her now, in the hall, telephoning Dr Jacobs.

Anna came into the bedroom moments later. 'Madam, the doctor, he says he will send the ambulance. He come now.'

Marie slid down between the sheets, ignoring the pain, beginning to fantasize about how it would be when there was herself, Dolph, and the baby boy.

Dr Jacobs arrived fifteen minutes later and helped her into the ambulance. 'I'll be following in my car,' he assured her, squeezing her hand.

'Is there anything wrong, doctor?' She studied his kind old face earnestly.

'There is nothing wrong, Marie. However, I know how much this child means to you, so I'm taking you to hospital for the birth. That way, if there are any complications, you'll be well cared for.'

'You know Dolph wanted the child born at home?'

'Dolph may be a leader of men, but I am an expert at bringing babies into this world. I will tell him I ordered you to go to the hospital.'

She lay in the back of the ambulance, listening to the screaming

162

of the siren and wondering why she should cause people so much trouble. Surely there were accidents to be attended to that were more important than a woman about to give birth?

As soon as she was settled in the labour ward, Dr Jacobs appeared above her like a guardian angel. The spasms were more frequent now, and she was scared. A sister came up to her and held her hand.

'Now, you must do what your body urges you to do. Push the little baby out of you, try to do it with the next spasm.'

She felt the life thrusting within her, the small being bursting to get out of her, and she pushed hard – but nothing happened. Again the doctor was beside her.

'Don't worry, it isn't easy. If it doesn't come we'll do a caesar.'

The word struck terror into her. Dolph had said that such births were unnatural and against the will of God. Well, she, Marie Klopper, would not have this caesar, she would give birth to her boy in the normal way.

Tears rolled from her eyes, the pain was so intense. Nothing had prepared her for this: some of her friends had attended antenatal classes, but Dolph had felt that giving birth should be instinctive. At the time she had complied with his wishes, but now a flash of resentment burned through her. Maybe it would have been easier if he had let her go to class. With the next spasm she pushed hard and sank back exhausted, her head on the pillow. She wanted to cry – what if the baby didn't come out? Suddenly, for a reason she could not explain, she wanted Anna next to her, not the doctor. Anna would understand.

She felt the next spasm coming, and was terrified, and pushed as if it were the last act of her life. The pain was worse than she could have imagined possible.

'Here it comes!' the nurse exclaimed. 'It's a boy!'

Marie closed her eyes and felt the pain subside. Suddenly she felt terribly alone, as if some part of her had been taken away. There was a terrible sense of loss.

The crying brought her to her senses – the crying of a little boy. Dr Jacobs brought him to her, still bloody from the birth and with his little eyes closed. A warmth suffused her body. She would die for this child. He lay close in her arms and his mouth sought the nipple beneath her gown, and when he began to suck the sensation was one of the most pleasurable she had ever known.

She did not see the look of anguish on Dr Jacobs' face, or the horror reflected in the eyes of the two nursing sisters. All she was aware of was her newly born son.

The woman had interrupted the meeting. He had turned to her angrily, demanding to know what it was that could be so important, but then she had shown him the note and he had been on his feet instantly, apologizing to the businessmen and farmers.

A son, he told them. God had blessed him with a son.

He had urged the big car on across the flat dirt roads, leaving a trail of dust behind him that rose into the air like a cloud. A thousand thoughts ran through his head. Already he could see the photographs of himself and his son on the front pages of the national newspapers. This was just the sort of publicity he needed. His public relations people had told him that he was appearing too hard – but the baby would change all that. Suddenly, he felt vindicated; he felt that now he was a man. The boy might have blond hair and blue eyes, like Marie. He would be a natural rugby player, a future leader of his country. Dolph almost ran over a herdsman and his sheep in his eagerness to get to the hospital.

As he drew into the hospital car park, though, Dolph made an effort to compose himself. The people who worked in the Kruger Hospital were all potential supporters, and he must not appear excited in front of them. The emotions that he felt must be hidden; he must behave like the future ruler of his country.

He could not help being surprised, all the same, that the woman in reception was not more helpful. Surely she must know that Dolph Klopper's wife had borne a son? He could not know of the message that had swept through the hospital, like a fire fanned by wind across the dry winter veld – a fire blazing out of control, vivid and terrifying.

He made his way along the corridor. He wanted to run, to scream, to sing with joy. But he walked, for one day he would rule South Africa, and rulers of men must be steady and grave. But the fierce emotion was there, just under the surface, and when, on the threshold of the maternity ward, Dr Jacobs came up to him and gripped his arm, Dolph spun round in anger.

'Doctor, I want to see my child, please!'

'Relax, Dolph,' the doctor said with a deathly quietness in his voice, 'he's fine. It's just that . . .'

'What, doctor?' Dolph demanded furiously.

'Nothing,' Dr Jacobs replied, backing away. 'He's a fine, strapping boy.'

Dr Jacobs stared across the rows of empty beds and thought of Marie, in the private ward beyond. What was needed here was a man of compassion – and that was not a description that fitted Dolph Klopper. He looked on despairingly as Dolph almost ran through the ward, to the room where his wife lay with their newly born son.

Marie held the baby tight in her arms. She hadn't understood what the doctor had said to her, but it didn't matter; whatever it was, it wasn't important. She could feel already that he would be a strong child, just the sort of child Dolph wanted. Now she could stand with her parents and her friends as an equal: she, too, was a mother.

The little boy started to cry again, and she held him close to her breast, gazing down into the beautiful dark eyes that stared up into hers. She knew that she was in love again. And perhaps this was the beginning of a new love affair with Dolph, too.

And then, looking up, she saw Dolph coming into the room. She felt a deep contentment. Life had been very good to her.

The smile evaporated from Dolph's face as soon as his eyes rested on the baby. Marie saw his confusion and sympathised with the shock he must feel as a new father. But to her surprise he started to back away, his whole body shaking. He raised his right hand and pointed desperately at the child.

'Whose baby is that?' he stammered. 'The truth, Marie, I want the truth!'

The voice was Dolph's, but it was not kind, it was ugly and cruel. The baby began to cry and she brought him to her breast.

'He's ours, darling,' she said, staring down at her child.

There was a terrible stillness in the room that made her look up again. The man she loved was glaring at her as though she were some foul, unwanted thing.

'Dolphie, what's wrong?'

'Marie, that's not my son. Whose is it?'

Why was he so angry? 'He's ours, Dolph. I want to call him Karl after your father.'

Dolph's lips curled back in fury. 'You'll do no such thing, you whoring bitch!'

She recoiled in horror, his words at last shattering her dreamy content. What was he saying? How could her husband speak to her like that? Call her a whore?

Dolph's face was filled with an animal loathing. 'Marie, you'll never sleep in my bed again, you'll no longer carry my name. Take that little bastard and go and live with his kaffir father.'

She started crying then, but hurriedly wiped the tears away. She looked anew at her son, and saw for the first time that his skin was a beautiful milk-chocolate colour. Then she looked back at the man whom she had thought loved her.

'He's your son, Dolph.'

It was then that Dr Jacobs burst into the room and grabbed Dolph's arm, trying to pull him away. 'These things happen, don't you understand? It is your son.'

But Dolph was beyond reason now. 'You slept with a kaffir!' he screamed at Marie. 'You whore!' And red-faced with rage, he threw Dr Jacobs to the floor and stormed out of the room.

Dr Jacobs dragged himself to his feet. There was no doubt in his mind that the boy was Klopper's child; Marie had been artificially fertilized with Dolph's sperm. There could be only one explanation, therefore, for the child's colour, and Klopper's dark skin and eyes confirmed it. But certainly he was not going to be the one to confront Klopper with the fact that one of his ancestors must have been black.

Dolph walked slowly out of the hospital, his fists bunched tightly. How could Marie have done this to him? He had selected her specially – a girl from the finest Afrikaans stock. But that was of no importance now, she had damned herself for ever. Naturally, he would tell Marie's father the reason why he had to leave her. The man would have to discipline his daughter, and find out the truth – for Dolph was already determined on meeting the man who had fathered the coloured child Marie now held in her arms. What black man could have dared to sleep with his wife? He would take his sjambok to him. Beat him till he screamed, and go on beating him . . .

As he left the hospital buildings behind him and drove off across the veld, he tried to think of other things – the referendum for example – but it was no good, his mind kept returning to Marie and the child. He thought of the scandal that the newspapers might make of this story. He must make some phone calls

. . . There must be immediate and total silence; the world must never know the truth about Marie and her coloured child – the child that, no matter what Dr Jacobs said, could not possibly be his.

Lucinda was not surprised when Rafe arrived over an hour late, and made no apology. He was just the kind of bastard she had taken him for. She had met him at a drinks party at the house of an old friend, and he had asked her out to dinner at one of Johannesburg's best restaurants, and she had declined. Once she had allowed the shock of her refusal to sink in, she had suggested he come to dinner at her house in two nights' time; all he needed to bring, she said, was some Veuve Cliquot, her favourite champagne. He'd accepted with alacrity, obviously relishing the prospect of adding her to his steady stream of conquests. Lucinda smiled now, as she ran to open the door for him. Rafe was in for a little surprise. She really enjoyed creating little surprises for men like Rafe.

He was better-looking than she'd remembered. His perfectly tailored casual suit, she could see, concealed a beautiful, finely muscled body, and he had a strong, chiselled face and dark eyes. When he kissed her on the cheek, she smelt his expensive after-shave.

She led him into the lounge, and let loose on him the anger she knew she was supposed to feel.

'Where the hell have you been, Rafe!'

He pushed her down onto the settee, kissing her on the forehead.

'You could at least have phoned.' She hoped her voice sounded suitably pained.

'I had a business meeting. I couldn't get away. Now, where are the glasses? This is a swell house, Lucinda. Is it yours?'

She could see the acquisitive gleam in his eyes. Definitely a gold-digger, this one, as well as a first-rate bastard. 'Yes. I inherited it,' she lied.

'Lucky girl.'

'Do you want dinner? It's in the oven.'

She knew he wouldn't want it, she just wanted to give him the satisfaction of refusing it. All men were the same in that way, they loved to humiliate a woman.

'I had a pizza earlier on,' he said. 'I'm not hungry.'

'Rafe, you know they say: it's bad to drink on an empty stomach – and I haven't eaten all day.'

He looked at her mischievously. 'You don't believe that old wives' tale, do you?'

'Not when I've got someone like you to spend the evening with, darling.'

She moved a little, so that her evening gown fell open to reveal her legs, sheathed in dark, sheer stockings. She saw his eyes drop momentarily, and lay back on the settee so that her whole body faced him.

He opened the champagne expertly and poured her a glass with a steady hand. 'Haven't you got some music?'

'Of course, Rafe darling. This room has everything, including me. Try the cabinet next to the drinks tray.'

He selected a Nat King Cole disc, slow and very romantic. Then he walked back to her, picked up his glass and touched it against hers. She drank the whole glass and giggled excitedly. As she had hoped, he followed suit.

'Pour me another, Rafe, I feel reckless tonight.'

He filled their glasses and she sat sipping the champagne, waiting for him to begin.

'I cannot believe that I am alone in the room with one of the most beautiful women in Johannesburg.'

'I'm that attractive?' Lucinda replied with feigned naivety.

She leaned forwards, exposing her bosom for him, and he moved closer. 'Lucinda, you walk into a room and every man turns his head.'

She lay back again on the settee. He wasn't drinking fast enough, she wanted him more excited, more stimulated. That was the way she liked her men.

'I think we should drink a toast, Rafe.'

'To Lucinda Loxton. The most beautiful woman in the world.'

He downed his glass, and so did she.

Rafe refilled her glass and then his own. Boy, this one wasn't much good at holding her liquor, if he wasn't careful he'd be making love to a drunk, and that was no fun. Perhaps it was time to make his first move.

He glided over and touched his lips against hers. She did not resist, and her tongue came forwards, searching for his. Not many of the beautiful women he'd made love to had sexual

168

passion to match their looks, but from the first touch of their lips, he realised that Lucinda Loxton was something special. Her taste was like an electric shock to his senses. He felt himself stiff with desire. He wanted her, wanted to dominate her. He was being drawn on by an attraction he could not resist.

Lucinda knew she had him: he was losing control. She felt his hands sliding over her buttocks and slipping between her thighs. This she enjoyed – but then he started trying to force her down onto her knees, and this was not what she wanted. Her pleasure must always come first.

'No, darling, no. Take off your clothes.'

His lips worked their way down between her breasts, and then lower. She breathed in with excitement and, still clothed herself, helped him to pull his shirt off. Soon he was completely naked, his lips pressed against hers and his hands reaching up, feeling her breasts beneath the flimsy material of her dress. She could see the sweat building up on his skin, and this excited her even more. Occasionally his hands would come up and try to pull her down, but always she resisted.

After fifteen minutes, Rafe fell back exhausted. She looked down at him.

'Tired, Rafe? No, you lie down. I prefer it that way.'

He lay on the carpet, his erection pointing upwards, and she eased herself on top of him. Then she rode him, ensuring that the pleasure was all hers, never his.

'Come on, Rafe, push.'

'Please, Lucinda, just keep that up.'

She immediately changed her movements. Then, lifting herself up, she began to tease him with her fingers. The moment she saw he was enjoying this, she tightened her grip. He cried out, and doubled over with pain.

'Oh, I'm so sorry! I got carried away!'

She pushed him down and mounted him again. This time she could tell there was no danger of him climaxing and she watched with satisfaction as he lay panting beneath her.

Her orgasms came fast now. She screamed out with excitement and pleasure. Then she looked down at Rafe. He was hurting now, she was sure of it. He wanted to come, but he couldn't – he was in torment! The bastard deserved it. They all did.

'What's wrong, Rafe? Don't I turn you on enough? I thought you could keep it up all night.'

She could see the rage building in him, the anger in his eyes. She glanced down at her watch; she had timed it perfectly. She pulled away from him and started to laugh.

'You should have told me you were impotent!'

He was on her in a second, forcing her legs apart, pushing himself into her. She let her hands work down again – waiting till she heard the key in the front door – then she squeezed his testicles as hard as she could.

'Oh my God! You fucking bitch!'

He rolled over, clutching himself, tears of pain running down his cheeks, and found himself looking at a pair of smooth, shapely legs. He looked up to see a tall, beautiful blonde staring down at him.

It was only then he realised that he was completely naked and that Lucinda was fully clothed. He dragged himself towards the settee and pulled on his underpants with great difficulty. He felt the eyes of the two women upon him.

'Lucinda, come into the kitchen with me.' Her voice was husky, controlled.

He waited till they had gone into the kitchen, then he pulled on the rest of his clothes, and made for the front door. That was the last time he would go anywhere near Lucinda Loxton.

In the kitchen, the two women sat on opposite sides of the table.

'Lucinda, what the hell do you think you're playing at?' Victoria found it difficult to keep her voice down.

'He tried to rape me, the bastard!' Lucinda pushed her flame-red hair roughly behind her ears.

'Don't try that on me. You wanted to hurt him. It looked to me as though you raped him.'

'Bitch!'

Victoria ducked as the fist came at her, and she grabbed Lucinda's hand across the table, staring into the flashing green eyes, trying to find an answer.

'Lucinda, I spoke to Stephanie Coltrane yesterday. You went out with her son – and he had to see the doctor after you'd finished with him.'

'He was a lecherous bastard. He tried to rape me, too.'

'What's wrong with you, Lucinda? Can't you have a normal relationship?'

She let go of Lucinda's arm and her sister stared at her angrily. 'A normal relationship, Vicky? Like you have with that old man?'

Victoria hit Lucinda hard across the face so that she fell to the floor, then dropped to her knees beside her and held her arms apart as she tried to hit back.

'Don't ever speak to me like that again, Lucinda. Ever.'

Lucinda burst into tears then, long sobs that racked her body, and Victoria helped her up and led her into the lounge. The young man, she was pleased to see, had left; she hoped he'd be all right. She left Lucinda on the couch and went to the drinks cabinet to pour herself a stiff Scotch. There was enough pressure in her life already, what with worrying about Kobus' health, supporting him in his bid to topple her father, and her own heavy court schedule; the last thing she needed was the additional burden of Lucinda. Then, suddenly, she felt guilty. She'd vowed that she would never return Lucinda to the mental hospital – but what had happened to her resolve to turn Lucinda into a normal, well balanced human being?

She went back to the couch with her drink and sat down next to Lucinda. Her sister had stopped crying now. She looked at the long red hair, the perfect breasts beneath the thin dress, the sensuous curve of the lips. Men would always fall in love with Lucinda, that was her fate.

'Lucinda. We have to talk.'

'If it's about men, I'm not interested.'

'You're a guest in my house, Lucinda, but you've just insulted Kobus, and you've tried to hit me. Now you can listen.' The only way to deal with her is to be firm, Victoria told herself.

'Men find you very, very attractive,' she went on. 'Most women dream of looking the way you do. Now, if you don't want a man, you don't have to have him, but if you invite a man to make love to you, don't abuse him.'

The sister who was partly a stranger to her, stared back at her. 'I . . . I wish I could tell you. I never want to be loved by a man. I have only met men with one thought in their heads. Even Dr Spratt at the hospital – he never did anything to me, but I could see he wanted to. Vicky, I want to move out and find a place of my own.'

171

Victoria softened. 'No, that's not necessary. But just think about what I've said, and if you want to talk about this again, tell me.'

'I shan't want to. I'm going to bed.'

Victoria watched her leave the room, then sat alone on the couch, staring down into her drink. Lucinda was more challenging than any court case she'd ever handled. Something had happened to her in childhood, that was obvious. Something terrible. If she could just find a key to that dark compartment of Lucinda's mind, then maybe she could open it.

Dolph had spent much time in prayer. For the first time in his life he was doing something of great importance without consulting his father. He did not think his father would understand what had happened. Worse, he feared that his father might demand he honour the marriage vows – although, on second thoughts, that was unlikely. 'For better or for worse,' he muttered the words to himself out loud. They had seemed so right on the day of his marriage to Marie, but now they seemed strange and forbidding.

A coloured child. He looked at the back of his hand. Yes, he did have a dark complexion, but to suggest, as Dr Jacobs had, that the child was his – unthinkable.

He had spoken to Marie's father, and the man had understood. The fact was that Marie was an embarrassment to all of them, especially now, on the eve of the referendum, and when so many challenges lay ahead of them. So now he was taking the action that was necessary. His contacts were excellent, and he had been astonished at the co-operation he had received. Of course, he was fortunate; everyone at the small hospital understood – apart from that fool Jacobs, and he was too frightened to talk. No, the truth of the matter was obvious: the devil had tempted Marie and she had succumbed; and now the devil wished to drag him down with his lascivious bride. But he, Dolph Klopper, would not be beaten.

He picked up the copy of *Die Burger* and read the deaths column again.

Marie Klopper. God took her gently by the hand and led her into the garden, 19th July 1989. Remembered by her loving husband Dolph.

Very satisfactory. And now he must complete the business

172

with a visit to the Department of the Interior. It would not take long, less time even than the signing of the wedding vows, he mused . . .

Japie Theron was what Dolph would have described as a grey man; thin grey hair, grey suit and grey shoes. He had not met him before, but had been reliably informed that he could be trusted – and that was what mattered.

'Ah, *Meneer* Klopper. It is good to meet you. Now, everything has been explained to me, so you do not have to tell me anything, nor do you have to sign anything. I shall just show you this so you can see that it's all in order.'

He handed him a green identity book. All South Africans carried one; it was commonly known as the Book of Life, and provided a complete classification of the individual according to race and colour. Dolph stared now at the black-and-white photograph of his wife. They'd done a good job with it, she almost looked like what she was about to become: a coloured person.

'Marie Klopper has become Marie Jantjies. She is a non-white from the Cape, with a small boy who has yet to be christened. Unfortunately her husband, Boetie Jantjies, who worked on the railways, was killed in an accident on 19th July 1989.' Japie Theron sniffed, and stared more fixedly at Dolph. 'Her husband left her a small house in the coloured suburb of Riverlea, just next to Soweto, and his railway pension amounts to R450 per month.'

'Make it R600.'

'You're a generous man, *Meneer* Klopper.'

'The pension is for the rest of her life?'

'Yes. She'll be living well once her son is grown up, eh!'

'Theron, let us keep to the facts – this matter is odious to me. My wife gave birth to a coloured son: I have arranged for her to be separated from me for ever, and she has agreed to this. Do I make myself clear?'

'I understand. I understand.'

'*Mevrou* Jantjies is in Baragwanath hospital at the moment. You must make sure that she is discharged in a satisfactory condition, together with her son.'

Japie Theron lifted his eyebrows and coughed. Dolph felt the spittle on his face and took out his handkerchief.

'Ach, sorry, *Meneer* Klopper. I couldn't help laughing. You

173

see Baragwanath is such a good hospital, as long as you're a kaffir!'

Baragwanath was the largest hospital in Africa, and catered specifically for blacks and coloureds. It was always in the news. Either the nurses were out on strike, or the doctors were up in arms about the appalling conditions.

Dolph said: 'My name has been removed from the records?'

'I don't know what you're talking about, sir. You're no relation to this Jantjies woman.'

'Good. I hope you continue to be so discreet – you may have to cope with a journalist or two sniffing round.'

'They'll discover nothing, man.'

Dolph Klopper found the dull grey eyes boring into his own strangely disconcerting; he did not want to have anything further to do with this man. He rubbed his hand nervously across his forehead. The strain of the whole business was sapping his energy.

'Then, er, there's the other matter, *Meneer* Klopper . . .'

Dolph took the tightly wrapped brown packet from his pocket. Ten thousand rands, a small price to pay for ensuring that his former spouse remained in lifelong obscurity.

The church was packed; there were even people standing outside the main doors.

Close to the altar stood Dolph Klopper, with Marie's parents beside him. As the Reverend Eldad Cilliers slowly spoke the words of the funeral service, Marie's mother began to cry, and the whole congregation felt deep pity for a woman who had lost her daughter so early in life.

Afterwards there was tea for the women, liquor for the men. Dolph, pouring himself a generous brandy and coke, felt a hefty slap on the back and turned to see the Reverend Cilliers standing behind him.

'Well Dolph, don't waste your time grieving. You've got to concentrate on helping Loxton put down Van der Post.'

Dolph stared deep into the old clergyman's eyes. No, the Reverend did not know the truth; Eldad Cilliers, like the majority of the congregation, believed that Marie had died giving birth to a dead child.

'You must marry again. You must have many sons.'

Dolph felt the fury rise within him. He did not try to fight it, but neither did he let it show on his face. There would be no more women in his life – now he would devote everything to the cause. God had shown him how easily the black races could pull down the white: when he ruled, he would reinstitute the law that made it a crime for a black man to sleep with a white woman. And he would make it punishable by death.

'I shall not marry again,' he said.

The Reverend Cilliers patted him on the shoulder again. 'A man needs a woman. God is cruel sometimes. I can only think that this has happened to give you strength.'

In his sumptuous office in the Packard Studios in Hollywood, John Packard settled back into his chair and glanced at the picture of Saffron on his desk. Then he looked up at the elegant Englishman opposite him.

'Well, what progress?'

The man smoothed back his fine black hair, adjusted his glasses and gave Packard a tight-lipped smile. 'Better than I'd hoped, old chap.'

John Packard laughed hard, and the man waited until he had finished. 'So,' he said, 'I think the time may be right to pull the rug from under his feet.'

Packard held up his hands. 'Not yet. I want the building to start, I want his emotional involvement to be at a high. I want him to believe that his dream is coming true.'

'But, my friend, I thought you wanted to bankrupt him?'

Packard's face, beneath the fine silver hair, became suffused with red. 'I want to destroy the bastard,' he said.

Eleven

Shuffling along the pavement in his filthy overalls, George Zwane approached the guardpost at the front of the police station. A young black constable looked out at him, and he shuffled over to him and cupped his hands together in the universal gesture of the beggar. The constable, thinking that the man in front of him looked as though he had been drinking heavily, and would probably use the money to buy more drink, dug dutifully into his pocket all the same.

As the constable looked through his change, George pushed the package in his right hand underneath the wooden table that stood in the guardpost. To replace it, he pulled a similar but empty packet from his pocket. Then he thanked the constable for the fifty-cent piece and shuffled away.

Now, though the first part of his mission was completed, he was extra vigilant. His training in Botswana had been good; the instructor in Francistown had told him that it was at moments such as this, when tension eased a little, that you could give the game away. He was tempted to start running – but instead he kept on shuffling slowly away from the guardpost. Of course, he had achieved nothing yet. The constable might spot the package under the table, and then they would come after him.

Not hurrying, he moved into some bushes and lay down on the grass behind them. No one would take any notice of him here. After all, it was quite natural for an out-of-work black man to lie in the grass in an all-white suburb.

He watched as the white Ford Escort pulled up outside the police station and the young white student, Marc, got out. The

176

Comrades had recruited him from the University of Witwaters-rand. They said he was naive, but very dedicated. Marc, unlike George, would be remembered afterwards – but that was all right because, being white, he could be spirited away to another country, given a new identity. Anyway, that was what Marc believed would happen to him; but in the Comrades' book he was disposable. He had hardly been admitted into the organiz-ation at all, he only knew George and a few juniors. If the security police caught him and put wires on his balls, they'd get very little out of him.

He watched Marc get slowly out of the stolen car with the false number plates, close the door and then sit on the bonnet. George pulled out a packet of cigarettes and put the packet to his mouth, pulling out one of the cigarettes with his lips. He lit it lazily, inhaled deeply, and smiled. So far, everything was going to plan.

A few minutes passed. Then, another car drew up outside the police station. George tensed. This was an unforeseen complica-tion. A white woman got out of the car, locked it carefully and fumbled the keys into her handbag. She went up to the black constable at the guardpost, who snapped to attention, then listened as she spoke. Meanwhile, Marc moved away from his car, walking somewhat unsteadily towards the street corner. He was almost out of sight, and the constable was now showing the woman round the side of the building to the charge office. George looked down at his watch. 12.45 p.m. Fifteen minutes to go.

'Hey, kaffir.'

George felt his fists tighten, then remembered where he was and who he was supposed to be. 'Eees, my baas?' he answered contritely.

The old man looking down at him had rotting yellow teeth and limp blue eyes. 'Get off my fucking lawn,' he said.

'Eeeh, baas, I was only sleeping.'

'Sleep somewhere else, you bloody layabout.'

Now he was in trouble – the old man might remember him. But there was nothing he could do about it, the man was not a target.

'Move on, man,' the old man said, 'you'll get arrested.' He started digging in his pocket, and to his surprise George found a R5 note being pushed into his hand. Then the man was gone,

177

shuffling back to the house, back into his comfortable white world. George moved away, further down the road.

The moment Marc rounded the corner he began to run. They had told him not to run, but he felt his bowels were about to explode. He staggered behind some bushes and yanked down his trousers; he felt a wave of relief pass through his body as his bowels gave way, followed by a feeling of intense nausea.

He had to get away quickly. They had given him precise instructions about the route to follow out of Johannesburg, and details of the crossing point into Zimbabwe. Now he crossed the main road and began walking towards the bus stop. Act normally, he kept reciting to himself, unconscious of the fact that he stank of faeces.

At the bus stop a couple of women were already waiting. After a few moments he noticed that one of them was looking at him, and was faintly puzzled by her animosity. He had no idea that she had been watching him all the time, revolted by his smell. She would be the one who gave testimony at his trial, saying where she saw him and how he looked at that moment.

Fortunately the bus was on time. Marc paid his fare and walked up the stairs to the top of the bus. He felt himself relax as the bus accelerated down the road, taking him away from the police station and the stolen car with the false number plates.

At one o'clock they came out of the police station. George couldn't see exactly how many, but there must have been at least forty. His intelligence had been good; as he'd been told, there had obviously been some sort of training operation going on inside. The woman he'd seen earlier was with them, trying to get past them to her car. There was nothing he could do about her: all the planning and the sacrifices could not be thrown away now.

They were almost at the guardpost now, ready to pass through. This was where there might be problems, for they might go through in single file, but he needed them in a group. The first bomb he'd planted was designed to affect the whole group of them, to make them run away from the station, towards the stolen car that Marc had parked outside.

Then George saw a car drawing up outside the station, and nearly jumped to his feet in terror. A black woman and her two teenage daughters in school uniform got out.

178

'Get out of the way! Oh Jesus!' George muttered the words, a silent, desperate prayer, but the woman stayed next to the car, talking to her daughters. She reminded him of his Brenda.

The policemen were out of the station sentry gate now, and waiting in a group. It was better than he had hoped – perfect. Except for the black woman and her daughters.

He slid the device from his pocket. It looked like the remote control for a video recorder, except for the small aerial positioned on the top.

Two goddamn women and two girls. This was the price. Was it too high?

His finger hesitated over the control button, then he thought of the Comrades. If he didn't go through with this, they'd never believe in him; they'd think the special training he'd undergone in Botswana was a waste of time. This was his chance to prove himself.

No. He couldn't do it.

Then he thought of his father, gunned down in cold blood. He had to find the killer.

His finger touched the button.

The first small bomb in the guardhouse exploded, and the policemen ran away from the blast. Two of them lay on the ground, dead and bloody, and the black woman was running, pulling her daughters desperately after her. There was the smell of blood, a sense of panic. The blue uniforms were swarming in the direction of the car Marc had left behind. Seconds were going by, seconds between life and death. With this action George would become a terrorist.

Coldly he pushed the second button.

There was one hundred kilograms of high explosive nestling in the boot and innards of the stolen car, and the fifty-litre fuel tank was filled to capacity. The red light of the control device glowed next to the spare wheel.

For a moment it seemed as though nothing would happen; then the sheet of flame spread out from under the chassis and seared across the tarmac. Some of the policemen turned. The black woman and her two daughters were enveloped in flames.

The explosion was like the thunder that so often fills the Johannesburg sky in summer, violent and chilling.

Within minutes, the smoke began to clear. George realised that he had broken the control unit in his right hand, he had squeezed it so tightly. The front two storeys of the police station had collapsed, the outer fence had disappeared and the guard-house was flattened. The black woman was lying in the centre of the road, both her legs missing, screaming uncontrollably.

George got to his feet and flung the control unit down the storm drain in the road next to him. He turned down a side street – and already people were coming out of their houses, looking around, trying to find out where the noise was coming from. The screaming continued, a long, high-pitched wail, followed by shrieks of anguish. God, what had he done?

The car was waiting round the next corner. George jumped into the back seat and lay down on the floor.

'*Amandla*.' The driver muttered the word and started the engine. He did not pull away quickly, but at the leisurely pace of a man on his way towards a business meeting. All the same, George vomited all over the car seat . . .

Back at the police station, a constable staggered out of the smoking, broken façade and stared at the devastation. He leant against the wall, crying uncontrollably, then he ran back inside.

As the last of the smoke began to disappear, the scream of ambulance sirens filled the air. A crowd of people began to gather at the other side of the road. Then the trucks came, full of riot police, armed to the teeth. They disgorged into the street and began to round up passers-by for the grim procedure of questioning.

Suddenly, above the devastation came a shadow, moving like a demon finger, and an avalanche of noise. The helicopter touched down at the side of the road, and an impeccably dressed man wearing dark glasses stepped out of the hold. He walked up to the body of the black woman and took off his glasses.

David Loxton cradled the bloody head in his hands. 'I will find them,' he announced. 'If it takes me a lifetime, I will find them.' Then he kissed her, and let her rest in peace.

The photograph was splashed across the front of every major newspaper in the world: the South African Minister of Justice kissing the dying black woman. It carried a message that appealed to the hearts and minds of millions of people. The photograph of David Loxton also appeared on the front cover of *Time* maga-zine, and inside there was a major article entitled, 'Anatomy of Terror. The South African Reality.'

180

In South Africa, house prices in white suburbs across the country took a startling dive. The reaction was even more pronounced than it had been during the Sharpeville shootings in 1961 and the Soweto riots in 1976. The Rivonia police station, where the bombing had taken place, was in the heart of South Africa's wealthiest suburb, and as a result the white elite no longer felt secure. An anger that had been building in the country for over a hundred years was ready to explode in their faces. On this, the eve of the national referendum on David Loxton's security bill, the dominant feeling among the white population was fear.

David moved slowly, taking his evening walk, as he always did, in the grounds of his Pretoria home. Above him were oak trees that had been planted a hundred years previously. He liked the sense of continuity they gave him, they reminded him of the length of time the white man had been dominant in South Africa.

David knew that all he had ever wanted was now within his grasp, less than a few weeks away. All he had to do was get the referendum over and done with. The bombing of the Rivonia police station and his tending to the dying black woman was the best publicity stunt he could have wished for.

He could offer the population security. And that was important, because the country was nervous. Unless the population supported the new security bill, the wave of violence would intensify.

David had always known that he could cut the correct profile with the overseas press. As an Englishman by descent, he knew he was more acceptable than an Afrikaner like Kobus van der Post.

David turned back to the house. His dream of becoming the most powerful man in Africa was close to fruition.

Anna's husband, Joseph, came to see her, as he always did, on Saturday morning. He'd caught the bus from Carltonville the previous evening, after the late shift. It was hard work in the mine, but he'd done well there, studying in the evenings to advance himself.

At over six foot tall, he was a proud, strapping man. Hard work on the mines for the last ten years had left his body lean and fit. He lived for Anna and their four children, and dreamed of getting a better job, of having Anna and the children to live

181

with him. As it was, the children had to stay with an aunt in Kimberley, and Anna had her job with the Kloppers.

Now, he knocked on the door of Anna's small room at the back of the Kloppers' house – but the door swung open, and to his surprise he saw that the place was bare. He felt as if someone was watching him, and spinning round, saw Klopper staring at him, wild-eyed, a shotgun resting in his hands.

'Don't look for her,' Klopper said. 'She's gone to Kimberley.'

Joseph trembled. What was going on? 'I'll be on my way, then, Mr Klopper.'

The twin barrels of the shotgun were raised. 'Unzip your pants, Joseph.'

'I'm going!'

'Kneel.'

'No. Please, no!'

Klopper's finger brushed the trigger, and Joseph dropped his underpants and knelt down.

Klopper fired, but the shot went wide, and Joseph urinated in terror.

'Got no balls, you black bastard. Screw my wife, but you've got no balls.'

He lifted up the barrel and pulled the other trigger. The noise was deafening but the shot flew harmlessly above Joseph's head.

Joseph's bowels exploded and he flopped face forwards, whimpering.

Klopper laid the shotgun on the kitchen table and walked out of the room.

Twelve

Thursday, November 5th was a cold, overcast day. Throughout the country there was an air of grim anticipation. By midday, in spite of the weather, it was clear that there was going to be a record poll. Across the country the polling booths were jam-packed with people keen to cast their votes.

In the affluent white community there was an air of expecta-tion, of silent hope, but the black people looked on sullenly at a decision-making process from which they, the majority of the country's population, had been excluded. The black townships were quiet. The people knew that at this time the police and army were especially vigilant, and to protest would be even more dangerous than usual. The Houses of Parliament were almost empty. Most MPs were at home. The result of the referendum on David Loxton's security bill was to be announced the follow-ing morning.

The baby woke her early, demanding his morning feed with an intense yelling that echoed right round the little house. Marie put on her dressing-gown, took Morgan from his cot, and went into the sitting room, where she immediately turned on the small television set. Today was November 6th, the day the results of the referendum would be announced.

She watched the faces on the black-and-white TV screen. Black-and-white – what a neat approximation of the South African world that was! How naive she had always been. But at least she had never been rude or callous to black people. And now it was Anna – her black servant, Anna – who had helped her through this terrible time, coming to see her regularly, giving her tender words of advice about Morgan and, best of all, just caring about her. Now Anna's husband was a frightened man. Marie shuddered again as she remembered what Anna had told her: how Dolph had humiliated her husband, Joseph. In her heart, Marie knew she, Marie Jantjies, would get her revenge.

She hugged the child tightly to her and felt his little face press against her bosom. She unbuttoned the front of her dress, slid out a breast and enjoyed the pleasant sensation of suckling him. Outside, the rain drummed on the tin roof; she could hear the noise above the sound of the TV. Her sitting room was sparsely furnished, just a couple of cheap sofas, and a red nylon carpet over frayed linoleum tiles. She looked down at her son, Morgan. He was her strength; with him she would survive, no matter what the hardship.

She had voted the previous evening, against the bill, in support of Kobus van der Post. Her new classification as a coloured still gave her the right to vote – it was only blacks who did not have the right.

Now, as she watched, the face of David Loxton flashed onto the television screen, followed by a footage of Dolph in full flow. Dolph thought she had slept with a black man – well, she wished she had. A black man would have been proud of his son and the woman who had borne him. It was Dolph who was abnormal, a perverted fanatic.

She carried the child, now sleepy with milk, over to the simple table in the corner of the room, and sitting down with him on her lap, opened her text-book and began to read. The house had been paid for, so the money Dolph had provided, R600 a month, made it unnecessary for her to work provided she was prepared to live in near poverty. That was fine, she didn't need much, and she had registered to read for a legal BA at the University of South Africa next year. Now she was studying in preparation.

She had been brought up to attend to the needs of a man. She had never really questioned that role till now – but now the desire for revenge against the callousness of her people burned in her soul. Her father had sided with Dolph. At first she could not believe it, then she had understood. He too was a man without feelings.

There was a knock at the door, and Marie started. Who could it be at this time of the morning? Anna had said she would not come again until the weekend, so it could not be her. Marie knew very few people in Riverlea. The coloured community was still suspicious of this white woman with the coloured child who had suddenly been thrust into their midst.

She got up, put Morgan down on the sofa and went slowly to the door. The child started to cry the moment he knew he was alone.

She stood a few minutes before opening the front door – scared. She knew she was being watched by the police, which was perhaps why the local people were so wary of her. At last she opened the door – and saw her mother standing outside in the pouring rain, ashen-faced. Marie realised the courage it must have taken for her to come. She took her mother in her arms, then led her into the little house and closed the door behind them.

They stood staring at each other. 'How did you find me?' Marie stammered.

'Anna told me . . . You thought I approved of this?'

'No, Ma, I could never think you capable of that.'

She looked at her mother closely, seeing this woman she had known all her life in a new light. She stared at the still-young skin, the gaunt figure that was such a contrast to her own, the black hair turning to grey. Then the baby cried loudly in the room beyond the tiny hall.

'I want to see him, Marie.'

They went into the sitting room, and her mother took the baby into her arms. She rocked him slowly, so that he stopped crying and began to gurgle. 'It's Dolph's child,' her mother said. 'His mouth. His eyes.'

Marie felt the rage building in her again. 'No, it's not. He doesn't deserve a child.'

'You're right, he doesn't. What's his name?'

'Morgan. Where's Pa, Ma?'

'Waiting with Dolph at party headquarters. Waiting to celebrate the victory of David Loxton's security bill.'

'Does Pa know you're here?'

Her mother looked up at her with an intense expression on her face. 'I don't care whether he does or not, Marie. I never thought he could be such a bastard.'

Marie was taken aback. She had never heard her mother swear, or for that matter say anything negative about her husband.

185

'I will not leave him, Marie,' her mother said now. 'But I will never abandon you as he has chosen to do. You see, I was married in the traditional way, so that everything I once owned belongs to him, and if I left him, that would be the end of me. But this way, if we are secret about it, at least I can help you. Believe me, it's the only help you're going to get.'

'I am going to become a part of Riverlea, Ma.'

'You are white – they will never accept you.'

'I will earn their respect, Ma. Morgan is one of them, therefore I am too.'

They sat and talked for a long time. Then Marie got up and went to the kitchen to get Morgan some apple juice, while her mother watched the television and rocked the child in her arms. Marie had almost finished filling the bottle when her mother ran into the kitchen.

'Come quickly! The news – you cannot believe what has happened!

It was only a matter of waiting for the official result now, because David Loxton was absolutely confident that his bill had been passed by the nation. After all, he had the full support of Klopper's followers now, and after the publicity he'd got from the Rivonia police station bombing, his image was at an all-time high, both at home and abroad. That was why he had arranged to make an address to the nation on the 7 a.m. breakfast television news. He supposed he should have discussed it with the other members of the cabinet first, but then he had many enemies within the cabinet and there was always the possibility that they might have stopped him.

The studio lights came on now, and he gave a sigh of relief. Nothing could stop him now. He watched the video-camera operator focus in on Don Kent, the goodlooking anchorman. Don had a remarkable ability to ask the right questions without looking like David's lackey.

'Good morning,' said Don Kent. 'Today is a time for hope and optimism. In anticipation of an overwhelming vote in favour of his new security bill, the Minister of Justice, David Loxton, is here in the studio to give a special address.'

David concentrated on projecting himself as effectively as possible. In his mind he cast himself in the role of the great leaders of his country, strong as stone and stubborn as an ox, a

186

bulwark against the tides of black political pressure and world opinion. He stared into the camera, heard the countdown in the hidden earphone, saw the indicator – and he was on the air.

'I feel deeply privileged to be here this morning. My security bill is a guarantee that you'll all be able to sleep easy at night, knowing that the police and army are in complete control . . .'

In the monitor he could see how strongly he was coming across. He looked the very essence of a Whitehall man, wearing a Turnbull and Asser blue-and-white-striped shirt with a dark blue double-breasted suit. He was in control.

Marie Klopper held her child close as she listened to Loxton on the television. Was there a God, she asked herself, if men like David Loxton were allowed to live and have power? Oh, but she had changed so quickly! She had always seen life from her own perspective – a wealthy, white, subservient housewife. Now, a woman alone, she saw South Africa through the eyes of another people – a people whose dignity had been stripped away by apartheid. Marie realised that if Loxton was behaving like this, he was thinking along the same lines as Dolph. They were in league, she knew it. But Dolph would use Loxton as a stepping-stone to the State Presidency. And if Dolph could treat her, his own wife, like a piece of unwanted baggage, then how would he treat the twenty million black and coloured people among whom she was now classified?

She made a silent vow to herself. However long she lived, she would fight this apartheid, this horrific doctrine of separateness.

Morgan looked up into her eyes, and she bent over him. 'Yes, my darling,' she whispered, 'you shall understand this horror. You shall never know who your father was. I will teach you to fight this thing, and you will be part of a better South Africa.'

She looked again at the face of David Loxton on the television screen. If there was anything she could do to thwart him or her husband, she would do it – no matter what the danger.

David Loxton had driven home directly from the television studio, and sat now in his study with a cup of coffee. He was feeling very good. Once the referendum results were announced, he would close in quickly on Van der Post – whose health would probably collapse under the strain! And after Van der Post was gone, he'd bring in Klopper.

The phone rang, and he picked it up immediately.

'Yes? Of course. I'll come over immediately. Thank you.'

When he put the receiver down, his face was drained of all colour.

It was nine thirty. Don Kent appeared on screen, red-faced and nervous. His normally sleek hair was in disarray, his tortoiseshell glasses perched precariously at the end of his nose. He owed his fame and future to David Loxton. If Loxton fell from power, Don Kent knew he would be out of a job.

And here are the final results,' he said. 'The new security bill has been defeated by ninety-seven votes!'

The room was shabby, dimly lit by a naked, dirty bulb. The walls had once been white but were now a dark yellow, and the table was scarred with coffee stains and cigarette burns. On the far wall a large map of Africa hung in a beautiful wooden frame that contrasted strangely with the rest of the room, and below it, at the head of the table, sat a man, slim and malevolent. He was dressed in a denim suit, his face hidden by a navy balaclava. Through the slits in the mask his eyes glistened. Next to him sat a fat man wearing dark-framed sunglasses. Against the wall, standing rigidly to attention, was George Zwane.

George was on edge. He had been summoned to this emergency meeting, in a disused warehouse just outside Soweto, in the early hours of the morning, and he didn't know why. He knew that by now he must be attracting the attention of the man who controlled the Comrades – and perhaps, his hour of vengeance had come. He had killed and killed again for the Comrades, and now commanded a large number of them. To the best of his ability he had emulated the force of evil behind the violence and murder that was running riot through the country, and his atrocities against the white population were making him a legend in the townships. His simple philosophy that the Comrades should vent their wrath against their oppressors rather than against their own people was catching on.

In the distance, now, he could hear fireworks celebrating Kobus van der Post's victory in the security bill referendum. He tried not to think about that. He knew that Van der Post could not stamp out the Comrades – and that would wreck his plans for a peaceful future.

The man in the balaclava rose from the head of the table, standing up in front of the map of Africa. He was very tall. The fat man sitting next to him pushed his dark glasses back up to the top of his nose as he stared at George Zwane.

The man in the mask spoke. 'Sit, Comrade.'

George did as he was told. This man unnerved him.

'Good – you can take orders as well as give them. I have watched you for a long time, Comrade. I can make or break you. My name to you is Kumalo.

'I know all about you, but let me tell you my story. I am the bastard son of a migrant labourer, born in Soweto in nineteen fifty-two. I never knew my mother. As soon as I could walk, I learned to survive on the streets. I fought. I gained power through terror: terror is my weapon. At fifteen I was leader of one of the biggest street gangs in Soweto. In the riots of seventy-six, I consolidated my power, and destroyed the homes of those who stood against me. Now I rule. I charge protection fees, and everyone pays. I control the supply of liquor, drugs and prostitutes in this town. Those who cross me, die in agony. And now I intend to control the whole country . . .'

There was a gleam in Kumalo's eyes. He went on quickly: 'Van der Post seeks to negotiate with the moderate black leaders, and these discussions threaten my power-base. I do not want these moderates in control of the army and the police force – it must never happen. I shall achieve what I want by killing, and I have decided that you, George Zwane, will be my new agent of death.'

Kumalo looked down at the fat man in the dark shades. 'Call Letsoko.' The fat man waddled to a side door, his enormous buttocks swaying as he moved, and whispered something into the darkness. George knew of Letsoko. He had heard people speak of him in hushed tones as the one being groomed to lead.

Letsoko came into the room, a short, ungainly man with greasy hair matted into dreadlocks. He looked at George with contempt, then at Kumalo.

'Letsoko, are you loyal to my cause?'

'Yes, Comrade Kumalo. I would die for you,' Letsoko answered confidently.

'Such loyalty must be tested. I have chosen Comrade Zwane to be your successor. Now you must die for me.'

Kumalo stepped back, picked up a sawn-off shotgun and pushed the barrel into Letsoko's mouth.

'Suck the barrel, my friend.'

The weapon exploded, and blood and brain spattered around the room.

George's face was plastered with this bloody debris. He felt the fear in his bones. This was the man behind the violence, now he knew for certain. This must be the man who had dared to kill his father.

Kumalo sat down, laying the shotgun on the table, and the fat man next to him rose with difficulty. 'Comrade Kumalo has spoken,' he said. 'He has decided that you will replace Letsoko. What do you say, Comrade Zwane?'

George stared at the bloody corpse of Letsoko, too stunned to utter a word.

Kumalo leaned back lazily in his chair, taking the shotgun and pointing it directly at him. 'I have your wife, Zwane – you will do as I order.'

George felt his bowels loosen.

'You, George Zwane! You will kill Van der Post!'

Kumalo grinned when he saw the expression on George Zwane's face. He wanted to destroy this smart-arsed lawyer. He knew Zwane had been friendly with the white bitch Victoria Loxton, and she was very close to Van der Post – he'd seen their picture in the papers. Killing Van der Post would destroy Zwane – and Kumalo liked to destroy his enemies, very slowly.

The torture had gone on for weeks now. It was the unpredictability of it that destroyed his soul.

Sometimes he remembered the last moments of his freedom, getting off the bus, walking away from the bus stop and thinking how easy it had been. The sirens in the distance seemed not to have anything to do with him, and it was only when they got closer that he had started to run.

They caught him minutes later. He'd been really badly beaten up. Three of them had got out of the car and started to kick him. Then he passed out, and woke up in the boot of the car, knowing that they were taking him to the police station. He was nauseous from the smell of petrol and the fear, and he could not move, for his hands and feet were firmly bound. He was grateful for that journey, all the same. It had given him a chance to compose himself, and it was then that he had made the decision to die rather than disclose any information on the Comrades. He had made a vow not to inform on Comrade Zwane, his controller, but now Marc knew that vow would be put to the test, and he was determined not to break.

At the station they had taken his fingerprints and his photograph, and then they'd taken him to a cell and given him another beating. They seemed to take great pleasure in it, smiling and talking to each other between blows.

He'd lost a lot of weight since then. He hadn't seen a soul except for the warders and the police. They'd let a doctor in once, but Marc was only allowed to answer the doctor's questions by nodding or shaking his head. And yet despite the torture and the isolation, he could feel he was winning. Of course, the best thing would be death; then they wouldn't be able to do anything more to him. Already he'd lost most of his teeth and quite a few nails, but he hadn't told the bastards anything worth knowing. He had always been such a coward at school, now he surprised himself. What else could they do to him?

As if in answer, the door of his cell opened and an attractive woman with dark hair walked in. She stood looking down at him and smiling.

'Hallo, I've come to look after you, Marc. My name's Jackie.'

She spoke with a slight Afrikaans accent. He did not reply. This, he had learnt, was the first important step towards non-cooperation.

'We know it wasn't you who did the bombing, Marc. They used you – and now they've abandoned you. You don't owe them any loyalty.'

He was bored with it. He didn't look at her. How could she work for them?

Two policemen came into the cell with a broomstick. They grabbed him, and handcuffed his wrists to his ankles behind his back, along the broomhandle. Then a rope was attached to the cuffs and the rope was put through a pulley on the ceiling. He was hoisted up, suspended by his hands and legs, facing downwards. He moved slowly round in circles.

The policemen disappeared as quickly as they had arrived, leaving him looking down at Jackie. He closed his eyes.

'Come on. You can tell me, Marc.'

He felt her hand on his face and smelt cheap perfume. She pushed him round, and he rotated like a propeller blade.

'Do you want to talk, Marc?'

He felt a bit giddy. She spun him more quickly, and he began to feel nauseous. She kept on spinning him, first one way, then the other, and he started to vomit. It was so painful, because of the way he was suspended.

'Why don't you talk to me, Marc?'

She started to spin him round again, and he wondered if he could handle much more.

Then she stopped, but his head was still spinning, and when she spoke he could not hear. She hit him hard across the face with something, and he felt blood running from his mouth. His vision cleared, and he could see that she was holding a telephone directory. She hit him hard again.

He was winning. She was the one who was losing control.

Her face was ugly, twisted with rage. 'Tell me who ordered you to park the car outside the police station, Marc. Who recruited you?'

He laughed. He had beaten her! There was nothing she would get out of him.

She pulled out a clasp knife and cut away the ropes that held him up. He fell down, his head smashing against the concrete floor. He was dizzy now, there was a ringing sound in his head. He stared at her calves, encased in the ugly blue stockings that were part of her police uniform.

Then he felt her hands undoing the waistband of his trousers, and tried desperately to move. She produced a pair of pliers, and now began slowly to crush one of his testicles.

'No! No! You fucking bitch!' He screamed out in agony.

He latched his teeth onto her ankle and passed out.

Major Piet Momberg looked at the woman in front of him. A very attractive brunette, he thought to himself, as long as you didn't pry too deeply, because inside, Jackie Steenkamp was sick.

'You overstepped the line, Steenkamp.'

'The prisoner was not co-operative, sir.'

'And the prisoner has now talked?'

'No, sir. But he will break.'

'When?'

'Next time, sir.'

He had been going to take her off the case, but they needed the name of the man who had organised the bombing. David Loxton had been putting on the pressure.

Major Momberg had seen another prisoner Jackie Steenkamp had interrogated, after the doctor had treated him: the man had been savagely and sadistically tortured. Major Momberg had thought that the doctor should have treated Jackie Steenkamp as well. But she was the best interrogator they had, and he really had no choice; if he didn't get the information out of that stubborn young man, his police career would be over. The word was out that David Loxton wanted to get the man who had organised the bombing and subject him to a public trial.

'One more chance, Steenkamp.'

He saw the sickly smile cross her face. 'Thank you, sir. That's all I'll need.'

He would not break now, Marc was certain of it. They would get nothing out of him. He felt secure now; he knew he would not break his vow.

There was a noise outside the cell door and he lay where he was. Probably the doctor again, he thought. The door opened, and two grim-faced young policemen came into the cell.

'Get up!'

He lay where he was, so they dragged him up and stripped off his clothes. Then they tied him down to the bed, so that he was spreadeagled, facing upwards.

He shivered as the cell door closed behind them and he was left alone. He did not know how long it was before it opened again. He felt like screaming when he saw her. She came up to the bed and sat down beside him.

'How are you, my poppet?'

He closed his eyes, his whole body shaking, out of control.

'I'm going to squeeze them again,' she said, 'but this time I won't be so gentle.'

His bowels caved in and, bizarrely, he felt ashamed of the mess he'd made beneath him. Then he felt the jaws of the pliers against the skin of his scrotum and started to scream.

'Zwane! Zwane! George Zwane!'

When he opened his eyes again, she was gone, and the cell door was wide open.

*

193

It was on the nine o'clock news that evening.

'Earlier this evening, the Minister of Justice, David Loxton, announced that investigations into the Rivonia police station bomb blast have revealed that George Zwane, the South African attorney wanted for murdering a policeman, was responsible.

'It is believed that Zwane is now living in Botswana, launching terrorist attacks against South Africa.

'The Minister has emphasized that the government will use every means at its disposal to bring this cold-blooded killer to justice.'

Marc had been faintly surprised that they did not give him the death penalty. Instead, it was a life sentence, and here he was, serving it. He had years and years of this to go, countless years of it . . .

The other prisoners gave him the cold shoulder. Of course, they were not politicals, so they would not understand him or his motives. To have no friends, to be shunned, was soul-destroying. And he couldn't walk properly, because there was constant pain from his crotch. He'd asked for a doctor, but the guards had just laughed.

Nothing mattered any longer. He wanted to die. He would be remembered as the Judas – the one who had turned the screw on George Zwane.

Now he pulled the piece of electrical cord from under his mattress and examined it critically. Then he stuffed it back as he heard the clomp, clomp of the guard's feet pass over the top of his cell. In his row there was no privacy, for there were no ceilings. Instead there were iron bars above him and a 40-watt bulb that glowed weakly all night long.

He had timed this guard often. It would be ten minutes before the man came overhead again.

He grabbed the cord from under the mattress and wrapped it round the bars above him, then tied the other end tightly round his neck. The next moment he was suspended, swinging in the air. He went dizzy as the cord bit into his throat. Then he blacked out.

The guard stared down at the man swinging by his neck from the bars. Then he pulled a clasp knife out of his pocket and cut through the cord, so that the body crashed down on to the concrete below.

194

He watched and waited. Sure enough, after ten minutes the prisoner started moving. That was fine. The bastard had no right to die – the policemen and the women he had killed at the Rivonia police station must be avenged. Major Piet Momberg's words echoed in his mind: this prisoner was not to die, he must be watched carefully because he would be a key witness when they caught George Zwane.

He looked down again and saw that the prisoner's eyes were open. They would move him to the cooler in the morning – the windowless concrete cell at the end of the row, so tiny that a man could not sit up straight in it. He laughed aloud, and resumed his patrol.

Kobus van der Post closed the door of the cabinet room behind him and walked grimly away down the corridor. He had seen the quiet smile on David Loxton's face as they discussed the escalating violence in the townships. Loxton had advocated a crackdown, a regime even fiercer than the one already in force – mass arrests and martial law. But Kobus had argued against him, and he had carried sixty per cent of the cabinet with him, and now the decision was made. On January 5th Kobus would address the the township dwellers at a public meeting, and would make an offer of conciliation.

It would be an historic speech. He would make it in the centre of Johannesburg, from the steps of the public library. He would put an end to Loxton's arrests without trial, and hopefully would win him the grass-roots support of the black population. And hopefully would finally stem the violence.

Treason was the word that kept beating in David Loxton's brain as he drove home from the cabinet meeting. All his plans overthrown! Van der Post could be in power for at least five years, during which time things would change a great deal. His chances of ruling South Africa were fading into nothingness.

Now he and Klopper must make new plans. They had the support of the army, at least. So one attempt to overthrow Van der Post had failed – but there were other ways, and these would now have to be explored.

So Kobus van der Post was to make a major announcement to the people on January 5th. What did that herald? Would anything

195

really change? George Zwane should have rejoiced in the feeling of optimism that was running through Soweto township, that vibrant, angry black scar to the south-west of Johannesburg. But George had been a frustrated man of peace for too long and he no longer believed in peaceful initiatives. He knew in his heart now that violence was the only answer – and it was violence he carried in the guitar case that was slung over his shoulder as he trudged along the dirty streets of the township.

George wasn't going to give power away to anyone. He was going to kill Kumalo, and take Kumalo's power for himself. He had chosen two of the Comrades, men whom he knew were loyal to him, for this task.

He came to the tin shanty where they'd agreed to meet, and knocked on the door, but there was no reply. He knocked again, and this time the door swung open, creaking on its loose hinges. A strange smell wafted out to him. He could not see much in the dark interior of the shanty; the only light came through breaks in the corrugated-iron roof, faint shafts of sunlight in the darkness. Then, looming in the darkness, he saw two men, both sitting, not moving or saying a word.

He went inside. He touched the first man, saw that his eyes were bulging. His shirt was soaked with blood and a noose of barbed wire had been wrapped tightly around his neck. The other had been killed with a bicycle spoke, shoved expertly between the ribs. Both bodies were still warm; they could not have been dead more than an hour.

Shit, shit, and shit again! How had Kumalo found out?

A loud whistle pierced the air. George came to his senses and bolted out of the door. From the other side of the dirt street, a young boy beckoned him, and now he could hear the sirens screaming in the distance. In an instant he was at the boy's side, following him into a shop, and they dashed behind the counter, the proprietor making way for them. The boy grabbed at George's pants, to hold him back.

Suddenly, from nowhere, police vehicles arrived, spewing out hordes of riot police, who headed straight for the shanty George had just left. They didn't open the door but started firing on the shanty immediately. George felt the sweat running down his face. He wouldn't have stood a chance.

In the distance, now, there was the sound of chanting. George saw fear written on the faces of the policemen. The commanding officer wrenched open the door of the shanty and ran inside. He appeared moments later, shouting orders.

'It's a set-up, man. That bastard Zwane isn't here, and the other two were dead before we drilled them. Let's get the fuck out of here.'

But the arrival of the police vehicles had attracted attention, and gradually a crowd had formed around them, mostly school-children and teenagers, staring angrily at the uniformed men. Now a stone hit the front light of the leading truck. There was the sound of splintering glass, and immediately the policemen were sprinting back into their trucks. Now the stones came like hail, banging against the bodywork, bouncing off the wire grilles that protected the windscreens.

Years before, the police trucks would have charged into the crowd. Now they reversed rapidly, speeding back the way they had come, and in seconds they were gone. George watched the angry children run past the front of the shop, still in pursuit.

There was another tug at his arm. He followed his new-found friend out of the back of the shop and into the narrow alleyway behind. As they walked briskly along, George saw people disappearing into their homes. An emptiness was creeping over the township: children on the warpath were a thing to be avoided.

The boy pushed him through the doorway of a brick house, and was gone before George could thank him. He made his way along the hall and came to a room where two men were sitting. Kumalo and Fat Man. They did not get up as he walked in, but merely stared at him.

Fat Man was wearing a smart blue suit, his belly flopping over the crocodile-skin belt holding up the trousers. Kumalo, tall and emaciated, was dressed in a black leather jacket and stove-pipe jeans. Both were lounging in armchairs; unrest was something they caused, not worried about.

Kumalo spoke, his voice soft and menacing. 'Sit down, Zwane. The security police want to find you so they can put the electric wires round your balls.' Fat Man farted noisily as Kumalo continued: 'They've got Marc in the solitary wing at Pretoria Central. He held out for a long time for a white boy, but now he's bleated like a lamb. Tried to kill himself, but they wouldn't let him. Do you know why?'

George looked at Kumalo's ugly face. For the first time he noticed that one eye was permanently weeping.

'No. Why?'

'Because they want him for your trial. They'll break you first, and then they'll put you on the stand. They'll hang you, Zwane!'

Kumalo raised the pistol he always had with him and levelled it at George's chest. 'I know what you were planning. That's why I had those bastards killed. I'd have let the security police take you, but I want you to kill Van der Post.'

George shivered.

'Bring the bitch in!' Kumalo commanded.

Two men dragged Brenda into the room in front of George. She was crying and could not look him in the eyes. In an instant he knew that they had raped her.

Kumalo grinned at George. 'You take my threats idly, don't you, Zwane? Well, all my men have had her. And there'll be worse if you try anything else!'

Brenda raised her head and looked into George's eyes – a look of desperation. It was all his fault. The tears began to run from her eyes, and he wished that he could die.

Fat Man contemplated the folds of his stomach. He was now alone in the room with Kumalo; the faint smell of burnt flesh was the only reminder of what had taken place earlier.

Fat Man handed Kumalo the hip flask. 'You should have had Zwane killed. What do we want with the stupid, idealistic bastard?'

Kumalo smiled. 'Fat Man, Zwane is merely a pawn in our game. He will be sacrificed, naturally.'

Fat Man took the hip flask back and pushed it to his lips, taking a big slug, then looked again at Kumalo. 'I always underestimate you.'

'Zwane is a hero, Fat Man. He's got too much power. I want him out of the way, but I don't want to be implicated. So, I let Zwane kill Van der Post. Then he'll be an even bigger hero! But of course, he'll be arrested, tried and hanged – and his arrest and trial will fuel the anger that we have been building in the township for the past year.'

'How can we be sure Zwane will be caught?'

'Because we will give him away!'

Fat Man roared with laughter. It was a good plan, even better than he could have devised himself.

He sat on the bench in the late afternoon sun, feeling dirty and depressed. He took another swig from the wine bottle wrapped inside the brown paper packet, then belched loudly. None of the white people walking from the library, trying to beat the rush hour, took any notice of him. All they were aware of was another dirty, impoverished black.

He lay back and cocked his eyes up to the skyline. He followed the upper edges of the smart new office blocks. They were of no use to him – on the new buildings the security was too good. He needed an older building, where people didn't care too much about what went on.

Just before sunset he made his choice: an old block built in the 1950s, with a discount bazaar at street level and disused offices above. Against the skyline there was a line of washing hung out to dry. Someone lived up there on the roof, and all he had to do was get to know them.

He waited till darkness to make his approach. There was an alley further down the street and he slunk into it, weaving in and out between the rubbish bins. He could hear the rats scuttling around in the darkness. There was a rickety-looking fire escape that clung tenuously to the back of the building like some strange plant. At the bottom of it was the usual combination of locks and barbed wire, but he climbed over these without difficulty and began to ascend the rusted metal steps as quietly as possible.

The roof was quiet and eerie. He pulled himself up over the parapet, unafraid of the drop below him, concentrating on the faint light that came from a small concrete structure in the centre of the flat roof.

He peered through the door. An old man with a grey, wrinkled beard sat trying to read a newspaper. Next to him was a paraffin stove, and on the table the remains of what had been his dinner. George saw from the man's face that he was a Zulu, and this was good – but he still wasn't going to take any chances.

He drew the knife from inside his shirt and moved noiselessly through the door. He was on the old man before he knew what was happening. As the knife blade was pushed against his throat, the man cried out in Zulu: 'No! No! I am an old man. I have two wives and many children to support.'

199

George pushed the blade harder against the wrinkled folds of the old man's skin. The first drops of blood slid down the blade. Such savagery was necessary. The man's body sagged against his own and George felt a great sadness. This man would probably die for what he was about to ask him to do, but George had no choice.

'Old man. In exchange for your life, you must help me.'

'Anything.'

'Are you sure?'

'Whatever you want. Take it.'

'I want nothing that you own. I want you to help me. I will live here for the next two weeks, and no one must know I'm here. If they should find me, tell them I'm your son. You will buy food for me, and collect something from a locker at Johannesburg Station for me.'

The old man was silent. Clearly he was perplexed, and expected something more.

'Do you agree?'

'Yes.'

'What is your name?'

'Solomon.'

'I hope you are as wise as King Solomon in the Bible, then you will live for many more years. Should you betray me, you will die.' He let the old man drop onto the floor, and waited.

At first George thought he might have overdone the strong-arm act, but eventually the old man rose to his feet and felt his neck. Then he stared at George.

'I thought you wanted to steal everything I had.'

'I want nothing of yours.'

'If you had asked me for a place I would have given it to you.'

'It is good, Solomon, that I forced you to give it to me. Don't ask any more questions.'

The old man nodded. Then he went to a cupboard in the corner of the room and pulled out a huge blanket. He indicated to George that the bed was his.

'No, Solomon. I am still young. I'll sleep on the floor.'

The old man turned out the light and without a word they both fell asleep – the terrified old man, and the young lawyer who was now an agent of death.

*

George was up with the first light of dawn, and out on the roof, staring down at the steps of the public library. The position was better than he had imagined it would be – he had a clear, uninterrupted view. Even better for his purpose was the housing of the lift winding gear on his immediate left, a sort of hut standing out like a miniature castle from the roof, with slits in the side to let in the light. He tried the door, but it was locked. He would have to get some tools and break in, unless the old man had a key.

The smell of cooking floated in the air, and he walked back across the flat roof to the dwelling at its centre. The old man was up, and cooking pap on the paraffin stove. He looked up sourly as George came in through the door.

'I have worked in this building for twenty years. It is a nice life. Now you come and threaten to take it away from me.'

'At least you are alive, Solomon.'

The old man's wrinkled hands shook as he served up the porridge. George steeled himself; he could not allow sentiment to sway him from his task. The old man handed him a plate of pap which George ate quickly, then Solomon cleaned out the metal pot and filled it with fresh water, and they both watched the stove in silence, waiting for the water to boil. A heavy, familiar sadness weighed on George, because of the old man's poverty, his dependence on the owner of the building for his livelihood, the lack of any security for his old age. Poverty was a part of Africa, there was no freedom from it. The only freedom that could be given to a man was his right to live where he wanted to, to choose a government, to own a house and to travel freely. But how many years would it be before those freedoms were achieved?

The coffee tasted good, and it brought George back to reality. He took the key out of his jacket pocket and handed it to the old man.

'Solomon, this morning you will go to the luggage lockers at Johannesburg Station. You will find number five hundred and eleven and open it. Inside you will find a guitar case and a large canvas bag. You will take both, and relock the locker.'

He took a wad of notes from his pocket and handed it to the old man. 'With this, Solomon, you will buy us food for the next two weeks.'

'It is too much,' the old man said.

201

'Buy whatever you want to.'

Solomon got up to leave, but George gripped him by the wrist. 'One more thing. The room that houses the lift winding gear – you have a key for it?'

The old man took a bunch of keys from his pocket and removed an old rusted key which he handed to George. Then he set off, down the building's internal staircase.

George waited a while. He was sure he could trust his host, but he did not want to give the game away. Only when he had seen the old man emerge from the bottom of the building did he return to the concrete room housing the winding gear.

The lock did not turn easily, and for a moment he thought that Solomon might have given him the wrong key. Then he heard a click, and he turned the rusty handle.

The inside was musty, and there were rat droppings everywhere. He was about to go inside when the winding gear started up with a deafening racket. George clutched the door of the room, sweating heavily. He hadn't realised his nerves were as bad as this. He must pull himself together. He was on his own, no one would help him if anything went wrong.

When he had calmed down again, he went back inside the room and saw to his delight that it was perfect for his purpose. He could see out through the slits in the wall and down to the steps of the library, but from the ground and from the air he would be invisible. It was perfect. Nothing could stop him now.

The 'death' of his wife, Dolph reflected, had had one unexpected benefit. Without his realising it, Marie had been drawing him away from his father, and now that she was gone, they were much closer. Maybe it was true, maybe Marie had been an agent of the devil.

The old coloured woman was waiting for him as he came up the drive to the family farm. As usual, she was grinning, but for some reason he had never resented her. He knew he should be grateful to her, because she had been with his father since he had been born and his mother had died. This kaffir had known his mother, and for that reason he was also deeply envious of her.

'*Môre*, Figi,' he greeted her, in Afrikaans. As far as he knew, she spoke no English.

'*Môre*, Dolph.'

'How goes my pa?'

'Well, master, he seems a bit down.'

Dolph could never understand why his father did not move into town. The old man wasn't poor, he could have bought a big house and had plenty of servants, but instead he chose to live out here on the farm, with no one but this ageing coloured woman for company.

He went in, and was pleased to see that everything was immaculately clean as usual. Figi was certainly a good house-keeper, he couldn't deny that. As always, the place was dark inside, but then it always had been, and he knew his way around the old crumbling farmstead from boyhood.

'Dolph?'

The old man's voice in the darkness thrilled his heart. Yes, it was better since Marie had gone, much better.

'Pa, it's me.'

'Sit down, my son. Are you over it yet?'

He hadn't told his father the truth about Marie, about the coloured baby. He was ashamed of the whole incident and felt that his father might say it was a punishment from God. So, instead, he had told his father the story that he had given to the world, that Marie and the baby had died at birth.

'The work is helping me to forget, Pa. I try not to think of it, I try to keep my mind on our cause, that is the best medicine for me.' He was silent for a while, staring down at his hands. 'I think I have the support of the army, Pa. They hate Van der Post.'

'That is good. I also have not been idle. I have talked to my friends in Europe – friends with influence.'

'What will they do?'

'The international support Van der Post seeks will not be forthcoming.'

Dolph sat in silence, wondering how his next comment might be received. 'Loxton has spoken to me again,' he said. 'He wants to join us.'

'This coalition – would it oust Van der Post?'

'No. But if something happened to Van der Post and the government collapsed, there would be an election, and we would win the majority.'

'You will kill Van der Post, then?'

'He's a traitor.'

'Act quickly, before he talks to the kaffirs.'

'That is precisely when we'll kill him, on January 5th when he gives his address. The world will be watching with their TV cameras.'

'It is good.'

'The speech will be on the radio too. Listen carefully, Pa.'

Victoria put the hot cup of coffee down beside Kobus on the desk, and he sat back from his typewriter, put his hands behind his head and groaned. She massaged his shoulders, slowly working the tension out of them.

'Kobus, you must get some rest – you can finish it in the morning. You mustn't worry about it, it's brilliant.'

They were in the office of Kobus' sprawling Pretoria house. Victoria had already read through the draft of Kobus' forthcoming speech, and had been deeply impressed by it.

'Yes, but will it do the trick, Vicky? I have to offer immediate and concrete solutions, but internal change is useless unless it's backed by the goodwill of the overseas governments.'

'The United Nations is behaving very strangely. I would have expected them to support you.'

'So would I. That announcement by Dr Klee yesterday completely threw me. They evidently regard me as a lying fascist.'

'It's almost as if pressure is being put on Dr Klee and the rest of the United Nations not to accept you.'

'But by whom?'

He got up from his chair and stood looking into her eyes. Then he was holding her against him.

'Vicky, I . . . I don't know what I'd have done without your support these last months. I . . .'

'I know. I feel . . . I . . .'

Her lips touched his and they kissed.

'Stay with me tonight. I need you. I feel so alone.'

She folded him in her arms.

Thirteen

The Secretary-General of the United Nations stood alone in his office high among the skyscrapers of New York and looked down at the street below him, trying to clear his mind. He'd been forgetting things lately: it was the tension. He turned back from the window and sat down at his desk. A large brown envelope lay on it – taunting, tantalising.

His buzzer sounded, and the cool, efficient tones of his secretary burst in upon the air-conditioned stillness of the room. 'Dr Klee, the meeting of the General Assembly begins in ten minutes.'

'All right, Megan, I know. I won't be late.'

'Just wanted to remind you, sir.'

The voice disappeared. He turned back to the envelope. Unable to stop himself, he took out the photograph. A young officer stared at three gaunt, naked bodies suspended from piano wire. In the background were the stark, ordered rows of the huts.

He was back there in an instant. It was always so cold there. But then there was warmth, too. It had come from the ovens next to the showers. He could still hear their screams at night in his sleep – the screams that came when they realized they weren't going for a shower. It had always amazed him, how they fought to get out of that sealed room. When they opened the doors after the allotted ten minutes, they had to struggle to get them ajar because of the bodies piled on top of each other – the men and women who had desperately tried to escape the poisoned gas.

He had been poisoned then, too. A young graduate, his head had been full of the philosophies of Schopenhauer and Nietzsche, of the primacy of the will and of a super-race.

The camp stench never left him.

He had been one of the lucky ones. He had realized that the war was fast coming to an end, and had asked for a transfer to a clerical position. It had come through a month before the Allies arrived at Dachau. Dachau, oh God, Dachau. Ulrich Klee remembered that time. He had gone into a church and started praying. He had asked God to forgive him for what he had done, and vowed that in return he would dedicate his life to peace.

He had never forgotten that vow. He had turned his back on a lucrative career and become Austria's delegate at the United Nations. Many years later he had been elected Secretary-General, on a unanimous vote.

He looked down at the photographs on his desk and knew that they would never understand – his wife, Sonja, his two sons and his daughter. What would they do if they knew?

The bastards had been clever. They must have been watching him for years, seen his steady rise to power, observed the dedication that went into everything he did. They had approached him the moment he was appointed, two years ago.

It had seemed simple, then. He had told them they disgusted him, that he felt no loyalty to the Führer, and they had gone away – and stupidly, he had thought they would leave him alone. Then they had sent him these photographs. There he was, yes, it was undisputably him – oh God – supervising people filing into the gas chambers.

They had smiled and said that he must do what they asked when the time came. That time had come a week ago, and he had done as they asked. Would God ever forgive him?

But that had not been enough for them. They had made further demands, and he had refused to obey them.

Then this further photograph had come. He had opened the envelope, unsuspecting. Where had they found it? It was of himself staring at those hanging Jews. He might have been able, somehow, to explain it away if he hadn't been smiling – a smile of pure satisfaction. . . If the press got hold of the photograph he would be finished. Sonja would divorce him, the children would hate him. All the work he had done over the years to atone for his crimes would be forgotten.

No, he could not face it. He had considered suicide, but they had told him that in that event they would make sure his name was disgraced for ever.

He could not understand what their interest in South Africa was. He himself saw Kobus van der Post as a final ray of hope. He liked what he knew of him – the man radiated an elemental goodness. But, on the instructions of his tormentors, he had advised the US and British governments to give Van der Post a hard time. He had hoped that they might ignore his advice, but naturally enough they had acted on it, and refused to acknowledge the Van der Post initiative.

Now the General Assembly meeting loomed. He had to speak; not his own words, but those of the Nazi party he had tried to escape. He was their mouthpiece now.

He hunched over the calf-skin top of his desk and wept like a child. 'Oh my God, help me!'

But there was no help. The room was quiet. The buzzer sounded, and he rose from the desk in sudden fright.

'You must leave now, sir, or you'll be late.'

He picked up the envelope of photographs, went over to his wall safe and locked it inside. Then he took a deep breath and composed himself. There was nothing he could do. It had been the same at Dachau; they had told him what to do, and he had done it. To fight back would have cost too much.

The conference room, when he reached it, was packed: there must be more reporters than there are delegates, he thought. The room had gone noticeably quieter as he entered, but now the hubbub was as loud as ever. He looked with annoyance at the long rows of seats filled with the representatives of countries that had no real influence in the world. They were like a pack of hyenas, waiting for a kill. Today he was about to dash the hope of peace in South Africa – and the smaller African countries would applaud his speech, giving little thought to what chaos in South Africa might do to their own fragile economies.

He rose from his chair, and immediately all attention was focused upon him. He tensed as he faced yet again the terrifying fact that what he was about to say would immediately be relayed to millions upon millions of people throughout the world, subtly influencing their thinking. His eyes swept round the room, resting briefly on the delegates from the Soviet Union and Cuba, from the USA, the German Democratic Republic and Great Britain. They all had respect for him, they would all, unfortunately, follow his lead.

'Ladies and gentlemen, we are here to implement Resolution

961/89 of the United Nations General Assembly. As the representative and leader of that body, I must advise you on the course of action I believe we must take.

'It has been said that the recent developments in South Africa herald major change. However, we have been promised major change many times before, without result.'

He looked over towards the South African representative, Jacob Snijders. He was a new appointment, had scarcely been here two days; Professor of Political Science at the University of the Witwatersrand. Dr Klee looked down at the papers on his table and wished he could explain to Professor Snijders what he was about to do.

'Even though Kobus van der Post has agreed to negotiate with the African Freedom Council,' he went on, 'I believe that, essentially, nothing has changed.'

Professor Snijders rose out of his chair as if to speak, and Ulrich Klee looked at him disapprovingly. The press cameras picked this incident up, and focused in on the furious expression that had now appeared on the Professor's usually calm face.

'Essentially, nothing has changed,' Dr Klee repeated. 'I believe, therefore, that our policy should take an even harder line than before. Stiffer sanctions; penalties for countries buying arms or any other goods from South Africa; the immediate closure of South African consulates and embassies around the world. In short, we must tighten the noose.'

He couldn't believe the outburst of applause. They were following him like a pack of lemmings and he felt like crying. Hadn't they read the reports of what Kobus van der Post was doing? There was real change taking place in South Africa, no doubt about it.

Sick to his stomach, he continued: 'Though this body stands for peace, on occasion, when human rights and peace itself are threatened, it must adopt a warlike stance. Now, I believe, is such a time. Our African friends need support and military assistance, and I would like to propose that we give it to them. The world has not seen a more abhorrent regime than the one currently in place in South Africa.'

How can I say this, he thought, when I remember the views I held in my youth? When I think what goes on behind the Iron Curtain, in the 'democracies' of Africa, in the South American military dictatorships?

'Gold and diamonds,' he said, 'are the lifeblood of South Africa. I propose a blanket ban on dealing in South African diamonds and gold.'

Now he saw fear etched in the faces of the British and American delegates. Neither of those countries could afford to sever their ties with South Africa completely. He was holding a loaded gun to their heads.

'Today, we have it in our power finally to snuff out this vicious and totalitarian regime. And so we will not talk to the new State President, we will merely spell out what needs to be done.'

He turned and faced the camera squarely, which was what they had asked him to do, and spoke his concluding words. 'Hand over power to the black majority immediately, Van der Post. Then we will talk, to *them*.'

Immediately, delegates were jumping over their tables, racing towards him, yelling with excitement. He looked over to Professor Snijders' chair: it was empty. The television reporters were on him in seconds. He must not avoid them – that was also a part of his orders.

An intense-looking young woman with long blond hair and tortoiseshell glasses thrust a microphone in front of his face. 'Dr Klee, how do you feel about the British Premier's stance against sanctions?'

'As you know, it is not our business here to approve or deplore the policies of our members. The British Premier has good reasons for doing what he does. However, I would ask him to re-examine his policy in the light of what I have just said.'

She pressed on. 'The British Premier says that Kobus van der Post's initiative is the most decisive step forwards in South African politics for years.'

'I think that's naive. What we are seeing in South Africa now is merely a new version of the policy that has been in force there since the Second World War.'

The reporter changed her tack. 'Are you trying to expurgate the guilt you feel because your father was a prominent Nazi?'

He felt himself trembling with rage. It was people like this who would destroy him if the photographs of him in Dachau were released. He hated what he was doing.

'The South Africans are not Nazis,' he said stiffly.

'Many sided with the Nazis during the war.'

'That is not relevant here. All we are concerned about is the present fate of the black people of South Africa. I find your reference to my father extremely tasteless.'

He was glad to see her disappear, red-faced, into the crowd of heckling journalists. He fought his way to a side door and retreated into the anonymity of a corridor. His personal body-guard followed.

'Please, Matthew,' Dr Klee said, 'I need a moment alone.'

The bodyguard still hovered in the passage while Klee went into the toilets. He locked himself inside a cubicle, and drew a hand wearily across his face. It had been worse than he had imagined it could be. He felt ashamed and degraded.

He heard someone else come into the toilets. It must be Matthew. He heard the outer door locking, the sound of foot-steps coming towards his cubicle.

'Come out, Klee.'

He recognized the accent immediately. He retreated to the back of the cubicle. 'Please, leave me alone.' But at once he regretted his cowardice.

'Not bad, Klee, not bad at all. Hide, if you want to.'

He heard the heels smack against the tiles. '*Heil Hitler!*'

'*Heil Hitler.*'

'*Ja*. That is better, Klee. You must have no doubt now who you serve. Your speech was excellent, but your comments to the press . . .'

'I'm sorry . . .'

'*Ja*. Klee, how would your wife like to see you laughing at the *Jude*? Or your children?'

'What is it that you want?'

'Your undying loyalty, Klee. You know what we will do if you do not follow our instructions to the letter?'

'Yes,' Klee replied weakly.

'Good. Now we want you to carry on as you have done today. Kobus van der Post must receive no support at all from the UN, and you must use all your influence to encourage destabilisation and war. And you must continue to emphasize your views to the United States and the other countries on whom South Africa depends.'

'But why?'

'Do not ask why, Klee. Just do it.'

He heard the footsteps going away and then the door to the

toilets closing. He sank onto the toilet seat, shaking badly. He would have to obey them, he had no choice.

'They must be out of their minds,' Saffron said.

She and Max had just been to dinner with Kobus, and were driving home along the Pretoria to Johannesburg motorway. Saffron's hair was pulled back, tightly plaited, falling like a lariat of black silk against the deeply tanned skin of her back. 'I don't understand it, Max,' she said. 'The United Nations seems to want Kobus out.'

Max's brow furrowed in concentration. He had been deeply concerned at Kobus' obvious tiredness. 'Everything hangs on this speech he's going to make. If he can just get the momentum of change going, I'm sure the rest of the world will back him.'

'But he's already had very positive feedback from the British ambassador and from the Premier.'

'I appreciate what they're doing, Saffron. But even though they're our biggest trading partner, they're just one country. What Kobus needs is the United Nations openly on his side – then this country can get going again. Then sanctions would start to be lifted, then there'd be more money, more jobs, and a chance for the black people to vote for government representation.'

'Kobus is taking it badly, isn't he?'

'Vicky told me he's not sleeping much.'

'Well, you're not, either. You must pressure Shelton to pay up.'

Max was annoyed. Saffron had obviously been looking into the development of the Okavango project, and really, it was unnecessary. 'There's nothing to worry about, everything's been signed,' he replied, a little too quickly.

'How much money do you have left?'

'I'm heavily overdrawn.'

Suddenly a truck cut in front of them, and Max had to brake hard to avoid going into it.

'What an oaf! Hell, people drive badly! All right, then, I'll call Shelton. I've shown my commitment, now he must prove his.'

In the murky confines of the little cement hut, George Zwane lifted the Dragunov out of the guitar case and cradled it for a moment in his hands. Then he moved up to the perch he had

211

made himself next to one of the slits in the wall, and raised the rifle to his shoulder. Carefully he focused the sight until the steps of the library came into view.

Perfect – a perfect line of fire down to the podium, which was being constructed now, out of scaffolding and planking. The bunting was already up. He was worried about the podium, though. Would they leave the top open? What if Van der Post was surrounded by bullet-proof glass?

'Not long now.' He muttered the words to himself. Eleven o'clock on Saturday morning, that was when the papers said the speech would be.

He repacked the guitar case and then unwrapped the large package that Solomon had brought him. Inside was the aluminium figure of eight he had asked for, a harness, and three hundred metres of nylon climbing rope. These he would use to abseil down the back of the building immediately after the assassination. He stowed them carefully inside a cardboard box which he put in one corner of the room, then he walked out into the sunlight and locked the door of the lift room behind him. He stretched briefly, released from the confines of the hut, then walked over to the parapet and stared down at the busy street below.

What if he had another chance to live again? Would he choose the same course? He thought of Brenda, of Kumalo, and wondered if he should have followed the example of his younger brother Malcolm and gone to live abroad, away from this hell on earth. What of his own children? God, his life was destroyed! But whatever happened, he would get his revenge on Kumalo.

He went back into the tiny servant's room on the roof and smelt the stink of the paraffin stove. At least he had to spend only one more night here, and then he would be away from this place for ever.

John Packard smiled to himself. He looked down at the computer print-out, then up at Shelton.

'Good work – he's hopelessly over-committed.'

'It wasn't easy, old chap.'

'You'll phone Proust?'

'My pleasure.'

Packard watched with satisfaction as Shelton dialled the

number of the Swiss bank. He knew Saffron – she'd come running back once Loxton was broke.

'Monsieur Proust . . . Very well, thank you. Er, how shall I put this . . .? I have a slight problem . . . That loan to Max Loxton . . .'

Packard listened, his lips thin with excitement. Max Loxton and his project had just become history.

In the thick darkness David Loxton turned his car down the long drive that led to the Onderstepoort veterinary school. He smiled wryly to himself; the last thing on his mind was animals and their welfare. The dazzling light of the front headlights picked up the oak tree with the bench under it. He drew up, and switched off the engine and the lights. It was pitch black now, and utterly quiet. He felt the comforting butt of the 9mm pistol under his arm, another product of his weapons factory, already achieving excellent sales in South America.

There was a tap against his side window, and he jumped. Hurst must have been there all along, waiting for him behind the bushes. He leaned across and opened the passenger door. The light came on inside the car as Hurst stepped in, then the door closed and they were in darkness again. From previous meetings, David put together in his mind a picture of the man he could not see: tall, dark-haired, with a lean, good-looking face. The mouth did not smile, but held a sardonic grin. Major Hurst must be about forty, but he had the body of a much younger man. He had an unusual smell about him – perhaps it was the smell of death.

They shook hands, and David winced as he felt the ice-cold grip. The less he personally had to do with Hurst, the better.

'You made quite sure no one was following you?' Hurst asked.

'Absolutely. Only one other man knows about this, apart from the General.'

'Who?'

It was like a gunshot in the darkness – a ringing question that suddenly made David feel he was the weaker. It was an unusual feeling for him, and not a pleasant one.

'Dolph Klopper,' he said.

'A good man.'

So Hurst was another Klopper supporter. Almost every day

gave David fresh cause to be glad that he had won Klopper's backing.

'You are clear about your target?' he asked the Major.

'Yes, very clear. It will be a pleasure.'

David thought back to the many strange things that had happened over the years – the people who had gone away and never come back. Major Hurst was the man behind those disappearances. He was always paid cash and there were never any problems.

'I have the money for you,' David said. 'It buys your silence?'

'My silence is guaranteed. Fifty-rand notes, as I asked?'

'In packs of twenties. Fifty thousand, as agreed. It's in the boot, in a black attaché case.'

The Major seemed to relax after he had heard this, and David offered him a cigarette.

'No thanks, I want to live.'

It was said without humour. David inhaled deeply on his own cigarette and watched the tip glow in the dark. 'This will be our last meeting for a while,' he said. 'There must be no mistakes.'

'I never miss.'

'Untrue. What about Max Loxton?'

Suddenly the Major's face was very close to his. 'If anyone should ever find out about me, you and the General are next. Understood?'

'I understand.'

He was gone in seconds, leaving David alone in the big car, silently smoking his cigarette. He smiled nervously to himself, then started the car. It was actually a case of getting two jobs done at once, he thought, bumping back down the long drive. After this, Victoria would cease to be a problem, too.

It was just barely light, and a cold wind was blowing. Victoria pulled her coat closer to her and looked around her, at the podium on the library steps, the long rows of chairs that had been set out. Already the principal streets leading to the library had been blocked off; already there was an air of anticipation.

Victoria liked the centre of Johannesburg, she always had; the pioneer spirit was still here. Usually, for her, coming into Johannesburg meant going to her chambers and then to the Supreme Court. Every day of her life she faced the vast machinery of the South African police force and military system. But today was Saturday – the streets were quiet and almost empty. Today was special, because today she was going to hear Kobus give his address to the people, and for some reason – she wasn't quite sure why – she had decided to come here early, on her own, just to look around.

A piece of newspaper was tossed up by the wind in front of her. She ran after it, caught it and placed it in a rubbish bin. Then, on some inexplicable impulse, she looked upwards. She saw a black face looking down at her, then it disappeared. She thought she recognised the face, puzzled over it for a few seconds, but then dismissed it from her mind.

She walked up the steps to the library and onto the wooden podium. Below her she could see the vast area that in a few hours' time would be teeming with people. She went up to the lectern, wondering what it would feel like to stand there and make the announcement that Kobus was about to make.

Then she looked at the lines of windows in the buildings that flanked the library square, and she shivered.

Why had she looked up? George asked himself desperately. Why had she, of all people, walked along this particular street on this particular morning, of all mornings?

What they had told him in the training camp was true. You had to distance yourself from the people you knew, because they were always the ones who betrayed you or weakened your spirit. That was why he had seen as little of Brenda as possible. But now he wished he'd seen more of her; he wished he had weakened.

The roof was empty but for him; he had sent Solomon down to Natal with a letter. He just hoped Solomon would stick to the story when the Security Police got hold of him. Of course they would question him, and in the letter he had told Solomon to tell them everything; to say that he had been forced against his will to share his pathetic little room-sized home with George Zwane, killer and revolutionary.

He went back to the lift room and pulled the Dragunov out of its case for the last time. He picked up the ten-round magazine. Each bullet had been carefully checked: he could not afford a misfire, there would be no excuse for failing.

He examined the weapon very closely. It was gas-operated, with the same rotating-bolt breech as the Kalashnikov, but the

215

trigger system and barrel were designed specially for this particular weapon. This Dragunov was also fitted with flash-suppressor and a recoil compensator to hold it firmly on the target. He drew the wooden stock into his shoulder and focused the telescopic sight. At target practice, they had said he was a natural.

There she was again, in the hairlines, standing on the podium where Kobus would be in five hours' time. God, why was he shaking so much?

He put the rifle carefully down and then went back to the tiny servant's room to make himself some tea. It was going to be a long wait. He had to steady his nerves.

The funeral-black, long-wheelbase Mercedes-Benz swept along the motorway. On either side, and to front and rear, motorcycle outriders kept pace with it, turning on their sirens whenever a vehicle blocked their way. Inside, behind the chauffeur, sat two men, both immaculately groomed, both exuding power.

Kobus turned to Max. 'Twenty minutes to go.'

'Yes, my dear friend,' Max said, with great emotion. 'How does it feel to be on the verge of setting this country on a new course?'

But passionately involved as he was in what Kobus was about to do today, Max couldn't seem to fix his attention on the present. He kept thinking back to the telephone call he'd received earlier that morning from Proust, the call that told him Shelton had pulled out of the deal.

He had contacted his attorneys immediately. Yes, they said, he could sue Shelton for breach of contract, but it would take at least five years to recover the money. He was broke, finished. How could he have been so stupid as to trust Shelton? But then Shelton's credentials had been excellent. In his gut, though, Max knew where he'd made his mistake. He'd been in love with the Botswanan project, he'd allowed his emotions to override his business acumen – and at a terrible cost.

That was when he'd received a second phone call, from Packard, to let him know that Shelton had been his front.

He had sat in his office alone after that, staring at the wall, opening and closing his hands.

He hadn't wanted to accompany the President, but Kobus had insisted, in fact demanded that Max be with him. He hadn't told

Saffron yet about the dealing turning sour, about Packard. He wondered how she'd react.

He looked across at Kobus, hiding his feelings with a genuine smile, and the big car swung off down the Jan Smuts Avenue ramp and past cheering students outside the University of the Witwatersrand. Kobus wound down the window and waved to them. He looked at the hope and courage written on their faces, he looked at the placards. 'Van der Post for Freedom.' 'Van der Post for Equality.'

'Hell, it makes me want to be young again, Max.'

'You're sure you don't want more security? It can still be arranged.'

'No. This has to be done openly or not at all. The foreign press corps will be there, so I don't want a heavy security presence. I must show confidence, not fear.'

'Here we are. Kobus – good luck.' Max pumped Kobus' hand, then hugged him.

They both got out of the car to face a barrage of reporters. Several cabinet ministers moved forward to greet them, microphones and video cameras were everywhere, questions were hurled – but Kobus, ignoring them, made his way calmly up the steps of the library and onto the podium.

The crowd contained both black and white, there was a carnival atmosphere. Max had never seen such spirit before, and he knew why. For the first time in his life he was witnessing a massed gathering in South Africa where the army and police were not present.

Saffron appeared from behind him, and gripped his hand tightly. God, how could he tell her about Shelton pulling out? She had told him he was overcommitting himself, and he'd ignored her. He bent down and kissed her, and simultaneously a flash bulb went off. They pulled apart and mingled with the crowd.

Kobus stepped onto the podium.

The crowd went quiet. Max could hear the pigeons cooing in the trees as Kobus moved to the front of the small stage. For a moment he seemed to hesitate, but it was only to turn and greet Vicky. After that he went forward to the lectern.

The applause was deafening. It filled the streets and swept around the square in waves. The film and television cameras

217

were madly filming it, overcome by the sheer exuberance of the people who had assembled here in the streets of Johannesburg.

Kobus angled the microphone towards his mouth.

'One people!'

The cry echoed through the square, followed by a wave of applause.

Kobus raised his hands in the air, and the crowd went quiet.

'There have been so many speeches made in this country that we have all got sick of them. Promises have been made, promises have been broken.

'I am going to ask something of every South African today. One simple thing: courage.

'There will be no more reform. Reform says that there is something to be reformed. I will scrap every single discriminatory law that has ever been passed. I will introduce black representation at the highest levels of government. You will be able to vote for your own people.'

Now it was deadly quiet. Max could hear the noise of the TV cameras as they relayed this startling speech to the world.

'Freedom, that is what I am pledging to every South African . . .'

The sound of the shot, and the sight of the blood erupting from Kobus van der Post's chest, were simultaneous. He sagged forwards over the microphone.

'Oh, my God . . .'

His last words echoed in the silence as the second shot hit him in the face and the third in the neck. He crumpled to the ground. Vicky was there in an instant, screaming, hysterical.

Max looked around desperately, but all he could see were cameras and reporters as he pushed through the crowd.

Vicky looked up at him, her face covered with blood. In her eyes there was an emptiness, a void that would never be filled again.

BOOK II

A tide of anger swept across the land like dark thunder clouds scudding over the highveld sky. In the townships the people rioted, destroying everything in their path – schools, buses, houses – so that for a few days it seemed as if the country was on the verge of anarchy. Then with well-oiled precision, the army moved into the townships, and long fences or razor-wire piled out of massive trucks, encircling the pockets of violence. The people turned on themselves then, looting, raping and burning; hundreds died victim to the necklace while the men in uniform looked on impassively. The television crews relayed it to an outside world which watched in silent horror.

Kobus van der Post's funeral was a dismal affair, a simple service and cremation attended by a few black leaders. For Victoria Loxton it seemed as if the world had ended. She handed her practice over to Ken Silke and took a one-way ticket to London. Everything in the country she loved so much reminded her of Kobus. In her womb she carried his child, and it was this child that gave her the will to carry on – to continue her legal career in Britain.

But in her heart was a heaviness that would not go away. The man who had killed Kobus had been one of her closest, most intimate friends – George Zwane, who now languished in Pretoria Central prison. All her life she had fought for the things that he believed in – for equal rights and representation for the black peoples of South Africa. These were things that she was prepared to die for. But as she looked into George's dark eyes when she visited him that last time in jail, she had found herself questioning the very substance of her beliefs. She had refused to give in to

221

these negative thoughts, but she had realised she must leave South Africa for a time – distance herself from the events that threatened to destroy her.

In England she would take on corporate work rather than criminal cases, and concentrate on bringing up her child. Lucinda went with her, also determined to forget the past; in London Vicky hoped to nurture Lucinda's very considerable artistic talent. Perhaps, just perhaps, things might take a turn for the better.

Max was a broken man. After Kobus' death he had started drinking heavily, and he had split up with Saffron, who continued to blame him for trusting Shelton too much. As a result Max had gone back to the Okavango, determined to try and salvage what was left of his project, and when Saffron followed, trying to persuade him to abandon it, he had refused to listen, letting Gumsa pole him through the beautiful waters on a makoro while he viewed the newly built foundations. Now he was in Zimbabwe, having won a tender to complete the new Houses of Parliament. He hoped the money from this venture would enable him to continue the project in the wetlands.

Saffron, Vicky knew, was making a big feature. And she also knew why: Saffron, too, was determined to make enough money to try and salvage what was left of Max's dream. Vicky passionately hoped that Max would come to his senses before too long; he'd never find another woman who loved him as much as Saffron – a woman who could stand up to him, too. He was destroying himself in his drunken despair.

Their father – Vicky's and Max's – had, together with many of his fellow ministers, defected from the ruling party to join Dolph Klopper's AWB. A general election was then held in an atmosphere of fear and intimidation, and the AWB gained power, with Dolph Klopper as State President and David Loxton as Minister of Justice.

One

She pushed the pram past Harrods, heading in the direction of Knightsbridge tube station, before turning left towards Hyde Park. She had to wait some time before she could safely cross the main road, and then she was in the park, walking among the people who lay sunning themselves on the rolling green lawns by the Serpentine. She walked up The Ring and over the bridge dividing the Serpentine from the Long Water. Eventually she parked the pram next to an empty green bench, and took the baby out. Sitting down with him, she kissed him on the forehead and then started to rock him.

A pleasant-looking old man in a Harris tweed jacket and a cloth cap sat down on the other end of the bench.

'Beautiful child,' he said.

'Thank you. Fortunately he's on his best behaviour.'

He could not quite place the accent. He glanced at her again. He'd always liked his women rather more voluptuous, but this one could certainly turn heads. He wondered who the lucky father might be.

'You obviously enjoy Hyde Park,' he ventured.

'I've come here nearly every day since I came to London a year ago.'

'Ah, your husband was transferred here from abroad?'

'No – I've never been married.'

At his age he could hardly approve of that, but really, it was so common these days that one just had to take it in one's stride. 'There's no better place in the world than Hyde Park on a pleasant summer's day,' he said.

The baby started to cry, a loud, bawling noise. 'There, there, Kobus, it's all right.' She hugged him close, and immediately he calmed down and nestled in to her.

The old man smiled, pushing his wire-framed glasses back up his nose. 'An unusual Christian name.'

'It was his father's. He was an Afrikaner.'

'Mm, a South African. Can't say I agree with their politics.'

'Nor did he.'

'Oh. That's why you came to London?'

'Something like that. I was a civil rights lawyer there. Now, I'm waiting for admission to the London bar, so I can practise here. And you? Tell me about yourself?'

'Ah, I've been with the army all my life. At Sandhurst. . .'

It was nearly dark when she got back to the house, a Georgian villa in a pretty little South Kensington square. She carried Kobus up the steps and unlocked the front door, and was pleased to see that Sarah, the nanny, was waiting to take the baby from her. Then she went back down to fetch the pram.

Sarah saw that her employer had been crying again. She wished she knew the whole story about Miss Loxton. She'd managed to glean some information from the articles in the papers last year, but there was still a lot she didn't understand, and Miss Loxton would never talk about it. Then there was her red-haired sister Lucinda, the artist, who lived on the top two floors and was always gallivanting. Sarah had to admit they were good people to work for, though. Never a dull moment, and generous to a fault.

Lucinda looked at herself in the mirror again. Perfect! She pulled her bodice a little lower to reveal some more cleavage. The black silk dress was her favourite; it felt good against her skin, and she knew it made her look sensational. She teased out a few more locks of her flame-red hair and winked at herself. It was time to go downstairs. She could eat later at the dance, but she'd sit with Victoria while her sister had her dinner.

Lucinda's dress rustled against the black and white tiles of the hall as she made her entrance into the dining-room. It was a room she particularly liked; Vicky had chosen pink walls, edged with white, and elegant japanned chairs. It had a feeling of cheerfulness, of optimism, which her sister particularly needed, Lucinda thought. She looked across at Vicky now, and thought how different she looked from the woman who had left South

Africa a year before. She'd had her hair cut very short, giving her face extra definition, emphasizing the features – the high cheek-bones, the full lips and clear blue eyes – so that her face looked more open. Since Kobus' death Lucinda had seen a new vulnerability too. It made men want to protect her, but over the last year Lucinda had sensed Victoria retreating into herself. She hardly talked to anyone now except very close friends. It would be good when she could start work again, it would force her to be more sociable.

'You were in the park a long time,' she said.

Vicky smiled. 'I met a charming old man.'

'He tried to chat you up?' Lucinda replied gaily.

Victoria's face took on a haughty look. Oh no, thought Lucinda, I've said the wrong thing again. She decided to change the subject. 'Well, my exhibition's certainly getting talked about,' she said. 'Good reviews and bad reviews.'

Victoria had been at the opening of Lucinda's first exhibition the previous day – over twenty different paintings were on show.

'Any buyers?'

'No one yet. I gather people think my style's outrageous! But I can't help that, I just paint what I see. It's only thanks to you that I've got this far, Vicky. And it seems terribly indulgent, you know. I think I should get a job.'

'Rubbish! You're very talented, and you know it. The gallery would never have shown your work unless they thought it had merit. Did you meet anyone interesting today?'

'Yes, I had lunch with Richard Belsham, and in the afternoon he showed me round his gallery. He specialises in modern art. I think you'd like some of the pieces he's got on show, Vicky.'

'Will he buy one of your paintings?'

'He's thinking about it. "Sunset in Turmoil", that's the one he likes.'

'Lucinda, that's your best! It's disturbing. It's so powerful that it frightens me.'

The painting depicted a tortured sun over the African bush. Lucinda had already decided she would not sell it. It was her own perception of Africa; the picture was a part of her soul.

'You like Richard?' Victoria asked.

Here we go, another lecture, thought Lucinda. 'He's a bit stuck-up but a real darling,' she said. She saw that Vicky was staring hard into her green pea soup. 'Vicky, don't look like that!

It's not my fault he's married. Anyway, he says he doesn't love her any longer – all she wants is his money.'

'And she has a title?'

'Oh yes, they're the perfect society couple.'

'You're in love with him?'

'What's this, Vicky? A thousand questions?'

'I was just interested.'

'Instead of cross-examining me you should go back to work. Surely you must be close to being admitted? When Ken Silke was here last week he told me they were most impressed by you – that your admission was a formality. You know Vicky, I think he's in love with you, but you always give him the brush-off.'

Vicky grimaced. She was sick of Lucinda's attempts to try and pair her off. 'Ken is a good friend,' she said.

'Vicky . . .'

'It's not that simple, Lucinda.' Vicky's voice was harsh. 'Now, let's leave the subject, shall we? Tell me where you're off to tonight.'

'The Honourable Sarah Bond's coming-out.'

'I thought you didn't like that sort of thing?'

'I love balls . . . And Richard will be there with his wife.'

'You are the ultimate bitch, Lucinda.'

It annoyed Lucinda that Vicky could make such comments with so little emotion. Didn't she ever get excited about a man? Couldn't she understand sexual attraction any more?

'I think you should leave married men alone,' Vicky said stonily.

'For your information, they're generally better in bed. Anyway, what are *you* doing tonight?'

'I've got a lot of letters to write, and then I'm going to bed. I'm tired. Kobus was difficult today.'

'How exciting!'

Suddenly Victoria was crying, great uncontrollable sobs. 'I loved Kobus, don't you understand that!'

Lucinda went over and hugged her. 'I'm sorry. I didn't mean it. You just seem so cold.'

'Don't you realise how hopeless I feel? I met a man I truly loved, I've borne his child – and he's dead! God, it's so unfair.'

'I didn't understand, Vicky, I'm sorry. You're just so different from me. Look, I'll stay with you this evening . . .' She held Victoria's hand and stroked her hair.

'No, you go, Lucinda. I'll be fine, really I will.'

Later, Victoria watched Lucinda getting into the cab, waved to her, then closed the door. She went up to the nursery and took Kobus from his cot, hugging him in her arms. She looked down into his big, brown eyes, his father's eyes, and watched him gurgle. His eyes opened, sleepily, and he let out a stifled cry, then his hand touched her face. He watched her for a few seconds, then his eyes closed again.

'You're all I have of him now, darling.'

Tears rolled down her face as she rocked the child backwards and forwards. Later she went to her bed, hugging the little body close to her own, and somewhere in her dreams she travelled back to Africa and was happy.

Two

The car tore along the Dullstroom road at a furious rate, giving way to no one. An old man slowly pedalling his bicycle, savouring the afternoon sun, was forced off the road as the car roared past and lay in the dirt, shaking his fist at the retreating dust cloud.

The car's front and rear plates carried army registration numbers, though the man inside was not wearing a uniform. He was a lean, hard-looking man, General Jurie Smit, with a crew cut. His face had a cold look, with long vertical lines running down either side of his mouth, and grey-blue eyes that were focused on the road ahead with singular determination.

Eventually he came to a long gravel drive and turned into it, giving the sign 'Balmoral' a cursory glance. He reduced speed, and became conscious of the giant pines which lined the long drive, their shadows flickering across his windscreen. For a moment he felt a touch of envy – then cut it out of his mind with that ruthless concentration on essentials that had characterised his entire career.

The house was nestling in the trees below him – built from stone blocks, with a green corrugated-iron roof that blended in with the surrounding countryside. There was a neatness, an order about the house and the surrounding lands that was pleasing to his eye. In the open garage he saw two cars, and smiled slightly to himself. At least they were both here, and his journey would be worthwhile. So often these meetings were cancelled at the last minute. He glanced over at the leather-bound report on the seat next to him. He had waited a lifetime for this opportunity and knew that the two men he was about to meet were the only ones who could give it to him.

The house was empty, except for the servants, one of whom showed him inside. 'They're fishing, sir,' she said quietly. He had brought his own rod, and unpacked it carefully – a Hardy that his father had given him years ago. He put on his sleeveless jacket and attached some flies to it, then he pulled on a pair of green boots and strode off down the path to the river.

It was winter, so that although the trees were still green, the lands were parched and dry. The later afternoon air was cool and fresh. He could smell the running water in the distance, and a smile crossed his usually stern face. On the skyline he made out the shape of a man in camouflage – one of the many bodyguards who would be constantly patrolling the estate. Then he saw the two men he had come to meet, fishing further downstream, and he waved his greeting. He strode out into the fast-flowing waters and prepared his rod to cast. . .

They returned to the lodge just before darkness, each with a net full of trout. They didn't talk much at first, the memory of the fishing was still with them, and a continuing desire not to disturb the tranquillity of mind it had brought them. All the same, the General used this period to good advantage – quietly summing up his distinguished companions. They were Mr Dolph Klopper, the State President of South Africa, and David Loxton, whom the General already knew – David Loxton, Minister of Justice, and the second most powerful man in the cabinet. An odd partnership, the General thought, an Englishman and an Afrikaner; yet it worked brilliantly. Together they had asked him to draw up his plan. They were men of action, these two. They had seen what needed to be done, and they had done it – so that now Van der Post was dead, and not a finger could be pointed at them. And now George Zwane languished in jail, waiting to hang for the act that had horrified the world. Yes, it had been a brilliant coup, handled with faultless precision.

And now the future looked most promising – the new Defence budget was the highest in the country's history. Klopper had also reintroduced blanket military conscription, so that every white person living in the country was obliged to be on permanent call-up. Jurie smiled to himself, and the vertical lines on his face hardened. That had got rid of all the foreigners, the Englishmen, the Jews, the Portuguese. Now the nation was united as never before. And Van der Post's supporters had either changed allegiance or left the country.

A wry smile crossed the General's face as he recalled that Kobus' biggest supporter, Dr Max Loxton – reportedly bankrupt and an alcoholic – was busy on a construction project in Zimbabwe, building the new Houses of Parliament. As for the sister, the lawyer, she was evidently in London with Van der Post's illegitimate son. Ironic, Jurie thought, that a bastard like Kobus van der Post should produce another one just before he died. One had to admire the old man though, at his age. And with such a beauty!

Altogether, General Jurie Smit felt very good. The men he was with were making history, and he was proud to be with them.

In the kitchen of the lodge the servants were already preparing dinner. He gave one of them his fish, then pulled off his boots and walked into the main room where a huge fire was already burning.

This lodge, three hundred kilometres to the east of Johannesburg, and one of the oldest in the Dullstroom area, belonged to David Loxton. The main room, with its high ceiling supported on massive wooden beams, and its plain stone walls, was hung with priceless paintings which reflected David Loxton's impeccable taste. From above the cavernous fireplace a huge stag's head silently observed the proceedings below. Though the house was old, everything in it had been refurbished. Each guest room had its own dressing-room and bathroom; the floors were all of red quarry stone, and scattered with animal skins. Everything was immaculate, in fact, in typical David Loxton style. He could afford it, of course, the General reflected. His company, Terminal, produced and supplied most of the weapons and ammunition for the South African army, and his arms were of such high quality that they had become South Africa's biggest foreign currency earner after mining. Loxton's private weapons collection was also among the finest in the world. The General knew that in the gun safe at the lodge were three sets of Purdeys he would have killed for.

He looked out of the window, which was misted up from the heat of the fire. A man walked across his line of vision, another of the camouflaged security men who kept constant vigil over the farm. No point in taking risks, mused the General, no point at all.

A few moments later, Dolph Klopper and David Loxton

entered the room. Loxton strode across to the butler's tray, and examined it to see that everything had been laid out correctly.

'What's yours, Jurie?'

'Double Scotch – no water, no ice.'

'I like a man who doesn't desecrate his Scotch. The usual for you, Dolph?'

'*Ja.*'

Loxton poured brandy into a glass, added some ice and handed it to Klopper. They settled down into the comfortable couches next to the roaring blaze.

Loxton turned to the General. 'A good day's fishing?'

'Magnificent, David. Your stream is well stocked. I've not fished so well in years.'

'And before this night is over, old chap, we'll have made arrangements for an even bigger catch.

The General wore regimental evening dress for dinner, and now he sat drinking port after an excellent meal. Norman's port, he noted – only the finest in the world for David Loxton.

'*Ja*, so now we come to the reason for your visit, General.'

Klopper would be formal to the last, he thought. David Loxton was far more urbane and polished, he was the one who always handled the foreign media people. Yet as a leader he did not quite command the popular following Klopper had.

'Mr President,' the General said, 'I have everything you requested – just give me the go-ahead.'

David Loxton looked away from the flames. 'It is all as we decided?'

'Yes. We followed Dr Preusser's instructions to the letter: a large number of small charges buried deep within the concrete superstructure of the new Houses of Parliament. There'll be no sound – the entire building will just cave in.'

Klopper sat forward, his elbows resting on his knees. 'This will eliminate the Zimbabwean parliament. There'd better be no bugger-ups, or you and Loxton will carry the blame.'

The General was mesmerized by Klopper's black eyes. 'There'll be no bugger-ups,' he said stoutly. 'Hurst has been working under cover in Harare for the last three months. But he will not activate the charges – that will be handled by his operative.'

'What do you think, Minister?' Dolph turned to David Loxton who had been watching them both in silence.

'It must appear an accident. Hurst's man will obviously wait till the main building is full – we want all the key people dead. The building destroyed.'

'There'll be no evidence of the charges, sir. But we've also taken the precaution of using Eastern bloc equipment – no one will think South Africa had anything to do with it.'

Dolph got up and started to stride up and down in front of the roaring fire. 'Your forces must be at the ready, General. The rebel groups we have been supplying with weapons over the last year will take control of Zimbabwe – but we must be ready to back them up, should they need help.'

'Sir, I've organised a dummy military exercise on the border for that week.'

'Good. And keep your men under tight control. There's nothing worse than a rabble,' Dolph warned.

The General stiffened. He was proud of the discipline he had instilled in his men.

'Outside intervention?' David asked.

'I will use my own contacts to guarantee that there is no trouble from the outside,' Dolph said dismissively. How could he be so certain? the General wondered. What was the source of his power?

David Loxton got up and refilled their port glasses, then he raised his own.

'Gentlemen! To the most powerful nation in Africa.'

The cell stank. The toilet was blocked; the food, when it came, was inedible. The beatings continued. Not for information but just to destroy his spirit.

He looked up at the light above him and thought for the millionth time of Victoria Loxton. Even though it was nearly a year ago, he could still remember every detail of their meeting.

The police had caught him just after he'd left the building from which he'd aimed the shot at Van der Post. He knew he'd been set up as soon as Van der Post fell . . . He'd been running down the side streets and the back alleys to the get-away motorcycle-scrambler, but when he reached the place they'd agreed on, it wasn't there. That was when he realised, in terror, that Kumalo and Fat Man had double-crossed him. A few minutes later, the police had got him.

They started on him the moment he was in the back of the police van. They pulled off his clothes and started hitting him – not so that anything would break, but just enough to bruise badly. He'd passed out before they got to the station. Then the interrogations had really started. First they tried the conventional method: keeping him awake all night, beating him, starving him. When that didn't work they gave him the injections. There were horrific nightmares, the terrible craving for whatever it was they were pumping into him. He'd lost a lot of weight and his flesh hung loosely on his bones.

Then came the electric shock treatment. He could tell they were beginning to realise that he just wasn't going to break. Anyway, they never asked him any meaningful questions, and he knew that to tell them the truth would be a waste of time. They'd hardly be interested. All the evidence counted against him, that was all there was to it.

Then, after about seven days as he remembered it, they said he had a visitor. He had been surprised; they usually kept people much longer in detention before allowing them to see anyone. But they were cleverer than he had imagined. He was surpised, too, that there was to be no guard present. He was pushed into the bare little room and the door slammed behind him; and then Victoria Loxton entered through another door and walked up to the table he was sitting at. She didn't say a word, just sat down facing him.

The tears were running out of her eyes. Vulnerable was the last word he would ever have used to describe her, but that was how she looked now. The silence was worse than any of the tortures he'd been subjected to.

'How could you?' she said.

'I . . . I had my reasons.'

'You betrayed our friendship, our trust – you've taken away my very soul.' She collapsed on the table, sobbing.

'I had to avenge the death of my father,' George said.

She sat up and glared at him. 'By taking away the life of the man who believed in him! The man who had him released! The man whose child I carry!' She paused. 'This is goodbye, George – don't make it worse by looking for excuses.'

He felt utterly empty and alone. He wanted to escape to his cell. 'Victoria . . .'

She had got up and walked to the door, banging on it loudly and screaming for the guard to let her out. Then she was gone, and he was dragged back to his cell . . .

They didn't interrogate him for a long time after that, just left him alone. That was the worst of it, because all he could do was think of her, and realise that she would never find out the truth – that he was innocent of Kobus' death.

The trial was a farce from the beginning. Every day the Supreme Court was packed, and he had used it as a forum in which to express his beliefs. He was asked about the history of his involvement with the Comrades and his reasons for joining them, and he told them. He told them, too, the names of Kumalo and Fat Man, knowing that they'd never find them. He told them about his training, and how he had bombed the Rivonia police station.

He didn't have a chance. The white cadre, Marc, whom he'd recruited for the bombing, testified against him in the witness stand. George hated to think of what they must have done to him: he was a walking wreck, his skin a sickly white, his eyes blank as he looked at George.

Passages from the Public Prosecutor's interrogation were engraved on George's memory.

'Did you shoot Van der Post?'

'I was going to – but someone shot him before I could.'

'Produce exhibit number one. The accused will stand down. I now call the witness for the state, Dr Lourens Louw.'

Dr Lourens Louw had given a very polished performance, thought George. A distinguished-looking man, with a silver streak running through his black hair like a parting, he said that he had examined the weapon-exhibit number one – and that three shots had been fired from it. An examination of the victim's body, followed by the autopsy, revealed that the bullets that killed Van der Post had come from this weapon – the weapon that was covered with George Zwane's fingerprints.

It had been like a well-rehearsed play, thought George. The only difference was that it hadn't ended in applause, with everyone leaving the theatre. Of course, the final act was still to come: his death.

Three

The white wall round David Loxton's house stood three metres high. In front of it were two lines of security fencing topped with razor-wire, and between the lines of fencing was five metres of open space along which guard-dog patrols passed every fifteen minutes. As if that wasn't enough, both of the wire fences were electrified.

The sun hung low in the late afternoon sky and the clouds on the horizon line shone russet gold. Max stared at them for a while, almost hypnotised by their beauty, then reluctantly pulled his eyes away. The sense of apprehension returned to him, but he willed himself towards the clump of bushes over the road from the wall. Memories of childhood came back to him – memories of playing truant. Was it still there, or had they found the old tunnel and filled it in?

The bushes were thicker than he remembered, the branches had intertwined in a lattice-work that was impossible to pull apart. He pulled a hacksaw out of his rucksack and went to work, glancing through the bushes every now and again, hoping the noise of his sawing wouldn't attract attention. Sweat trickled down his face. He reached inside his jacket, felt the Browning brush against his hand, and pulled out the hip flask. The whisky tasted good. What the hell was he doing? Saffron gone, the building schedule behind time . . . Hopelessly in debt, creditors moving in on the Botswanan project . . . It didn't pay to think too much. Just one fact he needed to keep in his head: the fact that George couldn't possibly have shot Kobus from that angle, even though all the evidence pointed to it . . .

Bloody, bloody bushes. God, someone was bound to hear him.

Another slug of whisky to steady the old nerves. The noise of the blade cutting through a particularly thick branch made him cast a few anxious glances along the wall before he concentrated on his work again.

There was something black in the distance. A guard in uniform! He stood frozen, hardly breathing. You could almost hear the dog's paws on the grass. Then silence, and he was cutting again, desperately, almost crying.

Now a patrol car was going slowly past. Oh God! Had he been seen? Then there was earth, and metal bars against his fingers, and he was pulling the grid up, fastening the rope to the grid and then letting himself down into the blackness and the stink.

He switched on the torch. The tunnel was full up to the halfway mark with dank black water. He belched loudly, and laughed the light uneasy laugh of fear. The memories came flooding back. Escaping along this passage with girls in the dark of the night; beatings from his father. How he hated the bastard! He waded forwards, the slime oozing around him, bubbles breaking on the surface. The tunnel banked slowly upwards – the slime was finally down at his ankles now. He played the torchlight along the brickwork, looking for the hatch. A glance at his watch. Damnit. No time left.

Then there it was, rusted metal rungs leading up a concrete tube. He climbed upwards and put his shoulder against the metal grid at the top. It gave easily, surprising him. And no alarm bells, no barking. He was inside the grounds.

Now he moved like a hunter stalking his prey, the balaclava covering his face, the slime of the tunnel camouflaging his body. This was an impulse that had come to him one night in a drunken stupor. Get George out, and get even with his father.

He heard the hated steps. His father was as precise as a watch. He was taking his walk in the garden now, after his evening meal, with his bodyguard at a discreet distance.

Max moved in behind the bodyguard. As the man swung round, Max hit him flat on the head with a blow that knocked him out cold. Then he pulled the chloroformed duster from his pocket and padded up behind his father. He lowered the duster over his father's face, whipped out the Browning and smashed the butt into his father's head.

Loxton gave a stifled cry, then collapsed in a heap, and Max dragged him off, picking up the chloroformed rag for later use.

He heaved his father's inert body over his shoulder and started running at an even pace till he got to the open manhole cover. He dropped the unconscious body down feet first into the tunnel, then followed carefully, positioning the lid so there would be no evidence of it from above.

Another slug from the hip flask. To George Zwane, and freedom!

David Loxton came to consciousness with a violent headache. He couldn't see anything, and he was firmly trussed. All he could hear was the noise of a vehicle moving at high speed. He tried to shout out, but discovered that there was a gag through his mouth. He was in the boot of a car, he realized. He could remember going for a walk after dinner . . . but after that, nothing . . .

Much later, the vehicle stopped. He heard voices. Perhaps it was the police – the tone sounded official. Or no – perhaps a customs post? He heard the doors of the vehicle being opened, and he tried to move but couldn't.

Then there was silence. He waited, terrified. What were the bastards going to do to him? The first opportunity he got, he would try something.

Someone got into the vehicle. The engine was started, they were moving again – and he hadn't a clue where they were going. What was happening? It was only a week to go before the opening of the new Zimbabwean parliament. The wiping out of the entire Zimbabwean cabinet was to be his crowning glory and the beginning of a new phase of power politics in Africa.

Had Klopper turned on him? He couldn't quite believe that. But what other explanation could there be? The security around the house was excellent – how the hell had his abductors managed to bypass the two electric fences, the dog patrol, and the alarm system that spanned every wall? Would they negotiate with him? At least, if money was what they wanted, he had plenty . . .

Hour after hour of driving. He dropped off to sleep at last – to wake in a cold sweat when, without warning, they came to a halt. Perhaps this was a death squad and he was about to be killed. The terrifying thought came to him that he might be necklaced.

The boot was opened. The sunlight blinded him, but he could see a man in a navy balaclava, and he could smell whisky. Then a chloroformed rag was placed over his mouth and nose, and he passed out again.

*

Dolph Klopper opened the letter and studied the note with interest. Was it a hoax?

He picked up his phone and dialled Loxton's personal number.

'Hallo. Hanli, how are you? No, I was not informed,' he lied, then continued, 'Is the man all right? But how did they get in? Of course I'll get him back. Please, we must remain calm – no publicity yet. Do you understand? Get your doctor to give you a sedative.'

He carefully replaced the receiver, and read the note again. How very, very convenient. The demand was simple enough: *Release George Zwane or Loxton will die. You have one week.* It was unsigned.

He got up from the green leather chair and locked the door. Then he walked across to the big oil painting of Van Riebeeck the first governor of the Cape. He smiled as he looked into Van Riebeeck's eyes, then pulled a cigarette lighter from his pocket and ignited the ransom note. He watched the flame devour it, then crushed the blackened remains in his fist, scattering them through the open window at his side.

'Ashes to ashes, dust to dust.'

He stared reflectively into the distance for a moment or two, and then returned to his desk. As he had expected, the phone rang again within minutes.

'Hanli, don't worry. I am calling for a nation-wide search. I'll have every policeman in the country put onto it.'

He put the phone down, dialled another number and issued a few commands . . .

Twenty-five minutes later, General Smit walked into his office.

'*Môre*, Dolph.'

'*Môre*. Be seated. Would you like a coffee?'

Once they were settled, Dolph told his secretary that they were not to be disturbed, then sat back in his chair and stared into the General's pale, blue-grey eyes. He liked the steely determination in them – definitely one of the old school, the General. His father had been a leading figure in the 1940s, pushing the South African government to declare solidarity with Hitler rather than with the Allies.

Dolph switched to his native Afrikaans, instinctively preferring the language to English. 'Loxton has been kidnapped,' he said.

'How convenient. As we have discussed before, this Englishman is only of short-term value. We really do not need him any longer.'

238

'You understand me so perfectly, Jurie!'

'But of course, we must act by the book.'

'But of course. There will be TV reports – a full-scale operation. I'll make a plea myself.'

'You have received a ransom note?'

'I have just destroyed it.'

'Good. Then after a decent interval of time I will say that we have heard nothing, that we believe Loxton is dead.' The General's face hinted at a smile.

'*Ja*, the kidnappers will kill him. Then it will only be you and I who are truly in control. How very convenient it is that this has happened.'

'Sir, these kidnappers, what did they want?'

'George Zwane.'

'Well, we have just about destroyed him physically.' This time the smile on the General's face was obvious. 'It's six months to the hanging, though. Perhaps he could . . .'

'Have an accident?'

Hanli could not stop crying. She had never felt so alone. She had phoned her sons, who were both abroad on business. Dirk had immediately booked a flight home, and Rory had said he would come as quickly as matters permitted, but he was busy tying up a large deal. So for the moment she was on her own, with only the servants and the men from the National Intelligence Service for company. She could not even use the telephone any more, in case the kidnappers made contact. There was a tap on the phone, of course, so that they could be traced – but so far the phone hadn't rung.

Hanli could feel herself growing more and more agitated. She couldn't stop asking herself why the kidnappers hadn't made a demand. She had a terrible suspicion that Klopper wasn't telling her everything. She'd never liked him, though she had always made an effort to get on with him for David's sake. She sensed a sinister side to him – and now, as she sat alone in David's study, she thought of that side again. It had not escaped her notice that Dolph did not seem to be in the least disturbed by David's disappearance.

She looked down at her watch. Eight o'clock; already time for the evening news. She switched on the television and leaned back in David's chair, clutching one of his handkerchiefs.

239

'Good evening. Here is the eight o'clock news. Yesterday evening, the Minister of Justice, David Loxton, disappeared without trace from the grounds of his home. A security guard was seriously injured during the abduction. We now go across to General Jurie Smit in our Pretoria studio.'

What a cruel, callous man that is, Hanli thought as General Smit's face filled the screen. She could almost smell him; when she had met him on previous occasions, she had been uncomfortably conscious of the unusual aftershave he always wore. He was like a bull terrier, lean and powerful.

'I personally have taken command of the search for Mr Loxton,' the General said now. 'I would ask any members of the public who think they have any information as to his whereabouts to come forward. For the person or persons who have abducted the Minister of Justice, I have one simple message: Release him immediately, for we will surely find you and then you will pay dearly.'

The newsreader returned to the screen with the rest of the news, and Hanli switched off. She felt better – they were making a real effort. And if David were being held for ransom, she knew the government would meet the conditions, whatever they were.

It was the first day he had not been beaten. They even gave him palatable food for lunch, and soon after that, a warder came to his door.

'Get up, Zwane.'

He got up dutifully. At first he had always resisted, but the beatings had taught him to obey.

'You are being moved.'

Stupidly, he allowed a smile to creep onto his face, and the warder grinned back at him. 'You're going to hang, you bastard! But not in this place. Somewhere a little less well-known.'

George tried to smile again, but a coldness had crept over his body. Even now, with his body beaten and broken, he did not want to die – in fact every beating had made him more determined to live.

'Come on, "Comrade". I haven't got all fucking day.'

He walked out in front of the warder. It felt strange to walk past the rows of single cells; he had come to this prison in the dark and had never seen outside the walls of his own small cell. Now he tried to remember everything very carefully, saving up

240

the details in his mind. These were the last precious moments of his existence. Or were they? They'd played so many games with him so often, it was difficult to know what to expect.

When they got out into the open, he was blinded by the sunshine. The only light he'd been conscious of in his cell was a forty-watt bulb. He tripped and fell – and was grabbed roughly and thrown into the back of a yellow truck. He hit the metal floor with his face. Like everything else to do with the prison, it stank.

The warder peered inside. 'Hope you have an early death, "Comrade".' He laughed – an unpleasant rasping sound – and slammed the door shut.

The truck started up noisily, then pulled away. George could hear the gears being changed, and was hurled round inside his steel box as the vehicle turned a corner. Were they leaving Pretoria? Where were they taking him? He had long since lost count of the amount of time he had spent in jail. In spite of himself, he began crying. He wanted to touch his children, he wanted to hold his wife. At least he could cry now in privacy, and not where they might mock him. This was his final gift from God – and he savoured every moment of it.

The interior of the truck was suddenly lit up, and he looked for the bulb that had created the light. It was only then that he realised the door at the rear had swung open – he was seeing daylight again.

He touched the door and it opened further, so that the dust from the dirt road blew into the compartment. He looked down at the ground moving fast below him. Difficult to judge how quickly the truck was going, but it was now or never. Fate had given him this last chance. He hurled himself out of the back, towards the side of the road.

He smelt the dust in his nostrils and then he hit the ground hard. He felt stunned. Had he broken anything? But there was no time, no time, no time. He got to his feet and started to run. He saw that the veld in front of him was dry. It must be winter.

In the distance he could make out a clump of wattle trees, and desperately he ran towards them. It was only now that he realised how much strength he had lost. He could not run, he had to walk, and more like a drunkard than a sober man. The smell of the earth was wonderful, dry and pungent. It was the smell of freedom: like nothing he had ever known. He willed himself ever closer to the clump of trees, longing for the comfort of their shade and their protection.

He reached them minutes later, and lay down to rest. Immediately, a shot rang out and the earth close to him rose up in a cloud. He was on his feet again, and this time he found he could run. Who had fired the shot? The question ricocheted through his brain. Perhaps it was only a farmer having a bit of fun.

The veld banked away steeply and he saw that he was heading down into a narrow gorge. He could see the white of water at the bottom, as it cascaded its way between rocks under a carpet of foliage. The longing for freedom kept him going. He could not stand the thought of being enclosed between four concrete walls again. He toppled forwards, landing painfully in a thorn bush. Hurry, hurry. The sound of the water drummed in his ears, echoing his own thoughts: hurry, hurry, hurry. A network of creepers snaked their way down the cliff face towards the stream.

Desperately he pulled himself out of the thorn bush and grabbed hold of a creeper. Another shot passed over his head. He moved down the creeper, hand over hand, his body hanging out over the gorge. Then there was an avalanche of shots all around him, and he stopped moving. He was running out of strength, he could feel it. The drop beneath him must be over one hundred metres.

A rasping laugh echoed up and down the kloof. George looked around to see where it was coming from, and saw an armed man with a rifle on the cliff opposite him.

'Jump, Zwane!'

It was a taunting voice that made the rage within him flare. He started moving again, heading deeper into the fissure. As his feet struggled to get a purchase on the vine, more shots exploded around him and he saw the sparks dance off the quartzite rock. Some shards hit him in the face, and for a moment he was blinded. He was crying now, he knew he was going to die. He had been set up. He should have stayed in the truck after all.

Gradually the strength in his fingers dwindled. He thought of his son, of his wife. He thought of Victoria Loxton, and of Max.

The rock beneath his fingers was crumbling. Desperately he scrabbled with his boots, but no comforting surface came up to meet his feet. Oh my God, it's not going to happen . . . He tried to traverse away from the centre of the rock face, and a bullet

242

slammed into the back of his left hand.

'No!' he screamed, as his fingers gave way.

The body lay on the rocks of the river bed, the water downstream running red with the blood. Major Hurst kicked it, feeling the thrill subside. But it had been good, making Zwane believe he had a chance when he had none. And, of course, making it all look like an accident: Zwane had run just where he'd wanted him to. Oh, the Major thought, if he could just relive those moments again! Perhaps he should have played it out longer. But no; there were others with him who must not know his weakness for killing – the intense, almost sexual pleasure it gave him.

'Is he dead, sir?'

He stared at the pasty-faced seventeen-year-old with the assault rifle. 'Quite dead.'

'You didn't give him a chance, sir.'

Hurst strode over to the boy and tore the rifle from his hands, then he picked him up by the scruff of the neck. The boy struggled, so he gave him a slap across the face and then pushed his head into the bloody water. He waited till the bubbles stopped coming from his mouth, and then glanced round at the other men, who were looking on with amusement. He winked at them conspiratorially.

'The youngster doesn't understand.'

He pulled the boy out and watched him retch up the water. He gave him a hard kick in the buttocks. 'What did you see?'

'What do you mean, sir?'

'The kaffir, how did he die?'

'He fell, sir.'

'You were the only one who saw it?'

'No, sir.'

Hurst picked the boy up again and held him close to Zwane's body. 'You were the only one who saw him fall, Conradie. As far as the inquest is concerned, we weren't here.'

'Yes, sir.'

Hurst let the boy go and gestured to the men. 'Get the body back to the truck. Not a mention of this to anyone. If I hear any gossip, you're dead.'

The men looked on grimly and Hurst was pleased. He'd selected them all carefully, the boy being his only oversight. He thought of the money, thirty thousand rands in used notes, that

243

he'd be getting for the job, less than he'd got for the Van der Post job; but he'd have done it for free. As far as he was concerned, Zwane should have died a long time ago.

Killing, he thought, that's the only way to live.

David Loxton came round feeling nauseous. He looked about him. Mickey Mouse patterns on the wallpaper, and a revolting orange carpet on the floor. Where the hell was he? The window had been carefully bricked in, the ceiling was concrete and the door was unmistakably steel. He got up with some difficulty and walked into the smaller adjoining room which contained a bath and toilet and – damn! – another bricked-up window.

Back in the main room he saw that on the table next to his bed there was some fresh fruit and a jug of water. To his surprise he found that he was hungry, and for the next five minutes concentrated on eating and drinking. After that he paced his way carefully round the room. They'd taken his watch and his wedding ring, which made him feel vulnerable. He lived by his watch. Time wasted infuriated him – life going by with nothing achieved.

Now he banged furiously on the metal door, but there was no response. Next he examined the furniture, going through all the drawers and cupboards, but he found nothing. He ran himself a bath, pleased to find that the water was very hot. The bathroom smelt strongly of disinfectant, and the walls were lined with ugly green tiles. He felt strange, taking off his clothes, but once in the water he felt both relaxed and refreshed.

Lying in the bath, he analysed his situation: there must be some clue that would tell him where he was. As far as he knew, he had travelled entirely by road, and had passed through some sort of customs post, which meant he could be in Botswana, Lesotho, Swaziland, Zimbabwe or Mozambique – any of the countries that bordered on South Africa. Of course, the sounds he'd heard could have been played to him on a tape, to mislead him; it was perfectly possible that he was still in Pretoria, having been driven round in circles.

At least, his captors, whoever they were, had not yet caused him physical harm, and the security forces would already be combing the country, looking for him. But this silence, this lack of contact – it could drive him crazy. Who the hell was holding him captive? What did they want? He was paralysed – for once in his life there was absolutely nothing he could do to alter his situation. The sense of emptiness scared him. He felt his head spinning.

He towelled himself dry, dressed, and then lay on the bed. For the first time in his long career he thought of the men his legislation had condemned to solitary confinement. Perhaps someone was exacting their revenge on him? Eventually he fell into a deep sleep. He dreamt of developing a new kind of tank – the most advanced tank in the world. His mind was filled with visions of wealth and power.

He woke up to see a very small, wizened man sitting next to his bed with an Uzi submachine-gun across his lap. From the man's appearance and his small build, David thought he might be a Bushman.

'Comfortable, sir?' the little man asked.

'I demand to be released immediately!'

The little man laughed, a dry laugh. David could not place him, yet he had the uneasy feeling that somewhere, deep in the past, he had had a connection with him.

'We've sent a note to Klopper,' the man said, 'but he's taking his time to reply.'

'What do you mean?'

'You have been kidnapped, sir. The trade is simple enough.'

David immediately felt better: now he knew the deal. But what was the price they were demanding? Hanli had only limited access to his funds, so the State would have to intervene. However, he must put on a tough face. The less money expended, the better.

'You realise you'll never get away with this, don't you? You may hold me to ransom, but the State will eventually catch you.'

'No, we do not want your money, sir. The trade is simple. Your life for that of George Zwane.'

David started sweating. Suddenly it was not so simple. Dolph would not drop the charges on Zwane, would he? But surely, if his own life was in danger, it would be different?

The Bushman got up. David estimated that he was less than five feet tall, but he handled the machine-gun pretty well, all the same.

'Where am I?' David asked.

The little man was staring at him, fascination in his eyes. David saw the barrel of the machine-gun drop – and launched himself from the bed towards the man's chest.

It was over in a second. The Bushman expertly side-stepped him, and David crashed head-first to the floor. He lay there, writhing in agony, staring at the man's tiny plimsolled feet. The machine-gun was trained on him.

The Bushman said: 'My father was Kotuko. Remember Kotuko, sir? He was a friend of your first wife's, and you killed him by shoving a red-hot rod up his arse. Remember? So don't try anything else, because killing you slowly would be my pleasure.'

David tried to hide his fear. 'Can I have something to read?'

'No.'

The door closed.

David dragged himself up from the floor, ashen-faced. Who the hell was behind this? Obviously they knew him, knew all about him . . . But it was no good worrying about that, he must concentrate all his energy on trying to think of a way to escape.

After a little while he had an inspiration, and searched the cupboards again. In one of the drawers he found what he was looking for – a newspaper lining. He unfolded it and examined the header. It was a page from the *Harare Herald*. Harare! Yes, all the evidence pointed to it, including the long drive and passing through the customs post.

He was trembling now. How long was it since he'd been kidnapped? The new Zimbabwean Houses of Parliament were to be opened soon, and then . . . The enormity of what was going to happen struck him like a thunderbolt. There would be civil war in the country – his life was in terrible danger.

He lay on the bed and started praying. He was powerless to stop what was going to happen . . .

Some time later the door opened and the Bushman came in.

'Food for you, sir.' He paused. 'And I have bad news for you, too. Klopper doesn't want you, sir. He's launched a nation-wide search for you, but he's made no mention of our demands.'

David sat up, shaking. 'He could be stalling for time – are you quite sure he got your note?'

The little man nodded.

Suddenly, David lost control. 'I've had quite enough of this farce!' he roared. 'I demand my freedom!'

'You! You demand freedom! You who have had so many men

246

sentenced to death! You who have arrested so many people without trial!'

David snarled his reply. 'You're naive. How would you rule a country that was being destroyed by terrorists? Encourage them, would you? Don't be a fool! The law exists to maintain peace, and anyone who threatens peace has to be eliminated . . . Am I in Harare?'

He caught a flicker in the Bushman's eyes. Good, he'd caught the man unawares. He grabbed his arm – but the barrel of the Uzi was pressed against David's chest, the Bushman's finger wrapped around the trigger.

'Killing you would give me great pleasure, sir.'

'Listen to me. If this is Harare, we are in great danger . . .'

'Don't try and get clever with me, Mr Loxton.'

'I'm serious! Tomorrow, if I'm correct in my estimate, is the opening of the Zimbabwean Parliament. Am I right? And the first item on the agenda is a discussion of the situation in South Africa.'

'I don't know what you are talking about.'

'Oh yes you do! Now listen, for God's sake! In twenty-four hours we could all be dead.'

Max poured himself a drink and switched on the television – though it was unlikely to tell him anything he didn't know. That Dolph Klopper obviously considered David Loxton expendable was causing him great anxiety: there had been no reply to the ransom note, not a word.

The black newsreader's face filled the screen. 'Here is the news from the People's Broadcast Centre, Harare. This is the eve of an historic event, for tomorrow morning our new Houses of Parliament will be opened by President Robert Mugabe. This impressive building was designed by Israeli architect David Isaacs and built by a Zimbabwean consortium headed by Dr Max Loxton. The first debate in the new parliament building will concern the situation in South Africa, and the growing strain on medical resources caused by the AIDS pandemic.'

Max took another sip of his whisky. He didn't like to think about the construction of the parliament building – everything had been done far too quickly to ensure first-class workmanship. But if he'd tried to slacken the pace he would have lost the contract, and he needed the money desperately.

He caught the presenter's next words and leaned forward in nervous anticipation. 'In South Africa, the search for David Loxton continues. The South African Minister of Justice was taken from his home on Sunday night, despite massive security. A search has been launched across South Africa, and in an impassioned speech today the State President, Mr Klopper, vowed he would not rest till Loxton was found.'

There was a pause. Then the newsreader continued: 'Also in South Africa, today, the activist and freedom fighter George Zwane, sentenced to death over a year ago for the assassination of Kobus van der Post, escaped police custody during transportation from Pretoria Central Prison. His body was later found in a river gorge in the Eastern Transvaal, where it is believed he fell to his death . . .'

Almost automatically, Max leant forward and switched off the set. So it had all been for nothing. George! Oh God, George!

He remembered the young legal student he used to spar with, and all the long years of friendship after that, the shared ideals. He remembered their last meeting in the grounds of the hospital in Francistown. Perhaps he should have talked more, tried to reason with him . . . There could be no more talking now. Just emptiness.

He thought about his visit to the scene of the shooting in Johannesburg. It had been some months afterwards, the police investigation into Kobus' death was almost over. He had stood on the library steps, where the podium had been, and looked across to the building from where George had fired the three shots. He had known at once, then, that something was wrong. He remembered Victoria being covered in Kobus' blood, and the direction in which Kobus had been thrown by the first shot: the angles simply didn't tie up. It was strange that he hadn't thought of that before, but then, like everyone else, he had assumed George Zwane was guilty.

After that, Max had investigated the building from which George was supposed to have fired the fatal shots. The lift was broken, so he'd trudged up the ten storeys to the flat roof. The glare of sunlight was intense here. On a line suspended between a television mast and the hut that housed the lift winding gear, a few old clothes were hung out to dry. There was a concrete block house with a tin roof. The door was open, and he had walked

248

across to it. Inside an old man was boiling a billy full of water on his primus stove.

'Greetings, old one.'

He had spoken in Zulu; he could see that the man was a Zulu. The look of dawning hostility on the old man's face was replaced with a smile.

'*Hau*. I thought you were the police.'

'This is where the shot was fired from, isn't it?'

Max had seen how the old man tensed up then, and decided to proceed more carefully. 'Old one, may I share some of your tea?'

He had sat on the cold concrete floor as the old man made the tea, and they had exchanged names.

'You have lived here a long time, Solomon?'

'I will live here till I die, boss. George Zwane promised me that I would not be forced to move after what happened.'

'He was always a good man.'

The old man's eyes lit up. 'You knew him?'

'We used to practise together, boxing.'

It was a good subject to bring up; Solomon was interested in boxing, and they spent the next hour talking about it. Then, without warning, the old man shifted the conversation back to George.

'"He was a good man." Why do you say that?' He pulled himself closer, and Max could smell the pipe tobacco on his breath. The old man grabbed Max's hand. 'I trust you, boss. I will tell you everything – but you must promise never to speak to the police.'

Max was taken aback. So much trust so soon! The old man might be giving him something that could destroy his own life.

'He told me to go away,' the old man said. 'He gave me money. He said I must go back to Natal for a few days. Naturally, I agreed. But something told me not to go. I took the money and went to the *Sangoma*.

'What the *Sangoma* saw in the bones scared me – and him. He said that George was a great man, and that his brother would be greater. The *Sangoma* spoke on. He saw death in the land. He saw a white woman, great pain, great suffering. She crossed a big sea.

'The *Sangoma* stared at me. He was frightened. He saw terrible things. He said I must stay, I must watch over George. He said I must then wait for a sign, a man would come. Then I must tell him, he said.

'You boss, you are the one of whom he spoke. Now I will tell you.'

The old man settled himself on the floor and pulled out his pipe from under the mattress. He stuffed it full of dagga, and lit it, then handed it to Max. It was an honour, to be given the first inhalation of the pipe. He smelt the curious, pungent odour, took the smoke deep into his lungs and let it lie there, weaving its mysterious spell, then he handed the pipe back to the old man.

'That night I stayed with a friend, boss,' Solomon continued, 'but the next night I came back. There is a place I often sleep in on the tenth floor, next to the hot water tanks, so I stayed there.

'I awoke in the morning to hear the sounds of many people. I looked out of the window to see the square in front of the library filled with men and women. I had heard there was to be a great speech, though to tell you the truth, at my age such things matter very little. I made my way carefully up to the roof – George had locked the door, but I had my key with me. I turned the lock as quietly as I could.

'The roof was empty. I wondered if he had left. Then I heard sobbing in the distance, coming from the lift house. I took off my shoes and made my way carefully towards it. There's an inspection ladder at the back. Often I lie right on the top and warm myself in the sun in the morning. So I pulled myself up the ladder and crept across the roof to the skylight.

'He was right below me – an enormous rifle on his shoulder. I looked down to the stage far below and saw a man with grey hair in a blue suit walking towards the microphone. George was watching him. All the time he was saying something. His words had become almost a chant: "I cannot do it, I cannot do it."

'He lowered the rifle, he buried his face in his hands. I could see that there was a battle raging within him. He must have been fighting the devil.'

Max readjusted his position on the floor and the old man took another long pull on his pipe.

'The shots caught us both by surprise. I fell over backwards, and he dropped the rifle, then snatched it up again quickly. He looked through the sight. A woman was crouched over the man who lay dead on the stage. George said "Oh my God, Oh my God."

'Then he was gone, over the edge of the building like a bird and bouncing smoothly down the wall on a thin rope. I was alone again, and I was glad I had listened to the words of the *Sangoma*.'

Max had said at last: 'Your secret is safe with me, old one.'

Solomon's hand had clasped his own. 'There was more. I have to tell you. This *Sangoma* said I must tell the man I was to meet – you – to beware of a cloud. It is evil, it will destroy you.' Solomon came closer to him, peering into his eyes. 'I have saved the spirit of George?' he asked.

'Yes, and far more,' Max had assured him. 'More than you will ever understand. I thank you.'

Max remembered the quiet desperation he had felt as he left the building. If it wasn't George, then who *had* assassinated Kobus? He hadn't told Victoria any of this – she was in London by then, and this would have been too upsetting for her, with the baby on the way and Kobus' death still fresh in her mind.

And now, because of what he'd learned that day from Solomon, here he was in Harare, having kidnapped his own father. But George Zwane was dead; he could no long trade David's life for George's. His captive was useless. Suddenly he thought that he would never have got into this appalling mess if only Saffron had been with him . . .

Maybe he should kill David. No, he couldn't kill his own father, however much he might hate him. The best course of action would be to hand David over to the Zimbabwean authorities, who would no doubt return him to South Africa.

Max poured himself another drink. He'd failed George – he'd promised himself he would get him out. He'd failed Kobus, too. And he'd failed in the Okavango. And he'd wrecked his relationship with Saffron. What the hell was happening to him?

Gumsa came into the room. Gumsa, whom he trusted more than anyone else he knew – more even than Saffron.

'Kaikhoe . . .' the old man began quietly. Then he stared at the glass in Max's hand. 'The poison will kill you,' he said.

'Gumsa, my old friend, we lost to Klopper. George died today, trying to escape.'

'How did he die?'

'I don't know, I don't care. We must release my bloody father.'

There was a bitterness in Gumsa's eyes, but Max knew the old

251

Bushman would not want David's death on his hands. 'Kaikhoe,' Gumsa said, 'your father has told me a story. I do not know if it is true. It is to do with the opening of the Houses of Parliament.'

'How the hell did he find out where he was? Go back to the room, Gumsa, and question him. I'll stand by the door.'

Outside in the passage, Max could hear the conversation quite clearly.

'Can you be more specific about what is worrying you, sir?'

'I can't tell you the details, but we have to get away from here quickly.'

'I will be open with you,' Gumsa said. 'Yes, we are in Zimbabwe, in the capital, Harare, to be exact. We'll be handing you over to the authorities today.'

'What day is it?'

'Monday.'

There was a lengthy silence, and then Gumsa appeared, closing the door of the room behind him.

Max shrugged. 'He was just trying it on, that's all. It doesn't mean anything.'

David lay on the bed, his body rigid with terror. He would be in the hands of the Zimbabweans when the Houses of Parliament collapsed. It was too much of a coincidence that he should be in Harare at the same time, and would be held as the number one suspect. He'd hang – no doubt about it.

His mind was made up, he knew what he had to do. He moved to the door of his room and started to drum on it with his fists.

No one came. He screamed out again and again, but still no one came. If only he had told them earlier! Maybe they had already arranged for the Zimbabwean police to collect him.

He couldn't remember when he finally gave up banging and shouting, and dropped off to sleep, but the next thing he knew was that the Bushman was in his room again.

'How are you, sir?'

'What time is it?'

'Eight thirty in the morning, sir. Time to hand you over.'

'No! Listen, damn you! The new parliamentary buildings will collapse during the opening session today. My son is involved in the project, and if I'm in their hands the authorities will blame me. Don't you understand? I'll die, damn you!'

David felt himself shaking with rage; the Bushman was leaving

252

the room without a word, he just wasn't going to believe him! There was another noise, and he turned to see his son Max burst into the room.

'Father, what the hell were you saying to Gumsa?' The time for deception was over. He hadn't bothered about the mask.

'Max! How did you find me?'

Max stared coldly at his father, who had turned almost white with shock.

'I didn't find you, I kidnapped you! Your life for George Zwane's – that was the deal. But Klopper didn't value you, and George is dead, so I'm handing you over to the Zimbabwean authorities.'

'No, for God's sake, Max, no! Your building's going to cave in.'

'You're crazy!'

'Max, one of our agents planted explosives deep in the concrete at all the key points in the structure. As parliament opens he will detonate those charges and the building will collapse. It will appear to be an accident caused by bad building.'

Max was on his father, slowly strangling him with his hands. He punched him in the stomach, then in the face. He was losing control, he couldn't contain his rage any longer. Only when his father was a bloodied heap on the floor did he stop.

'Why? Why?'

David dragged himself to his feet. 'To destroy this government. We've been backing a rebel Matabele group in Zimbabwe for a long time, and when the Houses of Parliament collapse, they'll stage a coup and seize power.'

'And who is this agent? Where is he going to explode the charges?'

'Why should I tell you? You're going to hand me over to the authorities and they'll sure as hell hang me when it happens. And even if I escape, Klopper will know I betrayed the project.'

'You're lying!'

'Listen, Max, we want a new government here and we intend to dispose of the current one, just as we disposed of Van der Post!'

'I can't believe it!'

'Zwane bungled it, lost his nerve at the last moment, so our chap shot Kobus and Zwane took the rap. Now do you believe me?'

Max felt his world falling apart. He'd been looking for a more complicated solution, but the whole thing was devastatingly simple. He had never quite realised how ruthless his father was; a lot of things fell into place now. Life was cheap to men like his father. There were no ethics for them. Suddenly his father's threat was real.

'You and your stupid ideals, Max,' David was saying. 'Van der Post would have destroyed our country. Look what these fools have done to Zimbabwe.'

Max dragged his father up against the wall and held his face close to his own. 'You will pay for this, you bastard. Do you know what you've done to Victoria? She was carrying Kobus' child!'

'Of course we knew she was sleeping with him – but the pregnancy, that did come as something of a shock.'

Max felt himself sobering up fast.

'It's nine o'clock now,' he said. 'How much time have we got?'

'The building will collapse when parliament is assembled.'

'How?'

'You agree to silence and my immediate release?'

'Yes, damn you.'

'All right, then. Detonation is radio-activated and silent. Our operative will be there, at the opening, disguised as a German magazine reporter. Now, Gumsa will take me to the border?'

'Get out of my life, you bastard!'

Four

The American TV news crew got out of their van in a hurry –
they were running late. Clark Allan, veteran political journalist,
would do the live broadcast straight after the opening ceremony.
A stocky, aggressive man, he liked to be where the action was,
and he was sure that the opening of the new Houses of Parliament
would be the occasion for some fiery speeches. He knew that
Zimbabwe was moving towards a tougher stance on South Africa,
and that there would be calls for stiffer world sanctions, and for
military support for Zimbabwe. Like an old warhorse, he smelled
battle in the air.

Clark searched his pockets for his cigarettes, and swore to
himself. He'd left them in his hotel room, and the thought of
surviving the next four hours without a smoke was unbearable.
He broke away from his party and hurried across the busy Harare
street to a corner café, where he bought two packets, enough to
last him till the evening.

Leaving the café was the last thing Clark Allan remembered,
for it was just then that Max brought the back of the pistol hard
down on his head. Dragging him into the alley, Max felt in
Clarke's pockets for his press card, taped his mouth shut, then
bundled him into his own waiting car and locked the door. With
a press card in his hands, Max knew that getting into the
parliament buildings would be easy.

He couldn't have been more wrong.

Max flashed the card at one of the armed guards, who looked at
it closely and then gestured for him to move to one side. While a

255

man checked his name against a typed list, the guard kept the barrel of his rifle trained at Max's head.

'I'm afraid, Mr Allan, that there are too many journalists here already. I can't let you in.'

'Holy smoke! My crew's already gone through,' Max muttered, in the best American accent he could muster.

This disconcerted the security man. 'They should have told me they were with you. All right, in the booth over there. I'll have to search you before you go in.'

Max felt the sweat beginning to run down his back. Tucked in the waistband of his trousers was his Browning, and in his pockets, extra ammunition clips. Like a man walking to the scaffold, he went into the booth, where another security man was waiting for him.

When Max spoke to him in Shona, the guard looked up from his frisking in surprise. He smiled – then drew back as he found the gun. Max let him have it, a hard right to the side of the head that dropped the man to the floor. He waited for a few moments till he heard the other guard call, asking if everything was OK. Max shouted out a reply in Shona, and breathed easily when it elicited a casual, unworried response.

So far, so good. Max walked out into the open, his bold steps belying the hammering of his heart. He glanced at his watch and saw that it was after ten. Not much time. The guard gestured up the stairs.

The place was packed. All around him were Zimbabwean dignitaries, and he saw a couple of familiar faces, but fortunately he wasn't recognised. How was he going to find a German magazine journalist among all these people? Oh God, it was useless.

Suddenly there was a cry in the distance, the sound of guards running. Shit, now he was in trouble.

Then he had it in a second – he knew exactly what to do. Memories of learning German at school came flooding back to him.

'*Die Bombe! Die Bombe!*'

He screamed it out, his eyes scanning the shocked crowd, and he caught a flash of blond hair.

He drew the gun and spun round. Then he saw the look of shock on the blond man's face. The man broke into a run, reaching for something in his jacket. Max guessed that that something was the detonator.

He knew the building back to front, and he guessed where the man was heading – to the fire escape. He pushed after him through the terrified crowd.

Up now. He was sweating, heaving foot after foot, the metal stairs ringing with his tread. Going higher and higher.

There was a single crack, and Max's left arm swung back with the impact of the bullet. He felt himself collapsing down onto the stairs. Another shot grazed his shoulder – and he raised the Browning and fired, double tap, then forced himself upwards.

He was on the roof now, the German crouching down in a corner. It was all coming back to him, his army training: he was rolling over and over now as the bullets smacked around him. Tears were running out of his eyes and he was gasping for breath. Almost incidentally, he found himself looking down through the skylight. There were people everywhere.

Fuck! The bloody German had the detonator in his hand. No time to lose.

Up, legs apart, Weaver stance, point, shoot.

The German lifting up . . .

Pulling the trigger again and again . . . Then silence.

Max staggered over to the bloody corpse and snatched the remote control unit from the man's hand. He smashed the plastic transmitter to pieces with the butt of his pistol.

Then came reality, the cold of a rifle barrel in his neck.

'Don't move. You're under arrest.'

The rifle barrel was trained directly at his head now, and the eyes looking down at him were none too friendly. The rifle moved in a gesture that indicated he should get up. Slowly he rose to his feet, and started calculating whether he had any chance of taking this guard out. The guard backed away, holding the weapon in the manner of a man who had used one often.

'Walk in front of me, slowly. Put your hands on your head.'

Max did as he was told. The elation of having stopped the German was fading rapidly. He was in big trouble now, and no one was going to give a damn.

General Jurie Smit sat in the air-conditioned comfort of the underground bunker, looking at a television monitor. The colour picture showed the interior of the Zimbabwean Houses of

Parliament, and the Speaker had just sat down. General Smit looked anxiously at his wrist-watch. It was now four minutes after eleven, the parliament hall was full, and nothing had happened.

Had someone botched the placing of the charges? It crossed his mind that the missing David Loxton might have something to do with this, but at this stage he couldn't work out why.

All around the General, massed along South Africa's border with Zimbabwe, was the biggest concentration of South African troops ever assembled. As far as they were concerned, it was just a very big training manoeuvre. Only the General and a handful of his closest aides knew that they were there to support a rebel coup in Zimbabwe. By General Smit's calculations, the rebels should have control of the entire country by the end of the day – but that was dependent on the destruction of the parliament building in Harare and the death of most of the country's leaders in the process – and right now that didn't look as if it was going to happen.

The General picked up the field phone, a hot-line direct to the State President's office.

'Jurie . . . what is going on?'

He tensed, hearing the aggression in Dolph Klopper's voice. He replied slowly, knowing he must disappoint the man who was his leader and his friend.

'I don't know, man. Maybe the charges malfunctioned. However, I think there's another explanation for this.'

'What?'

'Loxton.'

'It was his idea, he'd never have tipped them off.'

'To save his own skin?'

'*Ja*, you may be right, Jurie. But what do we do?'

'If there's no unrest and no violence, the rebels can't risk making a move, it would be suicide for them. And if we moved in, I'll bet you any money there'd be international intervention.'

'You *must* attack!'

'Dolph, we can't take on the United States or worse, the USSR; we wouldn't stand a chance. Our only course is to pull back. Isn't it?'

There was a long silence on the other end of the line. 'Damnit,' Dolph Klopper said. 'Hell. Yes.'

*

258

Hanli sat in David's study, looking out over the garden at a policeman in the distance. The whole house was filled with security people, and it unnerved her. She was so worried, she couldn't sleep. It didn't really look as though they were going to find David, and the recent arrival of several bills had forced her to realise that she must start to take care of his financial affairs. Of course, he had accountants for company finance, but they didn't handle his personal expenditures.

She sat at his desk now and examined the ledger, trying to analyse which payments had to be made where. She'd never realised how many clubs and associations he was a member of. One bill in particular bothered her: a large sum owing to the Prester John. The monthly membership fee was not particularly expensive, nor were the meals, but there were un-itemized expenditures of a thousand rands a time, eight of them in one month. They had been overcharging David, she was sure of it. She found the number for the club's accounts department, and picked up the telephone.

'Mrs Loxton speaking. I've been checking my husband's account for October and there are certain unspecified charges I'd like to query.'

'Can you hold on while I call up your husband's account on the computer, Mrs Loxton?'

She heard the sound of the keys being tapped.

'Mrs Loxton? You are querying the eight charges of one thousand rand?'

'Yes.'

'I can only tell you that the account is in order, Mrs Loxton.'

'But what are they for?'

'Probably drinks and food bills, Mrs Loxton.'

'But these charges should be itemized! Why are they not? I demand an explanation.'

'I'm sorry, Mrs Loxton. Perhaps you had better speak to the manager.'

Now she was really irritated. They were definitely on the make. She picked up the phone again.

'The manager, please.'

'Manageress, dahling. Speaking.'

'It's about my husband's account.'

'And who is 'e?'

'David Loxton.'

'Oh la la!' Hanli immediately sensed the change in the woman's attitude. 'Mrs Loxton,' she said, 'I'm sorry, we haven't met. Is your husband all right? I 'eard the terrible, terrible news.'

'The police are doing everything they can to find him, thank you. Now, please, about my husband's account.'

'It is not in order?'

'No. And your accounts department has been totally unhelpful.'

'I'll 'ave to get back to you, Mrs Loxton. I'm afraid I 'aven't got a copy of your husband's account 'ere.'

'That's just not good enough! I suspect that you people have been grossly overcharging him . . .'

'Your 'usband owns the club, Mrs Loxton – it would 'ardly be in my interests to cheat 'im.'

'I want an explanation by tomorrow, or I'll make sure you're fired!'

Hanli put the phone down, seething with anger. She hated the patronising tone in the woman's voice.

That afternoon she had a few friends over for tea. She was not allowed out of the house now, except under police escort, so it was company for her – though all her friends had to be searched before they were allowed on to the property. After tea, Hanli mentioned the problems she was having with David's account at the Prester John, and was astonished when one of her friends burst into laughter.

'I don't see what's so funny, Angela!'

'Un-itemized expenses!' Angela, an attractive blonde with a generous figure, flashed her blue eyes at Hanli Loxton. 'If you really want to know, dear, I'll tell you. When I was at Pretoria University someone told me I could earn a lot of money if I worked at the Prester John, and I did.'

'So?'

'You don't earn a lot of money at the Prester John just by waitressing, Hanli.'

Now all the women were staring at her with bemused expressions on their faces.

'What are you implying?'

'Nothing Hanli, absolutely nothing.'

*

260

The truck driver dropped David off at an intersection, half a kilometre from the house. Thirsty, hungry and exhausted, by the time he made it to the drive he was finished.

A policeman stepped out in front of him. 'That's far enough!'

'Watch your tongue.'

The man stepped back. 'Mr Loxton, sir! I didn't recognise you.'

'Take me inside, you oaf!'

Hanli, aware of a growing commotion, was beginning to feel she had really had enough of all this. Plainclothes security police were suddenly appearing from everywhere, sirens were screaming in the distance, there was the roar of a car in the drive. It was too bad!

And then David burst through the front door, and she was in his arms sobbing, the tears running from her eyes.

'Oh my God, darling! You're all right!'

'Relax, Hanli, everything's fine.'

'Did they hurt you?'

'A few bruises – nothing that time won't heal.'

'But what happened?'

'I was kidnapped. I don't know who did it – they used an intermediary. He slipped up, and I managed to escape.'

She tended to his cuts and bruises while he phoned Dolph Klopper. The conversation was stilted, and David put the phone down after only a couple of minutes.

Hanli looked up at him incredulously. 'Wasn't he pleased you were all right?'

'Yes. But there are problems.'

'Problems?'

'Nothing for you to trouble your pretty little head about. It's a matter of state policy; something didn't work out.'

David left Hanli for half an hour while he made a full statement to the police. He refused to talk to the press till the next morning on the grounds that he was emotionally drained. Later he rejoined Hanli in the lounge in time for the six o'clock television news.

'A report just received indicates that the Minister of Justice, David Loxton, believed kidnapped earlier this week, gave his captors the slip today and is now at home recuperating. There will be a more up-to-date report in our eight o'clock bulletin.

'In Harare today, amid the excitement of the opening of the

261

new House of Parliament, an armed South African breached security and shot and killed a German journalist. The names of the two men involved have not so far been released.'

David switched off the set and stared into space. If Dolph discovered he'd told Max about the plan to destroy the Zimbabwean Houses of Parliament, his political career would be over. But Max was a man of his word – their pact would be honoured. He still could not get over the fact that he had been kidnapped by his own son, and the knowledge that he was to have been traded for a convicted black terrorist filled him with disgust.

As for his own 'escape', it had been ridiculously easy. He'd hitched a lift to a point close to Beitbridge, on the border between South Africa and Zimbabwe, and not having a passport, had swum the Limpopo River.

The phone rang, interrupting his thoughts. Hanli was holding the receiver out to him. 'It's Dolph Klopper again.'

'Thanks. I'll take this alone.' He went through into the study and closed the door.

'Ah, David,' the voice boomed. 'I just wanted to ask you: where were you held hostage?'

Tired as he was, David recognised the danger. Obviously the grapevine had been working; perhaps the police had found the truck driver who'd taken him from Beitbridge to Johannesburg. Dolph was testing him – and he'd better play the game straight.

'A house in Harare,' he said.

'It is a tragedy,' Dolph's voice said, 'that the Houses of Parliament in Harare are still standing. I learn that there was a fight on the roof of the new building, and I think, David, that you may not be telling me everything.'

'Has it occurred to you, old chap, that the charges might have simply malfunctioned?'

'Then who were these men they caught? Hurst tells me his German operative was shot dead.'

'Listen, Dolph, the whole operation was my idea.'

'*Ja*?'

'Well, I'd hardly want to wreck over a year's work, would I?'

There was a long pause on the other end of the line. Obviously what he'd said to Dolph was making sense.

'All right, David, my friend,' Dolph's voice said. 'Rest now.'

David put the phone down with a sigh of relief. Now he would have time to refine the story of his captivity for the media.

262

He went back into the lounge and Hanli brought him a cup of coffee. 'David,' she said, 'while you were away I started to look into your finances.'

He was about to be quite sharp with her, but then something told him to be wary.

'Thank you, darling,' he said. 'Was everything in order?'

'I think they've been overcharging you at the Prester John. There are some big bills they don't seem able to account for.'

David smiled. That was all it was. He'd had a story prepared for just this kind of eventuality for years. Though the club knew how to keep its mouth shut, in certain circles its reputation was well known. Better to tell a half-truth than an outright lie.

'It's something I've never told you about, Hanli,' he said.

He saw her start. That was good; all prepared for some really horrific revelation, she would swallow his story with relief.

'In the arms business,' he said, 'I have a lot of clients to keep sweet. Some of them like to be taken on holiday, to go to my game ranch, some of them like to go gambling or just have a good drink. But there are others who demand a more basic form of entertainment: women. The Prester John is where I take them, because it's private, and the women are both attractive and reliable. Those particular clients come away well satisfied, and my business usually goes through without a problem.'

Hanli put her arms round his neck. 'Oh darling, I'm sorry to have been suspicious.'

'That's all right, darling, quite understandable.'

It was very cold in the hall, and Victoria wrapped her dressing-gown tightly round her as she went to answer the phone. She and Lucinda were enjoying a quiet breakfast in the conservatory of their South Kensington house; the baby was upstairs, still fast asleep.

It was Ken Silke on the line from Johannesburg. Victoria couldn't believe what she was hearing. Max had just called him, Ken said; he'd been arrested in Harare, and was on trial for murder.

'He hasn't got much of a chance, Vicky. Please, I need you as a character witness.'

She put down the phone and walked back to the conservatory. It was a beautiful winter's day outside, with the sun shining brightly on the snow that carpeted the garden. A few minutes ago she had been thinking how lovely it looked. Now it seemed entirely irrelevant, unreal.

Lucinda looked up. 'What's wrong, Vicky?'

'Oh God, Lucinda. It's Max . . .'

When she had told Lucinda what little she knew, Lucinda said at once: 'I'll look after Kobus, Vicky. You must go to him, you must.'

The maid came in with the morning paper, and Max's photograph filled half the front page of *The Times*. 'Mad Max Machine-Guns Innocent Journalist.'

Victoria read the headline out loud and then silently devoured the accompanying article. The more she read, the angrier she became. The closing sentence was the one that finally stung her into action. It said that Dr Max Loxton would receive a fair trial, but was certain to die for his crimes.

'I don't believe it,' Lucinda stammered, reading over her shoulder. 'I just don't believe it.'

Victoria ran up the stairs to her room and hastily packed her bags. There was no time to lose. She had to get to Harare as soon as possible and find out what had really happened. Not that she thought the truth would have much bearing on the proceedings . . . At least Max couldn't have a better advocate than Ken.

She phoned Ken and told him she'd be in Harare as soon as possible. Then she left in a taxi an hour later, with Lucinda standing on the steps to wave goodbye, and holding her beloved child . . .

Ken Silke, about to leave Johannesburg for Harare, had not told Victoria what he really thought: that this time Max was in too deep, that this time he didn't have a chance of saving him.

Saffron looked through the movie camera and turned to the assistant director. 'Honey, you call that well-lit? You're supposed to be the best. Prove it to me.'

The man went bright red, and she stormed off the set. They were on location in Scotland. The castle overlooking the loch was shrouded in mist, and a faint drizzle had covered all the equipment with moisture. Steam rose from the large lights that illuminated the set.

One of the runners came after her. 'Mrs Packard – long distance call for you, it's very urgent . . .'

When she put the receiver down, she was crying.

The assistant director came into the room. 'I'm ready now. I think you'll like – '

'Leave me alone, Ron, please.'

She gripped the sides of the table, her body shaking. Why had she left him in Harare? What the hell had she done? He sounded so desperate.

She felt a hand on her shoulder. Joe Morgan, her executive producer. 'Bad news, Saffron, love?'

'It's Max, he's in terrible trouble.'

'I know, love, it's in the paper.'

'Joe, I've got to go to him. I must.'

Victoria felt vaguely guilty about the elation she felt as her plane came in to land at Harare airport. It was now over a year since she'd left Africa, and the excitement of returning was intense. The smallness of the airport was what struck her first, after the vastness of Heathrow. The huge, modern aircraft she had just been travelling in seemed out of place here, beside the tiny terminal buildings. And the air smelt so good, redolent with life and energy. It was only now that she realised just how much she had been longing for Africa.

She was just about to ask the porter to load her baggage into one of the battered-looking taxis when she heard someone call her name. For a moment she could not see who it was, but then she smelt that distinctive, erotic fragrance. Saffron looked terribly drawn. They embraced for a long time, and tears ran down Saffron's face.

'Vicky, they won't let me see him. Ken's trying again now.'

They were interrupted by an avalanche of flashes and clicks, and a whirring of motor-drives. An eager American reporter shot forward, microphone in hand. 'Miss Loxton, do you have any idea why your brother should have wanted to murder the reporter for *Stern*?'

Victoria resisted the temptation to be rude. She knew she would need as many allies as she could get, and the press might be among her most powerful. 'I believe my brother to be innocent,' she said, 'and I have come here to help prove that.'

The reporter edged closer, glad to be getting an exclusive. 'Is it true that you were having an affair with Kobus van der Post just before George Zwane shot him? That Kobus van der Post is the father of your child?'

Vicky felt unsteady on her feet – she had not been prepared for this. 'Yes, that is true.'

In the sudden silence Victoria could distinctly hear the sound of pens scribbling. It was a good time to leave. She smiled at the reporters, then turned away, following Saffron. It wasn't going to be easy.

The prison governor shifted uncomfortably in his seat and lowered his eyes. The meeting with Dr Loxton's advocate, Mr Silke, and his sister, Miss Loxton, was not going well. It was the elegant Miss Loxton who really frightened him. Her questions had all been strictly to the point, each pushing him further and further into a corner. He could think of no real reason to deny her permission to visit the prisoner. He smiled as he delivered his final pronouncement.

'Miss Loxton, you must give us time to consider your request.'

He could see the flash of anger in her eyes. 'You have told the world that this will be a fair trial,' Victoria Loxton snapped, 'yet you will not let a member of the family visit the accused. Furthermore, you will not let his girlfriend see him. Do you consider him guilty before he is tried – is this your idea of "justice"?'

What to do? If he didn't watch it, she'd be making some comments to the press that would reflect very badly on him. They'd told him to let the prisoner have as little contact with the outside world as possible – but if keeping Miss Loxton away from her brother meant jeopardising his career, he wasn't going to do it. Besides, they'd said she'd be a pushover, whereas she and Mr Silke were the toughest nuts he'd had to crack in a long time.

'All right,' he said. 'You may see him, Miss Loxton. Just you.'

'And Mrs Packard?'

'No!'

Ken Silke chuckled to himself. He hadn't rated Victoria's chances of seeing Max particularly high, but then he hadn't been working with her for nearly a year. He'd forgotten just how good she was.

Victoria hardly recognised the shell of a man sitting opposite her. She knew about the drinking – Saffron had told her everything – but even making allowances for that, Max still looked terrible. For the first time she saw traces of grey in his hair, and his eyes were lifeless.

266

She embraced him awkwardly, wary of the guard who sat watching them. She was certain that everything they discussed would be relayed to higher authority.

'Are you all right, Max?'

'They haven't killed me – yet.'

To her surprise, his face broke into its characteristic grin. 'Thank you for coming, Vicky. You've always had a passion for the truth, haven't you? That makes you a unique commodity in these parts.'

Victoria looked anxiously across at the man in the corner, but Max shrugged. 'This is as much privacy as we're going to get,' he said.

She touched his hand. It was dry, the fingernails deeply bitten. Then she looked into the face that had always seemed to her so strong, so full of certainty. This was the man who had given her the will to go on after Kobus' death. Now she saw fear in his eyes, and perhaps madness. She wanted to cry, but she kept control of herself. He must not die. She squeezed his hand.

'Max, I'm afraid Saffron is not allowed to see you.'

She saw a glimmer of light in those dull eyes. 'I . . . Please . . .' He took her hand. 'Tell her I love her.'

'Oh Max, how did you get involved in this business?'

'I found out the truth, you see, Vicky. George didn't shoot Kobus.'

Victoria's jaw hardened.

'You're deluding yourself, Max. Besides, George is dead.'

Suddenly Max hammered his fist on the table. The guard in the corner moved towards him. 'Leave me alone, for Christ's sake!' Max shouted. 'I'm not going anywhere!' Victoria felt the violence in him, the anger, and the guard slunk back to the corner of the room.

Then Max told her the whole story, punching the air with his fist occasionally to make a point. He told her how he'd kidnapped David, and how they'd obviously had George killed before he could do anything about it.

Victoria bowed her head. What a crazy, naive plan of her brother's, and how horribly wrong it had gone. But at the back of her mind, too, came a sudden sense of relief. George hadn't failed her; he hadn't failed himself. Then she felt guilt, terrible guilt. He had died alone, thinking how much she must hate him for something he had never done.

She was silent for a long time. Then she said at last: 'There's no mention of all this in the press.'

'We made a pact, and I'm a man of my word. Father told me about the plan to destroy the Houses of Parliament in Harare, and in exchange I gave him freedom and my silence.'

'So he's the only witness who can save you.'

Max leaned forward earnestly.

'Vicky, he hates your guts, he hates my guts. He won't lift a hand to save me. And if I told the story, who the hell would believe it? Do you think they're going to demolish a fifty-million-dollar building to find evidence they don't believe exists?' He paused. 'I should have killed the bastard while I had the chance,' he said.

'There *has* to be a way.'

'Stop dreaming!'

Max was shouting now, and Victoria was glad; she wanted the fight back in him. 'I'm going to talk to Father,' she said.

Max stared at her. 'You're wasting your time,' he replied. 'These people want my death – and all the evidence indicates that I deserve it.' He grasped her hand tightly for a few minutes without saying anything. His voice, when he spoke again, was hoarse. 'It's inevitable, Vicky, the death sentence, you know that. But I appreciate what you're doing.' He swallowed. 'Just make sure that when it happens you look after Saffron. Promise.'

'I promise.'

'That's quite the most preposterous story I've ever heard, Victoria. Max must be hallucinating.' David Loxton got up from his desk and went over to stand by the window.

Victoria tried not to let her emotion show, because she knew David would see that weakness and relish it. She sat up, and stared at his back. She spoke slowly, emphasizing each word.

'You can't let Max die.'

David swung round and leaned on the desk, pushing his forefinger into her face. 'Listen, that bastard kidnapped me. He would have cut off my hand to get Zwane back. Remember George Zwane? Max's "best friend" – the cold-blooded killer who made short work of Kobus? The two of you should choose your friends a little more carefully, I think.'

Victoria knew that if she'd had a gun in her hand at that

moment, she would have shot him. '*You* killed Kobus,' she ground out. 'Just as you're going to let Max go to the gallows.'

A big smile crossed David's face. He returned to his chair and leaned back in it, putting his hands behind his head and gazing at her reflectively. 'I must say, I never thought Kobus had it in him to father a son.'

Victoria felt an animal loathing for the despicable man who sat opposite her. She ignored the jibe. 'So you'll let Max die?'

'Short of going into Zimbabwe with a full infantry battalion, there's little else I can do.'

She looked at him coldly. 'Can you explain why Max released you?'

'I don't have to answer that question.'

'What about the ransom demand sent to Dolph?'

'Dolph never received any ransom demand. As I say, I think Max is under a lot of strain. He's been drinking heavily, and that American tart he fell in love with has dropped him. In his position I'd be imagining things, too – not that I'd ever allow myself to get into that position, of course.'

Victoria got up, swept her hair back and closed her briefcase. 'You are the only witness who can save him,' she said. 'You can't condemn your son to death by not appearing in court. I'll just have to find something to persuade you to testify.'

'Mission impossible!' he laughed. 'Now, if you'll excuse me, Victoria, I have a busy schedule which you have already interrupted by over forty-five minutes.'

The smile remained on David Loxton's face as the door slammed shut. It was the smile of a man who has power over others. Max and Vicky had never got the better of him because they did not understand the basic principles of power. He had always controlled them – he always would. And in this case it was so simple. Max would never break the pact they'd made; and even if he did, no one would believe him.

Dolph and Jurie were highly suspicious, of course. They knew beyond a shadow of doubt that Max had killed Hurst's German operative – but they also knew that Max hated his, David Loxton's, guts. They'd never put two and two together. Anyway, the evidence was about to disappear, for Max would surely hang.

David picked up the phone, and issued a couple of terse

instructions. Everything he could do to mess up Max's defence would be to his advantage.

Victoria got to Jan Smuts airport by half past three, in plenty of time to catch the five o'clock plane to Harare, and everything went smoothly until she got to passport control. The inspector looked at her passport carefully, then at her.

'Miss Loxton, you're on our wanted list. I can't let you out of the country.'

'This is ridiculous!'

'Listen, lady, you're not going anywhere.'

'I am a key witness in an important trial that starts on Monday. I *have* to be in Harare. I demand to speak to your superior officer.'

After two hours of fruitless arguing, Victoria left the airport and headed back for Johannesburg. She was crying. Max's life was in the balance, and she was mucking things up. Apparently, she had not fully paid her income tax for the previous year, and would not be allowed to leave the country until she had settled her account – and she couldn't do that until Monday. Of course, her father must have organised the whole fiasco at the airport – but there was absolutely nothing she could do to get at him.

She booked into the Sandton Sun hotel, north of Johannesburg, in a plush residential suburb. Once she'd got to her room, she picked up the phone. Her first call was to Ken Silke: she wouldn't be in court on Monday, that was for sure.

Ken calmed her down and told her not to worry, and after ten minutes talking to him she felt a little better. At least it was not a total disaster. But she'd wanted to be there for Max, and he would feel desperate, not knowing what had happened to her.

She called Saffron. Saffron, of course, could not understand it. 'But David's his father, goddamnit!'

'He's my father too, Saffron,' Victoria said wearily. 'You cannot begin to imagine how cold-blooded he is. And remember, it was Max who kidnapped him in the first place. They made a pact – David's release, and the identity of the man with the detonator, in return for Max's silence about David's involvement.'

'Vicky, he's going to hang! You know that, your father knows that. Surely all your father has to say is that South African Intelligence knew there was a plan to blow up the building, and

270

that he told Max about it? I mean, that won't affect his political career.'

'David hates Max, Saffron – he hates all of us. And if he admits to letting Max know about the plan, it'll get him kicked out of parliament. There has to be something else, some other way in which I can force David's hand. Something I've missed.'

Victoria could hear Saffron sobbing. There was nothing she could say to comfort her. The failure of the Okavango project, Kobus' assassination, and now this. What comfort was there for such a sequence of tragedies?

After she had put the phone down, she sat in silence in the anonymous hotel room, and realised that she was now a prisoner in this country, kept here by her father – by his obsession with money and power. She thought of her baby, and picked up the phone again.

'Lucinda, is Kobus all right?'

'Fine, but he's missing you. How's Harare?'

As Lucinda spoke, Vicky could hear Kobus crying in the background. Something snapped inside her. 'I'm not in Harare, I'm in Johannesburg,' she sobbed, and then recounted the whole dismal story. 'Lucinda,' she said, 'David *has* to testify. But how the hell can I make him?'

'You'll have to force his hand.'

'Don't you realise how powerful he is? It's impossible!'

She heard Lucinda start to cry too. 'Lucinda, I'm sorry,' she said. 'I shouldn't have shouted.'

'There's something . . .' Lucinda's voice was almost inaudible.

'What?'

'Wait. Please don't push me.'

'But what are you saying?'

There was a pause, then Lucinda's voice came clear and strong. 'He'll testify, Vicky.'

'What do you mean?'

'Just get to Harare as quickly as you can. I'll make sure David's there.'

Afterwards, Vicky lay in bed, staring into the darkness. What did Lucinda know that could possibly persuade David to come to Harare?

The hand was on his shoulder, shaking him gently. He groaned softly and tried to roll away, but the shaking continued. He opened his eyes and focused blearily on Hanli, then the clock. Two in the morning.

'Lucinda's on the phone, David. She's demanding to speak to you.'

'Tell her to call back at a civilised hour.'

Hanli picked up the phone again and David turned over, his wife's voice receding as sleep took him again. 'He says he'll call you in the morning. Lucinda? What do you mean? He'd never do something like that . . .'

David was suddenly wide awake and sweating heavily. 'Give me the phone!'

He snatched the receiver from Hanli's hand. 'Lucinda? What are you saying! I'm transferring this call to another phone, I'll speak to you in a minute.'

'Tell her to call you in the morning,' Hanli said drowsily.

'You know how she is,' David said. 'I'm scared she might kill herself. Go back to sleep, my dear, I'll sort this out.'

He went quickly out of the room and closed the door. He took a couple of deep breaths, then went down to the phone in his study.

'Lucinda?'

'You fucking bastard!'

'How dare you! I'm not going to listen to your insults.'

'You'd better be at Max's trial on Monday, I'm telling you.'

He began to relax a little. Victoria had obviously spoken to her – a last desperate ploy. 'I'm not going. Whatever Victoria told you, it's not the truth. Whoever kidnapped me, it certainly wasn't Max.'

'Father, you can bluff your way through the court session in Harare easily enough. All that matters is that you save Max. But I can tell you there's one thing you can't bluff your way out of. Something that'll wreck not only your political career but your private life too. You'll lose Hanli, and the boys. You think I've forgotten all about it, don't you?'

He felt himself go cold. She couldn't have remembered. Not now, after all these years.

'You think I don't know what's wrong with me, don't you? But I remember every last fucking detail, David. And I know why my mother did what she did.'

He felt himself shaking, his world collapsing. Memories, long pushed aside, came flooding back; memories that were strangely shameful, but also thrilling. But, oh God, if those memories became public knowledge.

'Be there on Monday, David, or I'm going to make sure the whole world knows about you – and that includes your highly moral government colleagues. It'll break your political career. It'll make Dirk and Rory want to spit on you!'

'Lucinda, please.'

'Be there, or see how much your fucking tart of a wife loves you after she hears what you're really like. Think of how Dirk and Rory will look at you when they know what sort of a man you really are!'

'Lucinda!'

But the phone was dead.

Dolph Klopper sat in the dimly lit lounge of his father's house, and for the hundredth time in his life, wondered what it was like to be blind. 'The failure of the Harare project is a big blow, Pa,' he said. 'The opportunity has been lost for good. We need the army to fight the war inside our own country now. It's getting harder and harder to contain the violence in the townships.'

'My son, the kaffirs need to be taught a lesson. They are becoming too confident, eh?'

Figi, his father's coloured maid, walked into the room and handed the old man a cup of cocoa. She gave no inkling of having heard the insulting reference.

'I need to put them in their place, Pa,' Dolph said. 'But how?'

The old man shrugged his shoulders. 'You have the weapons.'

'But there'd be an international outcry if I used them.'

The old man clicked his tongue impatiently. 'Haven't I shown you that the Reich still controls the world.'

Dolph shifted uncomfortably in his seat. 'A major move against the blacks would require detailed planning, Pa.'

'You are running out of time, my son. In the nineteen forties we hesitated, we prevaricated, and look what happened. The Führer was advised against using the chemical weapons. The fool! If we'd used them we would have won!' He hit the table with his bony fist, and cocoa split onto the freshly polished wood.

Dolph said slowly: 'Pa, perhaps we can make a chemical weapon to destroy the kaffirs.'

'But first you must find the man who betrayed you, or he will do it again.'

'I suspect it might be Loxton. He was being held in Harare when the Houses of Parliament were supposed to collapse. But how can I be sure he's guilty?'

'Don't waste your time asking such questions. Just use him and his experts to develop a chemical weapon, and then, when it is ready, my son, kill him.'

Max watched the water dripping from the roof of his cell and thought of George Zwane. What a pathetic waste of a life. But had he himself achieved anything more? He thought of Vicky. She'd said she'd see him again, but she hadn't come. He thought of Saffron, the smell of her, the softness of her skin against his own. He thought of making love, the tingling feeling that came over his body when he was near her. And now, when he needed her most of all, he could not even talk to her.

Things had gone so wrong for them all. Kobus dead, George dead; his own bankruptcy, and the failure of the Okavango project. Then – in spite of the drinking – he had won the big contract to build the new Houses of Parliament, had fought to meet impossible deadlines. Then came the discovery that his father had sabotaged the whole project. And now he was on trial for his life, and he'd made a vow not to name in court the very man who could save him. And even if he did break that vow, who on earth would believe him?

He thought of his mother, Tracey, and all that she had taught him. At least he had remained honest to that teaching: he had always done what he believed in. Perhaps if she had lived his father might have been a different man. Perhaps.

Ken would conduct a brilliant defence, and Victoria would make an excellent character witness, but in the end Ken had nothing to hang the story of the sabotage on. There was no evidence. The essential player was absent.

What would it be like, to hear the death sentence pronounced? He'd discussed it with Ken, but it hadn't helped him come to terms with it. How would he take it?

Lucinda sat on the bed, hugging the baby close to her and smiling. She had not felt so at ease since she herself had been a child. Max would be all right. She knew how to control David now.

Little Kobus was so pretty. She would have a child of her own

274

before too long – she was determined. Her father had ruined her life up till now, but she would not let him take another day from her. And she would make sure that he never forgot what she knew.

She went to the davenport in the corner of the bedroom, and took out her pen and a wad of bonded paper. With the baby lying comfortably on her lap, she started to write. She would make sure that the story of what her father had done to her was not lost. He might try to silence her, but once all the incriminating evidence was on paper and safely stored at the bank, he would never be able to manipulate her, Vicky or Max again.

She smiled with satisfaction. At last the roles would be reversed.

Victoria had spent most of the weekend on the phone to Ken Silke, discussing tactics for the trial. She'd thought Monday morning would never come, but now, finally, she stood waiting outside the offices of the Receiver of Revenue in Rissik Street, Johannesburg. In her hand she had the sheet of official paper she had received at the airport. Money, she said to herself. Well, whatever it takes, I'll pay.

To her surprise, she was greeted by name and shown up to the office of a Mr Kleynhans on the second floor.

'*Mejuffrou* Loxton?' Mr Kleynhans was an elderly man with a crop of startlingly white hair.

'I must apologise, *Mejuffrou* Loxton. It seems the authorities made a mistake and you were confused with another person of the same name. You have your bags here ready for the airport?'

She nodded, scarcely able to believe this was all happening.

'Let me follow you to your car. I realise that you are in a hurry, so we have arranged to hold up the passenger flight to Harare for you.'

Two minutes later, they were transferring her suitcase from her hire car to a white BMW saloon with police insignias, and as soon as she and Mr Kleynhans were installed in the back, the car leapt off with sirens blazing and tyres squealing. As they headed out to the airport on the motorway, Victoria looked over the police driver's shoulder and saw that they were travelling at over 220 km/hr.

Mr Kleynhans leaned confidentially towards her. 'My apologies again, *Mejuffrou* Loxton. The gentlemen from passport control phoned me at the weekend, and I came in early this morning and realised that an oversight had been made. If you'll give me the keys of your hire car, I'll return it. Can you tell me the cost of your hotel accommodation and food over the past three nights?'

Victoria handed him the bills from her purse, and he pulled out a wad of fifty-rand notes from his pocket and passed them to her.

'But that's far too much!'

'The Receiver of Revenue believes he should pay for your air fare because of the inconvenience you have suffered.'

When they reached the airport, instead of depositing her at the passenger terminal, the car screamed out onto the runway towards a waiting Boeing 747. Mr Kleynhans insisted on carrying her bags up the stairway to the first class section.

'Thank you, Mr Kleynhans!'

To his surprise – and her own – she kissed him on the cheek before disappearing inside the plane. The door closed, the steps were wheeled away, and the plane immediately taxied onto the tarmac.

Kleynhans watched it disappear, then walked quickly over to the glistening black long-wheelbase Daimler parked next to one of the hangars. He heard the whirr of an electric window being opened as he approached, and saw David Loxton sitting inside.

'Good work, Kleynhans. From today you can start your retirement. Of course, no mention of this incident must be made to anyone.'

'I understand, sir.'

'You will receive an extra gratuity of twenty thousand rands with your retirement payout.'

'Thank you, sir!'

Victoria entered the packed Harare courtroom at eleven o'clock. The judge looked up in surprise as she came in, then returned to the argument being put forward by the counsel for the prosecution. Victoria winked at Ken Silke conspiratorially, and he handed her a page of notes.

'Thank goodness you're here, Vicky. The judge really gave me a hammering for not having my key witness on hand. Apart from that, the prosecution have taken the line we expected. They're not accepting Max's plea that he was stopping a man about to detonate hidden charges, they're going for the murder of the

German journalist. How did you get out of South Africa so quickly?'

'Someone must have decided that it wasn't politic for me to be held up after all. Did they let you see Max?'

'No, they've been quite stroppy. Your non-appearance was seen as a deliberate attempt to try and hold up the trial.'

'I must try and talk to Max during the recess.'

She looked across at her brother in the stand. His face was deadly still. She could not bring herself to look at Saffron. She felt guilty for having annoyed the judge, possibly prejudicing him further against Max.

When the break was announced, Victoria slipped quietly out of the courtroom and went down to the cells. It didn't take her long to get permission to see Max. Closer to, he looked white and haggard.

'Don't hide anything from me,' he said in a dull voice. 'Father wasn't interested, was he? I told you it was a waste of time.'

'That's not fair, Max! If you don't try, you never stand a chance of winning.'

'So, what's your defence?'

'You. Your life, the things you believed in and did. All those things indicate that you would never dream of trying to kill a man in cold blood – unless it was to stop him from killing others.'

'But Victoria, I was caught in the act!'

He turned away from her and gazed at the dirty white walls of the cell, trying to collect his thoughts.

'Does Lucinda know?' he asked. 'Does she realise I'll hang?'

'Max, please keep your spirits up. There's a long way to go yet.'

'How's Saffron handling this? I can't look at her in the courtroom, I can't stand the suffering I'm putting her through.'

They held hands for a long time, in silence. When she got up to go, she said: 'Max, promise me you won't give up.'

He nodded grimly.

On the third day Ken Silke was ready to lead the defence. As he'd expected, the prosecution had put a number of witnesses on the stand – the journalist Max had mugged, the guard he'd knocked out. And there had been some surprises too: his physics professor, his boxing coach. The overall picture they painted was of a man with a violent temper who was not afraid to act out his

277

feelings. Then there was the fact that Max had volunteered to serve in one of the most dangerous battalions of the South African army during his compulsory military service. There was the fact that he had been tried for public violence in Botswana. The link with George Zwane was also highlighted. Max was called to the stand four times, and each time he had answered the questions in a straightforward manner. However, the prosecutor was a shrewd man who argued convincingly that Max was a dangerous criminal.

Now Ken Silke stood up, and the packed courtroom went quiet.

'I have come to this country to represent my client, who is on trial for his life. It is my intention to show that Dr Max Loxton's whole life has been characterized by a determination to improve society in any way open to him, and that far from being treated as a criminal, he should be regarded as a hero, particularly here, in Zimbabwe. I call . . .'

There was an intake of breath in the courtroom, and Victoria spun round furiously to see who had dared to interrupt Ken's opening speech. She found herself staring into the cold eyes of her father. Next to him was the President of Zimbabwe, Mr Robert Mugabe.

The President walked up to the judge's chair and conferred with him. Then he left as dramatically as he had arrived. The judge spoke as the hubbub in the courtroom subsided.

'I find myself in an unusual situation, and though I do not fully understand the circumstances I cannot contradict the will of my President. Mr David Loxton will now make a statement. He refuses to be cross-examined. Our President has guaranteed him immunity, allowing him the right to leave the courtroom after he has given his evidence. His statement will be made in camera, so that I must ask all those in the gallery to leave.'

Victoria felt giddy with excitement. She stared across at Ken, who was smiling. The prosecutor looked nervous. The judge gestured to David Loxton. 'Mr Loxton, would you move to the stand.'

As the gallery cleared, David Loxton moved slowly towards the witness box, rather as a man who has received the death penalty moves towards the gallows. He was impeccably dressed as usual, Victoria noted, in an understated pin-stripe suit and

278

black Italian moccasins, and with his dark hair smoothly combed back. He turned to face the judge.

'I will make my statement under oath.'

A messenger of the court handed him a battered-looking Bible.

'I swear before almighty God that I will tell the truth, the whole truth, and nothing but the truth.' Then he squared his shoulders and faced the court.

'As you know, the man on trial today is my own son by my first marriage. He is not a friend of mine and I am not a friend of his.'

There was a pause.

'As you may or may not know,' David Loxton went on, 'I was kidnapped some weeks ago. My government kept silent about a ransom note that was sent to them by my kidnappers. This was because my kidnapper wanted to trade my life for that of George Zwane, the terrorist.'

Another pause. Victoria saw that her father seemed to be having some difficulty in continuing.

'The South African government does not give in to such tactics,' he said. 'Even if it had meant my death, they would not have released Zwane. However, George Zwane died while trying to make an escape from a prison truck, so that my kidnapper no longer had any use for me. It was then I discovered that the kidnapper was none other than my own son.'

The prosecutor clenched his fists so tightly that the half-moons of his knuckles stood out on the backs of his hands. Suddenly Max's story was no longer a pack of lies but the truth. The prosecutor raised his hand to place an objection, but the judge stared down at him coldly. 'I cannot allow this witness to be questioned.'

'My government, as you probably realise,' David continued, 'has the most advanced intelligence-gathering network in Africa. Often we gather information that is of no real use to us. We do not believe in interfering in the affairs of our neighbours.

'Shortly before my kidnapping I had been notified of the possibility that dissident elements within this country might be attempting a coup. It was rumoured that this was to be achieved by collapsing the new Houses of Parliament, with carefully hidden charges, during the opening session of your parliament, and then, of course, blaming the tragedy on us.'

Victoria knew this was probably a lie, but she also knew her father was speaking for the media as well as playing for his political life. She knew what this speech must have cost him, but she could not understand why he was making it.

'When my son decided to release me, he informed me that that very day was the day of the opening of your parliament. I feared for my life. I told my son about the possible coup, and he immediately took it upon himself to prevent it. I identified for him the agent who would detonate the charges – a German masquerading as a reporter for *Stern*. Max and I made a pact – that information, in return for my freedom and his silence. After that, I fled the country. You will see by his testimony – or rather, the lack of it – that my son is a man of his word. I have given Mr Mugabe detailed plans of how the explosive charges were placed, and investigation will prove the truth of what I have said.'

And then David Loxton stepped down from the witness stand and walked out of the courtroom, looking neither to right nor left.

Lucinda switched on the television set and watched the nine o'clock news, the baby ensconced snugly in her lap. Outside, snow was falling, covering the streets of London in a delicate white velvet. Life was looking a lot more promising for her than it had ever done. The previous evening she had managed to go out with a man and enjoy herself. She had not snubbed him or insulted him, and he had asked her to go out with him this coming weekend, and she had accepted. Perhaps, having faced what it was that had driven her over the edge, and confronted her persecutor, she could now live a normal life. Perhaps.

'Today in Harare,' the newscaster said, 'Dr Max Loxton was exonerated of all the crimes attributed to him. Summing up, the judge, Mr Justice Webster, said that in his view Loxton should be regarded as one of the heroes of the Zimbabwean revolution.' As the camera switched to a view of Max, Saffron, Victoria and Ken Silke at Harare airport, walking across the tarmac to their plane, he concluded: 'Dr Loxton refused to make any comment to the press. He is rumoured to have left the country already on a private plane. His sister, Victoria Loxton, who was a character witness at the trial, left for London this afternoon.'

Lucinda smiled: tomorrow night, she and Vicky would celebrate. For a moment she wondered what would happen to her father.

Five

David Loxton walked into the room and felt twenty pairs of eyes focus upon him. This is what it must have been like, long ago, to face the Holy Inquisition – but he certainly wasn't going to show any sign of weakness. The men he faced now represented the most powerful political force on the African continent; they were the Band of Brothers, the Broederbond, the Afrikaans elite, drawn from every quarter of South African society. Dolph Klopper was amongst their number. David, as an Englishman, could never be a member, and in fact had always regarded the whole thing as faintly ridiculous. Now, as he stood before them, derision was replaced by awe. Because of his testimony at the trial of his son, David was accused by the Broederbond of betrayal. There was nothing he could say that would change that. Only he knew the reason why he had testified, and if Lucinda had done what she had threatened, his political career would have been finished anyway.

There was no chair for him at the head of the long table. He would have to stand during the whole session. It was a deliberate device, to weaken and intimidate him.

The man closest to him, on the left side of the table, turned to face him. 'David Loxton, what do you have to say for yourself?' He spoke in Afrikaans. He was the Reverend Eldad Cilliers, one of Klopper's most important supporters.

David took a deep breath. 'Brothers, I was placed in an impossible situation. You would not release Zwane, but then you could not know that I faced certain death in Harare. My son was going to hand me over to the authorities on the opening day of parliament. I realised that if the demolition of the Houses of

281

Parliament was not stopped, I would be finished – and I was not prepared to die. I told my son, and he agreed to release me. I also made him take a vow of silence, and made him promise never to reveal that our government was behind the plot. He chose to prevent our operative from activating the detonator, and was arrested after killing him. The Zimbabweans now believe that the attempt was organised from within their country – we remain blameless in their eyes.'

Eldad Cilliers rose from his chair before David could say any more.

'He has spoken. Let us vote.'

But David was not prepared to be finished so quickly. 'No!' he cried – and immediately all eyes were upon him. He had dared to interrupt them!

'If you condemn me,' David said, leaning forward, commanding their attention, 'then you condemn yourselves with me. If you condemn me, I will release all the information I have to the world media, and when I do the whole world will know the true origin of the plot. I have tape recordings of my discussions on the matter with the State President. Let me tell you that I also have evidence that the assassination of Kobus van der Post was carried out by a South African army gunman acting under our orders. So make your vote, brothers. But do it in the full understanding of what I will do if it goes against me.'

He stepped back from the table, and saw an angry flash in the Reverend Cilliers' eyes. The dominee rose again. 'Those who say guilty, raise their hands.'

Not a single hand was raised.

But though he walked free from the Broederbond's tribunal, David Loxton was still a very worried man. Unless he did something about it, Lucinda would have a hold over him now for the rest of his life, and he simply could not afford to have her pulling his strings.

It was time to cut her down.

BOOK III

One

1992

The bells that had been ringing out so merrily, ceased, and many of the congregation in the elegant London church – men in morning dress, women in the highest fashion of the day – turned their heads to look back up the aisle. They did not have to wait long. As the organist began to play the wedding march, Saffron appeared in the open doorway of the church, on the arm of Lucinda's husband, Lord Milner. They paused a moment; then Lord Milner squeezed Saffron's arm, making her smile, and they started to walk together down the aisle, Saffron arrestingly beautiful in a body-hugging red velvet dress slit up the middle to reveal her long, slender legs. Max stood waiting for her at the altar, and next to him his best man – a statuesque black man, Malcolm Zwane.

'You look too good to marry.'

Max whispered the words softly in Saffron's ear as she came to stand beside him, then they both turned to face the cross that hung on the stone wall behind the altar. The music ended and the minister stepped forward, his lean face smiling.

'Please be seated.'

As everyone sat, Saffron heard a baby cry and turned to look at Victoria in the front row with Kobus. She and Max had given the baby a special invitation, and young Kobus had been ordered not to leave, however much noise he might make.

'We are gathered here today to witness the marriage of two very special people. I would like you to join in a silent prayer for their future.'

285

Everyone kneeled to pray. Saffron prayed that Max would forget about the disastrous Okavango project and devote himself now to his latest endeavour – an air travel business in London. She had lent him the money to get started. He had been reluctant to take it at first, so they had made it a formal business deal, with Max contracted to pay back the money with interest on a specified date. Work often took them both to the United States, and it was there that they had met Malcolm Zwane, who had become a dear friend. Max had known his brother, of course – but Saffron knew that he valued Malcolm not only for that, but for the man he was: a born diplomat, seeking conciliation where George would have looked for confrontation. Yet often, Max said, when Malcolm spoke it was George's voice he heard.

Saffron took one more look behind her, to where Lucinda sat in the front row, looking very beautiful, now joined by Lord Milner. They had been married some three months before at a glittering society wedding. She turned back again, to face the altar. She must try not to think about Africa, in spite of the memories that kept flooding back. Max had given enough to the dark continent; he must get on with his life here in London. She was determined to make him very, very happy.

An uneasy air hung over Soweto township in the early winter sunshine; pockets of dirty mist lingered between the houses, witness to the thousands of fires which had been burning there the previous evening. On the outskirts of the township, behind barbed-wire fences, sat stern-faced young white men in South African army uniform, armed to the teeth and ready to jump into their Casspir armoured cars at a moment's notice. Silently, they prayed that there would be no trouble today. Most of them were conscripts, and wondered what they were doing, fighting people they were supposed to protect.

On the better side of Soweto, outside a house in one of the immaculate streets of the elite suburb of Dube, a glistening Mercedes-Benz sports car stood parked, its bonnet still hot after a hard three-hour drive from Pietersberg in the northern Transvaal. Inside the house, two men sat in the comfort of black leather armchairs, in a room that was decorated with boxing trophies.

286

'So, Kumalo, you have good news to report from Pietersburg?'
Fat Man, dressed in a shining Saville Row suit, spoke heavily.

Kumalo's mouth tightened, making the vertical scar running down his face more prominent than ever. He looked in disgust at the folds of fat hanging over the other man's crocodile-skin belt, and his nostrils flared as he spoke.

'Our supporters are getting better organised. As we agreed, it will be soon.'

'Time is irrelevant. We have the Transvaal, we should strike now.'

'No! The command is clear. I went to the cave – I was given my orders. We must not move yet, our immediate objective must be to create further unrest. First we must hit Natal, then the Cape.' Kumalo stared out of the window at the sprawling shanties just visible on the horizon. 'But we must maintain the tension here,' he said, 'that is very important.'

'Who is it who gives you the orders?'

'Fat Man, I cannot tell you. But to ignore them is to die.'

Fat Man looked at Kumalo uneasily. Nothing fazed Kumalo. Perhaps it was because he knew how great was the power of the person who gave the orders. 'I learn something from you every time,' he said.

'You agree I was right over Van der Post?'

'Of course. Van der Post's initiative would have been a disaster for us. A peaceful solution would bring us no power.'

'Our money will buy weapons for the Comrades in Natal, Fat Man, and in the Cape. Our strategy will be simple. Those who do not co-operate will be eliminated; those who can be bought will be bribed; and those who want power will be promised it.'

'And what about our brothers who want peaceful change?'

'They are doing a good job abroad – let them continue. As a result of their efforts we have international sanctions against us – creating more unemployment, fuelling further discontent. What more could we ask for?'

'They could take the power from us.'

'They are only a handful in Lusaka, we are millions and millions. The people want blood, and we will give it to them. All true revolutions need blood.'

'We will eradicate those who stand in our way?'

'With the necklace and the panga.'

Later, Kumalo left, drawing his black Italian leather jacket closer to him, against the cold. Goodbye, Fat Man, he thought. You are getting too big for your boots, and when the time comes you will be sacrificed. Those, too, are my orders from Pietersberg.

'Managing Director at twenty-two. That's a significant achievement, my boy.'

'I've earned the position though, haven't I, sir?'

He had indeed, and David was proud to give it to him. He had given Rory carte-blanche at Terminal, and the boy had amply rewarded his confidence. Since the incident with Dolph Klopper and the Broederbond, his own political career had gone from strength to strength, but this had meant that he had less time to concentrate on business, and needed an able lieutenant for his weapons firm.

Klopper had given him a lot of power. David was now Prime Minister – a position and a title that pre-dated the institution of the State Presidency, and that Klopper had resurrected especially for him. One of his chief objectives now was to turn the South African army into a leaner fighting machine, and he had briefed General Jurie Smit to this effect. Plans for invading the rest of Africa had been dropped; David knew they could successfully invade anywhere they liked, the trouble was holding on to conquered territory after occupation – they were having enough difficulty controlling unrest at home. However, the practice of destabilizing neighbouring states was being stepped up. He was backing guerrilla movements in a number of adjacent territories, most of which were already battling with civil war and a stagnant economy.

David smiled at Rory, and they both looked at the weapon lying between them on the table – the latest Terminal product. It was based on a stolen – David preferred the word 'borrowed' – German patent, and was perfect for South African conditions.

'It will work, sir. I've had a design team refining this prototype for the last six months. Soon we'll be in production.'

'Reliability?'

'Better than the AK-47.'

David whistled through his teeth.

'I'm not exaggerating,' Rory said eagerly. 'Don't forget it doesn't carry conventional ammunition.' He picked up the weapon and pointed to the mechanism. 'The bullet is only formed at the moment of firing. An infantryman can carry over one and a half thousand rounds on him with this weapon. In a loose combat situation like the one in our townships, it will be devastating against conventional technology.'

He pointed the weapon down from the office window towards the factory floor. 'Any fool can use this,' he said. 'No training is necessary. You just point and squirt.'

'Very good, my boy. This means that when we come to using citizen-force troops who have been out of training for a long time, they can just pick it up and use it. How heavy is it?'

'That's the best part. Including the additional ammunition, this weapon is lighter than our current assault rifle.'

'What will you call it?'

'The LA – the Loxton Avenger.'

'I like it, Rory. I like it a lot.'

'And, there's something else I'd like to show you, sir.' Rory hesitated, then continued: 'I've always felt that we could market our products a little better.'

David's brow furrowed – Rory was overstepping the mark a little here.

'Relax, sir,' Rory said hurriedly. 'It was an idea I came up with when I saw Dirk a few months ago in Los Angeles.'

David thought proudly of his other son's progress. Dirk was already being referred to as one of Hollywood's most promising young directors after achieving a box-office hit with his first movie. *Time* magazine said he had a natural gift for capturing the intensity and excitement of action. Looking at his younger son now, David couldn't help briefly comparing his scruffiness with Dirk's lean good-looks – but Rory was the one with the most potential, no doubt of it.

'You remember our last trip to Chile,' Rory said, 'when we sold the G5? Remember you had to have the weapon shipped over there to give it a field test?'

'Everyone does that.'

'We're not "everyone", sir. We're Terminal – the biggest independent arms manufacturer in the world. Let me show you something new: an effective method of selling armaments without a live test.'

In the little lecture theatre – Terminal believed in keeping its staff up-to-date on developments at home and abroad, with films and talks about technological growth and new weaponry – Rory

289

sat David down in the middle row of the auditorium, had a few words with the projectionist, then took the seat next to his father.

The screen in front of them grew light, but as yet there was no image – only the sound of gunshots, followed by a scream. Then a soldier appeared on the screen, armed with a conventional assault rifle. He crouched, turned cautiously, and pulled the trigger. Nothing happened. Anxiously he searched for ammunition, but he had none, and fear was etched across his face. Then came the noise of returning gunfire, intensifying. Suddenly the soldier's body was riddled with bullet holes, and the camera closed in on his bloody, screaming face.

The screen went black, then faded up again on the same scene. A man, unarmed but in combat dress, walked into the picture and spoke directly into the camera.

'You have just witnessed a standard warfare situation. A good man, a conventional weapon, a typical problem: in a war you don't have time to reload; in a war you can't always carry all the ammunition you need.'

The man walked up to the corpse of the soldier who had featured earlier and turned it over, picking up the assault rifle.

'This is the problem, and until now there has not been an answer. Now Terminal has a devastating solution.'

The screen went black again. In the darkness came the sound of a single spurt of continuous gunfire. The projector began to roll again – and this time the setting was a black township. David hunched forwards. The camera was taking the role of a soldier moving into an urban terrorist situation. It was very, very real.

From the camera's point of view, clear bursts of fire kept erupting, as if from the protagonist's gun, gradually eliminating every aggressor who appeared. Finally a man ran out in the street, obviously believing the soldier's weapon to be empty. There was a final burst of fire, and the man's body turned as the bullets tore it to pieces, blood spattering across the camera lens.

Now the film cut to a fresh perspective. The soldier moved closer to camera, clasping a smoking weapon. He held it up. 'The LA,' he said. 'The Loxton Avenger. It doesn't carry bullets, it makes them. Lighter than a conventional assault rifle, it lets you carry the equivalent of one and a half thousand rounds of conventional ammunition.'

A shot interrupted the presenter's speech, and he swivelled to return the fire. The sustained and withering burst continued for over two minutes, after which a horrifying scream erupted from the building into which he had been pumping the shots.

The camera went to close-up on the presenter's face. 'The LA. The Loxton Avenger. With it you're invincible. Without it . . . you're dead.'

The picture faded, and David started clapping spontaneously. 'Magnificent, my boy! It's so realistic!'

Rory looked serious. 'It is real. It has to be. The weapons market is a tough one – you can't fool people, you have to deliver.'

David stiffened.

'Everything you saw was real,' Rory insisted. He grinned. 'The ultimate snuff movie, you might say.'

'You could be prosecuted for murder!'

Rory merely shrugged his shoulders – and David couldn't help a smile. His sons had learned their lesson well. They had become ruthless; perhaps more ruthless than he was himself.

'Sir, our customers buy our weapons for killing,' Rory said earnestly. 'They want power – they want proof that what they are buying can kill.'

'But if this film got into the wrong hands . . .'

'Then we just say we faked it.' Rory got up and walked to the front of the auditorium. 'I want to take this into the market now, sir. The deposits we get will cover the costs of our final research and development before the LA even goes into production.'

'Magnificent!'

'Then I want the weapon issued to one of your newly formed riot squads.'

'Jolly good idea. We need to make a show of force in the townships. You realise the problems we are facing?'

'I do. But now you have the technology to surmount them.'

But as David Loxton walked out of his factory into the sunlight, his head full of plans for total control of South Africa, Rory, sitting in his office and staring across the glistening factory roofs, was thinking quite other thoughts. His father was so obsessed with politics. This factory, these weapons, that was power, not a seat in the cabinet. As Rory saw it, he would be supplying tomorrow's rulers – no matter who they might be. Black government or white government – the colour of the ruling party's skin was irrelevant, as long as you got their business. His father was already a part of the past. His father, for example, would never sell weapons to both sides – which was stupid. Who cared who won? All that mattered was making money.

Rory had a simple, lucrative plan. He had developed a new market for Terminal's old weapons. The LA was an incredible weapon, but of course its inferior predecessor, the R4, would continue to be manufactured – it would be ridiculous to let all that investment go to waste. Those old R4 assault rifles could be sold to the Comrades.

As for the state of the country, well, as far as Rory was concerned the continuing unrest was good news: he was profiting from both sides of the struggle. He chuckled to himself. What a fool his father was! Money – that was the primary, the only issue. Money was power.

Lady Lucinda Milner saddled the sleek black horse, then stood back and admired the way his flanks gleamed in the early morning sunlight. The horse had arrived the day before, just after her husband left for a few days' business in the City, and it was strange that he hadn't mentioned to her this new addition to his stable. But she was longing to ride him! She looked at her watch: ten minutes before Jackson came on duty. She knew she should speak to the stableman before riding this stallion, but he was so beautiful, and she was an excellent rider, after all. She led him forward by the bridle a few steps, excited by his strength and beauty. She tightened the belt under the saddle, looking back along the long line of closed green stable doors. Apart from his racehorses, her husband owned over thirty thoroughbreds.

She put her foot into the stirrup and eased herself into the saddle. He was tall, and she felt powerful as she sat astride him. The frost-clad lawns stretched temptingly off into the distance, but she turned one more time to look at the house behind her, an elegant Elizabethan manor set in its own landscaped grounds. She loved it, and spent as much time here as she could despite a busy social life. That weekend, for example, after her husband had returned late this afternoon, they were to go away with their close friend, the Princess of Wales. They had the house in London, too, but Lucinda only went up to London for major social events and to see her sister and brother.

Lucinda turned her full attention back to the horse, stroking his glossy neck. Then she eased him into a slow rising trot and headed out towards the beech wood.

She liked to ride in the woods, exploring, with no one to direct her, and early morning was her best time. That was when she might surprise a squirrel hurrying through the frosted leafmould, or one of the deer that roamed the estate. This land had belonged to the Milners since Doomsday. Her husband's great-grandfather had had a brief foray abroad, principally in South Africa, but otherwise the Milner family had remained in the British Isles.

This time, on the new mount, she found the woods a little tricky, and felt more confident once they had left the trees behind. The horse was almost embarrassingly obedient. In front of her was the long field they used as an airstrip. Lord Milner did not like to fly in winter, so the aeroplane was under wraps in the hangar at the far end of the field. She leaned down over the horse's neck and whispered in his ear: 'Carry me as fast as you can.'

The horse shot forward without prompting, and she held the reins tightly, feeling the big animal unleash its power. Her long red hair was pulled back by the wind, there was a tight smile on her lips, and as the horse settled easily to the gallop, for a few moments she forgot where she was. She imagined herself on the veld on her father's farm in Zimbabwe, charging past a herd of zebra. In the distance a bright red African sun was setting . . .

From the trees came a low, shrill whistle. Lucinda hardly heard it – but her mount's mood altered on the instant, and she came to her senses to find the horse suddenly changing direction and bolting towards a copse on her left. She pulled on the reins, but to no avail. The animal was quite out of her control.

They shot into the trees. Branches started to smash against Lucinda's face, and desperately she tried to check her mount, screaming at him to slow down, the sweat running down her face. Then a big branch hit her.

She hit the ground hard and tasted blood in her mouth. Her foot was still in the stirrup. The horse dragged her through the undergrowth. 'Stop!' she cried to the horse. 'For God's sake, stop!'

Then her head hit the side of a tree, and the stirrup broke. The horse snorted with satisfaction, then bolted off, wild and uncaring. She lay with her long red hair trailing off into the leaves, her riding crop still in her hand, her face white and still.

*

The cabbie looked in his mirror and studied the big man in the seat behind. Very wealthy, by the looks of his suit and his mohair overcoat. They'd keep him nice and warm, too, on a cold winter's night like this.

'Unusual accent you've got, guvnor,' he said.

'South African.'

'Can't say I agree with their politics meself.'

He watched the man in the rear-view mirror for signs of irritation, but all the man said was, 'Very few people do.'

'So what do you think's going to happen there, then, eh?'

'I'm not sure. It's over a year since I left, and I haven't been back, though I often visit Botswana.'

'Botswana?'

'A smaller country, to the north-west of South Africa – a beautiful wilderness.'

'I don't like wild animals. OK behind bars in a zoo, but that's about as far as I'll go.' The cabbie sniffed vigorously. 'But what about this trouble in South Africa, then? Think it'll end in a bloodbath?'

'The army's very powerful, but there could be a revolution. I've never seen as much anger there as there obviously is now.'

'I can't blame those poor black buggers. It's that bastard Loxton, the Prime Minister.'

'My father.'

The cab driver started, and looked in the mirror again, but the big man seemed quite unruffled. 'Er, sorry,' he said. 'But everybody's entitled to their opinion, ain't they?'

'Relax. I agree with you. He's a bastard.'

After the cabbie had dropped him at the big house by the park, Max stood a moment looking across the dark lawns and trees. Every day in his heart he wished he could be back in South Africa; but Saffron was right – here at least he had a future.

Yes, his father was a bastard. But a revolution? The army was just too powerful. Internationally, the feeling about South Africa seemed almost one of indifference now. The economies of Britain and the United States were in recession, and though some sanctions were still enforced, the problems in the Middle East threatened to divert attention away from South Africa altogether. The townships had become cauldrons of anger and despair. He had seen from news reports that Soweto now resembled a concentration camp, effectively walled in by a cordon of barbed

294

wire and security controls. Curfews kept everyone except the army and police off the streets at night.

But he was all right. His air tour business had prospered. He was known as a man who delivered, the new London whizz-kid. He had more money than he knew how to spend.

He walked up the steps of his house and the big front door opened before he had a chance to ring the bell.

'Uncle Max!'

It was a body blow, and caught him off balance. Max picked the boy up and hugged him. Of course, he'd forgotten: it was New Year's Eve, Victoria was going out and was leaving young Kobus with Saffron. He was nearly three now, and so like his father. Every time Max looked at him, it hurt.

'Max, please can we go and see Big Ben tonight?'

'It's way past your bedtime already!'

'You promised!'

'Oh? Did I?' Max feigned surprise – and Kobus giggled.

'All right then, you be a good boy for the next hour or two, and I'll see what I can do.'

He looked up to see Saffron standing in the hall. She was in black slacks and a black jersey, more beautiful than ever, with her long dark hair cascading off her shoulders.

'And how's the film director?' he said.

'How's about a kiss, honey?'

Max put Kobus down and embraced her, and their house-keeper came into the room to get Kobus.

'Time for your bath, my boy!'

Later Max and Saffron went up to their bedroom to change. However many times he was with her, Max still could not help marvelling at Saffron's beauty, the long line of her body, the firm, full breasts, the long, slender legs – and a face that still bewitched him. Then he started thinking about his conversation with the cab driver. Had he copped out of South Africa? The faces came back to haunt him . . . Kobus and George. Both men had died for what they believed in. What was *he* doing, apart from making a lot of money?

'What's the problem, honey?'

Max turned, and looked at the beautiful, naked woman facing him. 'Nothing,' he said. He took her in his arms and pushed her on the bed.

'You want children, Dr Loxton?'

He kissed her, and went on kissing her. It was like being swept up in the dust of a Karoo storm and then standing in the cool, dry air after it had passed, watching the raindrops begin to patter in the dust, smelling the freshness, feeling that feeling of optimism, of life renewed. Her body arched and fell as the passion rose within her. 'Oh Max! Max!'

At last they lay still in each other's arms – and suddenly the other thoughts came flooding back to him. The hotel complex in the wetlands . . . Sharing a bottle of wine with Kobus . . . Sparring with George . . . The laughter, the camaraderie and the hope. Where was it now?

'Max, come on . . . What's eating you?'

'Memories. The cab driver started talking about South Africa on the way home. I feel I've failed my friends, Saffron – they died for what they believed in.'

'Oh, Max. You're always talking to Kobus and George in your sleep.'

'Ghosts.'

'No, they were real people, who mattered.'

He blushed. 'You begin to know me better than I know myself.'

'I understand how you feel – watching that place disintegrate, not being able to stop it.' She picked up a magazine and tossed it on the bed. 'Have you read the leader in *Time*? They say the townships are like a powder keg waiting for the match.'

'After a hundred years of oppression it's inevitable. But no doubt my father's got something up his sleeve.'

They went down to stand by the log fire in the huge lounge – a room Max was proud of, for it had been featured in *Interiors*. He walked through into the ground-floor nursery and took Kobus from the housekeeper.

'All ready, then?'

He picked up the intercom in the hall, and called the garage. 'James, we're ready to go.'

Outside the sky-blue Rolls-Royce pulled up on cue, and the three of them were driven silently off. Max sat back, waiting for the inevitable.

'We're going the wrong way!' Saffron's face wore a look of disappointment.

'A surprise.'

'But I want to go to Trafalgar Square, then walk through the crowds to Big Ben. You know that's how I want to celebrate New Year's Eve!'

The big car moved along the motorway westwards out of London, eventually taking the turn-off for Beaconsfield. Max smiled at the look of irritation on Saffron's face as James turned into a dirt road between beech trees. At last they drew to a halt. In front of them was a roaring log fire and a table set for dinner.

'A genuine *braaivleis*, Saffron.'

Saffron stared coldly at him. 'I want to see Big Ben.'

Half an hour later they were braaing meat contentedly in front of the fire, James rocking Kobus on his knee. Max looked up for the stars but could only see clouds. He remembered a time when he was a little boy and he had sat braaing on a New Year's Eve with his mother. That had been at the bush camp in the Okavango.

By eleven thirty Saffron was again looking at him indignantly. 'I'll never forgive you – you promised, goddamnit!'

'Time for a walk, I think.'

Max led Saffron through the darkness, followed by James with Kobus. Without warning, a blaze of lights erupted from the blackness. In front of them a jet-black helicopter sat in the middle of a concrete landing-pad.

'Step aboard.'

He took Kobus from James, and climbed in after Saffron. 'Let me introduce our pilot, Saffron – Captain Guy Hawkins of Loxton Aviation.'

Captain Hawkins pushed the starter and the helicopter blazed into action, taking off moments later. They skimmed the tops of the trees, then headed eastwards towards London. Saffron snuggled up next to Max in the huge back seat.

'I should have known better,' she said.

Max grinned. From under the seat he pulled out a bottle of Moet and two glasses, and Kobus giggled noisily as he popped the cork. 'A toast to my latest venture,' he said. 'This is the development of an exclusive holiday service. This helicopter and five others will take our clients to the most beautiful parts of the world, places no one else can possibly go to. A guarantee of both exclusivity and privacy.'

Now they were over the City, glowing with light below them, and full of people. St Paul's was bathed in light, Trafalgar Square was packed to the sides. They could sense the anticipation and excitement below them. Max pointed downwards to the crowds.

'They're going towards the Thames, to see Big Ben. We've got an advantage over them. We can get a lot closer.'

Captain Hawkins looked over his shoulder. 'OK, I'm going in. We've got three minutes.'

Saffron couldn't believe it. She felt she could almost reach out and touch one of the hands of London's most famous time-keeper. As the big hand touched twelve, the whole helicopter reverberated with the sound of the chime. They moved away, out over the hordes of people who were singing below them.

Captain Hawkins put the machine down expertly on a landing-pad next to the Houses of Parliament, and then Saffron, Max and little Kobus joined the crowds, sharing in the spirit of the New Year.

It was a glittering occasion. Around the long table sat the cream of the British legal profession, male and female. Chandeliers twinkled above them, and an orchestra softly played a back-ground of Strauss waltzes as conversation ebbed and flowed. Many of the women present were striking to look at, but none more so than Victoria Loxton, who was not wearing a dress but a black-tie suit like the men. She was now in her late thirties, and despite a number of overtures had stated firmly that she was not interested in men. Masculine rumour, though, had it that she was longing for an affair.

At the moment Victoria was talking to Miles Lanson about his Channel tunnel development. Lanson was a billionaire British entrepreneur and former lawyer, who never failed to startle the establishment with his bizarre projects – which nevertheless had the uncanny habit of succeeding.

Now a tall man rose at the end of the table. 'I should like to wish you all a very happy New Year.' He raised his glass, gazing intently at Victoria – and Victoria gaily returned the smile. Judge Dalling had been trying to seduce her for the past year, and was obviously about to launch a new attack. She ignored the hateful looks directed at her by his wife; if the woman thought she was having an affair with her husband, she was a fool. Suddenly Victoria thought of Kobus, and wished she had stayed at home with him.

Miles Lanson invited her to dance, and she took a turn with

him round the floor. When they returned to the table she found a note waiting for her.

'You must excuse me. A telephone message – urgent, apparently.'

Outside in the vestibule, she quickly dialled the Milners' Sussex number.

'Anthony . . .? Oh my God! I'm coming immediately.'

The Lotus – her one indulgence, it was the latest model – was waiting for her in the car park. She changed into first and floored the accelerator. The tachometer shot up, and she was pushed back in the seat as the machine surged forwards. It wouldn't take her more than an hour to get to the hospital . . .

Blades whirring, the helicopter touched down on the grass. The little hospital was a converted manor house, not far from the Milner estate. As Max and Saffron hurried across to the entrance they saw Vicky's car parked outside.

A tight-lipped nurse greeted them in reception. 'They're waiting for you, third door on the left. Please enter quietly, she's not good.'

The room was ablaze with lights. Anthony was hunched over the bed, holding Lucinda's hands, with Victoria beside him. She turned as Max and Saffron came in.

'Thank God you're here. Come . . .'

Max stared down into the white face of the little sister he had loved ever since she was born. The eyes gave a flicker of recognition.

'Max.' Lucinda spoke slowly, and with great difficulty. 'Max. You've always been so good . . .'

He heard sobbing, and saw that Anthony was crying. How strange it was to see such a big man crying. Victoria gestured to them all to move away, but then Lucinda spoke again.

'Max. Don't let him get away with it . . .' She looked away from Max, to her husband. 'Anthony, take my hand.'

Anthony stood up, wiping the tears from his eyes, and took her right hand between both of his.

'My love, you'll be all right,' he said.

But they all knew it wasn't the truth. Victoria saw that her sister's face was deathly white now. Lucinda had had such a hard life – there was no justice in this.

299

'Be strong,' Lucinda whispered. 'Anthony, I want you to be happy.'

Her eyes closed, and her face looked peaceful in death.

The first light of dawn was breaking, softly illuminating the windows of Lord Milner's drawing-room, where the four of them sat, weary beyond description.

'I don't know who delivered that horse,' Lord Milner said, for the third time.

Max looked exhaustedly across at Anthony. 'She was always impulsive,' he said.

'If only she'd waited for Jackson, he'd never have let her ride it . . . It was six hours before we found her, you see. At first I thought she was all right, but then her condition worsened. It seems her neck was broken, there was brain damage. She'd never have walked again . . .'

Victoria stared at him intensely. 'So you told the doctor to . . .?'

'Yes.'

Victoria put her arms around him, and he said: 'She was so active, Vicky. To have seen her crippled, a half-wit . . . It wouldn't have been fair.'

'Few men I know would have had the courage to make that decision,' Vicky said. 'And I promise you, this awful period will pass and you'll be left with the memories of the good times you had with her. Those are what count. I know, I've learned to live with death.'

Max got up. He was weary and depressed. 'We must go, Anthony. I hope you'll come up and stay with us. I think it would be good for you to get away.'

Later, he and Saffron walked out onto the dew-soaked lawn and watched the helicopter make its way down to them. On the way back to London they said little, but Max's mind was in turmoil. Thoughts of Lucinda haunted him; thoughts of Africa. He had a sense of loss that was almost impossible to bear. What the hell was he doing with his life?

As the big black car pulled up and the chauffeur opened the door for him, there was the sound of a large explosion in the distance. Both David Loxton and the chauffeur turned to see where it had come from. A couple of miles away to the south, a cloud of smoke mushroomed into the sky.

'Another bomb,' David Loxton muttered angrily under his breath, then turned to enter the sombre, red-brick portals of Voortrekker Heights, the power-centre of the South African military machine. A soldier snapped to attention as he walked in.

'At ease.' He liked the precision of the military. At least here everyone was vigilant.

In the small conference room he was glad to see that no one else had yet arrived. He liked to be early for a meeting, it gave him time to compose his thoughts. He sat down at the head of the ebony table and stared up at the portrait of Dr Daniel François Malan, the architect of apartheid.

'How would you have played it, Danny?'

David did not feel the optimism he usually felt with the advent of a new year. He had been immensely pleased with the achievement of Lucinda's death, but the events of the previous night had put that quite out of his mind. Last night, a huge bomb in Sandton City, the elite shopping centre of the wealthy northern suburbs of Johannesburg, had killed over seventy people who were welcoming in the New Year. There had been similar explosions, with similar casualties, all over the country – no city was exempt.

Well, David thought now, it's time to teach these bastards we mean business. He unfurled a map he had brought with him, and studied the area marked in red. Soweto had mushroomed in size over the past few years, now officially accommodating nearly four million people – he hated to think what the unofficial figure might be. And the nerve-centre of the unrest was there, in the centre of Soweto, he was sure of it. The majority of the black population were against violence, as they all knew, but someone was organizing disturbances in the township in order to foment unrest. Who was it? Whoever they were, they had to be dealt with, fast.

The trouble was that the army had to remain outside, and so could only control the movement of people in and out of Soweto. To go inside the township they had to use Casspir armoured cars filled with riot police, and every time they opened fire on the blacks, it was broadcast all over the world. Even with the intensive media restrictions he had imposed, word of the inevitable atrocities still got out. He thought back to a month before, when the troops had just been issued with the LA machine-gun. A riot had started in Meadowlands, a suburb of Soweto, and a riot squad had been called in. A young soldier, hit in the face by a stone thrown by someone in the mob, had gone berserk and unleashed the power of the new machine-gun. Two hundred and fifty people lay dead when he had finished, and it had made the front page of every newspaper in the world.

David smiled. At least there had been some benefit. That one incident had advanced sales of the LA from overseas buyers to meteoric proportions. But it had also resulted in a continuing backlash of black violence.

He looked down at his watch – and at the same time heard the other men arriving. First in was General Jurie Smit, the head of armed forces. He shook David's hand.

'I hope this is good news?'

'Better than you would dream, Jurie, old chap.'

Next was Dr Preusser, lean and hollow-cheeked, his grey eyes gleaming through his steel-framed spectacles.

Last came Major Hurst, who closed the conference room doors behind him. David rose from his chair and shook hands with him.

'Good to have you in on this show, Major.'

'My privilege, sir.'

David waited till the three of them were seated, and then began to speak, pacing slowly round the table.

'The problem is, gentlemen, that we are losing control of the townships. They have become "no go" zones. We all know this, but what we have to do now is decide on a course of action. The State President and I spent most of Christmas discussing this, and last night's bombings have crystallized our decision. We are going to hit the bastards where it really hurts. We are going to show them who does the fucking in South Africa!'

He was pleased to see that everyone was smiling. They all thought the same way, that was why he had chosen them for this operation.

'So it's we four and Dolph Klopper,' he said. 'No one else must know about this. Is that completely clear?'

The three men nodded, eager to hear what was coming.

'Right,' said David. 'Now I shall give the floor to Dr Preusser, head of research at Terminal. He will tell you about Project Cobra.'

302

Dr Preusser had waited a lifetime for this opportunity. He rose shakily to his feet, looking at the men before him, a faint smile appearing on his usually taciturn face.

'At Terminal,' he said, 've have been developing chemical veapons for over ten years. These ve have sold to the Middle East and South America. However, in a conventional war situation, as you no doubt realise, such veapons are of limited usefulness, and liable to kill as many of the invading force as of the enemy. But in an urban, civilian situation it is a different story! The consequences of exploding a chemical device in a city are incredible – total loss of life. And even better, the area becomes habitable again after just a few veeks.

'People present on release of the chemical agent vill die. Toxic sickness is vat I vill call it for your benefit: the technical details are secret. In short, gentlemen, Cobra is the ultimate weapon.'

General Smit stared intensely at Dr Preusser. 'Little damage?'

'None. No one vill know vat has happened. They vill just die – in a three-kilometre radius every living thing vill be dead.'

This last comment fell like a stone into a still pool. David gestured for Dr Preusser to sit down, then got up himself, and resting his hands on the table, made eye-contact with each man in turn before speaking again.

'Best of all,' he said, 'unlike a real cobra, this one spits out its lethal venom without warning. Today, there are predators in the townships whom we cannot locate. With Cobra we can strike at their heart, destroy their soul.'

Jurie Smit stared at David.

'One for each township, man?'

'Yes, eventually. But for the moment, I propose just one, for Soweto. A big one.'

He raised his hand towards Major Hurst. 'You, Major Hurst, through your exceptional exploits have earned the right to be the first man to place this weapon.'

'When will the opportunity come, sir?'

'Cobra vill be ready this month,' Dr Preusser interjected.

David's eyes narrowed as he stared again at Hurst. 'You have your answer, Major. You understand that you will have to enter Soweto under cover. My intelligence unit reports that the violence is organized from Soweto.'

'Is the weapon large?'

Dr Preusser looked across at Hurst. '*Ja*, that vas a problem.

303

But I have a liddle solution. It is a binary weapon; there are two parts, both safe and inactive until they are combined, when they react with deadly consequences. So, ve use two chemical tankers disguised as fuel tankers. Detonation vill be triggered by an electronic timer, with the option of remote control.'

David beamed at Dr Preusser. 'Thank you,' he said. 'Major Hurst, you may go now. You will be at these barracks on permanent standby for the next month.'

'Yes, sir.' Major Hurst marched smartly out of the room, leaving the other three alone.

'He looks forward to it,' David whispered to Jurie Smit.

'*He* won't bugger it up,' Jurie replied loudly.

David coloured. They would never forget that he, David Loxton, had been responsible for the non-event of the Harare project. That memory would always haunt him.

Major Hurst understood perfectly well that he was supposed to stay within the barracks, but he had always hated confinement. Anyway, how dare they think they could keep him caged in for a month? Didn't they trust him? It was now two days since his meeting with David Loxton, and the more he thought about it, the more it irritated him. He was merely a lackey – there was no honour to the task they had assigned him, and none of the satisfaction of a genuine kill. He'd had a personal briefing from Dr Preusser, and really, it was killing by remote control.

He pulled on his track-suit pants and told his commanding officer that he was going on a long training run. Then he jogged out of the barracks. In a few minutes he had slipped beneath the security fence. He had a car which he used on assignments, in a lock-up garage a few blocks away.

Settling behind the steering wheel, he felt the excitement coursing through his body. He was going to see *her*!

This obsession had started a few months before. He'd always liked prostitutes for sex: you paid, you got your satisfaction, and it was over. No long-term relationship, no emotional problems. But this was different, very different. To start with, she was a coloured. Now usually he didn't like coloureds, he regarded them as half-breeds. But she was very, very unusual – especially with those blue eyes of hers. In fact, if you hadn't seen her classification papers you'd think she was white, pure white. And in a strange way it excited him – the thought that he was crossing the colour bar. There was an element of mystery in it, of excitement.

He couldn't precisely remember where they'd first met. She just always seemed to be around when he had time off. Once he'd noticed her in the bar, then at a dance he'd gone to with his men. It was obviously just one of those coincidences – they were fated to meet. And she wasn't a prostitute.

He'd taken her out to dinner a few times. He didn't want to sleep with her – not yet. He'd take his time. He felt it would be worth the wait.

It was good to drive again, it gave him a feeling of freedom. In the distance a dirty blue sky hung over the sprawling expanse of Soweto. Perhaps he was making a fool of himself, coming to see her without first phoning. But he had to go to her straightaway. The longing to see her was a force he could not control, like the desire to kill.

Marie heard the knock on the front door, and sensed that it wasn't one of her usual visitors. A look through the spy-hole, and she stepped back. It was him – Major Hurst. Oh God! Then she was dashing to the back of the house, telling Anna to take Morgan away, get him out of here. Her visitor would be a long time: Anna must take Morgan to Brenda Zwane in Soweto

Then she was dressing herself up, making herself attractive, and all the time the thoughts were running through her head. Remembering how her hatred of the government, her personal need for vengeance, had led her to join the AFC. Remembering that first meeting with Brenda Zwane, and how Brenda had understood her hurt. And remembering the terrible feelings of guilt she had for the life she had lived with Dolph. Then making plans to work for a better South Africa. Meeting this man . . . Marie had waited for him at every place he went to, always trying to catch his eye, hoping he'd take an interest in her. Eventually he had. No sex, yet. Jesus, it was hard pretending she loved someone she hated.

More banging on the door. Ready now, she ran to open it. She allowed herself to appear shocked at first, but her mouth quickly turned to a smile.

'Ian . . .'

He kissed her on the mouth. 'I had to see you again, Marie.'

He walked into her little house, his eyes exploring everywhere. She felt violated.

'Would you like some tea?'

She was afraid of him. She had heard rumours of what he'd done. She had done many other things for the AFC before this – delivering important documents, smuggling weapons into the township in her car – anything she could do to help. But Hurst was a bigger project – a chance really to hurt Dolph.

'Have you got a beer?'

She brought him a can, and a cup of tea for herself. Then she took a deep breath and sat down next to him.

'Where's your child?' he asked.

'Morgan's at a friend's.'

Looking sideways at her, along the sofa, Major Hurst knew that she was his kind of woman, even if she was coloured: that generous figure with its large, firm breasts, the sensual curve to her mouth. Sometimes he thought he'd seen her somewhere before, but where and when he wasn't quite sure. He sipped at his beer and felt her eyes upon him. He turned, and her lips moved towards his.

Then they were kissing. It felt very good. His hands explored her body and she did not resist. But he didn't want to frighten her, he didn't want to rush it. He didn't want it to be over. Part of him was afraid, but another side of him was desperately excited. It made him feel weak, vulnerable.

'What are you doing in the army, Ian?' she said. 'Don't you hate being ordered around?'

'Not really,' he lied.

'But you're intelligent, you should be doing better. I know a major doesn't earn that much.'

'The army is my life.'

'The army? You can't marry the army. You've got to live as well as work.'

He was quiet. She was annoying him because she was making sense. Why was she insulting him, telling him that his chosen profession wasn't good enough?

'I may only hold the rank of major, but I'm entrusted with great authority.'

She stroked the dark hair, then looked into his eyes. 'Looking after the regimental colours?' She laughed, and prodded him in the stomach. But he didn't find it funny.

'The army runs this country,' he said stiffly. 'Most people don't know that. We have the power.'

'Come off it, you just obey orders given by politicians like Dolph Klopper. You're just a pawn in a bigger game.'

Why was he listening to her? He didn't need to explain. But he wanted to see her again. And most of all, he wanted her to respect him.

'Yes, I am given orders, but I'm a free agent. Whether I choose to obey them or not is up to me. I'm in covert operations.'

She pursed her lips, as if trying to suppress a smile then said, in his voice: 'My name is Hurst. I'm a special agent.'

Now he was irritated. 'Listen, Marie, it's not a joke. My name will never be mentioned in the history books, but I can tell you my latest project will be part of history!'

She got up and knelt down beside him. 'I'm sorry, Ian. I was just teasing you. You're so tense.'

The need for a friend – the need for someone to talk to, was something that had always been with him. Now he'd found such a person.

He felt strangely elated. 'Thousands of people, perhaps over a hundred thousand, are going to die in one go,' he said.

Suddenly she was distant from him. 'I'll make us some coffee,' she said.

In the kitchen, she gripped the sides of the table, her knuckles white. God, what were they planning? She had to go through with this, had to hold on to him – there was no going back now. She had to find out what was being planned.

She went back into the lounge with the coffee.

'What you just said – ' she put a touch of awe and excitement into her voice ' – that's incredible.'

'I take my orders from the top,' he said. 'And I mean the very top.'

He left the house an hour later, promising himself he would not come back again. He had said too much, he knew – but it was because she had goaded him. The trouble was, he knew now that he needed her.

He drove hard. It was time he got back to camp.

Alone again, Marie was asking herself what price she would have to pay to get more information out of him. And yet already their relationship had yielded so much. What terrified her was the knowledge that he had been telling her the truth.

There was a knock on the back door. She quickly pulled on a

towelling robe and flung the door open. There was Brenda Zwane, holding Morgan.

'Anna told me he came.' Brenda's voice was heavy.

'I loathe him!' Marie screamed. 'I feel disgusting when I kiss him.'

Brenda squeezed her arm. 'Relax, it's time Morgan had his sleep.'

Marie took her child and laid him in the cot, kissed him on the forehead, then went back into the living-room.

Brenda hugged her. 'I'm sorry, Marie. I'm sorry it had to be you.'

'Don't be sorry. How many of your people had to die to get this lead?'

Brenda made her sit down beside her. She looked into her dark blue eyes. 'Well, Marie?'

'I'll see him again. I've got enough hate in my body to last a lifetime.'

'Did he say anything?'

'Yes, but I have to find out more. Whatever it is they're planning, it involves killing thousands and thousands of people.'

'No! Please God.'

'The bastard's falling in love with me. He's supposed to remain in Voortrekkerhoogte till it's all over, but he sneaked out to see me.'

'He'll be back. You'll find out more.'

Major Hurst's commanding officer had bawled him out for going on such a long run, but he'd taken that in his stride. What really worried him was the thought of what had happened in Harare: how David Loxton had blurted out the story about the bomb to his son. And now he, Major Hurst, had fallen into the same trap.

How could he have been such a fool? She was a coloured, and coloureds were criminals by nature. No, she could not be trusted. He owed his allegiance to the army; the army, and the killing it allowed him to do, were his first love. Now he had betrayed them both; he had jeopardized the security of Operation Cobra.

He had no choice. He would have to kill her, that was all there was to it.

*

'The bloody fool.'

David Loxton stood in the early morning light on the frost-covered grass of the parade ground lawn. General Jurie Smit stood next to him, erect and precise.

'Thank God we had him followed, David.'

'I thought he was the best.'

'Every man has a weakness.'

This last comment stopped David from launching a further attack on Hurst. Instead, he started to walk. His mind was working quickly.

'Jurie, you must get the name and identity number of this coloured woman, and run it through the computer. Get her complete profile – relatives, friends, the lot. Don't let Hurst know – he must keep on seeing her.'

Marie's world had suddenly become very small. She was scared to leave the house in case Major Hurst came and she missed him. She worried about how to question him. Thousands and thousands of lives now depended on her. She would not, she must not, fall short of the task.

Late in the afternoon, two weeks after his first visit, the doorbell rang and she looked through the curtains to see Hurst waiting on the step. She said a short prayer to herself, then went to open the door, smoothing the see-through blouse against her naked breasts . . .

They were together for more than two hours. By the time he got back to his rooms, he was sweating heavily. He knew now that he couldn't kill Marie. He was in love with her.

It had happened very suddenly, creeping up on him and then taking hold of his whole being. He was trapped. But after all, did it really matter so very much? His secret was safe with her – of that he was sure. He trusted her completely.

The solicitor pulled up outside the imposing mansion and sat in the car, straightening his tie. He did not do much work for Milner, but he valued the contact highly, for it brought him much business from other quarters. The butler appeared to open the car door for him, and he got out smartly. At the top of the steps, looking every inch the English nobleman, stood Lord Milner.

'Good morning, Riley.'

309

He hurried up the steps and shook hands. 'My condolences to you, sir. It must have been a terrible shock.'

Lord Milner inclined his head. 'Please come inside. Nancy has prepared tea for us in the summer room.'

Previous Milners looked down on them with quiet composure from the walls as the solicitor followed Lord Milner down the long hall. The house reflected the immense wealth of its owner, and the summer room was a happy place, furnished with rattan chairs and tables, its huge windows framed by pale green chintz curtains. Lord Milner sat down near the window before a small table on which stood a tray set with a silver tea service and fine bone-china cups.

'Did you bring the will?'

Riley bent down and took a white manila envelope from his leather attaché case. 'The details are quite simple. However, you'll find she wrote you a private note which is in the envelope too.'

Lucinda had left everything she had to her husband, including two farms in Botswana from her mother's trust. It was a sizeable estate.

'I never realised she had so much money of her own,' Lord Milner said. He opened the sealed note; inside was a letter in Lucinda's long, flowing handwriting, and two further sealed envelopes.

'If you won't be offended, I'd rather read this alone.'

'Not at all, Lord Milner. Shall I arrange the transfer of the money to your account?'

'That will not be necessary. You can place it immediately in a trust fund for Victoria Loxton's child. That was what Lucinda would have wanted.'

Later, after the solicitor had gone, Lord Milner read Lucinda's letter.

> *Anthony,*
> *Don't be sad. Somehow I have always known I would die while I was still young, and that is why I am writing you this letter, preparing . . .*
> *You will find two envelopes enclosed with this. The first, addressed to David, you must not open. If either my sister or my brother is ever threatened by my father in any way, then*

*you must open it, but otherwise, keep it in a safe place and
leave it alone. That I beg you.*

*The second envelope you may open now. It tells you where I
have hidden a self-portrait I did just after I met you. I was
never happier than when I was with you, Anthony. Please go
and find the picture when you have finished reading this.
Promise me.*

*As you will have seen, I have left you the two farms on the
island in the Okavango. Max owns the other farms on the
island. Do not sell those farms, they are priceless. I have not
been back to them since I was a child. I could not go back, they
reminded me too much of my mother, Tracey, and that man
who calls himself my father.*

*Anthony, I want you to live when I have gone. You are not a
man who can be alone, so find another wife, another love.
Make her as happy as you made me.*

Lucinda.

He went up to the attic and found the painting where she had
said it would be, beneath a dustsheet, and carried it – still
covered – down into the summer room. Outside the sun was
shining – he could see the wind blowing through the trees. He
pulled the dustsheet from the painting. She was there – as real as
she had ever been. She had given him a part of herself for ever.

The tears started to roll down his face. It was going to take a
long time for him to get over her. A lifetime.

Max gripped the phone tightly. 'Go on, Anthony.'

The voice at the other end of the line was hoarse. 'Max, I've
talked to the groom who found the horse wandering on the
estate. Quite a docile animal, he thought it. Anyway, he stabled
the horse, and since then he's exercised him regularly – I know
some people would have had the animal put down, but I couldn't
bear to do that . . . No more deaths . . . Well, one morning, one
of the younger grooms was exercising him, when someone nearby
began to whistle. It was incredible: the horse went berserk,
almost killed the poor groom. You see, Max, that horse was
trained to do what it did. I think . . . oh my God, this sounds
crazy, but Max, I think someone did this deliberately. I think
Lucinda was murdered . . .'

After Max had put the phone down, he remembered how

311

David had suddenly appeared in the Harare courtroom. Why had he come? It was because Lucinda had something on him . . . something that David had decided he didn't want to live with . . .

God, it couldn't be! The bastard couldn't have done it! Could he?

Two

Brenda Zwane opened the door hesitantly and found herself looking at two men, both black. One was elegantly dressed and fat, the other was tall and dangerous-looking in a black leather jacket and leather pants. The face of the tall man was frighteningly familiar, and he spoke first.

'Comrade Zwane, you have information.'

'My information is for the leaders of our people.'

The tall man strode through the door and hit Brenda hard across the face. Then he picked her up and, followed by the fat man, dragged her inside. The door slammed behind them.

'You talk to me!'

Brenda felt the grip on her throat relax and staggered towards a chair. 'Don't sit down – bitch! Remember me? Remember what I did to you?'

'No. Please no.'

'We hear rumours. You're full of shit. You're friends with the white bitch who parades as a coloured – Marie Jantjies.'

'Am I not allowed to have friends?'

'Speak.' The fat man, who was now sitting, uttered the one word menacingly.

'She's just a friend,' Brenda said nervously.

Kumalo held out his hands, hunching up his shoulders. 'Friend? We know she does things for you . . . Brings in weapons, carries messages. Now she's sleeping with someone from the army.'

'That's her boyfriend.'

The fat man on the chair clicked his fingers, then sat back. Kumalo hit Brenda hard in the pelvis. Then, as she staggered, he

313

tore her dress down, and whipping out a knife, pushed it under her left breast. Blood ran down to her navel.

'Cut it off!' Fat Man screamed.

'No!'

Kumalo let her drop to the floor, sobbing.

'His name?' Fat Man asked coldly.

'Major Hurst.'

'Better . . .'

'They have a plan . . . We don't know what it is yet, but thousands of people will die.'

Kumalo sat down and stared dumbly at the picture of George Zwane above the fireplace. 'You must find out more. We know Loxton has been trying to find us. Perhaps he has decided that we cannot be found, and so . . .'

'. . . he decides to destroy Soweto.' Fat Man was pale.

'My thinking,' Kumalo said slowly, pulling Brenda up from the floor. 'You must use Marie Jantjies, Comrade, and find out what you can. And remember, if you should try to cross us . . .'

He neatly sliced off Brenda's left nipple.

Max looked at the balance sheet and tried to concentrate, but it was useless. He got up from his desk and walked to the window. Outside, the street was full of midday traffic. It was unmistakably London, with the red buses and black taxis, and standing on the corner, a bobby in his distinctive navy blue helmet. Max's eyes left the window and wandered along the wall to the portrait of George Zwane, done by a Soweto street painter. His mother's voice echoed in his mind. 'Max, remain true to yourself. Max, do what you believe to be right.'

Was that what he was doing now? He wasn't happy. Every day was a misery, spent fighting off thoughts of the place he loved. He was living a lie. He knew in his heart that David had had Lucinda killed. And someone must have influenced Shelton to pull out of the Botswanan project . . . He still wanted to make Botswana 2000 work. If he was honest with himself, it was the thing he wanted most in the world. He needed something to live for, to die for.

He was over the drinking now – and the London business could run itself. He was going back to Botswana. Back to Africa.

*

As General Smit entered the top-floor studio, all the operators stood stiffly to attention. He gestured to them to be at ease and return to their places at the bank of television screens in the centre of the room. This whole building at Voortrekkerhoogte was given over to surveillance, and from the screens in this studio it was possible to see into every room of Marie Klopper's house. As the General had demanded, the intelligence people had really done an excellent job.

'Everything is in position, sir,' said Captain Pieterse, who was sitting in front of the screens.

'When will Hurst be arriving?'

'I'm not sure, sir. Shouldn't be long.'

'She suspects nothing?'

'No. Ah, here he comes now, sir.' And the General saw Major Hurst come into view in the top left-hand screen . . .

An hour later, General Smit was having trouble keeping awake. Captain Pieterse smiled.

'Bored, sir? Imagine what I feel like after a week of this.' On the screens, the woman leaned over and kissed Hurst on the cheek, and Hurst opened his eyes and stared at her . . .

'. . . So, Ian. Are you still on that important mission?'

Hurst breathed in deeply. It was like taking a high dive. He had to balance the risk of telling her against the risk of losing her. For some reason she saw his secrecy about the operation as a barrier to their continuing the relationship. Why not tell her? But there were other, more important things he wished he could talk about.

'Marie, I . . .'

'Is it a car bomb?'

He ignored the question and tried to pull her close, but she resisted.

'What sort of a bomb, then?'

'It hardly matters – it'll annihilate every living thing for three kilometres.'

'But how, Ian?'

'It's a chemical weapon – I'm not sure how it works. I just suggest you stay away from Soweto in mid January.'

'Do you know what you're doing? Won't you get hurt?'

He drew her to him. This time she did not resist and that made him feel better. 'No, my love, it's very safe. One tanker drives to

315

a pre-arranged position, then I drive another to join it an hour later.'

'But how do you know where to go?'

'Radio link-up. Evidently this stuff reacts quickly, then rolls across the ground like a fog. The weather's important – the direction of the wind and the air temperature – these things will dictate where the tankers are positioned on the sixteenth.'

'Is it nerve gas?'

'I don't know. Dr Preusser calls it Cobra.'

Captain Pieterse lit a cigarette and settled back into his chair. The show was almost over. General Smit coughed noisily. He detested smoking, especially when he was in an enclosed area and had to breathe the smoke.

'Taking another few years off your life, Captain?'

'It's my life, sir.'

'You're a fool, Pieterse.'

Captain Pieterse hunched forwards and stared at the TV monitor closest to him. 'Hurst's buggered off. And she's leaving the house already.'

'No foul-ups!'

'There won't be. We've had her under twenty-four-hour sur-veillance. She's in with Brenda Zwane.'

General Smit laughed. '*Ja*, I can just see Brenda Zwane dismantling Cobra.'

There was a crackle on the radio monitor.

'I think she's going to the call box, sir. We've got her worked out, you see. That's the closest call box to the house, so naturally we've got it wired. My guess is she'll make contact with Zwane.'

'But Brenda, what can I do?'

Marie looked worriedly around the packed Hillbrow coffee bar, and outside to the traffic flashing past in the darkness. She was scared.

Brenda's hand rested on hers. 'Don't worry, Marie. Look, Morgan's safe with Anna, so I suggest you don't go back to the house – it's too dangerous. Maybe Hurst will get suspicious; maybe he'll come back.'

Something told Marie that Brenda was as scared as she was. Up to that moment she had always thought of her as being confident and in control. Suddenly she had a sense of the

316

enormity of what she was involved in, and her heart skipped a beat. 'Is there something wrong?' she said.

To her horror, Brenda started to cry. 'It's the Comrades. They want this weapon, whatever it is. They want to use it themselves.' She swallowed. 'You've got to keep going, Marie – and I'll have to keep feeding the Comrades false information.'

'I'll . . . I'll have to stop Hurst somehow, won't I?'

Brenda said: 'Could you kill him?'

'I don't know,' Marie said slowly. 'I just don't know.'

'But vy vorry, sir?' Dr Preusser said confidently. 'Once the chemicals make contact, no one can stop the reaction – Cobra's lethal venom will form in a millisecond.'

Klopper had just revealed to Dr Preusser the possibility that someone might try to locate and disarm the device, but Preusser wasn't worried in the least. Really, he thought, Klopper was a fool to imagine anyone could interfere with the Cobra once it had been activated.

Dolph Klopper, however, seemed unmollified. He looked at Preusser coldly. 'If Cobra does not work, if this woman should find some way to disarm your weapon, you are finished.'

'It cannot fail,' Preusser said confidently.

'If it does, you are a dead man!'

This was too much! He wasn't going to stay and be threatened! But as he rose to leave, Klopper's security man moved quickly forward and gripped his arm, and he was forced back into his seat.

Klopper grinned. 'Thank you, Jan, there'll be no more trouble, the doctor is not unintelligent.'

Dr Preusser felt himself shaking with rage. What did the man want now?

'Who else knows about the weapon?' Klopper asked curtly.

'You mean the vorkings of it? I am the only one who knows about the completed detonator unit. Ve deliberately hand the vork out in separate pieces, that vay no one can guess how the finished veapon functions – except for me.'

Klopper smiled good-naturedly. 'I must compliment you on your security, then. So it is only myself, David Loxton, General Smit and you who know about the Cobra? Oh, and of course our runner, Major Hurst, and his female informant.'

'Yes, sir.'

317

'Right. I think that concludes our business, then, doctor. See him out, Jan.'

Outside in the dusk, Preusser was bundled into one of the state limousines. Jan got into the back seat with him, and the chauffeur pulled off without command, heading north.

'Where are we going?'

'The President wants you in a safe place.'

'But I need to supervise ze final programme . . .'

But this would cut no ice; he had already told Klopper that the bomb was completed. Anyway, why was he worried?

They pulled off the main road and turned down a narrow track. In the darkness Dr Preusser was aware of a ring of mountains, and there were tall trees along the side of the road. They must be on a farm – obviously a safe-house that they had prepared for him.

Without warning the car pulled to a halt. Jan got out, but the chauffeur remained inside, the motor still running and the lights on full beam.

'Get out, doctor,' Jan said, opening the car door for him.

Dr Preusser stepped out somewhat reluctantly. 'There's . . . there's nothing here!'

'Oh yes, there is. The house is over the next rise. We'll leave the lights on so you can see your way.'

Dr Preusser looked worriedly at Jan, who gestured to him to move ahead. Reluctantly he staggered forwards, trying to make out the house in the distance. He reached the top of the rise but could see nothing at all.

There was a shout from behind, and he turned.

'Dr Preusser!'

He stared into the blinding beam of the headlamps, and was about to reply when a fusillade of bullets from the LA rifle he had designed hit him in the stomach and lifted him into the air.

David Loxton was furious. Dr Preusser, it seemed, had been spirited away without his consent. Really, he was not going to tolerate such interference in his affairs.

'Where is he?' he said.

Dolph Klopper got up and put an arm round his shoulders, which irritated him even more.

'Don't worry, my friend, he's in good company. We don't want any more leaks like last time . . .'

'That was different, quite different. My life was in danger.'

Klopper looked at him squarely. 'I will control world reaction, David. We have nothing to fear. I am sure your Cobra will strike as fatally as you have promised.'

Max sat contentedly in the back of the executive jet. In the end the decision to return to Africa had been surprisingly easy, and to his surprise, Saffron had supported him. He had settled back into the continent as if he had never been away, and now he was on his way to Gaberone in Botswana, for a safari to the wetlands. There, he would survey the foundations of his hotel complex and work out how to proceed. He was determined to resurrect the project, to make it a success. At last he would be doing something that mattered again, something that would help to vindicate his two dear friends, George Zwane and Kobus van der Post. This time, he told himself, his dream – the biggest conservation project on earth – would become a reality. He had failed before, but he was damned if he was going to lose again.

They landed in Gaberone that evening. As Max walked down the steps and onto the tarmac, the hot, spicy air in his nostrils, he felt very young and full of energy. A Land-Rover was waiting for him, and the airport staff helped him load the cargo into the back. There was no problem with customs; it was natural that Dr Max Loxton, who had done so much for Botswana, should return to the country to go on safari.

He drove through the evening to the Gaberone Sun. Two years ago it had been the Gaberone Oasis, and it had been his. Then, it had relied for success on its South African visitors, but now he could see that there was an international clientele. Botswana's economy, unlike South Africa's, was booming. Max walked into the casino and saw the croupiers hard at work at the packed tables. With a twist of nostalgia he remembered how he had first met Saffron here. That had been a time of hope and optimism – but so was this. He would not gamble tonight. He had a bigger game to play, and he knew he was going to win.

He could not guess how soon his plans were to be disrupted . . . That night, towards dawn, in the darkness of his room the telephone rang.

It was Brenda Zwane – a voice from the past, a cry for help. She wanted him to cross the border, to meet a friend of hers, Marie Jantjies.

There was no way he could refuse, but as he put the phone down he could feel himself breaking out in a cold sweat. Precisely what was he getting himself into?

It was getting hot. Max opened the vents on the dashboard and let the air blast against his face. He needed to be wide awake – and at times he felt as if all this was a dream.

Passport control on the Botswana border at Tlokweng Gate presented no problems, and he was through to the South African side in under thirty minutes. He slid the passport under the iron grille that separated him from the customs official, and the man picked it up with indifference. Then his attitude changed. He stared hard at Max.

'Don't I know you from somewhere?'

Damnit, problems already. Max kept his cool. Thank God he'd grown a beard.

'I'm Dr Loxton,' he said. 'I do a TV programme on conservation.'

The customs official fiddled with his long, drooping moustache, and lazily fingered the passport. 'Ach, that must be it, Dr Loxton. Welcome back to South Africa. It must be nice to get back to the real world.'

Max walked away, relieved, and drove off towards Zeerust, in line with Brenda Zwane's instructions.

Back at passport control, the customs official let through another three people. Then a sudden smile crossed his face. Dr Loxton! The Prime Minister's son! That's who it was! The smile changed to a frown. What could he be up to? Better let someone know about this . . .

Max approached the rendezvous point slowly. He was looking for a red car, with Marie Jantjies inside it. Could that be it? He could see a red car drawn up by the side of the road. He could also see, on the opposite side of the road, a Mercedes-Benz sports car, and a mini-bus. His mouth went dry. This was the place all right; it would normally have been a deserted stretch of road. Why were there three vehicles here? The mini-bus looked empty, but there were two black men in the sports car, sitting and talking.

What should he do? Surely the only thing was to proceed according to plan. Heart hammering, he drew up behind the red car, got out of the Land-Rover, and walked over to look inside it. It was empty. The two men in the sports car, he noticed, were watching him with undisguised interest.

Then he heard a muffled cry from the mini-bus. He rushed over to it – and the bloodied face of a blonde woman appeared at the window.

'Marie Jantjies?' he mouthed desperately through the glass.

She wound down the window. 'Dr Loxton?' Her voice was entirely without expression.

'That's enough, Marie.'

Max spun round. The driver of the sports car, a tall, thin black man, was standing right behind him and aiming a sawn-off shotgun at his solar plexus. The man smiled. 'Marie was the bait,' he said. 'You're coming with us.'

Marie screamed, 'No!' But now the other man from the sports car was climbing into the mini-bus, and holding a blade to her throat, he dragged her out. Max heard the menacing voice behind him again:

'If you want her to live – come with us.'

But there was a new sound, the sound of police sirens. In the distance, in the direction from which Max had come, they could all see a police car approaching fast, its lights flashing.

'Ah,' said the tall, lean man. 'More company for you, Dr Loxton. Perhaps you should have a word with them.'

And suddenly, he and his companion were gone; taking Marie with them, they had melted into the bush, and Max was alone by the side of the road.

Propelled so rapidly from one fear to another, Max hardly knew how to react to this new turn of events. He stood there in the heat and the sudden silence, and squared his shoulders as the police car drew up. The driver's door opened, and Max stayed put, swaying a little on his feet.

'Dr Loxton?' The officer had a riot shotgun in his hands. His partner stayed in the car, looking on.

Max nodded. The time for playing games was over.

'You are under arrest.'

Max felt his spirits sink. The whole thing had been a set-up. But why had Brenda done it? But perhaps she had had no choice . . .

And then, without warning, gunfire erupted from the bushes.

The policeman in the patrol car was hit: blood spattered across the car's interior as bullets tore into the bodywork.

The policeman next to Max crouched down, ready to fire, but uncertain of his direction – so that when the tall man leapt out from behind the mini-bus with his machine-gun, he was caught off balance. He screamed as the bullets tore into his body.

Max looked on, stunned. Before he realised it, the other black man was out of the bushes, dragging Marie with him. The tall man gestured to his comrade. 'Take her away in the mini-bus. Dr Loxton is coming with me.'

'We haven't got a chance,' Max shouted angrily.

'Into my car! You drive, Dr Loxton, and leave the rest to me. You've no idea how much power I have.'

Max got into the car and gunned it forwards, pushing the engine screaming to the limit as he crashed through the gears.

'Who the hell are you?' he shouted to his companion.

'Comrade Kumalo.'

The name had an ominous ring to it. Max glanced at the face of the man next to him. Charcoal skin, dark, restless eyes and a vivid facial scar – he looked as ruthless as the weapon he carried. This must be the one George had spoken of – the man who controlled the marauding street gangs of Soweto. The man who ruled by fear.

'Afraid, Dr Loxton? Forget the AFC and pawns like the Zwanes. They're the past, I am the future.'

Max gripped the steering-wheel hard. 'Listen, Kumalo, I'm here to see Brenda Zwane, not to take your crap.'

Max drove on, trying to control the anger that welled up inside him. The South African situation hadn't changed – it was still one group against the other in the struggle for power.

'We have Brenda Zwane,' Kumalo said. 'You do what we tell you, and she'll be just fine.'

'What do you mean?'

'It's quite simple, Dr Loxton. Your father plans to explode a weapon, the Cobra, in Soweto that will wipe out thousands of our people. We want you to find that weapon, disarm it and give it to us.'

Max nodded. If nothing else, he had to respect Kumalo's forcefulness. 'And where do I find this "weapon"?'

'The blonde bitch Marie will take care of that.'

'How much do you know about this "Cobra"?'

'It is made by your father's company. It is a type of chemical weapon. It should be easy enough to disarm.'

'My father makes some of the most sophisticated weapons in the world,' Max said.

Kumalo grabbed his arm. 'If I thought you couldn't disarm it, I would kill you now with my bare hands.'

Max struggled away from the lean, bony hand. 'Keep your personal feelings out of this, Kumalo. First things first – we have to ditch this vehicle. The police will be looking out for it.'

'Everything has been taken care of. Here, take the turn to your left.'

Max powered off along the dirt road, a cloud of dust in his wake.

'Another kilometre,' Kumalo said, 'and you'll see a barn. Drive straight inside it.'

Max pushed the sports car as hard as it would go, and soon, over the horizon, saw the barn appear, a modern structure whose galvanized roof shone in the sunlight. The surrounding fields were deep green, and pools of water dotted the dirt track. The car splashed through them, showering the windscreen with mud. Then they were in the barn.

They got out of the car, and as Max's eyes adjusted to the dim light, he could see another car in the barn, half-covered in sacking. He could also see, lounging against the far wall, half a dozen other men – obviously Comrades.

'Our get-away car,' said Kumalo with a grin. 'Hop in, Dr Loxton.'

'You're well organised,' Max said grudgingly.

'It is the only way we can fight the police. It's taken us years to build up our power-base and instill discipline into the Comrades. But tribal differences count for nothing now.'

'Then how come you and your men are all Zulus?'

Max saw an angry scowl cross Kumalo's face. 'I have heard it said that you are too wise for your own good, Dr Loxton.'

'Listen, Comrade, you may not give a damn about people's lives, but I do. All you want is control of the townships, I know that. But I have come here to save people's lives.' He knew these men were killers. They would use him and Brenda, then dispose of them.

Kumalo brought the muzzle of his shotgun up to Max's chest – but in an instant Max was on him, with a hard blow to his jaw.

Kumalo tumbled to the ground, the gun clattering uselessly on the concrete floor, and Max kicked it away.

Then Kumalo got to his feet, pulling out a knife.

'Are you yellow, Kumalo?' Max sneered. 'Can't fight without a weapon?'

Suddenly the barn seemed very quiet. None of the Comrades moved. Kumalo threw the knife to the floor and moved towards him.

Max was in good shape. Not a day had passed in London when he didn't work out in the gym, sparring to keep in shape, and the sessions had given him the reflexes and the stamina he needed to run his business. Now they might well save his life. Kumalo must be some five years younger than he was, and far more of a gutter fighter – but Max was prepared to fight dirty, too.

Kumalo's fist shot through the air, catching his ear. Max felt the blood running down his cheek and his self-control went. He hadn't come all this way to die in some outlying barn at the hands of a rabid street-fighter. His left connected with Kumalo's forehead, and he followed it with a hard right to the jaw. Kumalo reeled and Max closed in, hitting him again with his left, lifting him off the ground and laying him out on the concrete.

There was silence in the barn, and Max heard a plane fly low overhead. He ran to the doors and looked out. As he had guessed, it was an army spotter-plane. He and Kumalo had only just made it to the barn in time.

He walked back and helped Kumalo to his feet. Kumalo turned slowly, surveying his men. The look in his eye told them that if any of them mentioned what had just happened there would be trouble.

'All you! Clear out. Remember to stay away from Soweto tomorrow.'

Max shivered. That was the reality. He had to try and disarm a lethal weapon he knew nothing about.

'Let's get going,' Kumalo said. He handed Max a balaclava. 'Cover your face, Dr Loxton. You may have beaten me but you can't beat the township.'

They got into the car and drove out of the barn, heading for Soweto. There was a lot of traffic on the road; it was the evening rush hour.

They reached the border of Soweto. Max was astonished to see a huge wire fence with a patrol road on either side of it running along the edge of the township. He clenched his fists. God, what was his father hoping to do? Thousands of people . . . They were mad.

Peeping out from beneath a concealing groundsheet, he saw a white trooper, holding the dreaded LA machine-gun, wave them disdainfully forwards. He breathed a sigh of relief. They were in.

Staring at Marie's bloodied face, Major Hurst felt an uncontrollable urge to kill.

'I . . . I was mugged by a street gang,' she stammered. The Comrades had dropped her off at the house earlier, threatening to beat her to death if she did not get more information from Hurst. She was desperate. What would happen to Dr Loxton? Would they torture Brenda? But for now she must concentrate on Hurst. She saw that he was studying her wounds with concern.

'This "street gang", do you think they were with the Comrades?' he asked.

She nodded.

'Bastards! Can you walk all right?'

'I can move – just.'

'You must get away from here – you're too close to Sweto. Tomorrow Cobra will be in place for detonation, and I guarantee the bastards who did this to you will be dead.'

Thank God, he seemed to have bought the story that she'd been mugged. Now she must try to find out more about Cobra. Brenda's life was at stake, so was Dr Loxton's.

'It's not such a big weapon then, is it?' she ventured.

'It's two fuel tankers. I get a fall guy to drive one in, then I follow and we meet up – somewhere in the centre of the township. Not that it matters to you, eh?'

'But how do you get away?'

'Remote-control detonation – it gives me plenty of time, don't you worry. Where can I meet you when it's over?'

She was at a loss for words. She hadn't thought about his getting away – about what would happen if Max Loxton failed.

'Marie,' he said, looking into her eyes, 'I want to see you again.'

'Give me a phone number where I can reach you.'

Hastily he scribbled it down on a scrap of paper. He must get back to barracks now. She was all right, that was all that mattered. And she'd promised a story as far away as possible from Soweto and its environs.

'Marie, don't be afraid,' he said. 'I'll get those bastards, don't you worry.'

He kissed her softly on the lips, and left.

They took Max to one of their houses, gave him a sleeping-bag and told him to move into a side room. They must wait for Kumalo to come back with Marie, who would have more information about the location of the weapon. Tomorrow, on the day, they would overpower Hurst and take the weapon.

That, at least, was what Kumalo planned. But Max intended to de-activate Cobra and render it harmless.

For the time being, Max remained in the side room, thinking about Brenda and wondering where they had taken her. He was brought some white mealie pap and minced meat in a bowl, and ate the warm food hungrily. He needed it – the fight with Kumalo had taken a lot out of him. Afterwards, he stared out of the dusty window, across the dirt street at the shanties. In the distance, he kept hearing explosions, screaming – yet the people walking about in the street outside seemed unconcerned. How terrible, he thought, to have become so inured to violence.

He eventually fell asleep, thinking of Saffron.

David switched on the video-player, a smile crossing his face in the darkness of the room.

'I thought you'd like to see this for the record, Dolph.'

Klopper sat impassively, sipping his brandy and coke. 'How could Major Hurst have been such a fool?'

'He's given nothing important away. The location of the tankers is still to be decided. And the silly coloured bitch he's been screwing knows no one – well, almost no one, Dolph.'

David hit the play button. His contacts in intelligence had finally dug up the truth about Marie's past. It was very good. Something to use against Klopper at last; something to twist the man's soul.

Klopper's brandy and coke hit the carpet.

'Something wrong, old chap?'

'What is the meaning of this . . . sickness?'

'Sickness? Yes, I'd say that was a pretty accurate description.

326

Your wife, screwed by a black man, gives birth to a chocolate-skinned baby, then you disown her, reclassify her, and banish her to a coloured township. I'd say that was sickness.'

Oh, the satisfaction! The man was white with fear. 'Looks like you lost out, Dolph,' he went on. 'A lovely body, and look how she's enjoying it. She definitely likes being screwed by Major Hurst, doesn't she? Of course, not as good as a kaffir.'

'You fucker!'

'You say one word wrong, just one word, old chap, and I'll expose the truth about your wife to the nation.'

'What do you want?'

Klopper was shaking. Oh God, how he was enjoying this! David moved in for the kill. 'Stiff upper lip, old chap. Show a bit more self-control. What would your coloured step-son say if he could see you now?'

Brenda Zwane sat rocking Morgan to sleep; the child had been crying for his mother. She looked across at the hard-faced man who stood guard over her, a shotgun loosely cradled in his hands. Where had they taken Marie? Where was Max?

What is to become of us? she asked herself. What future could they look forward to in a country ruled by Dolph Klopper? Or by the Comrades? No future.

Ulrich Klee stood on the balcony of his New York penthouse and looked down at the street below. In his hand he held a sheet of paper. Though it was past ten at night, the traffic was still heavy, but at this height the noise was just a dull roar. How often in the past had he contemplated the desire to disappear into this view? To hurl himself into the noise of the city and vanish for ever? Yet he lacked the courage to kill himself.

A messenger had brought the letter an hour before. He trembled as he looked at it again. They wanted him to buy time for them, to stall any kind of world reaction, to resist a call to arms at all costs. Project Cobra. The carefully calculated killing of thousands of people.

He went back into his flat, swallowed four sleeping pills down with a neat whisky and lay on his bed, trying to relax. Things had been worse since his wife died; she had always had the ability to distract and divert him, and now that she was gone he was sometimes afraid to be alone in his own home. His children were

327

married, and weekends with them and his grandchildren were his life-raft. If they discovered the horrors he had perpetrated he would lose them.

The dreams started – the dreams of people screaming in the gas chambers. He covered his ears, he prayed, but the screaming continued in his head. When would all this stop? he asked himself. When would death free him from this horror?

Three

The morning sun rose over Soweto. It had rained late in the night, settling the dust that often blew round the streets in the early morning, so that today there was a freshness in the air. Not a breath of wind; the place seemed almost bearable.

Max looked out of the window and surveyed the street outside. By now the township was up and going. Nothing seemed out of the ordinary, and it occurred to him that they might all be the victims of some bizarre hoax. He felt an alien in this place. For the others here, Soweto was the place where they had always lived; it was a part of their souls.

He opened the door to the main room, and found himself looking at Marie. Behind her was Kumalo, holding a shotgun to her waist.

'Good morning, Dr Loxton,' Marie said quietly. Her skirt and blouse were torn. He didn't need much imagination to know they'd raped her.

'Marie, where's the weapon?' Max asked kindly.

Marie stammered: 'He said that would only be decided this morning.'

'All right, Marie, you did your best.' He turned to Kumalo. 'Let her go.'

Kumalo looked at him blankly, then a sickly smile appeared on his face. 'No,' he said.

'Let her go, you fucking bastard!'

'Two hours to detonation, doctor,' Kumalo said mockingly.

Max grabbed the barrel of his shotgun – and as he did so, Kumalo pulled the trigger. Max felt the shot scorch his arm as he smashed his left fist into Kumalo's skull. The shotgun clattered to the floor, and Max grabbed it. Kumalo was rising, drawing something from behind his back.

'One move, Kumalo, and you're dead.'

'Try me, white man!'

Max pulled the trigger, and watched the shot disintegrate Kumalo's stomach.

The black man rolled over, clutching at his innards, tears streaming from his eyes. Two Comrades ran into the room, and Max pivoted round, working the pump shotgun. The noise was deafening, and blood covered the walls as the men died. Max turned back to Kumalo, who was writhing in agony on the floor, blood pouring from his innards.

'Spare me!'

Then Max saw that Kumalo's first shot had taken Marie in the face. She staggered to her feet and came across to him.

'Dr Loxton, the man who's going to detonate the Cobra, his name is Major Hurst – he's dangerous. I'm sorry, I failed,' she cried, blood pouring from her mouth.

'No, you didn't fail, Marie. Cobra will never explode. I'll get Hurst. Now, you need a doctor . . .'

She sank down at his feet and rolled over on the floor. He put down the shotgun and held her head in his hands, crying. She was dead.

'Spare me!' cried Kumalo.

Max picked up the shotgun and pointed it at Kumalo. But he could not pull the trigger.

The huge doors rolled back, revealing the long tunnel that disappeared underground. The three of them moved to the elevator, and Dolph Klopper pushed the button for basement level 3.

'No point in taking risks,' he said. He looked carefully at David Loxton, but the man's face was expressionless. How Dolph hated him!

'There are no risks, Dolph,' David Loxton said. 'Dr Preusser would have told you that.'

Dolph looked knowingly at General Jurie Smit. David had been told that Dr Preusser had died in an accident – no point in getting on the wrong side of him. David really had too much on Dolph now – it was a job for Hurst; but right now Hurst had more important work on his hands.

They got out at basement 3, and David Loxton led the way through the labyrinth of studios and control rooms. Everyone was in position, and heads turned as they walked by. Dolph enjoyed the ripple of tension that ran through the staff as they passed. It was his right. After all, he thought, we are the three most powerful men in the country. Of course, none of the people who had been called to the operations centre had any idea what was to take place. There would be no leaks – not like last time, Dolph thought, glaring at David Loxton.

David showed them into the master suite. Everything necessary for living in absolute luxury had been provided: kitchen, bathrooms, bedrooms and a gym. Off the main lounge was a small viewing theatre with a bank of six television screens. From here they would keep up with world news and comment via a satellite link. Any world service could be accessed in just a few seconds.

'Where do I make my broadcast from?' Dolph asked.

David showed him into another room, a sound and television studio, softly furnished and utterly quiet. 'The whole room has been designed to reflect a relaxed attitude. You can sit over there and the interviewer will sit in the other chair.'

'He has been briefed?'

'Of course. But naturally he is totally unaware of the enormity of his task.'

'Very good.'

Klopper looked at his watch. 'Hurst should be entering the township now.'

'Two hours to go. And we're as safe as houses.'

David relaxed. They were over a hundred metres beneath ground level in the fall-out shelter built for the South African Broadcasting Corporation by David's company, Terminal. Whatever happened, they would still be able to stay in contact with the rest of the country and the outside world. And they could live down here for over a year. He thought about the information he'd received the day before – that his son had entered the country illegally. But there was no point in worrying about that. After all, what could Max possibly do to hurt him now?

From where they were sitting they could mobilise and command South Africa's giant military machine. Whatever destruction they wanted to engineer, it was theirs to command.

*

331

Major Hurst put the tanker into second gear as he approached the police check-point. Since the vehicle's registration number had been cleared with all the police and army units operating within Soweto, he naturally expected to be waved through, but the soldier indicated that he must stop. Hurst wound down the window.

'Get out,' the soldier ordered.

Bugger it. Obviously some administrative mistake. But the rifle barrel was pointing at his head. What the hell was he going to do?

'Phone General Jurie Smit,' he said. 'I'm Major Ian Hurst. I have special clearance.'

'Wait here. I haven't heard about this.'

What was going on? He started to get out of the cab. 'Put me through to General Smit,' he said, 'or I'll have you flayed alive.'

Max pushed Kumalo's sports car hard. He was heading north, and fast; on the seat beside him was a pistol and Kumalo's shotgun.

There wasn't much time. God, his plan had better work.

Major Hurst was wet from his own sweat. It had taken over an hour to get through to General Jurie Smit, and now he was late, horribly late.

He gunned the tanker forwards. Have to be careful – bloody careful. The stuff was lethal.

He had been inside the township often, and it always made him feel distinctly uneasy. There was no protection here. He had heard terrible stories of soldiers who had died at the hands of the Comrades.

He glanced at the map he'd been given that morning. Perfect conditions, no wind. He drove carefully, looking for the bus depot. There it was! And there was the other tanker. Ten minutes, and he could be away . . .

He drew up carefully, parallel to the other tanker. Then he pulled out his pistol and screwed on the silencer.

The driver of the other tanker came over to him. 'Good to see you, sir.'

Hurst levelled the pistol at the young man's chest and pulled the trigger twice. The man clutched at his chest and toppled over, dead.

Hurst felt good again. He dragged the corpse into the cab, then he lifted the motorcycle scrambler down and readjusted his balaclava.

Now to work. He screwed the tankers' pipes together, forming an umbilical cord between the two huge cylinders. Next he connected up the detonator and the two big extractor fans. This was going to be his biggest kill ever.

Max gunned the car towards the boom, then accelerated. The metal bar took the windscreen off the sports car, and two shots exploded into the bodywork – but he was past the guardpost and heading for the runway. The sports car cannoned across the concrete as he edged the speedo up past 240 km/hr and headed for the hangars.

Split-second memories came to him – of flying with his father, then on his own. The freedom, the joy of it.

He slammed on the brakes and broadsided into the doors of the hangar, smashing them down. Mechanics came running for him and he raised the shotgun.

'I want a chopper. A Schweizer 300C.'

Nobody moved.

'Get it out on the runway, or I'll . . .'

A man was coming out of the office, armed. Shit. Max raised the shotgun and fired. Suddenly the man was lying on the floor of the hangar, clutching his arm and screaming, and mechanics were pushing the chopper out into the sun.

'Fill it up.'

The man was still screaming . . .

And then Max was in the cockpit. Battery on. Fuel boost. Throttle closed. Press starter. Magneto on. The engine roared into life as Max continued the take-off procedures. Then he was rising upwards, into the blue, and heading for the black scar on the horizon – Soweto.

Hurst kicked the scrambler into life, then pulled over next to the back of the tankers. He checked the R4 rifle hidden in the rucksack on his back, then the two pistols, one holstered under each armpit. He was ready.

He flipped open the lid of the control unit and found the actuator switch. He hesitated for a moment.

333

Thousands, maybe hundreds of thousands of people. He went cold as he pressed the button.

Max had forgotten just how manoeuvrable the Schweizer was. Skimming the rooftops, his eyes searched for the tankers. Where the hell were they? Perhaps Hurst had suspected something? Maybe he'd given Marie the wrong information? He *had* to find them. He thought of Marie's face as she died – he was not going to fail her. But where, where in this urban jungle were the bloody tankers?

He brought the chopper in low again. He wasn't going to give up. Perhaps this was the place, for he was now in the heart of Soweto.

Hurst ignored the sound at first, but then the animal instinct that had saved his life on so many occasions caused him to look up. Yes, he knew that sound, and something told him that it signalled danger.

He pivoted round and scanned the horizon. First he could detect only the noise, then he saw the chopper, sweeping over the rooftops like an angry bee. Who were they searching for? Somehow he knew this was a threat – to him and to the Cobra.

He killed the engine of the bike, and in one fluid movement dismounted and drew the R4 from the rucksack on his back.

Then he rolled under the closest tanker and remained still. After all, it might be nothing. It could be one of the many people who hired choppers to look for their stolen cars in the township. It could be a police patrol.

The sound began to fade and he breathed a sigh of relief. He crawled out. And then, without warning, the chopper swept over him and he saw the pilot look down.

No! It couldn't be! He knew that face, and he knew it meant trouble. He brought the rifle up to his shoulder and aimed. The pilot was clear in the sight of the rifle. He caressed the trigger.

The bang caught Max totally by surprise. The pain shot up his left arm and blood erupted below the bicep. In an instant he saw Hurst on the ground, the two tankers side by side, and he knew he had found the Cobra.

His pulse was racing. Now he had a chance. Marie had not

been wrong. He brought the chopper low, sweeping the rooftops. Another explosion, and a second bullet creased the hair on his head. Hurst could shoot well.

His left arm was hurting, but he grabbed the shotgun with it and leaned the weapon out of the right side of the chopper. He swung the machine on its side and headed straight back towards Hurst – coming in hard and fast from behind.

Hurst started running and Max pulled the trigger.

Hurst was thrown across the ground. A shot grazed his back and he swore out loud. Dr Loxton knew how to look after himself.

Suddenly, Hurst was afraid. The possibility of death was real. He rolled and rolled till he was under the tanker, then he raised the rifle again. The bastard was using the tankers as a shield. He was coming down behind them.

Where the hell was he? Shit! Shit! The chopper was down and Loxton was on the ground.

Max was out of the cockpit and running towards the side of the tanker. Hurst burst from the side, levelling the R4 rifle at him. Max raised the shotgun with his right hand, fired, and ducked in behind the rear of the tanker.

How much time had he got? Had Hurst activated the Cobra? Just how good was this guy?

A shot ricocheted off the metal behind him. Max dropped to his knees, pumped the shotgun and ripped off a shot at Hurst's retreating form.

Hurst swore as the shot grazed his scalp. He drew his pistol and dragged himself up over the tanker cab. Without making a sound, he pulled himself onto the smooth upper surface of the tank. Loxton would never see him, and the moment Loxton moved out of cover, he could nail him. Now he was ready for the bastard.

Max cursed out loud. Where the hell was Hurst? He'd disappeared completely. Seconds passed, and still no sign. Cautiously Max moved out from beneath the tanker. He saw the shadow a fraction too late, turned, and Hurst crashed down on him, knocking him to the ground.

*

335

Hurst raised the pistol, ready to hammer it into the back of Loxton's skull. But he'd underestimated the power of his opponent: the bastard wriggled free – and then the blow came, like nothing he could have expected. His head spun, his mouth felt bloody. Loxton's eyes were filled with hatred. Hurst summoned up every last ounce of energy within him and hit back.

Max felt himself losing consciousness as the blow connected. But he held on, seeing Hurst vulnerable, his guard down. It was his last chance. Max hammered home a left to Hurst's torso. He kept on punching, blows to the head, one after the other in quick succession. He saw the pistol drop from Hurst's hand as he staggered away. Another hard left, and Hurst collapsed.

Max went up to the side of the tanker closest to him. Hurry, hurry. Where was the control panel for the detonator? A quick glance behind him told him that Hurst was still out cold.

He followed the side of the tanker, looking for some sort of control box. Hurry! Then he got to the back and saw the pipes snaking between the two vehicles. Desperately he looked at the mass of equipment, working by instinct, looking for the central control unit. Then he noticed a black box behind an outlet valve. It was locked.

Less than ten minutes left – and, it wouldn't open. Hurry! He raised the pistol and pumped a shot directly into the lock.

Carefully he lifted the lid and found himself looking at a stainless-steel case with a timer on the outside. His eyes took in the wiring. He was sure the device was set to react immediately if interfered with. In his mind he rapidly explored the possibilities: how the circuit linking the electronic timer to the detonation mechanism functioned. Less than eight minutes to go now! He would just have to take a chance. He sprinted to the chopper and snatched up the emergency tool set. Taking a set of hexagonal keys, he removed the glass cover of the timer, and lifting it gently upwards, started to sever the wires which linked the timer to its power source.

Nothing happened. Then he realized that was just what the designer had intended: the external wires were just a front. The real mechanism must be hidden beneath the body of the timer.

Hurry! The red figures of the timer danced in front of his eyes as he unscrewed the base plate of the device. Hundredths of a second were passing and he couldn't stop them.

Carefully he started to pull out the tiny integrated circuits that made up the control board. Less than one minute to go. Hurry, hurry, hurry. Shit. He'd blown it . . .

A drop of sweat fell from his forehead and landed in the centre of the control board. The lights on the timer went out, and he fell backwards.

Nothing happened. The Cobra was dead.

Hurst, coming round slowly, saw Loxton fall back from the timer. He crawled across to his R4 lying in the dirt a metre away. Then he rose carefully and aimed the rifle at Max Loxton's back.

'You're wasting your time, Loxton. Let's get out of here.'

Max turned and smiled at him. 'It's out of action. I know what I'm doing.'

'So did Dr Preusser, the man who designed it.' Hurst gestured towards the helicopter with his rifle. 'We're going to visit some friends of mine. You fly.'

Max raised the chopper into the air, a smile of relief on his face. He had succeeded. The weapon was dead.

Hurst said: 'Loxton, you don't believe me?'

'No. Believe *me*, it's over.'

'Let me introduce myself. My name is Major Ian Hurst, and I am working for your father, Dolph Klopper and General Jurie Smit, who organized Operation Cobra. There are two ways of detonating the bomb – a timer and a remote control unit.'

Max concentrated on flying. Major Hurst was irritating him.

'You don't believe me, Loxton, do you? Remember the Oasis Hotel? Remember the gunman who tried to kill you? Ah yes, I see you do. The gunman was recruited by myself under orders from your father.'

'You're lying.'

'He was a German professional, imported for the job. He failed – you killed him in Zimbabwe when you foiled the plan to blow up the parliament building in Harare. You see, he didn't know you were such a good fighter. He underestimated you, as you're underestimating me.'

Hurst had obviously read the newspaper articles about the incident – so long ago, oh God, how long ago! – at the Oasis Hotel in Botswana. Hurst was just trying to unnerve him, Max

337

told himself, terrorize him with words. Well, he wouldn't listen, he would concentrate on flying.

'Your best friend,' Hurst said, 'your confidant, Kobus van der Post. Do you think George Zwane killed him?'

Max went cold. 'No.'

'But you couldn't find out who did, could you? Your father is very, very clever. He used Zwane, Dr Loxton, and now he's using you. Believe me. Your sister, Lucinda. She died in a riding accident, didn't she?'

Max said nothing.

'It was a thoroughbred with a wild streak, kindly supplied by your father.'

Max felt his eyes burning. He knew all this, but to have the catalogue of his father's appalling crimes listed like this . . . It was too horrible.

'So perhaps now you'll believe me when I tell you that Cobra will detonate, Loxton. If the timer fails, they can activate it by remote control.' Hurst grinned. 'Put the chopper down here. I'll see you in hell.'

Max came round in darkness. The last thing he could remember was getting out of the chopper.

The place smelt revolting. He was lying on a blanket on some kind of bunk. He got up and made his way through the gloom to the door. It was locked, so he banged on it. There was shouting in the distance, and he banged again. He heard steps approaching.

A hole in the top of the door was slid open and a face peered in, a white face. 'Will you shut up, man? Do that again, and I'll beat you to a pulp.'

'Where am I?'

'You're in the jail, man.'

'Which jail?'

'Outside Soweto. You should have known better. It's illegal for whites to enter Soweto.'

Max thought quickly. Had the weapon gone off? He had to get out of here.

'I am Major Ian Hurst,' he said confidently. 'I am on a special assignment.'

'What?'

Max's confidence grew. 'I'm under direct orders from General Smit.'

The cell door opened, and he found himself looking at a young man of about nineteen. 'Where am I?' he said again. 'And how do I get out?'

'This is a secret detention centre. We're underground, man. There's a lift.'

'There'll be guards on the lift. Where are the stairs?'

'I'll take you out.'

The young warder led Max to a door at the end of the row of cells and unlocked it. Immediately Max pushed the young man away and sprinted up the stairs. At the top of the stairwell he came out into a passage. Not a soul about. He walked forwards into what seemed to be a sort of reception area.

There were bodies everywhere.

He thought how quiet it was. If this was Soweto, there should be the sound of cars outside, people. But there was nothing – only, in the distance, a sound like the wind rustling leaves. It was so quiet. And there was a peculiar smell in the air. He felt afraid – as if he were the only living person in this vacuum of silence.

He made his way through the revolving doors that led out into the open.

Everywhere, there were bodies.

He started to run. He ran, unchallenged, through the fortified gates of the detention centre and out into the township. There were people lying everywhere. Not all of them were quite dead; he could hear a child crying. He staggered over to a big black woman with a baby tied to her back that was still just about alive. He unwrapped the child and held it in his arms as it died. As he laid the child's body down next to its mother, he saw the woman's wristwatch – it had stopped just after 11.00 a.m.

Cobra had activated, unleashing its venom through the township.

A pack of young people were running down the road, directionless. For a moment Max thought they might attack him, but then he realised they were in a state of shock, like himself. He gestured to them. 'Come. We have to help the survivors.'

They moved as if in a dream, from street to street. But there was nothing they could do. Those who were still alive were slowly dying, and nothing could stop it. Some portion of Max's mind, still functioning with logical precision, told him how carefully his father had planned this devastation. None of the essential black labour force had died, they were out of the township, working. It was the people who didn't matter to the South African economy that Cobra had destroyed – the old, the young, the nursing mothers.

He ministered to the dying till he was so exhausted he could barely stand. Street after street of them. Animal corpses, too, lying strewn across the dirt tracks. He picked up the body of a young girl. She was like a doll, arms and head flopping uselessly. He cried. He could not stop the tears.

A strange mist hung over the township; the sunlight, filtering through it, created a bizarre rainbow. And the smell. The place smelt of death – and gas. Cobra's deadly poison still lingered in the air.

An emergency session of the United Nations was called that afternoon. First reports of the atrocity had already come in, and it was clear that some sort of chemical weapon had been used. The representatives sat grim-faced in the conference hall, waiting for the Secretary-General. But Dr Klee did not come.

Dr Klee's secretary, finding the door of his office locked, had to return to her own office for the duplicate key. When she finally entered Dr Klee's room, she found him suspended from the central light-fitting by a piece of wire. On the desk was a file with a Swastika on the front, and inside, photographs that filled her with horror.

Saffron and Victoria sat hunched in front of the television set, watching in disbelief. 'This is an urgent report from South Africa. Earlier today a chemical weapon was activated in Soweto. Preliminary estimates are frightening and indicate that as many as thousands upon thousands of people have died. Reporters have not yet ventured into the area, where the lethal gas is still active, but we have just received this televised report from the State President of South Africa, Mr Dolph Klopper.'

The screen showed two men sitting in armchairs, Dolph Klopper and an interviewer. The interviewer spoke first.

'Mr Klopper, what was the reason for today's action?'

Klopper leaned forwards, tugging at his beard. 'We suffer from over-population. The people who died in this experiment were unproductive – a drain on the resources of our country. The Cobra was the ideal solution.'

'Mr President, what you are saying is that South Africa has an advanced chemical weapon, a world first?'

'Yes, the Cobra is the weapon the world has been looking for, a real answer to the problem of over-population. It eliminates people, but it affects property only temporarily – in a year's time the area of contamination will once again be habitable. All the buildings in Soweto are still standing. And in our case the Cobra was deliberately timed to go off when the working population were out of Soweto – so you see, only unproductive people were affected.

'I must reveal now that we were aware of foreign interference in our plans: an attempt was made to disarm the Cobra. Naturally, it failed, and I must announce now that we shall activate the Cobra in the central city of any nation seeking to interfere further in our decision-making processes. South Africa is an independent state, and we shall go our own way. But our example should not be lost on the world. You, who watch us, are spiritually bankrupt, and have a lesson to learn from the decisive action we have taken today.'

Victoria stared at the television in horror. Saffron was shaking, tears rolling down her cheeks.

'Victoria, where's Max?'

'God! In Botswana – he must be in Botswana!'

'But he hasn't called. Oh, Vicky, I feel he's there, in South Africa. Oh, I can't stand it! I wish I'd never set foot in your goddamn country! All it's brought me is unhappiness.'

Victoria held Saffron in her arms. There was nothing she could say to comfort her. She watched the television set over her shoulder.

'The United Nations today convened to conduct an emergency session on South Africa. Dr Klee, the Secretary-General, failed to attend, and was later found to have committed suicide. Documents found next to the body indicate that he was a former Nazi. It is believed that Dr Klee may have been the victim of blackmail, and an investigation has been launched.'

The commentator looked tersely into the screen. 'We cross to Washington now for an emergency address by the American President.'

The rugged, good-looking face filled the screen. The President's brown hair was disarranged as usual, but he looked very strained.

'Anyone who can tolerate what happened in South Africa this morning is beyond the reach of morality. The news release just issued by the South African government can only compare with those issued by the Nazi party during the Second World War. As a member of the free world I find it utterly repugnant.

'Following a security resolution passed by the United Nations just over an hour ago, I have ordered mobilisation of our military forces. We shall be launching a full-scale invasion of South Africa. I have taken this action after consulting my Soviet colleagues; its purpose is to install a government that is representative of all South Africans, whatever their creed or colour. I ask other nations to give us their full support in this and I only wish I had taken action earlier, so that this horrific atrocity might have been avoided. I speak now for all of the oppressed peoples of the world when I say that we Americans will always protect the rights of those less privileged than ourselves.

'As for Mr Klopper's threat to explode a chemical weapon in one of our cities, all movement of chemicals inside the United States will now be monitored, and our experts reckon Mr Klopper's chances of success, should he attempt such a move, as negligible.'

The television picture now showed American Stealth bombers taking off from a secret military base in the United States, then American aircraft-carriers in the Indian Ocean, cruising towards the east coast of Africa. The impression was of overwhelming military power advancing towards South Africa.

Kobus toddled into the room then, climbed onto his mother's knee and looked across at Saffron. Victoria switched off the set.

'Where's Max, Auntie Saffron?'

'I don't know, Kobus. I wish to God I did.'

Brenda Zwane's captors had fled. Since they left, she had been feeling very strange. A listlessness had overtaken her as the afternoon wore on, and now she felt very tired – she kept overbalancing and toppling over. And Morgan kept crying . . . Perhaps they were both ill. She staggered towards the phone and rang a friend, but there was no answer. When she switched on the radio for the three o'clock afternoon news, she was surprised to hear a cold voice repeating the same instruction over and over again:

'Please remain where you are. There is no reason for panic. The authorities are taking care of the situation. Please remain where you are . . .'

She put Morgan in his pram and let herself out of the house. It was then that she saw the bodies. She picked Morgan up and held him close to her.

Everything was so still. There was a haze in the air, and sunlight filtered weakly through. Everywhere there were bodies, and she felt so bad, her limbs dragged so that she could hardly move, and she was crying uncontrollably.

She caught sight of a group of men in the distance, and made her way towards them. She was running out of strength now, and found it hard even to remain standing. She recognised the one who seemed to be in charge. It was Max, Max Loxton.

'Max?'

He spun round and stared at her. Then he drew her close and looked into her face. His voice was strangely comforting.

'Don't worry, Brenda. Just rest, lean on me. I'm sorry, I failed you. I've failed George, failed Kobus. I failed Napoleon . . .'

She could not focus on his face – it seemed to recede, draw near, recede again. 'Oh Max,' she said, 'you haven't failed.' She stared at his eyes, felt herself fading. 'George admired you . . . we all did . . . What could you do against your father, against this system? Madmen . . .'

She collapsed against him. Her last words were: 'Look after Marie's baby . . .'

Max took the child from her as she died. He stared across the street, and then lifted his eyes to the horizon. The strange haze that had hung over the township all afternoon had condensed into a deadly mist that was rolling towards them. He felt weak from the effects of the gas.

He looked down at the child Brenda had given him. It was dead in his arms.

David Loxton got up from the armchair and went towards the door. The General and the State President looked up.

'Don't be long,' said Klopper. 'I have another announcement to make shortly.' He looked supremely confident – he thought the American threat of retaliation was nothing more than bluff.

343

'I just need to freshen up,' David said, and as Klopper returned his gaze to the TV monitors, made his way quickly out of the room. He looked behind, to make sure he wasn't being followed, then proceeded down the passage.

It had all gone horribly wrong. The American President was coming on strong. Placing the Cobra in one of their cities had seemed the ultimate threat as far as the Americans were concerned, but now he was not so sure. If the Americans did invade, they would all be finished. He had to save his skin and get out fast.

At the end of the passage was a security door. David placed a magnetic card in the slot at the side, and it slid back to let him pass, then closed behind him. Facing him was the base of a metal ladder that went up into a long shaft. He started to climb slowly, knowing how far he had to go. He looked down at his watch and estimated he had at least five minutes before anyone came after him.

Soon he was at the top, and opened the inspection cover above him. He emerged in the room behind the main control centre. He pulled the pistol from his hip holster and screwed on the silencer, then opened the door to the control room very carefully. One man stood watching the television monitor, with his back to David, who moved silently up to him and squeezed the trigger.

A spurt of blood covered the monitor, and the man slumped forwards. Another guard burst into the control room – and David squeezed the trigger twice more. Two tiny holes appeared in the guard's forehead as he collapsed to the floor.

Swiftly, David locked the outer door of the control room, then he went over to the control panel and punched a set of commands into the central computer. Seconds later, the read-out came onto the screen:

'Final Nuclear Protection. Do you want to activate: Yes/No?'

He pressed the 'Y' key, and listened as every hatch and door in the building began to close. He got up and let himself out of the control room, closing the door carefully.

'Three minutes.' He muttered the words to himself as he hurried towards the entrance. A guard ran in through the double doors, looking panic-stricken. 'Get back inside, sir!' he shouted at David.

'Don't worry. I've something to sort out.'

The man looked at the Prime Minister as though he were crazy, then hurried past him.

Moments later, David was out in the sunlight, walking across the lawn to his car. Sitting in the driver's seat, he watched the doors to the underground broadcasting centre close electronically. He smiled.

He was free, and they were trapped inside.

'Where the hell is David?' General Smit glanced angrily in the direction of the bathroom.

'Relax, man,' said Klopper. 'He's not going anywhere.'

'I've never trusted that bastard.'

'*Ja*, I know. But he has his uses. This centre, for example.'

'I've had enough of him.'

'He has served his purpose, like Dr Preusser. It's time to dispose of him.'

An alarm sounded in the distance. General Smit stared anxiously at the computer monitor next to the television screen. It displayed the operating status of the underground broadcasting centre's control system

'Prepare for attack.' The words flashed up on the monitor repeatedly. Dolph Klopper hunched forward, nervously smoothing back his dark hair and fiddling with his beard. Then he got up.

'I'll find Loxton. He'll know what's going on.'

It did not take him long to discover that David was not in the underground suite. He was starting to run back to the main lounge when he heard the sound of the doors being electronically bolted.

His mind worked swiftly. He and Jurie had to get out, and fast. In the lounge he saw Jurie struggling to open the outer door.

'Bloody thing's sealed, we're trapped.'

'No! Loxton said there was another way out, an emergency tunnel that runs inside next to the lift.'

They both ran for the door that David had locked ten minutes earlier. There was nothing they could do to open it.

'He's double-crossed us! But there has to be a way . . . We *have* to get out!'

'This place was designed by Terminal, and David Loxton is the only person who can get us out.'

They made their way back, ashen-faced, to the lounge, and grimly sat down in front of the TV screen.

*

345

As the sun began to set, Max felt the effort of the previous seven hours beginning to catch up with him. He felt so helpless amid the death that surrounded him. Already the looters were moving in – ready to pillage from the homes of the dead.

He staggered round a corner and walked into an army patrol dressed in protective clothing. He didn't put up any resistance, accepting his arrest without a word. They locked him in the back of the armoured vehicle, and he was thrown around inside as they drove out of the township at a furious rate.

It seemed hours later that the vehicle finally drew to a halt and the doors were opened. Max staggered out into a floodlit field and saw that the ground was littered with half-dead people. He moved towards them, but was stopped by a vicious kick in the backside.

'This way. You're to be interrogated.'

He was dragged towards a grey concrete building covered with barbed wire, shown into a large room and, to his surprise, given a cup of coffee. He sat drinking it silently, unaware that someone else had entered the room. Then he looked up, and felt the hair rising from his head.

'You bloody fool, Max,' David Loxton said. 'You've never understood me – never taken the time to examine what I've been doing. You've always been a sucker for the underdog. Well, you've come to the end of the road, my boy.'

'You're worse than Hitler. Do you know what you've done? Have you seen the bodies?'

'They'd have starved to death anyway; there wasn't enough food to feed them all. You've never understood this continent, have you? It's the Darwinian law – survival of the fittest.'

'You believe that!'

'I've won, Max. You've lost.'

'You think the outside world will sit back and ignore this?'

'That's Dolph Klopper's particular problem at the moment.'

David Loxton got up and dusted off his immaculate suit. Max could see that he was smiling. The bastard was actually enjoying himself.

'You'll never get away with this,' he said.

'I already have.'

Max tried to get up but he was too weak.

David smiled at him. 'You're just like your mother, full of idealistic shit, and no idea how the world operates.'

346

'I know you sent that horse to Lucinda.'

'She was another pawn in my game. Just like you.'

David walked out of the room; Max heard him order the guards to keep him in solitary confinement till he died. With a mighty effort Max staggered to the door, pushed it open and was almost on his father when he was grabbed and held from behind. He spat hard, and the spittle landed on his father's face.

'I hope you rot in hell.'

David Loxton wiped his face and walked off, smiling. Max was wrong: Hell was not for him. That was waiting for Klopper and Smit.

Kumalo left Fat Man in the car at the base of the mountain slope. He had only been to this place once before, and he felt none too easy about being summoned to it again. He had failed, he knew that. But why this meeting now?

He ran his eye across the rocky slopes and picked up a flash of sunlight. He could see no one, but they were there. One wrong move and he would die. He increased his pace.

Fat Man heard the rear door of the car open and someone get in behind him. He didn't even dare look round; this was a terrible, sinister place – who knew what demon might have got in the car with him?

Then the garrotte was round his neck.

'No! Please!'

He raised his hands to try and pull away the wire that cut across his throat, but the grip tightened and he started to choke. His hand went for the pistol in his belt, but he didn't have the strength to draw it out.

A minute later, Fat Man was dead.

Kumalo went forward into the darkness of the cave. A long way away, at the far end, a fire burned. He moved towards it, reluctant but determined. This place frightened him, even the shadows seemed sinister. But he had no choice: he had failed, and knew that unless he appeared here, they would find him and kill him.

'Sit down in front of my fire.'

The voice – a female voice – startled him as it had before.

This was the voice that gave the orders; she was the one who could always supply the weapons.

'What do you say, Kumalo?'

He couldn't see her, only a procession of shadows on the wall. But then there was a brilliant flash of light, and there on the stone in front of him was Fat Man, naked, his throat slit.

This was as she had said it would be. But had she found out his plan? His plan to mobilise the Comrades across the country – to remove her, to hold the power himself.

'He thought he could defy me,' the voice said.

'No!'

'Everyone thinks he can defy me. You think you can defy me.'

'No!'

'You promise to do all that I command, then? Never even to think of betraying me?'

'I promise.'

'Then you will see the light of another day.'

'David.' Hanli's voice was trembling with pain and confusion. 'It's Victoria on the phone. I told her you weren't available, but then she said something about you and little girls . . .'

David pushed past her to the phone. 'Victoria, what – '

'Where's Max?'

'I don't know.'

'Yes, you do. The BBC says he was picked up in Soweto by your soldiers this evening.'

'Really?'

'Listen, you bastard. Lucinda may be dead, but her secret didn't die with her – she left a will. You animal! Tracey didn't have an accident in her car, she killed herself. You were screwing Lucinda. It's all here. Oh God, how could you do that? Lucinda knew there were others, too. You even made money out of it. Oh my God, David, how the hell could you have done that to her?'

'It's lies.'

'You raped her when she was eight years old. Do you want me to tell Hanli some more? Dirk and Rory will love it, too. You pervert! You child rapist!'

He thought quickly. His plan now was to get abroad as fast as possible. There was going to be a lot of bad publicity, a lot of unwelcome media attention, and he wanted that centred on

Klopper and General Smit, not on himself. The helicopter was waiting for him – but so was Victoria, and she was holding a loaded gun at his head.

'What do you want?' he said.

'I want Max.'

'If I let him go?'

'I'll keep the story quiet.'

'You have a deal.'

'Where is he?'

'In the Benoni police camp. I'll order his immediate release.'

'Good. And now you can go to hell, David. If Max isn't out in ten minutes, you might as well be . . .'

But David had already put the phone down on her, and was dialling the number of the Benoni camp.

'Yes. Max Loxton. Release him immediately. If you fail, I'll have you shot.' He ended the call, and as he did so, heard explosions in the distance.

Hanli came into the room, her face white. 'Little girls,' she said. 'You like little girls. Is that why you married me? You animal!'

'Come here, Hanli. It's all lies.'

'Oh God, you're disgusting. Those payments to the Prester John, I know what they were for now. They weren't for your clients, were they? They were for your little girls.'

'Shut up!'

Behind them, the window pane suddenly shattered. As Hanli turned, David saw Major Hurst moving fast towards her, and the next minute he had her in the crook of his arm, a pistol pointed to her head.

'Loxton, wherever you're going, I'm going with you, or she dies.'

David pulled the snub-nosed revolver from his belt.

'Try me, Hurst.'

As David raised the revolver Hurst fired – and Hanli lay on the floor, covered in blood and screaming. Then David pumped three shots into Hurst. Hanli was still screaming: David shot her in the forehead.

Hurst was dying. He looked weakly at David. 'I thought you loved her,' he faltered.

'Love is for fools.'

'You're the fool,' Hurst said softly, and his eyes closed.

A soldier burst in through the hall door. In an instant David realised he was an American. He crouched, and fired again, and the soldier toppled over. David was on him at once, stripping off his uniform as quickly as he could. Time was running out.

The bombers came in from the east. Key military installations across the country were destroyed. Waves of fighters overwhelmed the South African air force in hours. Dolph Klopper decided it was time for another nation-wide broadcast. After all, no one else knew that he and Smit were trapped. What would his father do? The old man would fight on to the end.

Dolph walked calmly into the TV studio with Jurie and sat down in front of the camera. He gestured for the editor to begin broadcasting, and then spoke in his usual direct style – though not with the confidence that generally accompanied it.

'The Americans are merely trying to scare us. There is no danger of an invasion; our army is quite capable of repulsing any attack. The situation in Soweto is almost back to normal. I ask you, as loyal South Africans, not to panic. Everything is under control. I pass you over now to General Smit, the commander of our armed forces.'

The camera focused on the General. Dolph saw that General Smit looked haggard; even his normally immaculate uniform looked dishevelled. His heavy, guttural English-Afrikaans accent reflected fear, not confidence.

'The army is in control of Soweto,' he said. 'The area will be safe by tomorrow morning, when residents can return to the area. In the rest of the country conditions are as normal . . .'

No one ever saw or heard the broadcast, because the South African television centre had been bombed half an hour before . . .

American ground troops took control quickly, and the South African army was rudderless. Cut off from General Smit at central command, they had no idea what was happening or how to react. Across the Witwatersrand, especially in Johannesburg and Pretoria, bands of marauding youths ran amok. People were necklaced in their homes, shops were looted.

More and more American and then British troops were flown in to restore order. A new hatred had sprung up, like lightning in the Highveld sky. A feeling of desperation, of futility, seized the country.

*

350

Saffron was seated at the controls of the chopper. She'd hired it as soon as she'd arrived in Botswana the previous night, after discovering that no one would fly her into South Africa. In the distance flames and smoke soared into the sky. She felt desperate. Max had sounded terrible on the phone. What had happened to him?

She put the chopper down at Lanseria airport, and was immediately surrounded by troops; American and British soldiers were everywhere. Eventually she managed to make contact with the commander of the American force, General Henderson. He looked desperately tired.

'Mrs Loxton, you're out of your goddamned mind. We're having one hell of a time here – these guys are really on the rampage.'

'I have a favour to ask of you, General. I'm looking for my husband.'

His hand fidgeted nervously with his ear. 'Yes – your husband. I know. He's . . . It's the after-effects . . . It was a combination of bacteriological agents and nerve gas.'

'Where is he?'

'He was released from a police camp in Benoni two days ago. I'll get one of my men to take you to him. He's organising relief workers in Soweto . . .'

As she travelled in the jeep towards the south of Johannesburg, Saffron could scarcely believe the destruction. Cars were overturned and burning, factories destroyed. It had all happened so quickly – the city of gold had turned into a war zone. How long would it be before any sort of order prevailed?

As they approached Soweto, the atmosphere changed. The driver handed her protective clothing. 'Please be very careful, Mrs Loxton. Our scientists still haven't quite worked out what the agents and gases are.' She followed his example and pulled on the mask.

There were few people in the streets and there was a deathly stillness about the place. Eventually they pulled up outside a hostel.

'He's inside there,' the driver said tersely under his mask.

Saffron climbed out with difficulty, weighed down by the special clothing. 'Won't you come with me?'

'Lady, I don't want to go in there, all right? You'll find him soon enough. I'll wait for you.'

She entered the yard – and suddenly there were people

everywhere. There was the smell of death in the air. In the corner of the yard was a big man crouched over a body, with a nurse at his side. Max. Heart singing, she ran towards him.

She lay next to him in the single bed, staring at the concrete ceiling above.

'I had no idea it was this bad,' she said.

'Perhaps as many as one hundred thousand dead by the latest estimates and more are still dying.'

She looked at him. The flesh hung loosely on his face, he'd lost a lot of weight and there was grey amongst his blond hair.

'What is it, exactly that's killed them?'

'It's bacteriological poisoning. There's nothing anyone can do.'

'Where's your father?'

'They took his house, but they only found Hanli, dead. Major Hurst and an American soldier had also been shot. My guess is he's out of the country.'

Saffron looked down at the black and white television in the corner of the room. 'Look, Max . . .'

The Americans were blasting open the doors to the underground broadcasting centre of the South African Television Service. After the time-locks had been detonated, the huge metal doors at last came open and a team of crack combat troops ran inside. Ten minutes later they reappeared with two men. Max recognised them clearly.

A television camera zoomed in on Klopper's face. He stared defiantly at the camera, and a reporter moved in on him.

'Mr Klopper, did you authorise the chemical bomb in Soweto?'

'*Ja*. I am proud of it. You people don't know what you are doing. It is the end of the civilised world. Give these people the vote and you are signing your own death warrant.'

'How do you feel about the thousands and thousands of people who lost their lives?'

'A mass of unproductive, inferior people only. Don't you understand?'

Klopper and Smit were bundled into an armoured vehicle before any more questions could be put to them, and the camera switched to the American President in Washington addressing a room packed with reporters. He seemed to be in good spirits, and smiled confidently.

'I'd like to say first how pleased I am to announce the capture of President Klopper and General Smit. We have taken control.'

A wave of applause followed this announcement.

'My first duty will be to visit Soweto,' he continued, 'to see the relatives of the people who lost their lives on January 16th. The men responsible for this unspeakable atrocity will be brought to justice, that I promise you. I also promise all South Africans a free and fair election, and the right to choose whatever political system they want as long as it grants the basic freedoms to every man irrespective of creed or colour.

'South Africa is a great country. To all of you, black and white, I bring a message from the people of the United States of America: we wish to see you prosper and grow in strength.'

Max walked into the doctor's room. It was time for the results of the tests. Relax, he told himself, relax.

Dr Katz was a wiry man with curly, jet black hair tinged with grey, and a wrinkled face that broke easily into an infectious grin. He inspired confidence.

'Sit down, Dr Loxton.'

Max stared into the dark eyes that scrutinised his own.

'You're a strong man,' Dr Katz said. 'I've always admired you. At least you tried, when none of the rest of us did. I am proud to have met and spoken to you.'

'You don't have to butter me up, Dr Katz. I know what I was exposed to.'

Dr Katz rose from his chair and gestured to Max to join him on the couch at the end of his room.

'Dr Loxton, strangely enough, it's when I meet someone like yourself that I find my job particularly hard.'

Max felt a cold stab of fear pass through his heart. 'Please, be direct with me, Dr Katz.'

'You're going to die.'

Max tried to laugh, but couldn't. 'How long have I got?'

'Two weeks. Perhaps a month.'

'That little?'

'Yes, that little. I'll give you some advice. Most people don't take my advice, but take it all the same – for what it's worth.'

Max found he was gripping the sides of the leather couch, his whole body rigid. He was scared.

353

'Go to somewhere you love,' Dr Katz said. 'Go with someone you love. Please. Be kind to yourself.'

Max got up and walked over to the window. He watched some children playing outside on the hospital lawn. He thought about children – how he loved them, how he wished he had one of his own.

Dr Katz was standing behind him. He put his hand on Max's shoulder. 'Listen, I'm sorry. For all you've done, you deserved more than this. You're the one who's made the sacrifices.'

'Thank you, doctor. For your advice especially.'

He left Dr Katz standing by the window.

'Now for the hardest part.'

Max muttered the words to himself as he got into the car and drove back to his house. He felt that the longest journey he ever made was the one from the bottom of his drive to the top.

Saffron came out to meet him and – hell – he found he was crying. She stood looking at him, and knew what it was he had to tell her.

Once they were inside, she poured him a stiff whisky. 'Don't hide anything, Max. How long have you got?'

'A month at the most.'

She looked up at the ceiling. 'Goddamnit, it's not fair. Here you are dying, and they can't even find your goddamned father who's responsible.'

'Easy, Saffron. He wasn't responsible alone. There were plenty who supported him.'

She looked him squarely in the eyes. 'What do you want to do?'

'I want to be alone with you, at the camp in the Okavango.'

They were off within the hour. The hardest part for Max was leaving the house, knowing he'd never return. Tuli had cried helplessly and Max had held her for a long time. Then she'd stared into his eyes and smiled. 'You're a good man, Dr Max, a great man.'

Victoria was there to see him go. She was acting as an adviser to the international force now controlling the country.

'I'll be thinking of you, Max. Always.'

He was walking to the chopper, not looking round, feeling the earth under his feet. Then they were up in the air, looking down at the city and flying over the silent morgue that was Soweto. Max took a last glance at the city, then steered the plane north-westwards, towards Botswana, the town of Maun and the Okavango Swamps.

They were at the hotel in Maun that evening, and sat out in the dying sunlight, watching the lazy curve of the Thamalakane River beneath them. But Riley's Hotel was still civilisation, and Max longed to go on.

'I need to be right in the bush,' he said to Saffron. 'I don't want any more people, any more demands.'

'Unwind, Max. Tomorrow morning we'll be there.'

The next day he felt much better, and smiled as he brought the chopper down on the tiny bush landing-strip. Gumsa was waiting for them with the Land-Rover.

'It's been a long time, Kaikhoe.'

'Too long, Gumsa.'

'How long are you staying for?'

'One month, maybe even two.'

'You have finally come to your senses. Take a drive – I'll secure the chopper.'

They got into the open Land-Rover and Max drove slowly down the track. For some reason he remembered back to years before, when his mother had driven him along this very same road. He pulled over.

'What's wrong, honey?'

'I just need to be alone – just for a few minutes.'

'OK. I'll wait here for you.'

He walked out into the bush, and kept going till it engulfed him. Then he sat down and looked up at the sky.

'Who are you, God? I loved my mother. I loved this land. You took one away from me, now you're taking the other. Is that just?'

There was no answer. The bush remained as it was. He thought of Tracey, how she'd taken him to this exact spot and shown him his first lion.

He was getting up to return to the Land-Rover when a fleck of brown caught his eye among the bushes. He moved stealthily towards it and smelt the animal smell. He was looking at a lioness with three cubs. There was a contentedness about them. One of the cubs rolled over, and mother rested her paw on it. The cub yelped with delight. Then the mother roared, and somewhere in the distance, a lion roared in reply. Max shivered, and wondered

355

where the lion was lurking. Then he realised that he had seen some sort of sign. He had been given an answer.

He walked back to the Land-Rover and to Saffron, and they drove on to the camp. He knew he had come to the right place.

Victoria had watched the whole trial impassively from the gallery. Now, on the fourteenth day, the judge was about to give his verdict. At no point had either Klopper or Smit shown any remorse. They seemed completely unmoved by what they had done. It was clear that to them, the one hundred and twelve thousand people who had died in Soweto were an irrelevance. Bizarre details that had unfolded during the trial included the assassination of Dr Preusser, the designer of the Cobra.

Judge Blair walked into the courtroom and asked everyone to be seated.

'I have practised as a judge for over twenty-five years,' he said. 'I have seen the worst that one person can do to another. But never, in my entire career, have I come across an action as cold-blooded as the one that has unfolded before me over the last two weeks.

'The two men who stand before you in the dock are quite unrepentant and, it seems, even proud of what they have done. Counsel for the defence has argued that they were merely performing a task which they were elected to do, but I must concur with the counsel for the prosecution in saying that the white South African electorate can hardly be blamed for the cold-blooded murder of over a hundred thousand people.

'I am reminded, in giving judgement, of the Nuremburg Trials over forty years ago. I sense, in my reading of those trials, the same desperation in the minds of those presiding as I feel now. How does one deal with something that seems beyond the realms of possibility?

'I am empowered to give the death sentence. However, I believe that to pronounce the death sentence on the two men who stand before me, unrepentant and unforgiving, would be to do them a kindness.' He stared coldly at Klopper and Smit. 'No death sentence. Life imprisonment. The two of you will spend your lives working with, and caring for, the dying. Such work is dangerous. It requires contact with people who have a high level of bacteriological poisoning.'

The two accused men seemed to waver on the stand. Then, to everyone's astonishment, Klopper squared his shoulders.

'There is a sickness in mankind,' he said forcefully, 'a failure to understand the laws of nature. It is you who cannot see it.'

The words echoed coldly through the courtroom, and the judge turned his back on the two men.

One morning at breakfast, after two weeks at the camp, Max pulled out one of the many maps he kept permanently in the lodge.

'I want to take you somewhere that's very special to me,' he said to Saffron.

'I don't want to leave.'

He saw the concern on her face and hastened to reassure her. 'It's not far – a day or so's drive to the west. Gumsa knows the way.'

'A sacred place?'

'Yes. For the Bushmen people. It's also a water-hole. I've always wanted to take you there.'

'I . . . let's go.' Her voice faltered; unspoken words crowded the air around them. He placed his hand over hers and she gripped it tightly.

That night their love-making was tinged with desperation. Saffron cried afterwards.

'I'm scared! Afraid to live without you.'

'You must come here, often. When you come here you will always find me.'

'Goddamnit – it's so unjust.'

They slept in each other's arms and rose with the first light of dawn, packing a few last things into the Land-Rover. Then they were off, Saffron glancing wistfully back at the camp. She knew now that she would never go back there with Max. Strangely, that knowledge did not depress her as it might have done. It felt surreal, like everything else that morning.

At first, as they made their way between the waterways, following the faint track, their progress was slow. In some places there were long stretches of water and the Land-Rover had to move cautiously, though it was never more than three feet under water. Eventually they came to dry land, and the bush began to thin out. The palms became few and far between, sand more prevalent. Saffron realised that she was entering a totally different world.

The Land-rover gradually picked up speed and they moved across the open plain on a scarcely discernible track. Far in the distance she could see the hills, like a mirage on the horizon. Gumsa, who had been talking most of the time, became silent as they got closer to a series of round hillocks that seemed to dominate the entire area. They stopped for a while to pick up firewood and stow it on the roof-carrier above the vehicle.

It was almost sunset before they reached the base of the hills and Max ordered Gumsa to stop.

'This is fine. We've come far enough. We'll camp here – we can go into the hills in the morning.'

That night, after eating round the campfire, the three of them sat together. Saffron took Max's hand and smiled.

'You were right to come here. It has a special quality.'

There was a noise close by, and she tensed. Gumsa smiled. 'Do not worry. It is my people. They have come to see who has invaded their sacred place.'

'Should we have come?'

'Of course. They have been expecting Kaikhoe.'

She stared into Gumsa's eyes and saw that he understood everything she had not explained to him. He knew that Max was dying.

Suddenly she became aware of a small figure crouched by the campfire – an old, wizened man with closely cropped hair and wrinkled features. He was smiling. Max spoke in the clicking language he used with Gumsa, and the old man replied:

'We have been waiting for you.'

Max looked at the lean, strong legs of the old man, and at his tiny bow and arrows. These were a people who demanded very little of life, and respected their environment.

'You are safe here,' the old man said. As he spoke, a woman, children, and then some younger men appeared. 'You are welcome to camp with us,' Max said. 'To share our food.'

'Such a big fire, Kaikhoe.' The old man stared at the roaring blaze, and Max knew why. When the Bushmen lit a fire they used very little wood, just what was needed to cook their food and no more. Everything to them was precious.

Saffron awoke with the dawn and stared at the hills in the red light of sunrise. There were four of them, set roughly in line; the one furthest to the north was a flat, bare rock rising three

358

hundred metres above the plain. Max had explained to her that the Bushmen called the largest hill the Male, with his companion the Female, and the closest of the smaller hills the Child. The Male rose blue-black out of the trees beneath it, and it seemed to Saffron to contain the essence of the mystery of the place. She went over to the fire and put on a billy, watching the water boil as the sun rose gradually in the east.

A faint line of cloud formed a wispy line above the horizon and she stared at it in fascination. She felt Max's hand on her arm, and he leaned over and kissed her on the forehead. Together they watched the sunrise until their bodies were bathed in the yellow light and gradually warmed by it. They ate a simple breakfast of pan bread and mealie pap. Then the old Bushman appeared. He spoke to Max for a long time.

'He will show us the hills,' Max told her. 'He says that you are very lucky to be my chosen one. He also says that you are very beautiful, like the first stars of the night.'

Saffron blushed.

'Tell him I am honoured by his praises.'

The old man led them across the sandy plain, then up towards the hills. At last they came to the green vines that clung to the base of the hill and passed through a crack in the rock.

Max whispered in Saffron's ear: 'This is a great honour. He is taking us to see one of the secret springs. You must never tell anyone about this place. It is sacred.'

They walked through a dark cavern, and then, in front of them, the sunlight burst through a hole in the rock above and lit up a pool of water that was blue and clear. Moss and small trees grew around the edge of the pool. The Bushman knelt down and drank slowly from the water. He gestured to Max and Saffron to follow his example, and Saffron thought she had never tasted anything as sweet and pure in her life. Max watched as she drank, and the Bushman spoke in subdued tones.

'He says that this is the source,' Max told Saffron. 'The beginning of life. He says he knows that I am ill, and I must drink to strengthen my soul for what is to come.'

She got up and looked at the Bushman, into his inscrutable eyes. For once in her life she truly felt envy – that someone with so little could be so content.

'He says you are the sun, your day is long, but I am like the moon. You can survive without me, but the nights will be empty.'

'How does he know so much?'

'Because he knows so little. His mind is free of the clutter that we carry around with us. The Bushmen are a spiritual people, that is why they have managed to survive so long. Come, he has something else to show us.'

From the spring they walked along a narrow valley, under huge overhangs of rock. Saffron stared at the rock face in fascination: It was covered with pictures depicting every aspect of the Bushman's existence.

'So beautiful! Did his people paint these?'

'No, not these. They do still paint, but you are not allowed to see those paintings. These were done long ago.'

They returned to the camp in the light of the setting sun, and after they had eaten hungrily round the campfire, some of the Bushmen gathered to play them a song. One played a hunting bow, tapping the string to create a low, hollow note, and against this rhythmic, hypnotic background, two other men played four-stringed *gwashis*, while the rest sang. The music was plaintive and hauntingly beautiful.

Max and Saffron fell asleep watching the burning embers, but when Saffron woke later, the place where Max had been was cold beside her. She got up in a fright, and Gumsa came up to her.

'He is gone. You must not worry.'

She shivered. She wanted to cry, but there was something about Gumsa that calmed her.

'When will he come back?'

'No, he will not come back. You will see him much later.'

Saffron lay down in her sleeping-bag and stared up at the sky. The tears rolled down her face. She felt Gumsa's hand touch her own.

'Do not cry. His body might leave you but his spirit never will. Africa has taken him into her soul.'

Four

Dolph Klopper lay in his cell and stared at the ceiling. Each day was worse than the last. He did not want to think about what had happened to his country. The world was weak. How could they have handed over control to the black people?

The bolt on the door of his cell slid back, and the warder stepped in and stared down at him.

'Get up, Klopper. You have a visitor.'

'Visitor?'

'Yes. A coloured woman.' He said it almost mockingly.

'I don't want to see her.'

'I think you will.'

He was led down the corridors of Pretoria Central Prison and shown into a small room with a single window. In the centre of the room, sitting at a small table, was his father's maid, Figi. She smiled at him as he came in, but he did not acknowledge this greeting and remained standing: he would not demean himself to sit with a coloured.

'Hallo, *Meneer* Klopper.'

He grunted a reply.

'I bring bad news, I'm afraid.'

Suddenly his senses were alert. Pa. No, not Pa!

'Your father died a week ago.'

Dolph swallowed hard. 'He was an old man,' he managed at last. 'Did he die peacefully?'

'In his sleep. He left you a will.' She took a piece of crumpled paper out of her bag, and he snatched it from her.

'Thank you.' His tone indicated that she should go, but she

361

ignored it. 'You must read it now,' she said. 'I know what's in it. I helped him write it.'

'Then why do you want to stay?'

She screamed at him: 'Read it, you bastard!'

He was tempted to hit her, but something in her eyes stopped him – something familiar that he had not seen before. He sat down and read the paper, his fingers curling round the edge of the table as he did so.

She spoke when he had finished. 'Your father was a strange man, but I loved him always. I was just another woman to bed. Of course, he couldn't see, but he knew that I was coloured. I was two women to him. First, I was his kaffir maid, and second, I was his wife, the mother of his only child. You.'

Dolph felt the room spinning around him. 'It is a lie,' he whispered.

'Your life has been a lie, Dolph. I loved you – but I hate what you have become. He did that to you. I made him promise that you must know the truth, if only for Marie's sake.'

'What are you telling me?'

'The coloured child she bore you, Morgan. His darkness was yours. You never knew his name, did you? I went to see her after you threw her out; I tried to help her. She is dead now, of course, killed by the gas – by you.'

'And the boy?'

'He died as well.'

Dolph got up and walked out of the room, the old coloured woman staring after him. The warder showed him back to his cell, and before he closed the door offered a last passing comment:

'So, Klopper. You're a kaffir.'

AMERICA

John Packard was in his Hollywood office at seven in the morning, as he always was. His manservant placed a copy of the *Wall Street Journal* on his desk, and he sat sipping his coffee and staring out at the early morning sun shining on the roofs of his studios. He felt very, very good. The deal he had closed with the Japanese the week before had fulfilled his ultimate ambition, to be the most powerful man in the electronic communications business. Now he was not just films, videos and broadcasting networks, he was computers and satellites too.

One of the phones on his desk rang – his personal line.

'Shelton! How are you? What . . . But it was watertight! I don't believe this. No, I haven't . . .'

He snatched up the fax that had landed on his desk moments before. It was the proposed text for a newspaper article headed 'Saffron Packard Bares All', and the article itself fulfilled the promise of the headline. 'Saffron Packard has come clean about her former husband's ruthless business dealings. How he paid people to work for rival networks and sabotage them, so he could buy them for next to nothing. How he engineered the destruction of Max Loxton's Botswana project by loaning money through an intermediary, then reneging on the agreement. . .'

Packard put the fax down and snatched up the phone again. 'Shelton, this will never be published. I'll sort it out . . . What do you mean, you're under arrest by the Swiss authorities . . .?'

He slammed the phone down just as there came a brief knock on the office door – and, Saffron walked in, tight-lipped.

'I guess Shelton spoke to you, honey. I don't care about him – he'll get fifteen years. Your sentence may be different . . .'

Packard half rose from his chair. 'I'm not about to . . .'

'John, I could contact the FBI. They can arrest you, provided I testify and produce the necessary evidence, which I hold. I've been advised that you'll get twenty, maybe thirty years.'

Packard looked up at her. 'What is it you want?'

'An advance of fifty million dollars – to start with. Then . . .'

'That's enough!'

'No. You'll pay for it every day of your life.'

Packard stared up at his former wife. 'You have a deal, you bitch!'

ARGENTINA

It had been a good game. The billionaire from Texas leant over to congratulate his host. 'David, that's the best polo I've seen played in many a year.'

'Thank you, Jim, old chap. I'm flattered.'

'When I came to Argentina, I had no idea I'd be entertained so magnificently. You have a beautiful estate, and a most charming wife.'

Gabriella was a twenty-one-year-old former beauty queen. David Loxton looked over at her where she sat talking to Jim Calhoun's wife, and smiled.

'Thank you. I'd like to show you my mines, too, if you have time.'

'Yes indeed, but let's get the arms deal sorted out first. Have you always lived in Argentina, David?'

'Oh yes, though I did spend a few years in Africa once.'

PIETERSBERG

Kumalo staggered up the slope to the mouth of the cave. He did not want to go inside. He did not want to confront the future. Then he looked around him, at the men who stood amongst the rocks, armed with high-powered rifles. He had no choice. There was no escape.

Inside, in the darkness, he smelt blood. He willed himself forward into the tunnel till he sensed that he had entered the big cavern.

'What have you to say?'

Her voice echoed against the cold wall of the cavern and penetrated his very soul. He felt frozen.

'Speak up, Kumalo. You have had four years.'

There was no choice. He must speak.

'We have fought hard all that time,' he said. 'But Malcolm Zwane has fought back. He is State President. He has the military machine that the international task force built up on his side. He knows that the Comrades want to overthrow him, and he has put us down ruthlessly.'

'You told me there was a weapon with which you could retaliate. The same weapon that destroyed Soweto a few years ago. The Cobra.'

'That is correct. With Cobra I can destroy Malcolm Zwane's army.'

'And where did you get this Cobra?'

'I bought it from the red-haired one, Rory Loxton.'

'How much did you pay him?'

'Millions.'

'How much?'

'Seventeen million rand.'

'And you have the Cobra?'

Kumalo collapsed sobbing on the cold floor of the cave. 'No! He cheated me!'

'Your time is over.'

A fire flickered into life in the centre of the cavern, and Kumalo saw her face in the distance. 'And so is yours,' he said softly.

As the men advanced towards him from the shadows, he moved his hand to the detonator, feeling the packs of explosive taped to every part of his body. A blade penetrated his back. He screamed – and activated the detonator.

He felt the white heat sear through his body, but smiled as he saw the look of horror on her face.

In the second before he died he knew that she no longer had the power. He had taken it from her.

EGOLI

As the plane landed at Napoleon Zwane Airport, Johannesburg, the massed military band began to play. Steps were wheeled up to the fuselage and a red carpet was unrolled. As the door of the plane opened, the crowd burst into song, and a tall, distinguished-looking woman waved to them. Her long blonde hair was lifted by the breeze and flashed in the sunlight.

Dr Malcolm Zwane, the President, walked along the carpet to greet Victoria Loxton with a kiss. Next down the steps was Saffron Packard in a black dress, her dark hair severely plaited. The President kissed her too.

'Congratulations, Saffron, both on your film and the success of the Okavango project.'

A young boy, smartly dressed in a dark suit, walked down the steps. His eyes reflected wonder at a continent that he had never seen before. Dr Zwane waited till he was at the foot of the steps, then pumped his hand.

'Kobus, you will always be welcome here. I had the privilege of knowing your father – a truly great man.'

The whole party walked back into the airport buildings. A fleet of stretch-limos transported them towards Egoli, the city of gold that stood amongst the yellow mountains of mine-waste in the stark sun of the Highveld.

In the leading car, Victoria turned to her host. 'Malcolm, honestly, you didn't have to make such a show.'

'On the contrary, Victoria, your return to this country is an historic event. For me it is the attainment of a goal I set myself when I was elected to office.'

Victoria thought about what Malcolm had achieved since that time. He had returned to Africa after the international force had withdrawn, and had spearheaded the formation of a new government. He had been elected President in the first general election, and had proved himself to be a great and able leader. But the country was still in turmoil. There were violent elements that refused to recognise the new government.

'Thank you,' Victoria said. 'But I still don't know why you brought us here.'

'You cannot guess? Well, let me keep you in suspense.'

'I don't think that's fair,' Saffron interjected mischievously.

Malcolm smiled. 'Ah. And I know I have to watch my step with you, Saffron. Your reputation for getting your own way is notorious.'

Saffron squeezed Malcolm's arm. 'If you're referring to the way I manipulated John, that's true.'

'And as a result he's funded the entire Okavango Project.'

'And he'll keep paying for the rest of his life, Malcolm. He's also backed my feature.'

'Kaikhoe.' Malcolm pronounced the name softly.

'It's my gift to Max – a film about him, and everything he believed in.'

Victoria stared across at Saffron and saw that her eyes were bright with unshed tears. She felt the tears start in her own eyes. Malcolm took her hand.

'Believe me, Victoria, I know what it cost you to come back. But you are more a part of this country than most of us who live here. I'm so glad you've brought Kobus with you.'

Victoria stared out at the country that was such an enigma to her. They pulled onto the highway that traversed the length of Egoli, and she gazed at the city, her memory returning to Kobus' assassination – so many, many years ago.

'Victoria, I'm sorry,' Malcolm said. 'I have been unkind – I am asking too much of you. I will take you to the hotel now, and we will go to Soweto tomorrow.'

She looked up. 'No, Malcolm, you mustn't. I want to go there now. This is a great honour for us. Max and your brother and your father should have been alive to see this. It was what they dreamed of.'

The car passed into an area of grassland, with just an occasional house set amid the bush.

'But it is not over yet, Victoria,' Malcolm said. 'Violence lives in the soul of my people, and their bitterness has not gone. I face new troubles every day . . . But that is not for you to think about now. See how Soweto has changed.'

'I thought you would have left it as it was, as a reminder.'

'Wait.'

The car approached a section of battered houses made of corrugated iron, with a dusty street running between them. At the end of the street was a huge bust of a man's head, cast in bronze and already darkened by the weather. It looked out to the north, and on the man's face was a look of determination, of almost religious zeal.

They pulled up and got out. Saffron walked slowly up to the monument, and Kobus was about to follow, but Victoria drew him back.

'Leave her alone. This is for her, you must understand.'

Tears were streaming from Saffron's eyes now. It was a brilliant likeness. At the base of the bust there was a simple plaque. Malcolm read the words out softly.

'*To Dr Max Loxton, 1949 to 1992. He was a part of our soul. He will be with us always.*'

Saffron was near collapse, and Malcolm put his arm round her shoulders, and stood with her, waiting for the crying to stop. Then Victoria came up with Kobus, and Malcolm stood in front of the monument and addressed them all.

'I invited you here to see this. I had to find a way to pay tribute to all that Dr Loxton believed in and did. Now I give you all the freedom of Egoli, and I hope that one day you will choose to live here.'

Then he looked intensely at Victoria. 'Now there is something I have to ask you.'

'I'm not going to stay,' she said.

'Wait, Victoria. I know you are happy and successful in London – but we need you here.'

'What is it you want to ask?'

'It isn't just me, it's parliament itself. We have appointed you Minister of Justice.'

Victoria looked away from him, at the bust of her brother.

'You know me so well, Malcolm,' she said. 'I accept.'

370

They all fell silent as Zwane stepped up on to the shallow plinth on which the bust of Max stood. The sun rested now just above the horizon line, colouring the clouds gold and red. Malcolm spoke with passion the words of a Bushman poem he had chosen as a last tribute to Max.

> The Wind has the bird with him and he walks a little way
> but no more: from the earth he rises,
> into the sky he shoots up, he soars
> and he takes the grass and whirls it far,
> scatters it so it falls a great distance.

A faint breeze blew up. The redness of the sun was on warm on Vicky's face. Now they were no longer exiles.